"I want out, Nick. This mission has brought everything back into perspective. There are no threats and no bribes Unit One can offer to make me change my mind."

"Melody, you haven't heard yet what's on offer."

"I don't care. Wallis Beecham is already behind bars and there's nothing more they can offer me. I don't want to be a government agent. I'm leaving Unit One."

She still had a lot to learn about the power of Unit One, Nick thought. The threats were more real and the rewards more gratifying than she dreamed of. What's more, Unit One was masterful at blurring the line between threats and promises, blending the whole thing into an enticing package.

"You're wrong in suggesting that Unit One has nothing to offer you," Nick said. "We can offer you something you want very badly."

Melody shrugged, torn between puzzlement and a healthy hint of impatience. "I can't imagine what that might be. I don't have many burning wants, Nick."

How little she knew herself. Nick drew in a slow, deep breath. "How would you like to know who your father is and where you can find him?"

The air in the room was suddenly thick with tension. Melody didn't respond for at least ten seconds, and when she spoke, her calm was deadly. "Do you know who my father is, Nick?"

JASMINE CRESSWELL

FULL PURSUIT

MIRA®

MIRA

ISBN 0-7783-2066-9

FULL PURSUIT

Copyright © 2004 by Jasmine Cresswell.

All rights reserved. Except for use in any review, the reproduction or utilization of this work in whole or in part in any form by any electronic, mechanical or other means, now known or hereafter invented, including xerography, photocopying and recording, or in any information storage or retrieval system, is forbidden without the written permission of the publisher, MIRA Books, 225 Duncan Mill Road, Don Mills, Ontario, Canada M3B 3K9.

All characters in this book have no existence outside the imagination of the author and have no relation whatsoever to anyone bearing the same name or names. They are not even distantly inspired by any individual known or unknown to the author, and all incidents are pure invention.

MIRA and the Star Colophon are trademarks used under license and registered in Australia, New Zealand, Philippines, United States Patent and Trademark Office and in other countries.

www.MIRABooks.com

Printed in U.S.A.

For John Malcolm Candlish,
with much love.

One

It took Melody Beecham less than ten seconds to jimmy the lock on Judge Lawson's study door and slip inside the book-lined room. Not quite a record, but satisfyingly close to her personal best. After six months of field experience with Unit One, she was getting pretty damn good at this breaking and entering stuff, even if she said so herself. Home invasion, burglary, wire tapping and computer hacking weren't exactly the skills she'd expected to develop into a career when she graduated from the University of Florence with an honors degree in fine arts, but she had to admit that carrying out missions for Unit One had a certain seductive appeal. Sometimes—often enough to be worrisome—she forgot that she was still working under duress and not because she was committed to their goals.

Relocking the study door behind her, Melody tucked the electronic pick down the cleavage of her black cocktail dress and switched on the microlight she wore disguised as a jeweled wristwatch. She directed the narrow beam around the room, checking for anything that didn't conform to the information she'd been given during her briefing early that morning. Everything looked exactly as she'd anticipated.

"I'm in," she murmured into her mike, crossing to the desk, the sound of her footsteps swallowed by the thick Persian rug. "No surprises. The judge's laptop is on the desk. I'm ready to start the download."

Nikolai Anwar responded. "The judge is talking to the governor's wife and the PR crew is still with them. They're taking photos. Lots and lots of photos." Nick's voice sounded clearly in her ear mike, even though he was at the other end of the house, on the ground floor, where the party to celebrate Judge Lawson's nomination to the Supreme Court of Connecticut was in full swing. "Go for it, Melody. I estimate you have at least fifteen minutes."

Fifteen minutes was more than she needed. Still, Melody's heart was racing as she opened the laptop and waited for the operating system to load. Since Judge Lawson was in the midst of a PR binge, the chances of him walking in on her were slim to none, but there was always an adrenaline rush at this crucial stage of a mission. She drew in a long slow breath, imposing calm. She knew from experience that an adrenaline high could spiral out of control with dangerous swiftness.

The moment the judge's computer was functional, Melody began to download the contents of his hard drive using a high-speed device developed by Unit One's own technical division. Unit One had accumulated significant intelligence to the effect that Judge Lawson's verdicts could be bought, despite his golden reputation for integrity. However, his recent appointment to the state supreme court was widely popular and Unit One needed rock-solid evidence before approaching the FBI with their accusations. The fact that Judge Lawson's verdicts were almost never overturned on appeal made it extra difficult to convince law enforcement authorities that those judgments were often bought and paid for. A wire tap, in operation for the past two weeks, had suggested that concrete proof of his corruption would be obtained if Unit One could get hold of the contents of the judge's hard drive. Hence tonight's mission.

The laptop buzzed and whirred its way through the download. The screen flashed Melody a message that one more minute was required to complete the transfer of information. She barely had time to heave a sigh of relief before Nick spoke again.

"Senator Lewis Cranford is coming upstairs. Judge Lawson just gave him a key, and he's coming directly to the study." Nick delivered the bad news with the sort of calm that warned Melody this was a major crisis. During an operation, Nick sounded more tightly controlled the more serious the threat.

"Abort the mission, Melody." His order was low and uninflected, but she could feel his urgency. "Get out of the study—now."

"Get out how?" She saw that only twenty seconds remained on the download and left the computer humming its way through the last vital moments. "If Senator Cranford's in the hallway, he's blocking the only possible exit."

"Go out of the window. You need to climb out onto the ledge, Melody. I'll be waiting to let you into the room next door." If possible, Nick's voice became cooler, quieter and even more calm—a sure sign to Melody that full-blown hysterics on her part were distressingly appropriate.

He wanted her to climb out onto a window ledge? In Melody's opinion, being caught by the senator was a significantly preferable alternative to crawling out onto a narrow slab of concrete, thirty or more feet above ground level. She had many skills useful to an undercover agent, but making like Spider-Man on the side of a building was definitely not one of them.

"Melody, get out of there." Nick's voice became clipped and she could tell that he was moving fast. "You're not just compromising yourself. You're compromising the entire mission."

"I'm leaving now." The computer burped to a halt. Melody ejected the super-capacity disk, clicked the mouse to shut down the laptop and banged the lid closed. It seemed that the habit of obedience died hard because she ran to the window and pushed it up.

Holy God. The ledge couldn't be more than six inches wide, and it was drizzling with rain, which meant that it was too narrow and slippery to support a cat, let alone a human being wearing a skimpy satin cocktail dress and evening sandals with two inch heels.

"Jesus, Nick, if I'd wanted to commit suicide I could think of more enjoyable ways than climbing onto this damn ledge."

"Get out, Melody, and that's an order."

The sound of footsteps approaching down the hallway finally jolted her courage—or her fear—to the point where she could obey Nick's instructions. Stepping behind the drapes, Melody drew them tightly closed behind her. Then she swung around and sat backward on the windowsill, pulling herself out until she could tuck her feet underneath her body, rest them on the outer ledge and push herself upright. Once vertical, she stretched her arms wide and clung to the ornamental shutters, her body pressed flat against the upper half of the window. Rain splattered on her head and naked shoulders, but as long as she had the minor comfort of solid surface against a portion of her body, she didn't give a damn about getting wet. There was no need to remind herself not to look down, since she was incapable of movement.

She'd escaped just in time, Melody realized as she heard the sounds of a key turning in the lock, followed by footsteps moving around the judge's study and a dim glow of light seeping out into the darkness. Given that she could see the lights Senator Cranford had switched on, she wondered if the silhouette of her body might be visible to him through the thickly lined drapes. Fortunately she was already so terrified that the prospect of being discovered on the ledge added barely a quiver to the overall level of her fear.

Nick's voice spoke into her ear mike. "Melody, don't answer me because the senator might hear your voice."

Since her vocal chords were paralyzed along with the rest of her, there was no danger that she might disobey Nick's order. No doubt he was about to announce their escape plan. She sure as hell hoped he had a magic carpet handy, otherwise she was going to be stuck here for the rest of her natural life, because she had no intention of ever making any movement that involved turning her head, lifting either of her feet, or releasing her death grip on the window shutters.

"I'm actually up above you," Nick said. "But I'm climbing down as we speak."

Climbing? He was seriously expecting her removal from this ledge to involve climbing up or down or along the brick facade of the judge's house? Hah! The man had a truly amazing sense of humor.

"So, here's the plan," Nick said, his voice soft and faintly amused in her ear. "Don't respond, or the senator may hear you. Unfortunately I just discovered the room next door to the study is occupied. The judge's son is in there. He's busy seducing one of the hired help."

Melody hoped it would be a very long seduction, since the prospect of edging across the side wall of the house was worse than remaining glued to the shutters by a factor of at least a hundred.

"I'm switching to plan B," Nick continued. "Remember when you were kidnapped by Wallis Beecham and he had you locked inside his office building in Lower Manhattan?"

Melody gave a strangled murmur of agreement.

"Okay. Remember how you expected me to have organized an escape route that involved rappeling down the side of the building, in the rain, with one thin safety line between the two of us? Well, that's exactly what we have to do this time. And, honey, please don't make any more spluttering noises. You have to be really, really quiet or Senator Cranford is going to hear us, and since he's determined to shut down Unit One if we give him half a chance, you know how many problems that would cause."

Melody heard a slight scrabbling noise above her head, no more than a squirrel might cause. A moment later, she felt Nick's arms around her waist, and his body pressed reassuringly against her back, the steel waist clasps of the rappeling cord comfortingly hard between them.

Feet braced against the wall, his weight supported by the line, Nick reached up and silently pried her hands from the window shutters, then wrapped them around the line just above his. His torso and legs formed a cradle in which she could simply sit and leave him to do all the work of climbing down, but Melody's panic was sufficiently alleviated by his presence that her training kicked back in. Her brain clicked into functional mode and her muscles unglued to the point that she was able to look up. She saw where the line was anchored around the chimney stack and calculated how she would have to cooperate in order to get safely down.

"We're lucky it's raining," Nick said as soon as they reached the ground. "Otherwise we might have had an audience waiting on the ground."

Melody was more than willing to be appreciative of the rain, or any other natural phenomenon that indicated she was still alive, with both feet firmly on the gravel path. She turned her back to the wall and pushed her soaking wet hair out of her eyes. "Thank you," she said.

Nick gave her a smile. Not one of his patented, curl-your-toes sexy smiles that he dished out to ninety percent of the women who crossed his path. This was one of his slow, sweet smiles that Melody sometimes hoped might be reserved only for her.

"You're very welcome," he said. "I'll have to see if I can't strand you on the top of a few more buildings. It's the only time you ever cling to me as if I'm your last best hope of heaven."

If only he knew how often she would like to cling to him, Melody reflected ruefully, and not just when she needed help overcoming her phobia about heights. If it weren't for the fact that she still retained some pathetic remnants of pride, combined with a primitive urge toward self-preservation, she would probably spend all her free time curled up in his arms. If Nikolai Anwar ever realized just how far in love she'd fallen with him over the past six months, she suspected there would be smoke billowing from his heels as he dashed for the nearest escape route from their relationship.

"Take your rewards where you can," she murmured, kissing him with a casual passion that contained no hint of the deeper emotions seething inside her. He kissed her back, his passion as fierce as hers, his emotions just as difficult to gauge.

There was no way to remove the anchor from the chimney stack without climbing back on the roof, so Nick quickly cut the line and concealed the harness and steel hooks under his cummerbund. "There's no point in going back to the party, even if we weren't soaking wet," Nick said. "Let's go find the car."

Melody was more than happy to leave. She patted the front of her dress, where the disk and the lock pick were rubbing uncomfortably. "At least we got what we came for."

"You managed to finish the download?" Nick looked cheered. "That's great news."

When they reached the sweeping circular driveway at the front of the house, the parking valet made no comment on the fact that they were both drenched with rain. Fortunately, since it was May and the night was warm, Melody's lack of a jacket or a wrap didn't appear too suspicious. The valet returned with Nick's Mercedes sports coupe, showing no sign that he would remember either one of them five minutes after their car rolled out of the driveway. Nick tipped him just enough to remain uninteresting.

Melody leaned back against the soft leather of the passenger seat, yawning. Reaction to the adrenaline rush of the mission, and the panic of being perched on the window ledge, was leaving her sleepy.

Nick handed her his cell phone. "Call headquarters, will you? Let Mac know that we're coming in and that we have the disk."

Melody pressed the speed dial button that connected her

with Martin McShane, Unit One's chief. "Hi, Mac," she said blithely when the chief answered. "Nick and I are on our way back to New Jersey. The mission was successful, and we'll see you in about ninety minutes."

"Congratulations. I need to speak to Nick."

Mac was always abrupt, but this was carrying curtness unusually far, even for him. Melody offered the phone to Nick, her sleepiness dispelled by a twinge of apprehension. "Mac needs to speak with you."

Nick took the phone. "Yes, Mac." He listened, his face hardening into an expression of such granite neutrality that even Melody couldn't imagine what he was hearing, except that it wasn't likely to be good news.

"We'll discuss options as soon as I get back," he said to Mac and hung up the phone, for once almost as curt as his boss.

"What is it?" Melody asked. "Nick, what's happened?"

He kept his gaze fixed on the road. "Mac has just been informed that David Ramsdell has escaped from custody."

Melody felt her stomach heave. Dave, once a field operative for Unit One, had betrayed his former colleagues so badly that the idea of him roaming free was sickening. "Oh, no! How in the world did that happen? We warned everyone often enough that he represented an extreme flight risk."

Nick shrugged. "The military brass are full of excuses, but the bottom line is that they underestimated him. Dave's one of the best." He gave a laugh that held no mirth. "Unit One trained him, remember?"

"What happened exactly?"

"Dave was being escorted back to his cell block in Leavenworth by a couple of young enlisted men. Apparently he'd just attended a judicial hearing regarding his case and he was shackled, which must have given the soldiers a false sense of security. He overcame the two guards, stole their Jeep, and was last seen heading toward the Interstate. The Jeep's already been found, abandoned at a rest stop thirty miles down the road. Presumably he hitched a ride out on a truck, headed who knows where. I think we can safely assume that regular law enforcement officials aren't going to have much hope of catching him."

Melody doubted if Unit One would have a much better chance of finding Dave than the rest of the law enforcement community. Dave was a master of disguise, an ex-military special ops officer and a twelve-year veteran of Unit One. He had all the skills necessary to hide in plain sight, so he wouldn't even need to go underground to evade capture. Since Dave had spent so many years working for Unit One, he knew exactly how most law enforcement agencies functioned and could take all the necessary steps to protect himself from capture.

Fear shivered down Melody's spine. Dave Ramsdell had been ready to kill her only six months earlier, and she realized that she was reacting with a lot more than intellectual frustration to the news that he was on the loose.

With the disconcerting ability Nick had to read what she was feeling, he reached out and rested his hand briefly on her knee. "Dave isn't going to risk coming anywhere near you or anyone else in Unit One," he said quietly. "Don't worry, Melody. He's way too smart to risk his freedom for the sake of revenge."

Melody hoped very much that Nick was right.

Two

It was rumored within Unit One that Martin McShane owned a house in New Jersey's upscale Monmouth County, built close enough to the beach to have fabulous ocean views. Another rumor suggested that Mac's niece lived in the house, acting as caretaker while she tried to establish her career as an illustrator of children's picture books.

Melody had serious doubts about the rumors. It was difficult enough to visualize Unit One's chief in the role of benevolent uncle, but as far as she was concerned, the wildest rumor of all was the one that suggested Mac actually spent the night in his own home at least a couple of times a month.

If Mac really did sleep away from headquarters from time to time, Melody was convinced it could only be for a token catnap, rather like a roaming tom taking a few moments to mark the boundaries of his territory before bounding off again in search of fresh prey. She had started her training as a Unit One operative in late September last year. It was now mid-May, and in the intervening seven months she had never detected a trace of evidence that Mac grasped the alien concept of having a personal life outside work. Whenever she was at headquarters, however late or early, Mac was also there, his finger firmly on the pulse of Unit One activities, his hair bristling in a halo around his head, outrageous clothes slightly crumpled, his beloved espresso machine hissing, and his underlings jumping to do his bidding.

Tonight was no exception. It was close to midnight by the time Melody and Nick arrived back at Unit One's New Jersey headquarters. Mac greeted them at the door of his office, pixie face lined with fatigue, but his eyes bright and his short frame almost visibly twitching from a combination of tension and round-the-clock injections of caffeine. He wore gray sweatpants and a matching sweatshirt, both stamped Illinois Department of Corrections—Inmate. His feet were stuffed, sockless, into a pair of brand-new Prada loafers. By Mac's sartorial standards, this could be counted as one of his more conservative outfits.

A man of few words, Mac nodded toward the leather sofa where Bob Spinard, director of intelligence for Unit One, was tapping his fingers restlessly. Bob adjusted his glasses and peered blankly at Melody and Nick before giving them a distracted nod. Without a mouse nestled under his palm, Bob always tended to look edgy. Tonight, he looked positively fraught.

"Debrief," Mac said, waving his coffee mug in a gesture that was subtly commanding. His appearance might be eccentric, but he had a firm grasp on the reins of power. "Nick, anything you need to tell us about tonight's mission before we move on to the issue of Dave Ramsdell's escape?"

"Not much," Nick said. "Everything was pretty routine. Senator Cranford was a guest at Judge Lawson's party, as Bob had warned us to expect. Cranford went upstairs while Melody was still inside the study, which blocked her exit. She was forced to escape via the window. Fortunately the download of the judge's hard drive was complete by the time the senator put in an appearance, so the mission achieved its objective."

"Good. Let's hope we've finally nailed Lawson. I despise judges who are on the take, and I smell corruption thick and deep around this one." Mac tossed back the dregs of his coffee.

"Any reason to suspect that Senator Cranford went to the study in deliberate pursuit of Melody?" Bob Spinard asked.

Nick shook his head. "I was monitoring Judge Lawson's conversation with the senator right before he went upstairs. The two of them were discussing a Justice Department memo that had them pretty riled up. They wanted to refresh their memories about the precise wording of a key paragraph. Since Lawson was busy with his PR crew, Cranford volunteered to fetch the memo, which the judge had left sitting on top of his in-tray. I'm confident neither of them had any idea Melody was in the study when Cranford decided to go up there."

"Here's the disk I downloaded from Judge Lawson's computer," Melody said, handing it to Bob, who barely glanced at it before mumbling a word of thanks and shoving it into his shirt pocket behind his row of pens.

As recently as a few weeks ago, Melody would have been irritated by Bob's casual acceptance of her efforts. Tonight, she felt scarcely a qualm. Her sense of perspective was becoming as warped as everyone else's in Unit One, she reflected wryly. Three hours earlier she'd been making an illegal entry into the home office of Connecticut's newest supreme court justice. A few minutes later she'd been escaping through his office window and scrabbling down thirty feet of slippery brick wall. Now, she found herself agreeing with Nick's assessment: their invasion of Judge Lawson's home had been a routine mission, barely worth discussing.

"I'll get to the Lawson disk as soon as I can," Bob said, tapping his pocket. "I'm afraid it's going to take more than twenty-four hours to complete a full analysis. Unfortunately we've got even more important issues than a corrupt high court justice to confront right now."

"Which brings us straight to the problem of Dave Ramsdell," Mac said. "Bob and I have been assessing the impact of Dave's escape on Unit One and our conclusions aren't pretty. Here they are. First of all, it's going to be tough to recapture him. Law enforcement agencies across the country are already overburdened, especially the FBI. It's unlikely they'll waste much energy tracking down a rogue Unit One operative, even though he's an escaped federal prisoner. To add to our difficulties, we can't identify Unit One as Dave's former employer or we blow our covert status. Plus, Dave is a master of disguise. Not much use circulating photos to law enforcement, since he won't look like them—"

"And that's before you take into account the near certainty that he'll head straight to a plastic surgeon," Bob interjected gloomily. Never a man to look on the bright side, Dave's escape seemed to have sunk him deeper into pessimism than usual. "Ramsdell will order up changes to his features that will defeat our software recognition programs. We're going to have a hell of a time identifying him until he's actually in custody and we can check fingerprints or DNA."

"Maybe we shouldn't waste too much effort trying to catch him," Melody suggested.

"And let him get away with selling us out?" Nick didn't attempt to conceal his outrage.

"That might be our smartest move." Melody refused to let emotion overwhelm her judgment. "Unit One will be playing right into Dave's hands if we become obsessed with tracking him down. In some ways, isn't it to our advantage if we just let him disappear into the sunset?"

"Are you kidding?" Bob was irate enough to be jerked out of his gloom. "No way I'm willing to let that bastard roam free. Dammit, we trusted him with our lives and he sold us out to Wallis Beecham! He tried to kill you and Nick! He's a goddamned *traitor*."

Nick gave a wry grin. "Hey, don't hold back, Bob. Why don't you share how you really feel? "

"Don't tempt me," Bob muttered.

Nick's expression sobered. "His treachery sticks in my craw, too. Still, Melody has a point. However frustrating it might be to know Dave has avoided punishment, he's not going to cause us any trouble lounging under a tiki hut in Tahiti. That's more than we can say if we close the net so tightly that he can't leave the country. If Unit One shuts down Dave's escape routes, he's going to erupt. And Dave erupting is likely to scorch a lot of earth."

"You're dreaming if you think Dave plans to retire." Mac rejected the notion with a snort. "You know Dave. For Christ's sake, what are the chances he's planning to sit on a beach, nursing drinks with paper umbrellas stuck in 'em?"

"I can't calculate the odds," Nick said quietly. "Because I *don't* know Dave. Nobody in this room knows Dave anymore. Obviously, or we wouldn't be having this conversation."

Mac scowled into his mug, clearly unwilling to admit that Nick was right. He turned abruptly and made his way to the espresso machine, tugging at his sweatshirt as he went. Mac and clothes never had an easy time getting along together and he'd already pushed the sleeves on his sweatshirt up and down so many times that the wristbands had lost their elasticity and hung down over his knuckles.

"We can't just sit around on our backsides hoping Dave goes into retirement," Bob said. "That's an incredibly high-risk strategy. He knows too much about how Unit One operates."

"Plus he knows the names of two-thirds of our field agents." Mac stared glumly at his canister of coffee beans, as if hoping for a miraculous revelation of where to look for Dave. "He can blow our organization out of the water if he decides to sell those names to the wrong people."

The drumbeat of Bob's fingers on the arm of the sofa increased. "For all we know, Dave bought his way out of prison by selling those names. Seventy percent of our operatives may already be compromised."

And that seventy percent included her and Nick, Melody thought grimly. The two of them had discussed the disastrous ramifications of Dave's escape during the drive back to headquarters, but that didn't stop a fresh chill rippling down her spine at the potential threat Dave represented, both to Unit One and to the two of them personally.

"Let's look at the best-case scenario for a moment," Nick said. "Maybe we're overreacting. Who would Dave sell his information to? Since Unit One targets corrupt individuals, rather than organizations, he might discover there's no market for what he's trying to sell. Individuals rarely know they're in our sights until the mission is over."

Mac shook his head. "Wish you were right, Nick. Don't think you are. I'd feel more confident about the safety of

Unit One personnel if Dave's escape had been spur of the moment. But it wasn't. It was planned and he had help. That suggests somebody who knows his way around the system believes Dave is too useful to leave locked up in Leavenworth."

Nick's eyes narrowed. "How sure are we that he had help?"

"Too damn sure for comfort." Mac paced the area in front of his desk. "A witness—a young woman—saw Dave arrive at the Interstate rest stop. She'd been hanging out with her dog, a black lab that had eaten his way through the contents of a trash can. Dog kept throwing up so our gal didn't want to put him back in the car and drive on. She saw Dave abandon the Jeep and transfer to a late-model gray Ford pickup truck. She's fairly sure the truck had been waiting at the rest stop for at least an hour and she remembers it had Missouri plates. Unfortunately she doesn't remember any part of the license number. Can't describe the driver except that it was a woman. According to the witness, there was nothing memorable about the woman's appearance."

Bob pushed his glasses up onto his forehead and massaged the bridge of his nose. "Bottom line, the fact that there was a getaway vehicle waiting for him means that Dave wasn't acting alone. Someone decided it was worth their while to help him escape. Who's the someone? That's the million-dollar question."

"Maybe Dave has a girlfriend?" Melody suggested. "That would tie in with the driver of the getaway car being female."

"Dave doesn't have a girlfriend." Mac watched steam hiss into his milk, the froth blooming in a mushroom cloud at the top of his mug. "He's a grieving widower, remember? Neurotically grieving, or he wouldn't have wanted any part of the Bonita project. His parents are dead, too."

"He has a brother," Nick said. "His brother's name is Ian, I think."

"Dave's brother is with the military in Iraq." Mac paced the square of carpet in front of his desk, leaving his foamed milk untouched on the counter by the espresso machine. "We already double-checked and Ian is definitely with his unit in Mosul, repairing oil pipe lines."

Bob scowled. "However Dave escaped, and regardless of who helped him, we need to hunt him down."

"I want to be in charge of the hunt," Nick said quietly. "I was Dave's closest friend. We worked together on at least a hundred missions. Hell, he taught me ninety percent of what I know about conducting an undercover op. Even though I don't have a clue about what motivates Dave these days, I understand exactly how he's been trained. The operational habits he developed while he was with Unit One are a lot harder to change than his appearance or his ethics. Let me work full-time on bringing him in, Mac. I'm the best chance we have of finding him."

Melody had been expecting Nick to make the request. She hadn't been expecting Mac's instant and emphatic denial. "Can't do that," Mac said. "I need you elsewhere."

"To do what?" Nick didn't bother to hide his frustration. "As far as I know, there's nothing waiting for my attention that's more urgent than finding Dave Ramsdell."

"Something's come up. Top priority. Talk to you later." Mac scowled at his cuffs, then shoved them up over his elbows. They immediately started their downward slide again. "Don't worry, Nick. I've put every agent we can spare on Dave's trail. These are smart people. A lot of them knew Dave. They're familiar with the survival techniques he's going to adopt. You wouldn't add much, if anything, to the hunt."

Bob spoke before Nick could refute Mac's point. "My department's already working to turn up some leads," he said. "I have Jerry reviewing every mission Dave carried out for Unit One. He's cross-checking for anyone who might have both the motive and the means to help Dave escape. There are already a few names that have cropped up more than once. That gives us a core group to focus on."

Nick and Melody exchanged glances. She wondered if her expression was as bleak as his. They both admired Bob's grasp of electronics and technology. Melody freely acknowledged that without Bob's gadgets and the comprehensive intel his department generated, most of their missions would be impossible. But Bob was mentally deskbound, the quintessential analyst. Neither she nor Nick shared Bob's faith in the power of software to take the place of field operatives on the ground, conducting a real-world investigation. As for Jerry, Bob's deputy, he was the ultimate computer nerd. If you wanted to circumvent a security protocol or climb over somebody's electronic firewall, Jerry was your man. But if Jerry cross-checking past missions was Unit One's best chance to find Dave, then they were in deep trouble.

"Have you considered the possibility that Wallis Beecham is behind Dave's escape?" Melody asked Mac. To her, Beecham seemed the obvious culprit, although she recognized that personal hang-ups might be affecting her judgment. She had believed that Wallis Beecham was her father for the first twenty-eight years of her life. Having learned that he wasn't, along with many unsavory revelations about his lust for power and his complete lack of moral boundaries, she now despised him so much that she tended to see his dirty fingerprints smeared over every pot of mischief.

Mac perched on the edge of his desk, feet dangling off the

floor. "Until today, I'd have said that the security around Beecham is so tight that he couldn't organize a charity drive for starving orphans, let alone assist in the escape of a federal prisoner housed miles away in a military facility. But I'd have said the same thing about Dave Ramsdell, and obviously I would have been wrong. Why do you suspect Wallis Beecham might be involved? Dave failed him once, and Beecham isn't a man who forgives failure."

"That's true as a general rule," Melody conceded. "But Wallis is quite capable of springing Dave simply to wreak revenge against Unit One."

Mac shook his head. "Beecham doesn't strike me as a man who wastes time on revenge for the sake of revenge."

"He has a lot more time to waste now that he's locked up," Melody pointed out. "Besides, he might be trying to undercut Unit One's efficiency so that the legal case against him will be more difficult to prosecute."

Bob tugged at his lower lip, his expression doubtful. "If Beecham has the resources to arrange Dave's escape, why not cut out the middleman and escape himself?"

"Because Wallis doesn't have Dave's physical abilities," Melody said promptly. "In order to escape, Dave had to overpower two armed guards while he was handcuffed. For Dave, that was ho-hum—all in a day's work. For Wallis Beecham, it would have been impossible. Wallis has zero athletic ability and no skill in unarmed combat. He could never have made the break."

"That's true," Nick said, looking thoughtful. "Dave, on the other hand, might have more difficulty than Beecham in arranging for a getaway vehicle to be waiting at the nearest highway rest stop. It could be they decided to pool their talents."

"Pool their talents to do what?" Bob asked.

Melody grimaced. "To cause mischief. Create chaos. Wreak vengeance."

"To destroy Unit One," Nick said slowly. "That's one goal Wallis Beecham and Dave Ramsdell have in common."

"And that's a goal they're never going to achieve," Mac said grimly. "I'll get Beecham consigned to maximum security solitary confinement if I have to, but I'll not let the pair of them cause us any more trouble. So if Dave's escape is step one in a plan he and Wallis Beecham were working on for the destruction of Unit One, consider that plan quashed as of now."

Melody found Mac's confidence less reassuring than usual. "What if Dave doesn't need any more input from Wallis to carry out their plan?" She finally gave voice to the fear that had been lurking uncomfortably close to the surface ever since she heard of Dave's escape. "With Dave gone, the prosecution has already lost one important witness in its case against Wallis Beecham. What if Dave's mission is to wipe out the only other major prosecution witness? In other words, what if his mission is to kill me?"

"I considered that scenario and rejected it," Mac said coolly. "From Beecham's perspective, it's way too complicated to spring Dave just to get you killed. There's plenty of muscle Beecham could hire to eliminate you without jumping through hoops to spring Dave from Leavenworth."

Melody sincerely hoped Mac was correct in his assessment, since being the designated target for Dave Ramsdell was not a role she relished. If Dave had decided to kill her, he was likely to succeed. In fact, Melody couldn't help worrying a little about the possibility that Dave might decide to come after her entirely on his own account, without any encouragement from Wallis Beecham or anyone else. She and Nick were, after all, the two people most directly responsible for the fact that he'd spent the past six months languishing in prison. Revenge, at this point, had to look mighty appealing to him.

"In my opinion, what we need right now is to do the research and get some facts," Bob said. "At this point, further speculation isn't going to take us anywhere useful. We've covered all the obvious bases. Whatever the motives behind Dave's escape, our focus has to be on fortifying the safety of Unit One and its personnel. My people have volunteered to work double shifts and we're actively reinforcing Unit One's security firewall. Plus, I've already assigned Linda to design and set up a program that scrutinizes any seemingly minor or random mishaps in all our missions from here on out. We're going to follow up on every anomaly, no matter how small or seemingly insignificant. If a pattern of failure develops, we'll spot it, you have my guarantee on that."

Mac finally picked up his steamed milk, wrinkling his nose at the deflated froth. "We're also scrutinizing the physical safety of headquarters to make sure there are no vulnerabilities for Dave to exploit. Sam is working right now on developing even tougher security protocols. We should have those new protocols in place within twenty-four hours."

"In other words, we expect Dave Ramsdell to attack us, but our only defense is to retreat behind our barricades, and hope they keep him out," Nick said.

"That's about the sum of it," Mac said. "For the simple reason that we have no better choice. We don't have enough people to cover ongoing operations at the same time as we mount a physical manhunt for Dave."

Nick muttered something in Russian, a sure sign of extreme stress.

"If I understood what you just said, Nick, I'm sure I would agree. The situation sucks." Bob rose to his feet. "Well, that just about fills everyone in on the extent of the mess we're looking at. I'm going to try to grab a couple of hours' sleep unless you need me any more, Mac?"

"No." Mac grimaced as if his coffee and deflated milk froth tasted as bad as it looked. "You know how to reach me if anything urgent crops up over the next twenty-four hours."

"Sure. I'll be in touch tomorrow morning with a progress report." Bob bobbed his head vaguely in Nick's direction, blinked even more vaguely at Melody and slouched out of the room. He left a pool of uneasy silence in his wake.

Three

Melody could sense Nick's frustration at Unit One's help-lessness in the face of Dave Ramsdell's escape. His frustra-tion added to her own, but there was nothing she could do until Bob's team generated some leads for the operations di-vision to follow up. Breaking the momentary inertia that fol-lowed Bob's departure, she rose to her feet.

"Are you going home or spending the night here?" she asked Nick. She was tired enough that even one of the Spar-tan sleeping cubicles at headquarters seemed inviting, al-though if Nick planned to drive back to Manhattan, she would go with him. These days, she reflected wryly, it seemed as if she could barely keep up the pretense that she enjoyed spend-ing time apart from him.

"Don't leave yet," Mac said, halting her in midstep. "Sorry, but I need to brief you on another mission. You, too, Nick. I have to be in D.C. for an 8:00 a.m. meeting at the White House, or I'd hold off until morning."

"You're going to Washington?" Nick had been slouched in a chair, presumably brooding about Dave, but shock forced his eyes wide-open. "Good grief, Mac! Hell just froze over."

Mac shuffled his feet, looking as close to embarrassed as Melody had ever seen him. "Gotta go. This one's important," he mumbled, but added no explanation as to why.

Melody was as astonished as Nick. Mac despised bureaucrats and made it a rule to avoid official briefings, testimony before secret Congressional subcommittees, and any meetings involving representatives of the FBI or the CIA. In short, his list of people to avoid encompassed the attendees at virtually any important meeting ever occurring in Washington. Mac insisted that the moment he crossed inside the Beltway, he broke out in hives—his allergic reaction to the quantities of bullshit free-flowing in the nation's capital.

Mac's reluctance to deal with Washington's power elite didn't matter much, since Jasper Fowles, the commander-in-chief of Unit One and Mac's immediate boss, took care of the necessary brown-nosing. Jasper was a complete contrast to Mac, at least superficially. Where Mac had trouble speaking in whole sentences, not to mention keeping his shoes matched in pairs, Jasper was elegance and smooth polish personified. He got along well with politicians and prided himself on having a real talent for strategic ass-kissing, plus he was more than cunning enough to trap the Beltway Boys in their own silver-plated deceptions.

Melody was currently furious with Jasper, but even she was forced to concede that his handling of Washington's political flaks was brilliant. According to Nick, it was Jasper who had single-handedly kept funds flowing for Unit One when other covert organizations had been forced to scale back in the budget crunch that followed the formation of the Department of Homeland Security, the ascendancy of the Department of Defense, and the protracted, expensive aftermath of the Iraq War.

Melody wondered why Mac was submitting himself to the sort of Washington-insider meeting that he hated. Maybe Jasper couldn't go? That would be surprising, since she'd seen Jasper yesterday at the gallery, where she still maintained her cover job as his executive assistant. Jasper had even invited her to lunch, and Melody had refused with the insincere courtesy that was their standard method of communication these days.

She was well aware that her excessive politeness hurt Jasper, precisely because it was such an effective way to keep him at a distance. At least rage and yelling might have precipitated a certain honesty, which was probably why she avoided it with such determination. Melody recognized that in punishing Jasper for the role he'd played in her forcible recruitment into Unit One, she was also punishing herself. But her sense of betrayal was so deep that it wouldn't heal, and she couldn't seem to find the way forward to forgiving him.

Her success in bringing down Wallis Beecham had come at a high price, Melody reflected, including the shattering of her relationship with Jasper, a friendship she had valued more than any other in her life. She was glad when Mac spoke again, drowning her painful reverie.

"I had a long conversation with Senator Cranford this afternoon," Mac said, pressing the switch that brought down the projection screen on the wall opposite his desk. "He has a mission he wants Unit One to tackle as a personal favor to him."

"Senator *Cranford* is asking for our help?" Melody said. She and Nick exchanged another astonished glance. If hell hadn't frozen over when Mac agreed to go to Washington, it surely must have when Cranford requested Unit One's assistance.

"Cranford is setting us up," Nick said immediately. "He's going to double-cross us. He's been looking for an excuse to cut off our funding ever since we exposed him as one of the founding partners of the Bonita project. He's asking for our help as an excuse to suck us into an untenable position, and then he's going to screw us over. Count on it, Mac."

"My initial reaction was the same as yours," Mac said mildly. "But I think in this instance Cranford's request for help is sincere." Mac slipped a tape into the VCR. "Watch this and you'll understand why. He had this tape couriered to me yesterday. Get the lights, Nick. The quality of the images isn't good."

Nick dimmed the lights and Mac set the video in motion. A grainy image of a meeting hall filled with people of both sexes and varying ages flickered onto the screen. Mac paused the tape as a tall, handsome man in his early forties walked to the podium and picked up the mike.

Mac took a wooden pointer and stabbed it at the man's nose with a force that suggested he wished he were poking the real thing. "This is Zachary Wharton and what you're watching is the Sunday evening gathering of his followers, a pseudo-Christian sect called the Soldiers of Jordan. They don't allow filming or recording of their worship services, so this footage isn't authorized. It was taken six months ago by Jodie Evanderhaus, an enterprising journalist who used to work for the *Idaho Chronicle*. She was filming the service clandestinely, hence the dubious quality of the images."

"You said she worked for the *Chronicle,* past tense," Nick said. "What happened to her?"

Mac used the pointer to scratch his head. "She died."

"Of natural causes?" Nick asked.

"Supposedly she died of carbon monoxide poisoning. Investigators discovered she had a faulty furnace, so her death was officially declared accidental. It's possible that's true."

"Or not?" Nick suggested.

"Or not," Mac·agreed. He set the tape in motion again, but he kept the sound low so that he could continue speaking while Zachary began the service with a series of prayers.

"Okay. Background on the Soldiers of Jordan." Mac whacked the screen with his pointer, indicating the bowed heads of the congregation. "They're legally registered in Idaho as a church, which gives them considerable protection under the law, of course. Their campus is located in White Falls, a small town south of Boise, about twenty miles off the Interstate. It's a rural area, scenic but not extraordinary by Idaho standards. Makes money from agriculture rather than tourists. Zachary Wharton, their founder, is a lawyer. Member of the bar in Michigan, with no criminal record. Not even a parking ticket that the FBI or local law enforcement have been able to turn up. I'll let you listen to him for a few moments, then I'll cut the sound and you can watch the rest of the film while we talk about why Senator Cranford has sent this to us."

Zachary Wharton began his sermon as Mac turned up the sound. The audio was as scratchy as the images were blurred, but despite the occasional inaudible sentence, Wharton obviously had a compelling speaking voice and an effective manner of delivery. In fact, the total package of good looks and great voice was spellbinding, and Melody had to force the analytical portion of her brain to click in and stay operational. Zachary Wharton was not only a mesmerizing speaker, she realized, but he was also a clever one. Without podium thumping or shouting, he was efficiently whipping his audience into a frenzy of fear about the dangers of Islam.

The Christian democracies of the western world had been under siege by the forces of radical Islam since at least the 1920s, Wharton told his rapt audience. For years, America and the West had slumbered, unaware of the ravenous beast at their gates. They had focused on fighting the evils first of Fascism, and then of Communism while radicalized Muslim missionaries pursued a relentless strategy of building their army of fanatics by converting the poor and the disaffected throughout the world.

Islam had been so successful in gaining converts during the second half of the twentieth century that it had become the world's fastest-growing religion. Contrast this with the world picture a hundred years earlier, when Christianity had been the dominant—and growing—religion.

Zachary gazed at his audience more in sorrow than in anger. Christians had only themselves to blame for their loss of power, he said. Too often, they ignored the call to help the disenfranchised and the downtrodden. As a result of the Christian neglect of the poor and the weak, Islam gained converts not only in distant lands, but right in the heartland of America. Tragically, many African-Americans fell victim to the false promises of Muslim clerics who preyed on their hopelessness and their exclusion from mainstream society.

Zachary's voice took on a new and deeper tone of sorrow. It was no coincidence, he said, that a Muslim soldier serving in the Iraq War had shot his commanding officers. Or that an army chaplain and Arab interpreters from Guantanamo Bay had been arrested for spying on behalf of Al Qaeda. Muslims gave their loyalty to their religion, not to their country. Every Muslim in the United States represented not just an alien way of life, but also a threat to American national security. Terrorism wasn't the bogeyman that the government should be fighting. Radical Islam itself was the enemy, the deadly venom that threatened the two hundred and fifty years of American freedom.

Unfortunately the American government had abdicated its first duty, which was to protect the safety of its citizens. Mosques all across the nation were infected with fanatic, extremist versions of Islam. Imams taught hatred instead of peace. They had allowed consecrated ground to become headquarters for the plotting of slaughter and mayhem. As a result of the government's blind indifference to what was going on under their noses, disaster was guaranteed to follow. The events of 9/11 were just a foretaste of the destruction that would soon be unleashed on hardworking Christian families in America.

Zachary continued his sermon, changing the words, but not the message. Melody remained reluctantly fascinated. She was impressed by the slickness with which he progressed from chiding his congregation for not helping the poor to the point where all Muslims were suddenly a threat to the security of the United States. She'd heard other preachers—not to mention secular pundits on cable TV—delivering the same message, some of them in even more blatantly prejudiced forms. But Zachary had a beguiling, low-key method of presentation that made his views sound reasonable, almost scholarly.

His sermon reached a crescendo, and the congregation surged to its feet. Led by Zachary in a mellow baritone, they started to sing a robust chorus of "Onward, Christian Soldiers."

"Their theme song," Mac said, cutting the sound with a grimace of distaste. "Okay, you've heard Wharton's basic message. He goes on for another half-hour with riffs on the same basic theme. But he's damned good. Watch. You'll see he has the congregation dancing and praising Jesus and vowing to defend the homeland with their lives by the end of his rant."

"God knows it looks like a group that merits checking out," Nick said. "But I don't understand why Senator Cranford—of all people—has asked Unit One to help. Given the suspicious death of the newspaper reporter, surely there's grounds for the FBI to launch at least a preliminary investigation?"

"The FBI did launch an investigation," Mac said. "They already sent in two undercover agents, but neither agent had much success. Zachary Wharton spotted the first guy—Jerry Bostwick—within five days of his arrival on campus."

"What happened to Bostwick?" Melody asked, afraid she might hear the agent was dead.

Mac gave a wry grimace. "Zachary asked him to leave— very politely. Unfortunately Zachary is smart. Way too smart to attack an FBI agent and give law enforcement an excuse to arrest him or his followers."

"Did Bostwick pick up any useful intel during his five days on campus?" Nick asked.

"Not much." Mac expelled a frustrated breath. "Bostwick reported that he and the other men underwent compulsory military training each morning while he was on campus. He also said there was too much money sloshing around, suggesting outside sources of financing. He reported that there were permanent guards posted in front of Zachary's private office to prevent intruders. Gut instinct warned Bostwick that the Soldiers are planning something dangerous, but he could only speculate about what. Based on Zachary's sermons, and a few whispers from the men during military training, he's guessing that they plan to blow up a mosque somewhere. However, he admitted it's just as likely that they're going to blow up a Christian church somewhere and blame it on the Muslims. Or they might go after the mayor of White Falls who's made no secret of the fact that he'd like them to leave the area. We just don't have enough solid information to pinpoint their target."

"With fanatics like these, their logic can be tough to unravel," Nick said grimly. "Usually you don't find out what rat is chewing on their toes until after they've hit their target and paramedics are walking through the wreckage picking up body parts."

"Exactly." Mac scowled. "Since Bostwick couldn't come up with anything concrete before he was tossed off campus, the Bureau waited four weeks and then sent in a more experienced guy, Ted Cooper. They hoped Cooper would uncover some sort of concrete criminal activity the Bureau could act on. Cooper had penetrated half a dozen other extremist religious groups and he's considered brilliant at faking devotion to the cause. Seems he wasn't brilliant enough to deceive Zachary Wharton, though. Took Zachary less than three weeks to identify Cooper as another FBI informant."

"That's astonishing," Melody commented. "Usually these cult leaders are so puffed up with their own conceit that they never detect insincerity in the people around them."

"I agree." Nick's gaze narrowed. "In fact, it's surprising enough to be suspicious. I'm guessing somebody inside Bureau headquarters tipped off Zachary Wharton."

Mac shot him an approving glance. "My reaction precisely. Of course the Bureau denies Zachary was warned. They're huffing and puffing with outrage at the mere suggestion, but I'll give odds of a thousand to one that somebody slipped Zachary a warning."

"If Zachary knew Cooper was an FBI agent, I'm assuming he made sure the guy didn't see anything suspicious," Nick commented.

"You've got it." Mac shrugged. "Zachary seems to have worked a complete snow job on Agent Cooper. The guy went back to D.C. and filed a report that contradicted everything Bostwick had said. Cooper insists he never heard the Soldiers plotting anything remotely seditious. According to him, they're sincere Christian believers, trying to build a peaceful community—"

Nick rolled his eyes. "Which is why they have armed guards protecting Zachary's office 24/7? Because they're so peaceful?"

"According to Cooper, that's easily explained. The Soldiers don't believe in banks, so they deal in cash and keep several thousand dollars on campus. Naturally a sum of money that large needs to be guarded."

"How about the military training for the men? How did Cooper explain that away?"

"Zachary informed Cooper that commando training is a good way to keep the men physically fit. Works off excess testosterone and keeps the community humming along in harmony."

"And Cooper fell for such an obvious line?"

"Is it so obvious?" Mac said. "Yes, the Soldiers of Jordan play commando five days a week, but so do thousands of other kooks who are never going to shoot anything more dangerous than a wild turkey."

"What about sexual misconduct?" Melody asked. "That's often a point of vulnerability for these fanatical religious communities. The men in charge try to marry off the girls before they're old enough to know better."

"Apparently the single men and women live in separate

dormitories, and Cooper swears there's no evidence of under-age sex. Even Jerry Bostwick agrees that the kids don't appear to be at risk sexually. As for the adults, Zachary Wharton preaches celibacy, and he seems to live in accordance with what he preaches, at least on campus."

Melody tipped her head to the side. "And off campus?"

"Who knows?" Mac twisted an elastic band around his wrist in an effort to prevent his sleeves dangling over his knuckles. "Nobody's ever tried to find out. Cooper's glowing report was accepted by the brass in Washington and that was the end of official interest in the Soldiers of Jordan. Jerry Bostwick found himself reassigned to a horse doping investigation in Kentucky. As of today, the Bureau has no plans to reopen their investigation."

"And yet Senator Cranford suddenly wants Unit One to pick up where the FBI left off," Nick said. "Why? Cranford is best buddies with the Bureau's director, and he's mad as hell with us. So why would he second-guess the official conclusion of an FBI investigation—much less send in Unit One to expose their mistakes?"

"I'm getting to that." Mac poked his stick at the screen again. "The senator was sent this video by the *Idaho Chronicle* four weeks ago. Since then, he's read every scrap of information in the FBI files. He's talked to Bostwick, and was impressed by the guy's competence. He's also talked at length to Agent Cooper. He concluded the guy has a dangerously inflated opinion of his own brilliance. Cranford believes that Zachary Wharton and the Soldiers represent a clear and present threat to national security. His guess is that they're planning a major attack against Muslims somewhere in this country."

"Do you agree with Cranford?" Nick asked.

"Yes," Mac said. "Having studied Bostwick's original reports, before they got edited by his superiors, I believe the senator is right. Zachary Wharton is building a religious community in White Falls as the cover for a paramilitary operation, target unknown at this time, but probably a mosque full of worshippers. I don't have to tell you two that if the violence were brutal enough, the consequences of such an attack would be disastrous. Can you imagine how it would be viewed in the Arab world if Muslims in the United States were blown up by Christian extremists? Our country is already radioactive from the point of view of ninety percent of the people in the Middle East. Having Christians attacking harmless Muslims at prayer would be the equivalent of launching a nuclear bomb into the middle of Baghdad. Al Qaeda could hang out a shingle and young Muslim boys would be lining up to sign on for suicide missions."

Melody shuddered, the potential for disaster all too clear. "If we can't shut down the Soldiers directly, can't we be devious? Couldn't local law enforcement get them closed down for zoning or building code infractions?"

"Or how about the IRS going after them for tax evasion?" Nick suggested.

"Wish it were that easy." Mac grunted. "Zachary's a lawyer by training, and he's damned smart. He isn't going to get caught for anything obvious like failure to pay taxes, or overflowing septic tanks. Unfortunately."

Nick turned to watch the screen where Zachary was stretching out his arms and inviting his congregation to pray. A hundred heads bowed in instant obedience. Nick's mouth tightened into a hard line. "The Bureau may have given up, but what about local law enforcement? Are they still investigating the Soldiers?"

Mac shrugged. "White Falls has a three-man force, trained to cope with drunks, traffic accidents and the occasional case of shoplifting. They have lots of suspicions, but zero evidence of criminal activity."

Nick raised a disbelieving eyebrow. "With all those weapons stashed on campus, surely the cops could drum up a couple of weapons charges?"

"Nope, not even that. The mayor of White Falls has been vocal in his opposition to the group and some of his farm machinery was vandalized. The cops used that as an excuse to pressure a local judge into issuing a search warrant. All three cops went on campus to execute the warrant. They searched for hours and found nothing. The weapons Zachary hands out to his recruits all appeared to be legally bought and legally registered."

"Or hidden where the cops didn't manage to find them," Nick said cynically.

"That, too. But it's a big place, and there are only three cops. If the Soldiers want to hide incriminating documents or illegal weapons, they probably can. I tell you, the most important fact to remember about this group is that it's acting *smart.*"

Melody watched the screen in fascination as the Soldiers of Jordan rose to their feet, heads tilted worshipfully toward Zachary, and arms thrusting forcefully into the air. Even without sound, the gestures seemed to represent an unpleasant mixture of hysteria, rhapsody and anger. The chairs were pushed back and the worshippers linked arms in two circles— one of men, the other of women. They danced around, stamping hard every third step. Mac turned up the sound again, and she realized that the dancers were chanting *Cast out the devil. Stomp on his head. Cast out the devil. Stomp on his head.*

The mindless frenzy of the worshippers repelled her and Melody turned away from the screen, suddenly bone-weary. "I still don't understand why Senator Cranford wants Unit One to investigate these people. It's totally out of character for him to have approached us. Why doesn't he just go yell at the director of the FBI? That would be his usual style."

"You'd be right, except for one thing," Mac said. "He wants some serious action, and he wants it not only fast, but discreet. This is personal for Senator Cranford."

Mac stopped the tape, silenced the soundtrack and used his computer to change the focus. He zeroed in on a young woman gazing up at Zachary Wharton with complete adoration. "Here's why the senator wants action. Three months ago, Cranford's daughter ran away from home, supposedly after a fight with her sister. When she surfaced two weeks later, she was in Idaho."

Mac drew a circle with the pointer around the young woman's face. Like all the other women, her hair was braided, and she wore a high necked white blouse teamed with a pale blue skirt and plain sweater. "That's Rachel Cranford," he said. "The senator's eldest daughter. And as of ten weeks ago, a baptized follower of Zachary Wharton and the Soldiers of Jordan."

Four

In a departure from normal procedure, Mac didn't ask Nick to plan Unit One's mission to infiltrate the Soldiers of Jordan. Instead he issued flat orders about what he expected Nick and Melody to do. Mac's power grab would have been bad enough if Nick had approved of the operational profile, but he didn't. In fact, he couldn't remember any occasion when he and Mac had disagreed so completely about the parameters of a projected mission.

An hour had passed since his final heated exchange with his boss, but Nick's frustration still simmered. Unable to tolerate the prospect of sleeping at headquarters, he'd chosen to return to Manhattan, hoping the drive through dark and deserted city streets would work some calming magic on his jangled nerve endings.

Unfortunately the journey was almost over and the magic hadn't happened. Melody sat curled up in the passenger seat beside him, pretending to doze. Nick was grateful she had chosen to feign sleep, since it provided him with the excuse he needed to remain silent. However, they were already through the Holland Tunnel and into Manhattan. At this pre-dawn hour they were probably less than ten minutes away from Melody's apartment on East 31st. That meant she would soon have to stop pretending to sleep and he would soon have to speak. Nick wasn't at all sure he'd be able to open his mouth without saying something he'd regret later.

It was a hell of a long time since he'd been this angry. Nick glossed over a sudden flare of doubt as to whether what he felt was really anger. Much better that this churning in his gut should be rage directed at Mac and Unit One rather than fear for Melody. Or, God forbid, jealousy over what she had been ordered to do.

Nick buried the word jealousy before it could rear up and demand further examination. Why the hell wouldn't he be angry? There was no need to search for hidden reasons to explain what he was feeling right now. In his professional opinion, Mac's plan for investigating the Soldiers of Jordan was seriously flawed, and he'd wasted an entire hour at headquarters arguing the point—to no avail.

Nick didn't believe the excuses he'd been given to explain why he'd been cut out of the planning loop for this mission. He'd been with Unit One long enough to understand both the politics and the unspoken rules. He knew exactly why Melody was being sent to Idaho. Mac—with or without prompting from Jasper Fowles—had decided that Nick and Melody were becoming too emotionally involved for the smooth maintenance of social cohesion within Unit One. Therefore it was time for their affair to end. Everything else followed from that, right down to the fact that Mac was making an "urgent" trip to D.C. Nick was willing to bet there was nothing especially urgent happening in Washington tomorrow morning. Mac was simply leaving town in order to escape Nick's frustration at the blatant undercutting of his authority. Not to mention his anger at the even more blatant interference in his private life.

Nick sucked in air, but didn't feel any calmer. Quite apart from the personal issues, he believed Mac was being willfully blind to the dangers of cooperating with Senator Lewis Cranford. In Nick's opinion, the senator was a snake. Not a relatively harmless rattler, who at least made enough noise to give warning of his intent to strike. Cranford was a powerful boa-constrictor, hiding in the thickets of the Washington political jungle until he could slither down from his perch and coil silently around Unit One, choking it to death.

Mac had insisted that Rachel Cranford's recruitment by the Soldiers of Jordan changed the equation. The presence of the senator's daughter on the White Falls campus meant that Unit One could trust Cranford to be sincere in his plea for help. Nick considered this sheer wishful thinking on the part of his boss. Cranford had been venomous in his opposition to Unit One ever since the arrest of Wallis Beecham and the ensuing negative publicity. How in hell could Mac trust the senator's sudden decision to enlist the help of an organization Cranford had been vilifying only a couple of months earlier?

Far from being reassured by Rachel Cranford's presence in Idaho, Nick considered her at best irrelevant and at worst an added danger. The senator was more than capable of exploiting his daughter's involvement with the Soldiers of Jordan if it suited his purpose. It wasn't as if Rachel were in real danger. She hadn't been kidnapped. She wasn't being held for ransom, or locked up against her will. The senator admitted that his wife had spoken to Rachel a couple of times in the past month, and their daughter had made it plain she was in White Falls because she wanted to be. At almost nineteen, she was an adult and legally entitled to hang out with creepy religious fanatics if she chose to.

Nick drew to a halt at a cross-street traffic light, shifting restlessly. In retrospect, the night had been unsettling from beginning to end. From the strange, melting sensation he'd experienced when he realized Melody would have to overcome her phobia about heights and rappel down the side of Judge Lawson's house, to the devastating news that Dave Ramsdell had escaped, and on to Mac's plan for using Melody to infiltrate the Soldiers of Jordan, all three events might have been designed for the express purpose of forcing Nick to confront truths about his relationship with Melody that he would have preferred to leave unexamined.

The driver of the delivery truck behind him leaned on his horn, impatient because two seconds had passed since the traffic lights turned green and Nick wasn't already moving. The blast of the horn caused Melody to stir, but she gave no sign of waking up.

Perhaps she was genuinely asleep, not just faking it. She was such a good actress that sometimes even Nick couldn't be sure what she was really feeling. Her acting ability was part of what made her such an effective agent for Unit One. It was also part of what was starting to frustrate him in terms of their personal relationship. While Nick took care never to reveal his own feelings, he was accustomed to understanding everything about the women who shared his bed. It had been a humbling experience to spend six months partnering a woman who was every bit as smart, and every bit as good at dissembling, as he was.

Melody's feelings toward him remained a mystery, despite the fact that their affair had already lasted longer than any other he'd had. She was passionate in bed, she shared his offbeat sense of humor and she seemed to enjoy quiet Sunday mornings in his apartment as much as accompanying him to A-list parties and glittering first nights. Did her willingness to hang out with him mean that she cared about him? Or did it simply mean that she was a woman with plenty of inner resources, capable of entertaining herself? Nick didn't know, but he accepted that he had no right to ask Melody to bare her soul when he wasn't willing to give any confidences in return, so he tried not to obsess about all the things she still kept hidden from him.

Tonight, however, he'd been shoved against the self-imposed limitations of their relationship. When Mac ordered Melody to seduce Zachary Wharton and infiltrate the Soldiers of Jordan, her response had been cool, controlled and entirely professional. She'd expressed some reservations, but she hadn't refused the assignment. It had bothered Nick that he didn't know what she was really thinking. It had bothered the hell out of him that she appeared so willing to contemplate having sex with another man.

In fact, it still bothered the hell out of him. Nick started to sweat. He didn't understand why he was feeling this way. Or perhaps he did, which was even more frightening. He always cautioned new recruits about the dangers of getting emotionally entangled with a fellow operative. He had a great lecture about how successful undercover missions produced adrenaline highs, often followed by an intense need for sex. The trick was never to confuse the urgent desire for sex with falling in love, especially when your sexual partner was a fellow agent. The only thing messier than two operatives who'd fallen in love was two operatives whose love affair was over. Unit One was an emotional pressure cooker, he reminded recruits, and affairs tended to end with an explosion that destroyed not only the effectiveness of the individual operatives, but the mission readiness of the entire Unit.

Nick wasn't willing to concede that he'd broken his own prime rule. His feelings for Melody hadn't reached the point where they were interfering with his work. It simply wasn't true that his relationship with Melody had caused him to lose his edge, as Mac asserted. Dammit, there was no justification for Mac's decision to separate them. He and Melody were great in bed, they enjoyed each other's company and they worked well together. End of story. He wasn't becoming possessive where Melody was concerned. Okay, he hadn't assigned her to a single mission without him for the past three months, but that was sheer coincidence. And despite Mac's claims of personal bias, Nick was opposed to having Melody infiltrate the Soldiers of Jordan for reasons that had nothing to do with the fact that he couldn't bear to contemplate the possibility of her having sex with another man.

He swallowed over the sudden constriction in his throat and turned his Mercedes onto 31st Street, where Melody had found an apartment after she moved out of Jasper's penthouse. He reached out and rested his hand on her knee. Unit One had trained Melody to be a light sleeper and that was all it would take to wake her, even if she wasn't faking it.

He felt her muscles contract beneath his palm and she sat up, rubbing her eyes. She gave him a sleepy smile as he drew the car to a halt outside her building, an older one favored by doctors who worked at the nearby Bellevue Hospital. She yawned and blinked, gazing out of the window as if she hadn't yet fully recognized where they were.

He loved the way Melody always looked so drowsy and confused when she first woke up. Love being simply a figure of speech, of course. Nick shook his head, dispelling the unwelcome sentimentality. He needed to get home to his own apartment before something disastrous happened. For a man whose adult life had been built on a foundation of never allowing uncontrolled feelings to muscle their way into his relationships, spending this particular night with Melody would be a seriously bad idea.

He cleared his throat, determined to keep his voice and attitude brisk. He needed to get the business arrangements out of the way and deal with the personal issues later, when he wasn't tired and strung out, and all too likely to say things he'd later regret.

"I'll call you tomorrow so that we can start planning exactly how we're going to stage our official breakup within the parameters Mac has outlined." Nick looked at his watch: 5:00 a.m. "Will you be awake by eleven? Is six hours enough time for you to sleep?"

That sounded pretty crisp and businesslike, Nick decided, pleased with himself. Jasper Fowles was throwing a party tomorrow night. They'd been ordered to use the party to stage a public argument, followed by a public split. New York's gossip columnists would be there, as well as enough social luminaries to insure that word of their breakup would spread far and wide. All part of Mac's compressed timetable for ending their public affair, and introducing Melody—a newly unattached and highly desirable Melody—into Zachary Wharton's orbit. Melody might be naive enough to believe that their private affair could continue despite the public breakup. Nick knew better. For reasons of operational efficiency, Unit One had decided to separate them. There was no court of appeal against such decisions.

Melody didn't respond to his scheduling question. Instead she reached out and rested her hands against his chest, fingers spread wide. Nick shivered at her touch, unable to control the visceral reaction.

"Stay with me tonight," she said and her amazing violet-blue eyes were suddenly dark with sexual promise. "I...need you here."

Stomach clenching, Nick gazed at her, struck as always by the sheer perfection of her bone structure and the erotic allure of her sleep-tousled hair. He hesitated for a few fatal seconds. "I'd like to stay," he heard himself say, turning away from her. Turning from the truth of what he already knew.

"You have your set of keys?" she asked. Her voice remained husky with the remnants of sleep and Nick had to resist the urge to take her into his arms right there and then. He wanted to cradle her head against his chest, and kiss her mouth, and stroke his fingers along the taut, smooth flesh of her inner thigh....

"Yes, I have keys. You go on up." He spoke abruptly, putting the car back into drive, which gave him something to do with his hands other than ravish her. "I'll park in that new garage near the hospital. They usually have space there."

Melody had already showered when he finally made it up to her seventh-floor apartment after dropping off his Mercedes and walking the couple of blocks back to Third Avenue. She greeted him at the door, dressed in a short toweling robe, belted tightly around the waist. Her legs and feet were bare, and her hair was damp, so that it hung down past her shoulders in a heavy cascade.

Nick breathed in the subtle scent of shampoo and talcum powder that enveloped her and his protective barriers, already battered, were swept away. An image of her seminaked, walking into Zachary Wharton's bedroom, flashed across his mental screen. Something hot, sharp and exquisitely painful sliced through him.

"You look as if you could use this." Melody handed him a glass filled with iced Stoli, and he saw that she'd poured a similar drink for herself. That wasn't totally out of the ordinary—she enjoyed the occasional shot of vodka or glass of wine—but it wasn't routine for her, either. Maybe she wasn't quite as unconcerned as she appeared.

"Here's to Dave Ramsdell's swift recapture," she said, holding up her glass.

He acknowledged the toast with a clink of his glass. Astonishingly he'd almost forgotten about Dave.

"Na zdorovia." He tossed the vodka back in a single long swallow. The icy liquid raced down his throat, spreading welcome heat through his veins. He desperately wanted another drink, so he very deliberately put the empty glass down on the table.

Nikolai Anwar, master of self-discipline, he thought mockingly. *Totally controlled in every area of his life. Except one.*

"Would you like another vodka?" Melody asked, still nursing most of hers.

"No." He realized how curt he must sound, but he'd moved beyond the possibility of social courtesies hours ago, some time during his useless argument with Mac. In fact, words in general seemed to have slipped out of his grasp. How could he speak, when he had no clue what he wanted to say?

Since he couldn't find any words, he took refuge in action, pushing aside the niggling doubt that there had always been too much action and too few words in his relationship with Melody. He stepped toward her, removing the glass from her grasp and setting it down on the table. He folded his arms around her, closing his eyes as he absorbed her familiar softness. She relaxed into his embrace, fitting against him perfectly, as if their bodies had been designed for the express purpose of giving each other sexual pleasure. After a moment or two, she gave a tiny sigh—he thought of contentment—and her hands moved in a slow, intimate caress across his back and shoulders.

Quite often in recent weeks Nick had found himself enjoying the unspoken tenderness of their lovemaking. But tonight he wasn't willing to settle for slow or gentle. Fighting an onrush of foreboding, he tugged at the belt of Melody's robe, loosening the knot so that he could reach inside to touch her bare skin. He lowered his head to kiss her breasts and desire instantly ripped through him. His muzzy brain produced the thought that by now he should have become accustomed to the near-narcotic power Melody asserted over his senses, but it seemed that he was invariably caught off guard by the intensity of his desire.

The thought burned away, unable to survive the heat of passion. Despite the fire, Nick felt oddly cold inside. He held Melody close so that his erection pressed hard against the flat plane of her belly, and kissed her with an urgency that bordered on the brutal, forcing her lips apart, thrusting his tongue into her mouth, trying somehow to draw her warmth deep inside him. Trying to get close enough to fill the hollow ache in his gut. The ache that had started when Mac ordered Melody to infiltrate the Soldiers of Jordan by seducing Zachary Wharton. The ache that had been growing bigger and more painful every moment since.

Melody kissed him back, but tonight nothing quite satisfied him. The deeper their kisses, the hungrier and emptier he became. The ache in his gut wasn't being soothed, Nick realized; it was intensifying.

Desperate for…whatever…he pushed the robe off her shoulders and tossed it aside. With her robe pooled at their feet, he ripped off his own clothes, aware with some analytical part of his brain that his hands were entirely steady, and that he didn't fumble with a single zipper, hook or button as he shed his clothes.

That was Unit One training for you, he thought with bitter self-mockery. It didn't matter what you were feeling, nothing could interfere with the efficient completion of your mission. Making love to Melody? No sweat, man. Here's the Unit One manual that demonstrates how to insure your designated sexual target has a truly great orgasm.

"What is it, Nick?" Melody drew away from him, her hand reaching up to stroke away the hair that had fallen onto his forehead. She slid her hands down the length of his body, savoring the feel of him. He tried not to notice the implicit intimacy of her actions. God knew, he had enough experience to understand that sex was the easiest way possible for one human being to lie to another.

"Nothing's the matter." He kissed her again, with slightly more control than his earlier effort. This was likely to be his last chance to have sex with Melody for several weeks. *Perhaps forever?* Better make sure they went out on a real high. He'd been seducing female targets on behalf of Unit One for a dozen years. With all that experience, he at least ought to be able to make tonight memorable for Melody. Of course, from his point of view, memorable wasn't necessarily good. In view of what Melody would be doing over the next few weeks, the sooner he forgot what it felt like to make love to her, the better.

"I want you." She murmured the words against his mouth, her skin flushed, already moist with the heat of desire. Even now, after six months of sharing each other's beds, they didn't talk very much when they had sex, so the admission was far from routine.

"I want you, too." *I always want you.* Nick didn't say that part out loud, of course. Hell, no. Why risk honesty, when he could just be silent? Instead he gathered her closer, burying his face in her neck, smothering the other truths that lay hidden behind the simple acknowledgment.

After so many months, he knew Melody's body intimately. He knew how to make her nipples taut and how to bring a sheen of sweat to her skin, so he did it. He knew how to send the blood rushing through her veins until she was hot with passion. He knew how to turn her heat into chills, so that she shivered with longing, and he did that, too. He knew how to hold himself back so that he could draw out those last few exquisite moments of pleasure until she trembled violently, then shattered around him, her entire body convulsed by the intensity of her orgasm. He did all of that, and more.

When she was finally quiescent, the ripples of pleasure subsiding, Nick collapsed on top of her, his head resting on her breast. Her heart raced, and he could feel the accelerated rise and fall of her diaphragm as she struggled to regain her breath. Her climax had been so intense that she was completely spent.

Yeah, no doubt about it, he could grade himself an A-plus on this particular sexual encounter. He'd shown Melody a really great time.

For one horrifying, appalling second, Nick was afraid he might cry. After a few moments, he rolled to one side, removing the pressure of his weight from her. But they still lay wrapped together on the sofa in a tangled heap of cushions and limbs, their breathing heavy, neither of them speaking.

The ache in Nick's gut became a pain that threatened to tear him apart. He got up abruptly and went into the bathroom, locking the door behind him. He stood under the shower, scalding hot water pounding on him until the images of Melody having sex with Zachary Wharton were steamed away and the pain in his gut retracted to a tolerable level. It took a very long time.

Five

Nick emerged from the bathroom, a towel tucked around his waist. Melody had cleared away the vodka glasses and straightened the sofa cushions, but she hadn't gone to bed, as he'd hoped she might. He wondered what his colleagues would say if they ever realized that Nikolai Anwar, Unit One's resident daredevil, was actually a rank coward.

Melody, unfortunately, was a lot braver than him. "I know it's late, and we're both exhausted, but we have to talk," she said.

Nick almost made the stupid mistake of pretending not to understand what she wanted to talk about. Fortunately he caught that betraying evasion just in time.

"You mean your assignment to infiltrate the Soldiers of Jordan by seducing Zachary Wharton." He managed to sound almost matter-of-fact.

"Yes. And the fact that we've been ordered to stage a public breakup. What do you think of the mission profile, Nick?"

She hadn't been in Mac's office when he expressed his outrage. Ever the dutiful Unit One employee, Nick had followed protocol and invented an excuse to get her out of the room before he ripped into Mac and tore the plan to shreds. Now, less than three hours later, Nick felt no more than a faint twinge of surprise when he realized that he was going to fall into his habitual role of Organization Man and defend Mac's decisions.

In a moment of stark self-awareness, Nick finally recognized why he'd been so furious ever since he left headquarters. His rage had very little to do with Mac, or even the fact that Melody had been ordered to seduce Zachary Wharton. On the contrary, he was furious with himself because he'd known all along that he was going to put his professional obligations to Unit One above his personal feelings for Melody.

He was just like every other prisoner, Nick reflected bitterly. He had learned not only to love his jailors, but also to defend them against attack. His prison didn't have steel bars and chained gates, but the mental straitjacket of devotion to Unit One was just as effective and controlled him equally well.

He had joined Unit One straight out of college, recruited by Mac, who had once worked at the CIA with Nick's father. "This is what your parents would want you to do with your life," Mac had told him. "They were both great admirers of Unit One. They both believed passionately in working for justice."

Nick, lacerated by grief, had needed to believe Mac was right: that by fighting corruption, and crimes committed by the powerful against the weak, he would be pleasing his parents. Over the years, he'd convinced himself that his dedication to Unit One helped to redress some of the evil in the universe. Each successful mission became partial repayment for the fact that he alone had survived the car bomb that slaughtered his parents and little sister. Now, with a sense of self-loathing, he realized that years of devotion had brought him to the point where his whole life could be summed up in his job title. He was Nikolai Anwar, chief of covert operations for Unit One. End of bio.

"I have reservations about Mac's plan, but only at the margins," Nick said, finally responding to Melody's question. He wasn't sure whether to feel pride or disgust that his voice revealed none of the turmoil he felt about her assignment. "I question Senator Cranford's motives, rather than the operational details of the plan itself."

Melody sat on the sofa where they had just made love, tucking her legs under her. "Mac believes the senator's request for help is sincere, but you're still convinced the senator is setting us up?"

He nodded. "Even Mac acknowledges there's a chance that we're being set up. Given the senator's record of animosity toward us, I don't trust his sudden change of heart. Cranford is corrupt, and he's afraid Unit One is going to expose his corruption. Somehow—and I can't specify how—Cranford plans to use our investigation of the Soldiers of Jordan to get rid of us."

"Whatever the senator has planned, he may not succeed. Perhaps he's underestimating our abilities."

"I'm sure he is." Nick met Melody's eyes. "Mac has decided to send in one of our best undercover operatives to handle the situation."

Her cheeks flushed almost imperceptibly at the unusual compliment. He was no more generous in praising her professional abilities than he was in any other area of their relationship.

"Then what's Rachel Cranford's role in all this?" Melody asked. "Do you think she's a plant?"

"She could be. Or her devotion to Zachary Wharton might be genuine and Cranford is just using her to provide convincing cover for his sudden interest in the Soldiers of Jordan. In any event, don't trust her. In fact, when you're in Idaho, don't trust anyone except yourself. Assume that nobody is what he or she seems, and that everyone is lying."

Melody sighed, looking worried, as well as exhausted. "I appreciate Mac's confidence, but this mission sounds way over my level of expertise, Nick. If I screw up, the Soldiers of Jordan might kill dozens of people. Not to mention that Senator Cranford could get the budget for Unit One cut to zero. Our whole organization might be shut down because I was too incompetent to recognize what was really going on."

To hell with self-discipline, he needed another drink. Nick crossed to the sideboard where Melody stored her liquor and splashed vodka over ice. "You're ready for this mission, Melody—"

"Then why did you tell Mac the opposite? I'm sure you did, otherwise you'd never have used such a feeble excuse to get me out of his office."

"You're right. I wanted you out of the room. I was angry that Mac finalized the mission profile without consulting me—"

"And that's all? You sent me out of Mac's office so that you could indulge in a professional spat about turf?"

Nick forced a grin. "Hey, there's nothing more likely to get a couple of bureaucrats roiled up than a turf war. But as it happens, Mac also convinced me that if any agent in Unit One has a chance of getting intimate enough with Zachary Wharton to find out what's really going on with the Soldiers of Jordan, then you're the one."

If only his feelings about the mission were as simple as that explanation made them sound!

Melody frowned. "That's the part I don't understand. I'm the new kid on the block. I have no experience running a solo mission. Why send me?"

"Zachary Wharton is known to prefer women who are tall, slender and blond. You're tall, slender and blond—"

"So are at least three other Unit One agents with a lot more experience."

"Yes, but Zachary is known to have a real fondness for the Brits ever since he spent a year as an exchange student at Oxford University. His fiancée who died was English. You're half English. Plus he's a World War II buff and his greatest hero is Winston Churchill. You have grandparents who are not only Brits, they're the Earl and Countess of Ridgefield, and they met on the battlefields of Nazi-occupied France. They received medals for personal bravery straight from the hands of Churchill himself. You're a mighty attractive bait to dangle in front of a guy from inner-city Detroit with delusions of grandeur."

"Okay, my background story fits well," Melody conceded. "But even if I'm the perfect bait, surely Zachary won't take it?"

"Why not?" Nick was genuinely puzzled by her comment.

"If Senator Cranford is trying to set Unit One up, he'll warn Zachary that I'm a government agent. After which, Zachary will avoid me like the plague."

"Not true," Nick contradicted quietly. "Senator Cranford can't double-cross us if we never manage to get a Unit One agent onto the Soldiers of Jordan campus. He needs to have an agent in White Falls if he's going to lead us into a trap. It's a safe bet that the senator isn't going to pass on any warnings to Zachary Wharton."

Melody got to her feet and began to pace. "Let's assume

for a moment that everything works the way you've outlined. That Zachary is attracted to me and Cranford doesn't warn him I'm a spy. So I go with Zachary to White Falls and become his mistress—"

"I'm sure he'll have a better word for it than mistress," Nick interjected dryly. "How about acolyte? Or disciple? Or vessel of God?"

Her mouth turned down in distaste. "Whatever fancy name he gives our relationship, you and Mac are both assuming that if Zachary has sex with me, he'll let down his guard enough that I'll be able to discover what the Soldiers are plotting. You're counting on this despite the failure of two experienced FBI officers to uncover evidence of anything illegal. Not to mention the fact that Senator Cranford probably has some scheme going that's specifically designed to fool any Unit One operative infiltrating the Soldiers of Jordan."

"Yes, you're right," Nick said tersely. "We're expecting you to do better than the two FBI agents and we're expecting you to outwit Cranford."

"Why? How? What's my advantage over two FBI agents with twenty years of combined experience?"

"Sex," Nick said succinctly. "Sex always changes the equation because it automatically entails some degree of intimacy—"

"Coming from you, that's almost funny." Melody smiled with no trace of mirth. "You, of all people, should know that sex and intimacy have nothing to do with each other. What if Zachary just takes me to bed, has sex and then sends me straight back to the girls' dorm?"

"You'll have to make sure that doesn't happen, won't you?" Nick took a hefty swig of vodka, deliberately blanking his mind to pictures of Melody seducing Zachary Wharton, and then lying wrapped in his arms, tempting him into postcoital pillow talk.

He drew in a deep breath, since the vodka wasn't helping. "Obviously you and Zachary having sex doesn't solve all our problems. Zachary isn't going to take you to bed and immediately announce details of his master plan to control the world. You'll have to create your own opportunities and exploit every tiny advantage that comes your way, just as you would in any other mission. Having a sexual relationship with Zachary gives you an edge, that's all. You'll be with him in places and situations where no male agent could hope to penetrate without spending months—maybe years—gaining Zachary's confidence. To put it bluntly, exploiting your sexuality cuts the time investment Unit One has to make in this investigation. And right now, Mac and I are both afraid that we don't have too much time before something significantly bad happens."

Melody had poured herself a glass of sparkling water while he was in the shower. She sipped it now. "You make seducing Zachary sound so impersonal. Doesn't it bother you that in order to succeed in this mission, I'll be having sex with another man?"

Six months ago, he would have lied to her without a qualm. Three months ago, he'd have lied but felt a qualm. Now, he couldn't even lie. Rather than look at her, Nick stared into his glass of melting ice, but he admitted the truth.

"Yes, it bothers the hell out of me."

"Me, too."

The silence in the room was suddenly suffocating. "It's only sex," he said finally. "You have to keep your attention focused on the big picture."

"Only sex?" She gave a wry laugh. "My God, Nick, is that

how you view it? Is that why seduction in the line of duty is so easy for you?"

For a moment Nick wished it was still 1950 and he could tell her sex was different for a man. "Sex with Zachary Wharton doesn't have to entail personal involvement on your part."

"You're getting twisted in your own rhetoric, Nick. A few moments ago you were explaining to me how sex always involves intimacy."

"It would have been more accurate to say that sex always involves the *potential* for intimacy. As an agent, on a mission, you have to exploit that potential without allowing any encroachment on your emotions."

She drew the tip of her finger around the rim of her glass, her distress apparent. "The more I think about this assignment, the less sure I am that I can go through with it, Nick. I'm going to ask Mac to find somebody else."

His heart felt as if strips were being torn from it without benefit of anesthesia, but a dozen years of intensive training impelled him to worry about the dangers represented by the Soldiers of Jordan rather than the threat to his own relationship with Melody. "There is nobody else. Unit One has excellent training sessions you can take—"

"Training sessions?" Melody's expression was disbelieving. "Unit One has training sessions on how to seduce a religious fanatic?"

"The sessions provide general insights rather than specific instructions." And he sure as hell wasn't going to be the person teaching the class as he usually did. "Zachary's a man, as well as a cult leader, and you're a very desirable woman. Until he got religion after his fiancée died, he had an active sex life, with multiple partners. I don't anticipate that you'll have any difficulty seducing him—"

"Well, I do. The woman Unit One sends up against Zachary Wharton has to be absolutely confident of herself, her motives and her sexuality. I'm not that woman, Nick. I've done several things in my life that I've regretted later, but I've never had sex with a man I didn't care about. I don't think I can seduce Zachary Wharton just so that I can betray him."

"You need to stop focusing on the seduction," Nick said. "Move past it. Think about Jodie Evanderhaus, who ended up dead at the ripe old age of thirty-nine. Focus on the death threats against the mayor of White Falls. Remind yourself that Zachary Wharton is very likely a man who's already committed murder. Above all, focus on the likelihood that Zachary is a fanatic who holds human life cheap. He's quite possibly planning to kill dozens of American citizens whose only crime is to be Muslim. And that's if he doesn't have some even more ominous mission in mind that we can't begin to fathom until an agent from Unit One manages to get close enough to him to climb inside his head."

Melody flicked her hair away from her eyes. "I agree those are important issues. I understand Zachary Wharton needs to be stopped—"

"Good. Then remember that seducing a target is often the quickest and most efficient method of achieving the desired results. With everything that's at stake here, the speed with which we can obtain answers matters. It matters a lot."

"I understand all that," she said quietly. "I just don't know if I'm willing to prostitute myself, even if I agree with the merits of the cause."

"You're not *prostituting* yourself." Nick spoke calmly, as if Melody's protests weren't tying his gut in knots. "That's the sort of word people use to make themselves feel guilty. You're a Unit One agent and you've been assigned to a mission. You're working in the service of your country. You're hoping to save innocent people's lives. Your personal feelings don't strike me as especially relevant."

Melody stared at him, her expression hovering somewhere between frustration and disbelief. "Personal feelings are always relevant, Nick. They're the lodestone that keeps us from going so far off track that we end up damaging ourselves."

"Maybe for most people. But you're not most people. Personal feelings are a luxury you can't afford to indulge on the job." Before he met Melody, Nick would have believed what he was saying. The fact that he was now merely mouthing the words scared the hell out of him. What if Mac were right? Had he gone soft? Lost his edge? As chief of operations for Unit One, he absolutely couldn't afford to be squishy around the margins.

He spoke with renewed force, trying to convince himself. "If Zachary Wharton is planning the sort of massive attack against the Muslim community that Unit One suspects, then you need to go after him with all the skill and all the assets you have at your command. Your sexual allure is one of your biggest assets. As chief of Unit One, Mac would be derelict in his duty if he ignored your potential for succeeding with Wharton where two highly trained FBI agents have failed."

Melody retied the belt of her robe, pulling the lapels across her chest as if she felt chilled, although it was warm inside the apartment. "In theory, I accept everything you say, Nick. But in practice, I believe I'm going to resign. This assignment brings home to me how unsuited I am to work for Unit One. The mission isn't at risk if I quit. There are other female agents on the roster who would do a far more competent job of seducing Zachary Wharton than I'm capable of."

"Your resignation won't be accepted." For the first time

that night, Nick was a hundred percent sure of the accuracy of what he was saying.

She looked up at him, puzzled. "Why not?"

"Unit One is a paramilitary organization. You've signed a contract, and you're legally obligated to serve three years—"

Melody's gaze narrowed. "Quite apart from the fact that I signed under duress, those contracts are almost never enforced. Sam told me that months ago."

"Yours would be enforced," he said curtly.

"Then I'll go back to England. I still have a British passport. What's Unit One going to do once I'm out of the States?"

"Extract you."

"Extract me?"

"Yes." Nick's smile took on a dark, lethal edge. "And when you've been returned to the States, you'll be charged with desertion. The trial will take place before a secret military tribunal, and I can assure you the verdict won't be in doubt."

"Why in the world would Unit One go to all the trouble of extracting me?" Melody stared at him in bewilderment.

Because I would order the mission. Because even if we're not going to be lovers anymore, I need to know you're somewhere close to me.

"Because you're too valuable to lose," Nick said. He took comfort in the knowledge that he was speaking the truth, if not the whole truth. "You're a natural as a covert operative, Melody. You have a unique background and skill set. In the past three months, you've successfully completed assignments that agents with ten years' experience might have fumbled."

She didn't look happy with the compliment. "Am I supposed to be flattered because you think I have an innate talent for lies, theft, deception and betrayal?"

"Yes, if those talents enable you to put an end to activities that threaten the security and well-being of civilized society."

"You have an answer for everything, Nick. But right at this moment, I don't care much about the security of civilized society. I care about Mac's order that I'm to seduce Zachary Wharton." Her voice lowered. "I care about...us."

Nick had been waiting to hear her say something like this for much longer than he cared to acknowledge. But now that she'd suggested her feelings for him were important, he panicked. He'd been backing away from commitment for so long, he'd lost his capacity to handle a relationship that threatened to move out of the limited and short-term into something more significant.

"Unit One isn't the sort of workplace that encourages marriage and cozy family values," he said, after a pause. "Mac has been divorced twice. Ditto for Sam and half the other staff at headquarters."

"I didn't ask you to marry me, Nick. There are a lot of commitments friends can make to one another that fall short of marriage."

"Meaningful, long-term commitments aren't possible within the context of Unit One."

"I hope you don't really believe that."

"I believe it because it's the truth."

The look Melody directed at him was pitying. "Then I'm sorry for you, Nick, but it doesn't change my decision. You may be willing to sacrifice your personal life for the sake of Unit One. I'm not."

"As I explained a moment ago, you don't have any choice—"

"There are always choices, and I've made mine. I resign. I quit. I'm out of here. You and Mac will have my resigna-

tion in writing first thing tomorrow morning. To hell with
threats. If Unit One decides to enforce our contract and have
me prosecuted, let them go ahead. I don't believe any judge
in the country is going to put me behind bars because I refuse to prostitute myself with Zachary Wharton. Not even the
judge at one of your infamous secret military tribunals is
going to order me to have sex with a man I don't know, who
may be crazy and is quite probably planning to blow people
up."

She wasn't going to change her mind, Nick realized. Not
willingly, at least. He knew her well enough to be sure that
her threats weren't empty. In which case, the details of Zachary Wharton's mad plans would most likely be discovered
only when the bomb squad and the paramedics were picking
up body parts.

Nick did, however, possess one surefire weapon to coerce
her cooperation.

Maybe he should have left it for Mac to reason with her
when he got back from D.C. Maybe he was too tired to be
smart. Or maybe he had a masochistic urge to be the person
who delivered the final body blow to their relationship rather
than simply waiting for it to disintegrate under the pressure
of Mac's order for Nick to back off. In any event, he hesitated
only a few seconds before launching his attack.

He forced his mouth into a sardonic smile. "I should have
remembered that bribes work better than threats where you're
concerned," he said.

Melody shook her head, suddenly looking exhausted. She
held up her hand, as if warding off his words. "Let's not fight,
Nick. I don't want that. Truly. But you and Mac need to understand that I've made my decision. I'm not denying that I've
enjoyed the past six months, but that just shows how I've al-

lowed my judgment to become warped. This mission has brought everything back into perspective, and I want out. There are no threats and no bribes Unit One can offer to make me change my mind."

"You haven't heard yet what's on offer."

"I don't care. Wallis Beecham is already behind bars and there's nothing more Unit One can offer me. I don't want to seduce Zachary Wharton. I don't want to be a government agent. I'm leaving Unit One."

She still had a lot to learn about the power of Unit One, Nick thought. The threats were more real and the rewards more gratifying than she dreamed of, even after six months' exposure to the system. What's more, Unit One was masterful at blurring the line between threats and promises, blending the whole into an enticing package that kept even the most reluctant operative toeing the party line.

Nick realized he faced one last chance to back off and leave Mac to do Unit One's dirty work. It took only a second of reflection to decide that he preferred that the bribe to Melody—the betrayal?—should come from him.

"You're wrong in suggesting that Unit One has nothing to offer you," he said. "We can offer you something you want very badly."

Melody shrugged, torn between puzzlement and a healthy hint of impatience. "I can't imagine what that might be. I don't have many burning wants, Nick."

How little she knew herself. Nick drew in a slow, deep breath. "How would you like to know who your father is and where you can find him?"

The air in the room was suddenly thick with tension. Melody didn't respond for at least ten seconds, and when she spoke, her calm was deadly. "Do you know who my father is, Nick?"

He'd burned his bridges, so he told her the truth. "No, but other people within Unit One possess that information."

"How could they possibly know? My mother's dead. She told nobody that Wallis wasn't my father until she made the announcement in her will. I've searched every document, every scrap of paper she left behind. You couldn't have accessed her papers before I did…"

He didn't reply, but after a few moments, she answered her own question. "Jasper," she said with icy certainty. "It's Jasper, isn't it? He knows who my father is, and he's recorded the information on some file at headquarters."

Nick's silence was all the admission she needed.

Melody's voice ached with the enormity of Jasper's deception. "My God, despite everything that happened last year, I thought Jasper was my friend. How could he possibly have kept such important personal information from me?"

"He's the commander of Unit One."

"That's it? That's your answer? He's the commander of Unit One?" Melody stared at him, her expression shading from shock into despair. "How could *you* keep it from me, Nick? We've been lovers for almost six months. Doesn't that mean anything at all to you in terms of honesty and trust?"

He excused himself with the literal truth, the last refuge of a total coward. "I already explained, I don't know who your father is. I didn't have the information to give you."

The acid of her scorn dissolved his feeble excuse. "But you could have found out, couldn't you? In about two heartbeats."

"Yes." He didn't explain that he had deliberately avoided acquiring the information for fear that he would divulge it. In the last resort, he'd played by Unit One rules and he deserved her scorn.

Melody turned away. Judging by the glimpse he'd had of

the cold fury in her eyes, Nick guessed he'd just hammered the final nail into the coffin of their relationship. Not to mention her love for Jasper Fowles. Nick could almost feel sorry for the guy. Because, whatever Melody believed to the contrary, Jasper loved her as the daughter he'd never had.

Not that he needed to waste sympathy on Jasper, Nick reflected grimly. He had his own problems to worry about. Right now, he was guessing he had about as much chance of ever renewing his relationship with Melody as he did of celebrating his next birthday on one of the moons of Jupiter.

Melody stopped her furious pacing and swung around to look at him. Her eyes flashed with so much contempt Nick could feel himself shrivel.

"Congratulations. Your bribe has worked," she said with icy disdain. "I withdraw my resignation. By your standards, I guess you could say you've just won the battle. I'll seduce Zachary Wharton and squeeze out the information you're looking for—"

"I'm delighted to hear it—"

She wasn't willing to let him speak. "In exchange, the moment I hand in my final report on Zachary Wharton and the Soldiers of Jordan, I expect to be given the name and current address of my biological father. There, are you happy?"

"No, far from it. But I am relieved that the best possible agent is going to be investigating Zachary Wharton and the Soldiers of Jordan. I believe that a hell of a lot is at stake here."

"And that's all that matters to you, isn't it?" Melody drew in a shaky breath. "The mission always takes precedence over individual moral qualms. Not to mention individual happiness."

"If I said no, you wouldn't believe me." Unfortunately Nick wasn't sure he believed himself. "Dammit, Melody, we're talking about a situation where dozens of lives may be at stake. Perhaps hundreds of lives."

She ignored his attempt to justify his actions. "I would ask for a written promise that Jasper will reveal the name of my father as soon as I've completed my assignment, but I know how little Unit One's promises are worth."

"They'll give you the name," Nick promised. "You have my word."

"Well, now I'm completely reassured." Melody's sarcasm was biting. "Just make sure that Mac and Jasper understand I'll rot in jail for the rest of my life before I undertake another mission if Unit One doesn't uphold its end of the bargain this time."

"I'll make sure they get your message." Nick desperately wanted to say something that would redeem him in Melody's eyes, but he couldn't come up with any justification for what he'd done that she was likely to understand, much less accept. Why would Melody feel any more kindly toward him because he admitted that he was neurotic, unsure of himself and still angry with fate for snatching away his family? Melody had suffered tragedies and betrayals in her own life, and far from needing Unit One in order to rebuild her sense of self, she had enough inner strength to define Unit One as the enemy.

Nick steeled his heart. When you got right down to it, he'd had no choice. He was number three in the Unit One chain of command and he had a sworn duty to perform. Right now, he needed to reestablish a working relationship with Melody, even if their sexual relationship was shattered.

"It might be easier for us to decide on the parameters of tomorrow's mission if we hold our planning meeting at head-quarters," he said. "I'll expect you in my office at 1300 hours. Our first priority is to work out the details of how we're going to end our affair. The breakup has to be dramatic if it's going to make a splash in the media."

"Maybe I could stab you in the middle of Times Square."

"No, that would get you arrested."

"Pity. Although on second thought, a lifetime in prison might be a small price to pay for the satisfaction of seeing you dead at my feet."

"Then you'll never know who your father is."

Melody didn't speak. Her eyes said it all.

Nick ignored the sick feeling in the pit of his stomach. "I'm afraid you'll have to put up with being the victim in the public breakup of our relationship, since victims are more appealing to Zachary Wharton. Tentatively I'm planning to have you discover me in Jasper's guest bedroom with another woman."

"How is that going to make a splash in the media?"

"The woman will be Jacyntha Ramon."

Melody betrayed not a smidgen of surprise or interest in the fact that Nick was about to humiliate her with one of America's media darlings. She gave a curt nod of acknowledgment and walked quickly across the living room to the front door. She didn't ask how he could be sure that the star of the summer's hottest movie would be willing to play the role of the Other Woman and Nick sure as hell wasn't about to admit that Jacyntha had been trying to get him into bed for the last three months.

"I'm tired," she said, opening the door to her apartment. "We'll finalize the details in your office tomorrow. Please leave now."

Nick made one last despairing search for something to say or do that might redeem him in Melody's eyes. He came up empty.

Melody held out her hand. "I'd like my apartment keys back, please."

Nick gave them to her and she closed her fingers around them, clenching her fist tightly enough for her knuckles to turn white. Then she slipped them into the pocket of her robe. Her smile as he walked out into the corridor was mocking, impersonal, devastating.

"So long, Nick. See you around."

"Good night, Melody. I'm really…sorry."

"What for? Achieving your goal?" Before he could respond, she shut the door behind him, closing it with a firm click.

Nick pressed the elevator call button, his vision blurring, but his emotions flattened to the point of blankness. He'd experienced this sensation once before, when his family were blown up, and he recognized its return with a sense of dread.

It was despair, he realized. Utter, complete and total despair at the realization that he'd just lost Melody. Worse, that he hadn't really lost her; he'd deliberately thrown her away. And all because he was too damn scared to tell her that he loved her.

Six

Senator Lewis Cranford was working in the spacious library that he used as a home office when he was unexpectedly disturbed by the intrusion of his wife. He suppressed a quiver of annoyance at the interruption, and gave her a tepid smile. Until recently, Eleanor had been a model political wife, and he was willing to do his part to preserve marital harmony.

Eleanor was a woman of slender build, regular features and a conservative taste in clothes. She reminded male voters of their sisters, and wasn't sexy or fashionable enough to threaten female voters, a winning combination from the senator's point of view. She seemed to have no opinions on issues of the day that contradicted his own, or if she did she was smart enough never to express them. In return, the senator treated her with unfailing courtesy and paid off her bills each month without questioning too closely how his money had been spent.

This agreeable working relationship had frayed around the edges in recent weeks. Ever since Rachel had dropped out of college and taken off for Idaho, the senator had noticed worrying signs that Eleanor was no longer entirely reliable. She had not only argued with him about how they should deal with their daughter's flagrant failure to live up to her family obligations, but she'd even disagreed with him on a couple of policy issues. Although never, thank God, when there had been anyone important around. The senator was fully aware of the fact that a man who couldn't control his own wife had no hope of achieving higher office.

"I need to talk with you, Lewis."

The senator made a fuss about putting down his Montblanc pen and taking off his glasses, just so that Eleanor would realize she'd interrupted a vital train of thought.

"Is something wrong?" he asked. "You look a little agitated, my dear."

"I'm very worried, Lewis. I tried to call Rachel this morning. The man who answered the phone said she was unavailable to take my call."

"That hardly merits a rush to panic stations, Eleanor."

"Well, I called back again just now and they passed me around from one person to another. Finally a woman came on the phone. She told me Rachel had the flu and wouldn't be able to talk to me for the next couple of days."

"I'm sorry to hear Rachel is sick. Although if she would come home where she belongs—"

To the senator's amazement, Eleanor actually interrupted him. "How do we know Rachel's sick?" she demanded. "How do we know those crazies don't have her locked up so that they can perform some weird religious ritual? For all we know, she's going to come on the phone next time I call and tell me that she's been married off to some lunatic who spends half the day praising Jesus and the rest of his time blowing heads off scarecrows in potato fields!"

Truth be told, the possibility of Rachel marrying one of the Soldiers of Jordan had caused the senator several uneasy moments. Still, a daughter enmeshed in a Christian cult wasn't likely to generate as much bad publicity as politicians whose adult children were in drug rehab, or were campaigning for the legalization of gay marriage. If governors and vice presidents could survive that sort of negative PR, he could survive having a religious fruitcake for a daughter. In fact, he was counting on it.

"You're overreacting, Eleanor. The truth is, Rachel probably has the flu, exactly as you were told—"

"Then let me fly to Idaho and see for myself. I've checked the flights and if I leave right now, I can still get into Boise tonight."

The senator let her ramble on about hiring a car and driving to White Falls while he took a moment to think. Smart men always took a moment to check their impulse to blurt out the first thing that popped into their heads. "We have a dinner at the French embassy tonight," he said finally.

"I know." Eleanor sent him a pleading glance. "I just want to see for myself that Rachel is well and happy. I thought maybe you could ask Caroline Quentin to go with you in my place."

Caroline Quentin was his chief legislative aide, a woman as smart as she was ambitious. Lewis looked at his wife closely, but decided she couldn't possibly know that he and Caroline were having an affair. He noticed that his fingers were playing with the earpiece of his glasses and he stopped the telltale gesture at once.

"I can't believe a trip to White Falls is necessary, Eleanor.

I've read all the FBI reports, and while I agree that this Zachary Wharton fellow is a charlatan, I'm quite sure Rachel isn't in any danger."

"She's barely nineteen. She may be smart academically, but she doesn't have a grain of common sense." Eleanor's voice had an audible catch to it. "There are plenty of ways she can be hurt other than physical injuries. Please let me go, Lewis. In another week Megan will be coming home from prep school, so this is my last chance to get away."

There was always the risk that his wife would persuade Rachel to come home, which would undercut his professed reason for calling in Unit One. The risk of Rachel quitting Idaho seemed slight, however, and the benefits substantial in terms of getting Eleanor off his back. Unit One hadn't yet initiated its investigation. Steve Johnson—his ace in the hole—was not yet on campus. On balance, he saw no reason to forbid Eleanor to make the trip.

The senator gave his wife an indulgent smile. "Well, my dear, if it's so important to you, of course you should go and see our daughter. Don't worry about tonight's dinner. I'll make your excuses to the French ambassador."

"Thank you, Lewis. Thank you for being so understanding." He was glad to see that Eleanor at least appeared properly grateful. "I'll call you from White Falls as soon as I get there. Perhaps I'll even be able to persuade Rachel to come home."

"Don't get your hopes up on that score. You know how stubborn she is."

"Yes, unfortunately." Eleanor paused on her way out of the library. "Oh, by the way, I took a call for you about an hour ago, while you were outside in the garden. From a Mr. Johnson. Steve Johnson. He said he'd be stopping by the house to see you this afternoon at three. He said you were expecting him, but you hadn't confirmed the precise time. He didn't leave a phone number."

The senator drew in a long, slow breath, covering his excitement. "Thank you." He almost made the mistake of inventing an explanation as to who Mr. Steve Johnson was, then stopped himself just in time. His wife, after twenty-one years of marriage, was too well-trained to expect explanations about his constant stream of visitors and he didn't want to do anything to fix Steve Johnson's visit in her mind.

Cranford glanced at his watch. "Two forty-five. You need to hurry. I'll just have time to phone Caroline before Johnson arrives. It's such short notice. I hope she's free to join me tonight."

"For you, I'm quite sure she'll be free."

Cranford decided he must be imagining the sardonic note in his wife's voice. He looked up, directing a searching glance at her, but there was nothing in Eleanor's expression or her meek body language to confirm the outrageous suspicion that she was mocking him.

Frowning, the senator pressed the speed dial on his desk phone, nodding to his wife as he waited for his mistress to answer his call. He found the juxtaposition amusing and his good humor was restored. "Have a safe trip, Eleanor. Don't stay too long. I'll look forward to seeing you by the middle of the week."

At one minute past three, the live-in housekeeper tapped on the library door. "Zayer iz Meest' Yonson in liffing room, Senator." The woman's accent was so thickly eastern European that he wouldn't have understood what she was saying unless he'd been waiting to hear that Steve Johnson had arrived.

Cranford smiled warmly at the housekeeper, whose name temporarily escaped him. He was careful to be friendly to the help, although he was equally careful to hire people who spoke barely adequate English—not a challenge in D.C., where ninety percent of the people looking for work seemed to be foreigners. In Cranford's judgment, a combination of treating servants well and making sure they couldn't understand what was being said provided a valuable insurance policy against gossip, backstabbing and unwanted leaks to the press about his private life.

"Thank you. Would you show him in here, please?"

She looked blank, so he repeated his message with gestures. She gave a relieved smile. "I go fetch."

She returned almost at once, followed by a middle-aged man of uncertain ethnicity and nondescript appearance, wearing the Washington weekend uniform of khakis and a navy-blue blazer.

"Senator, thank you for agreeing to meet with me." The man walked across the study, hand outstretched, and Cranford rose, leaning across his desk to shake the man's hand.

"Steve Johnson, I presume?" Cranford certainly wouldn't have recognized him. He turned to the housekeeper, whose name finally popped into his head. "Thank you, Kaija. Close the door as you go out, please."

Neither man spoke until the housekeeper was out of the room and had closed the door as instructed. "I trust the last few days have been uneventful?" Cranford said, scrutinizing his visitor for familiar features and finding none.

"Excuse me," Steve said, walking quickly and quietly back to the door. He opened it and leaned his head out, scanning the hallway.

Satisfied it was deserted, he returned to the study and sat down across the desk from the senator without waiting to be invited. "Just making sure we weren't being overheard," Steve said. "Infiltrating agents into the domestic staff is one of Unit One's favorite tricks."

"Kaija's been here for months."

Steve looked faintly amused. "That's not necessarily proof of her innocence, you know. Unit One has both the funds and resources to be patient. Speaking of which…" He reached into his briefcase and took out a small electronic device, which he set on the desk.

Cranford sensed that he'd already lost control of the meeting but wasn't sure how to regain it. Damned Unit One operatives, he thought. They're all arrogant bastards, even the corrupt ones.

"What's that?" he asked, pointing to the device.

"One of Bob Spinard's favorite toys, although you can buy them anywhere these days. It overrides virtually all eavesdropping and listening devices. Blankets the airwaves with white noise so that you can't distinguish speech patterns even with voice-enhancing equipment. If your house is bugged, I don't want to have our conversation monitored. This little device operates with eighty percent efficiency even when confined to a briefcase, but with almost a hundred percent efficiency when freestanding."

"Of course my house isn't bugged!"

"How would you know? When was it last swept?"

"It's never been swept," Cranford muttered. "But how could anyone get access to plant a bug?"

Steve merely sent him a pitying look. Cranford thought about all the plumbers, electricians and other service personnel who wandered through his home on a regular basis. He made a mental note to hire a bug-sweeping crew first thing on Monday morning.

"Let's get down to business, shall we?" Steve said. "I'm running tight on time."

Cranford wasn't going to jump just because Steve Johnson told him to. Dammit, the guy needed to remember who was hiring whom. "You've changed your appearance but there hasn't been time for plastic surgery since you escaped. How did you do that?"

Steve said nothing.

Cranford tried again. "Is this how you're going to look when you join the Soldiers of Jordan?"

"Of course not." Steve sounded impatient at the suggestion. "Look, I have to be on a plane leaving Dulles in three hours, so can we cut the chitchat? You have some money waiting for me, I assume."

"First, I need to know what your plan is once you arrive in White Falls."

Steve's smile disappeared. He leaned forward slightly in his chair, and his easygoing attitude changed into one of subtle menace. "No, Senator. You already have a general idea of what's going to happen. I've made a promise that Unit One will be brought down. You have absolutely no need to know what the specifics of my plan are."

Cranford had conducted enough negotiations with thugs and criminals—not to mention politicians—to realize that it was now or never in terms of asserting his authority. Instead of backing away, he, too, leaned forward. "I'll remind you that you're one phone call away from being returned to Leavenworth. If you want my money, *Mr. Johnson,* I want some details of how you're going to earn it."

Steve's eyes narrowed, but he finally surrendered at least a snippet of concrete information. "I've been hired as the new training coordinator for Zachary Wharton's army, and that's all I'm going to tell you."

Cranford started to protest, but Steve cut him off. "No, Senator, you really don't need to know anything more about the specifics of the plan. If you were smart, you wouldn't *want* to know anything more. But I will guarantee my results. Here's what I'm promising you. Within one month of Unit One inserting an agent into the Soldiers of Jordan, their army will mount an attack against one of the larger mosques in Detroit. Our designated target will be in attendance at that mosque at the time of the attack. There will be a pitched battle, and when the battle is over, copious numbers of religious fanatics and government agents will be dead. The outcome is guaranteed."

Cranford felt a faint tightening of his stomach muscles. "You'd better make damn sure that my daughter is miles away before your battle starts."

"That's part of our deal, Senator. Your daughter will be leaving the campus five days before the battle erupts. Her return home will be your signal that we've entered the final countdown for the climax of the operation." Steve leaned back in his chair. "Now, I'd like the money you owe me."

Cranford crossed to his wall safe, hidden behind an enlarged photograph of himself and the owner standing alongside last year's winner of the Kentucky Derby. His safe was state-of-the-art, with no combination to remember and therefore no chance that somebody with fancy electronic equipment could override the locks. The safe could only be opened by two methods: blowing it up—or a biomatch of his right thumb and left index finger, touching the keypad in sequence.

The safe door swung open in response to his touch and Cranford removed the shrink-wrapped stack of cash from the safe. He carried it back to the desk and handed it to Steve.

"Here you are. One hundred thousand dollars. Give me an account number, anywhere in the world, and another three hundred thousand will be transferred into that account by close of banking hours on Monday, eastern time." He spoke blandly, although he had to admit his heart was pumping pretty damn good. Not to beat around the bush, Steve Johnson scared the shit out of him.

"The agreement," Steve said with deadly quiet, "was for half a million dollars. Up-front. In cash. Another two million to follow when I've achieved the destruction of Unit One."

For once Cranford told the simple truth. "I can't access that many U.S. dollars without drawing attention to myself. The bulk of my money is overseas and I have to be careful about bringing it into the country. You know as well as I do that the government is scrutinizing cash transactions with a great deal more intensity since they realized just how Al Qaeda uses so-called charities to send operating funds around the globe. If you don't already have an offshore account, and I assume you do, you need to open one this weekend and provide me with the number. I'll transfer the funds from my account in Russia. It's safer for both of us that way."

Steve didn't look appeased. "Even if I accept your explanation as to why you haven't lived up to our bargain, your method of payment still leaves me short a hundred grand."

Cranford shook his head. "On the contrary, it leaves you overpaid. Getting you out of Leavenworth cost me more than a hundred thousand in bribes and other expenses."

"And I'm worth every cent," Steve said softly. He rose to his feet, stuffing the money into his briefcase. "I could walk away from you right now, but I'm an honorable man." He smiled mockingly, although Cranford couldn't decide where the mockery was directed.

"I'm cutting you a major piece of slack, Senator. As a gesture of appreciation for the fact that you did facilitate those

Leavenworth arrangements on my behalf, I'm willing to wait until Monday for the money you owe me. At which point I expect to find four hundred thousand dollars transferred into my account in the Caymans. Not three hundred thousand, Senator. Four. Got that? Four. Count 'em. Four."

Cranford scowled. "I hear you."

"Good." Steve held out a sheet of paper that contained multiple sets of numbers, apparently grouped at random. "My account number appears in the seventh line from the top, first ten digits. You can find the bank code for the electronic transfer by looking at the ninth line, last six numbers. That's line seven, first ten digits for the account number. Bank code is line nine, last six figures. Please don't highlight or mark those numbers in any way. And get rid of the sheet when you've made the transfer, Senator. Just remember you have a hell of a lot more to lose than I do if anyone ever figures out who helped spring me from Leavenworth. I can disappear. You wouldn't have a clue how to do that. Okay?"

The senator found Steve Johnson's attitude infuriating. However, he would have been a lot angrier if he hadn't expected all along to pay the full half-million up-front. As for the two million bucks on completion of the assignment, he was way too smart to contemplate double-crossing Steve on that deal. Lewis planned to pay the guy sufficient funds to stay out of prison and enjoy his freedom for a long, long time. That way, he would have no incentive to inform anyone of his business partnership with Senator Lewis Cranford. Bottom line: two and a half million Russian oil dollars—all he had left of his dealings with Nikolai Anwar—was a cheap price for getting rid of Unit One. Lewis had things to do and places to go, and Unit One was the custodian of information that could drop him in his tracks.

Despite Steve Johnson's irritating attitude, Cranford concluded that their meeting had gone pretty damn well. And tonight he'd be having hot sex with Caroline, which sure as hell beat having boring marital sex with his wife.

His mood unexpectedly upbeat, Cranford escorted his guest personally to the front door. Hell, it was the least he could do for the guy who was going to take down Unit One and make America safe for Lewis Cranford.

Seven

Seventy-five-year-old Howard Cartwright, self-made billionaire, died while making love to his forty-year-old wife, Amelia, whose bloodlines were true blue, but whose family coffers had been emptied by two generations of wastrels. At the time of Howard's death, his marriage to Amelia had lasted a mere eight months. Fortunately for her, Howard had already rewritten his will, leaving the bulk of his vast fortune to his new wife.

In the four years since that literal stroke of good fortune, Amelia had been thanking God for Howard's timely demise by hosting lavish fund-raisers for a variety of worthy causes. The charities she supported ran the gamut from starving African children, through endangered Asian elephants, to American senior citizens who couldn't afford their medications. The one thing her causes all had in common was that Amelia invited only A-list guests for the privilege of consuming vintage burgundy from Howard's famous wine cellars, eating food catered by Bernadin and handing over thousand-dollar donations to noble causes. She saw no point in insulting the Almighty by allowing the hoi poloi to muscle their way into her program of good works.

Tonight's party on behalf of Zachary Wharton's mission to inner-city teens followed the usual pattern for Amelia's fund-raisers. Zachary's charisma quotient was off the charts and the guest list was stellar. Ninety-two people had paid to attend her party, which meant ninety-two thousand dollars straight into Zachary Wharton's treasure chest, since Amelia bore all the costs associated with hosting the event. In return for her generosity, Amelia was more than willing to receive Zachary's personal thanks as soon as the last guest had left the party. However, in keeping with the truly noble spirit of her charitable endeavors, the provision of sexual favors wasn't a precondition for being taken up as one of her causes.

And what a fine selection of guests she'd assembled tonight! Amelia eyed the crowds flowing through her Park Avenue penthouse with deep satisfaction. No boring social climbers or overjeweled Hollywood starlets had elbowed their way into this distinguished throng. On the contrary, these hand-picked guests were distinguished by their understated elegance and their abundant supply of money. Mostly gracious old money, but if not old, then such huge quantities that the tainted odor of newness could be forgiven.

Elegance, however, could take an ambitious hostess only so far. You needed excitement, too, especially for a fund-raiser, and excitement didn't mean hiring a reggae band instead of a harpist. Excitement meant a prime selection of celebrity guests and Amelia had achieved miracles in that department.

The chairman of the Stock Exchange, the attorney general of New York, and the conductor of the New York Philharmonic were all undisputed A-list, but her greatest coup tonight was the much-anticipated arrival of Melody Beecham. Even old-money Americans were impressed by British aristocrats, and Melody's grandparents were the real thing. The Earl and Countess of Ridgefield still lived on the Wiltshire land that had been given to their family by Richard I in the eleventh century, and much as sophisticated New Yorkers liked to pretend otherwise, you couldn't help being impressed by a family that had managed to defend its territorial acres for more than a thousand years.

Melody, however, had a lot more going for her than mere good looks and lustrous ancestors. Her media star, always radiant, had gone supernova since the mysterious death of her mother, the gorgeous Lady Rosalind, and the titillating revelation that billionaire Wallis Beecham wasn't her father. Her well-publicized liaison with Nikolai Anwar—no slouch himself in the celebrity department—and the arrest of Wallis Beecham on charges of kidnapping and conspiracy to commit murder had fanned the flames of public interest and kept her name in the gossip columns for months. But it was last week's spectacular breakup with Nikolai Anwar that had precipitated the sort of wall-to-wall media coverage usually reserved for Ben and J-Lo, or mass murderers who ate their victims.

The details of the Melody-Nikolai breakup varied according to who was telling the story, but the main outline was clear. At a party thrown by Jasper Fowles, owner of the prestigious Van der Meer Gallery, Melody had ventured into one of the guest bedrooms, accompanied by a reporter from *People* magazine. The idea, apparently, had been to find a quiet corner in which to talk. Unfortunately the corner Melody had chosen turned out to be anything but quiet. She and the journalist had walked in on Nikolai Anwar, who was romping naked on the bed with Jacyntha Ramon, the star of *Red Ocean,* last summer's giant box office smash.

No doubt fearing a flurry of lawsuits, *People* magazine had been annoyingly tactful in reporting what happened next. However, the tabloids had been less discreet and they informed their avid readers that at least a dozen of Jasper's guests had seen Nikolai emerge from the guest bedroom wearing clothes that didn't fit, and sporting an extremely bloody nose. Nikolai's own clothes, according to the *National Enquirer,* had been tossed off the balcony by an infuriated Melody, where they had immediately been scavenged by passing pedestrians. Nikolai, usually a poster boy for urban chic, had been forced to borrow slacks and a sweater from Jasper Fowles in order to slink home to his own apartment.

Melody must have left Jasper's penthouse via the service entrance because she hadn't been seen again that night, and she had refused all subsequent requests for interviews. Jacyntha Ramon was keeping equally quiet. According to TV reports, she had returned to L.A. on the first available flight, and nothing had been heard from her directly since the party. But a couple of her loose-mouthed friends had been quoted as saying that, based on her interrupted tryst with Nikolai Anwar, Jacyntha could understand why Melody Beecham was so furious about losing him. He was, according to Jacyntha, seriously well-endowed in all the areas most calculated to keep a woman happy.

Amelia was justifiably thrilled that Melody would be making her first post-Nikolai public appearance right here, at her fund-raiser. In Amelia's vast experience, there was nothing more calculated to get upper-crust hearts fluttering than a totally vulgar scandal about one of their own. The granddaughter of a British earl punching her errant lover in the nose was a tasty enough morsel. The fact that Melody had tossed Nikolai's clothes—every last stitch of them!—over the balcony of Jasper Fowles's penthouse was almost too delicious. Betrayed women everywhere could only sympathize. Errant men could only shudder.

It was almost eight when Melody finally put in an appearance at the party. Even though she'd arrived an hour late, Amelia rushed to welcome her. "Melody, you're here at last! I'm so glad you were able to make it. Oh, my God, is that an *original* Balenciaga you're wearing?"

"Yes, it was my mother's," Melody said. "She was given it on her eighteenth birthday. How clever of you to recognize a designer who closed up shop in the sixties."

"Darling, Cristobal Balenciaga is unmistakable. His bead work is unique." Amelia kissed the air near Melody's cheeks, nobly deciding not to feel jealous of the dress, or of how fabulous Melody looked. Amelia was naturally petite and dainty, and she worked hard to stay that way. In her opinion, verve and charm were feminine attributes that appealed far more to men than being tall and overintelligent like Melody. Who wanted to take a beanpole to bed? Especially if the beanpole was likely to start discussing the state of democracy in Africa at the slightest provocation. Of course, Melody also had perfect skin and hair to die for. Not to mention a body that tonight looked as if it had been poured into the incredible midnight-blue Balenciaga dress, glittering with antique crystal embroidery. Amelia couldn't help frowning, despite the threat of wrinkles, and the looming specter of Botox.

"You look wonderful, too, Amelia. That shade of green is lovely on you." Melody smiled as if she meant it, although she could already feel the stares of curious guests boring into her back. Fran and William Deneuve, notoriously avid gos sipmongers, even made a feeble excuse to stroll past so that they could scour her features for any hint of vulnerability.

Fortunately nobody would see anything Melody didn't want to reveal, however hard and long they stared. She'd learned to hide most of what she was feeling by the time she was shunted off to boarding school at the age of eleven, and her training with Unit One had honed her deceptive skills to a new level of competence. More to the point, she had no emotions she needed to hide. Her devastation at Nick's betrayal had lasted barely twenty-four hours before turning to anger, and even anger had passed over into numbness several days ago. At Jasper's party to be precise.

Melody had gone into the guest bedroom believing she was fully prepared to "discover" Nick wrapped in Jacyntha Ramon's arms. Why would she be upset, when she and Nick were no longer lovers, and the assignation was faked— cooked up in Nick's office with Melody agreeing to every detail of the plan?

Apparently, though, she hadn't been quite as prepared as she'd assumed. In one nightmare glance, Melody had absorbed the whole scene: the two of them stark naked, Nick's body so achingly familiar, Jacyntha's so threateningly voluptuous; the rumpled bedcovers, and Jacyntha's throaty little murmurs of contentment as Nick's hands ran over her luscious, surgically perfected breasts.

Melody had experienced a moment of searing, white-hot rage. If the sexual tension vibrating in that room had been faked, it was the best damn fake she'd ever been exposed to. It had been agreed in advance that she would slap Nick's face for the benefit of the *People* magazine reporter. The swinging punch she delivered to his nose had been no token gesture, however. It had packed all the force of the hurt and anger that had been building ever since Nick told her that Unit One knew the name of her biological father. That he could have found out the name if he'd wanted to.

Melody had watched the blood spurt from his nostrils as her punch landed, and she'd felt a heady mixture of chagrin and exhilaration. Grabbing Nick's clothes and tossing them over the balcony had been no part of their agreed script, any more than the hard-hitting punch, but it felt equally wonderful. As had the only remark she addressed to Jacyntha.

Make sure Nick never finds out what you want most in the world. He might promise to give it to you, and then you'll be left paying the price.

Melody's invigorating burst of rage had dissipated even before she left Jasper's penthouse. Numbness had set in, freezing her so completely that she was surprised when her body managed to get through the motions of daily life with its usual competence. Nothing had happened in the days since the party to precipitate an emotional thaw, which was probably fortunate in view of the mission that loomed ahead of her. For the next few weeks, Melody realized she needed to stay focused and not drift off into gloomy reveries about Nick or any of the other people in her life who'd betrayed her. If seducing Zachary Wharton was what it took to squeeze the name of her biological father out of Unit One, then she would seduce him. And as soon as she'd completed her assignment, she was going to quit Unit One. She was *really* looking forward to the pleasure of telling Jasper and Mac and Nick to take her job and shove it right where the sun didn't shine.

Since she wanted the chance to observe Zachary Wharton from a distance before the two of them were introduced, Melody made no protest when Amelia paraded her from one group of curious guests to another. Resigned to her role as a

live trophy in Amelia's battle for the title of Manhattan's pre-
miere hostess, she allowed the guests to poke and pry into her
split from Nick with the polite cruelty that sometimes seemed
to be the hallmark of upper-crust good manners. She parried
the most intrusive questions, occasionally let drop a deliberate nugget of gossip, all the while keeping at least half her attention focused on Zachary Wharton. Who, she noticed, was
permanently surrounded by a cluster of admiring women.

It was hard to be sure at a distance, but his attitude toward
his fan club struck Melody as courteous rather than flirtatious.
If she'd had no background information on him and had been
asked to read his body language, she would have described
him as mildly bored by all the attention.

Melody fielded one verbal thrust after another—mainly
comments on the beauty and charm of Jacyntha Ramon—and
a remnant of pride poked its way through the ice of her emotions. She yearned to flatten her inquisitors with a sharp retort, telling them in no uncertain terms that her heart had
been left unscathed by Nick's defection. Unfortunately the reality of what she needed to accomplish didn't allow her that
luxury. Unit One's mission required her to portray herself as
a betrayed woman, bravely hiding a broken heart. Melody despised the role almost as much as she despised the fact that
it was true, but she was enough of a pro to stick to the script.
Grimly focused on the assignment, she pulled out all the
stops, treating Amelia's guests to a portrait of a woman at
loose ends, searching to find a new center for her life after
the debacle of her split from Nikolai Anwar. A woman, in
other words, who might easily be vulnerable to the appeal of
a religious commune headed by a bachelor overendowed with
both sex appeal and easy answers to life's problems.

"Well, that's enough circulating," Amelia said after what

seemed to Melody like several hours of sophisticated group torture. "Zachary is relatively free of hangers-on at the moment. Let me take you to meet him."

"I'd like that." It was a relief to be on the brink of making contact with her quarry. "How did you first learn about Reverend Wharton's work with inner-city kids, Amelia?"

"From Cassie Lehigh. Do you know her? Her great-grandfather founded the Dresden Manhattan Bank." Amelia had the habit, ingrained in her social circle, of identifying people by the achievements of their ancestors.

Melody shook her head. "I don't believe Cassie and I have ever met."

"Well, the two of us went to prep school together. She married an industrialist who made engine parts or something equally dreary and she had to move to Michigan." Amelia pulled a face, clearly overcome by the enormity of her friend's sacrifice. "Anyway, last year Cassie helped to raise funds for the summer camp program Zachary was organizing for teen addicts from Detroit's inner city. She called me a couple of months ago and told me Zachary was hoping to start a similar program for kids living in the New York area. I haven't raised any money for drug rehab projects since Howard died, so I agreed to sponsor Zachary's visit here."

"He's going to have his work cut out for him," Melody said, making her comment sound admiring rather than doubtful. "Navigating the bureaucracy in the five boroughs is an art form all by itself. Especially for somebody like Reverend Wharton, who isn't a New Yorker. Or is he planning to move here permanently?"

Amelia shook her head. "He lives in Idaho." She paused for a moment, brow wrinkling. "Or is it Iowa? I always get those states in the middle of the country mixed up."

"Whichever one it is, do you think he'll be able to manage complex projects in Detroit and New York from so many miles away?"

Amelia rolled her eyes. "Fortunately, darling, Zachary's as much on the ball as he is good-looking. He'll have no problem staying on top of things." Amelia gave Melody an arch look. "Knowing your preference for super-smart men, I think you'll find him fascinating. He's single, too."

Melody laughed lightly. "Thanks for the recommendation, Amelia, but I'm not in the market. Especially for a minister-with-a-mission living in Iowa. Or Idaho. Or wherever it is."

"Darling, at least wait until you've said hello before you reject him. He's scrumptious."

"I'm sure he is. It isn't him, Amelia. It's me." Melody lowered her voice as if imparting a confidence. "You probably won't be surprised to hear that I'm somewhat off men at the moment."

"Nikolai Anwar is pond scum, that goes without saying. But you have to trust me on this, darling. The perfect antidote to a man who's a pig is to find one who isn't."

"Great advice, Amelia, but hard to follow. In my experience, the supply of men who aren't pigs is limited. The only men who seem to keep their pants zipped are the ones who have nothing behind the zipper."

Amelia gave a trill of laughter. "Well, we agree on that! Which is why Zachary is your perfect answer. He's truly an angel. There's something so erotic about priests and ministers who are handsome *and* smart, don't you think? Not to mention dedicated. It almost makes their poverty seem bearable." She paused for a moment. "Well, almost."

"I agree," Melody said with false enthusiasm. She decided to risk at least a smidgen of honesty. "But if Zachary Wharton is so smashing, why aren't you interested in him for yourself, Amelia?"

Her hostess whisked Melody around another group of would-be inquisitors and bypassed a cluster of men discussing the stock market. "Darling, I've no idea why I'm being so generous, except that your need right now is obviously greater than mine. So in the spirit of Christian charity, which is what tonight is all about, I'm offering you first bite of the apple."

That probably meant Amelia had already tried to attract Zachary's attention and been rejected, but Melody wasn't about to say or do anything to spoil such a convenient opening. Amelia arrived at her goal and infiltrated the two of them into a trio of women listening with rapt attention to a tall, dark-haired man whose compelling brown eyes sparked with intelligence. Melody barely had time to reflect that Zachary Wharton up close was even more impressive than he'd been on Jodie Evanderhaus's video before Amelia was introducing her.

"Zachary, I know you'll be interested in talking to Melody Beecham. Her grandparents, the Earl and Countess of Ridgefield, live in Wiltshire. My geography is hopeless, but Wiltshire's not too far from where you were studying in Oxford, is it?"

"No distance at all in miles, but quite a long way in travel time, especially for a grad student too broke to own a car." Zachary smiled as he shook Melody's hand with a firm, cool grip. "It's a pleasure to meet you, Melody." He gestured in turn to each of the three women standing nearby. "Do you know Catherine Delon? And Alice Marconi, and Louise Tauber?"

Melody noticed that Zachary had the women's names

down pat, although he must have been introduced to at least fifty people so far tonight and Amelia would have fainted at the thought of anything as tacky as nametags. She murmured greetings to the women, two of whom she already knew. All three were clearly torn between an avid desire to question her about Nick's affair with Jacyntha, and an equally avid desire to continue their conversation with Zachary. Amelia, demonstrating her exceptional talent as a hostess, solved their dilemma by convincing them that what they really wanted to do was sample the gourmet goodies on the buffet table. Belying her fluffy appearance, she scooped the women up with the determination of a bulldozer operating at full throttle, and escorted them into the dining room, leaving Zachary and Melody alone.

Zachary turned to Melody, his manner perfectly pitched between formality and intimacy. "Thank you for coming tonight," he said, managing to sound appreciative rather than bored despite the number of times he must have delivered the same thanks. "I'm overwhelmed by everyone's generosity and enthusiasm. There are many underprivileged teenagers in New York City who have cause to be grateful to Amelia's friends."

"It's a pleasure to be able to help. It's wonderful to know that you've managed to build such a remarkable intervention program, and in such a short time period, too." Melody took care not to allow a sarcastic edge to creep into her voice. "Most drug rehab programs don't achieve anything like your success rates. How do you manage such stellar results, Mr. Wharton? Or should I call you Reverend Wharton?"

"Just Zachary, please. I'm not here as a pastor tonight. Tonight I'm simply a man who is very appreciative of the support Amelia and her friends are willing to offer to young people in need." His voice was as open and friendly as his gaze. "As for the high success rates you're talking about, to be honest, those great results have almost nothing to do with us. The actual rehab programs are financed and run by professionals in Detroit who have years of experience in counseling underprivileged kids. The same structure will apply here in New York. Our church will only step in when the kids are already in recovery. Really, all we contribute is the healing power of a loving community. That and a beautiful campus in Idaho where addicts can spend a few weeks away from the pressures of life in the inner city."

"I've heard those pressures can be intense," Melody commented.

"Enormous," Zachary agreed. "You live in Manhattan, so I'm sure you know how stressful city life can be. Now imagine all those same stresses without the cushion of money to ease the pressure. Add in a few mental health problems and you're looking at a recipe for disaster."

"I read an article last week that claimed life expectancy for people living in the inner-city is twenty years less than for people who live in the suburbs," Melody said. "People who are barely middle-aged are dying of heart attacks and strokes and diabetes because of the trauma of living in run-down housing, located in dangerous neighborhoods."

Zachary looked at her with a visible sharpening of interest. "You're absolutely right, Melody. Living in the projects is hazardous to a person's health, which is one of the reasons I'm so excited about this summer vacation program of ours. I truly believe that spending a few weeks in White Falls gives these young people a chance to see their lives from a whole new perspective."

"A summer vacation is better than nothing, of course. But

what poor families really need is a permanent improvement in their living conditions."

"Once again, you're absolutely right." Zachary gave her an approving smile. "You sound as if you've devoted some serious time to thinking about the problems of children raised in the inner cities."

She gave a slight shrug, as if flustered by his compliment. "I've thought about some of the problems, but that's all I've done. I haven't taken any practical steps to help out."

"I disagree," he said warmly. "By coming here tonight, you've made a generous donation to a very worthy cause. Without financial support from donors like you, our programs would simply remain dreams that never make it out of the planning stage. I know there will be failures as well as successes this summer, that's inevitable, but you and other good people like you have given hope to a lot of young people who until now had very little to hope for."

"You sound so passionate about what you're doing," Melody said, and although the admiration she injected into her voice was feigned, she wasn't completely immune to his charms. In the flesh, Zachary was powerfully persuasive. She mentally stepped aside and tried to analyze what angle he was working. Why would he launch a scheme to transport former teen addicts into White Falls? she wondered. Was it something as mundane as wanting money? Was he stealing funds as fast as they were raised? Or were the boys fodder for his army? And what about the girls? Child brides for loyal followers, maybe? Melody made a mental note to check the statistics on his summer camp program. How old were the kids he sponsored? And how many of the recovering addicts stayed on in White Falls when their official vacations were over?

"I hope that describing me as passionate isn't a polite way

of telling me I'm coming on too strong." Zachary's smile displayed even, strong white teeth, and Melody was sure that, despite his disclaimer, he had no doubts at all about the favorable impact he was making on her. The guy might genuinely care about underprivileged teens, but he was smugly confident of the effect he had on women.

"Oh, no." She worked up another shy smile. "Not at all—"

"Good. I have no sense of moderation where my kids are concerned. Push a button and I launch into immediate preaching mode."

"You have nothing to apologize for. I don't think much is achieved in this world by people who aren't passionate about their causes. The young people you're working with are lucky to have you as their champion. Personally I find your enthusiasm inspiring to watch."

"Thank you. And it's good to know I wasn't boring you to tears." Zachary returned her smile, his gaze openly admiring. "But I have to give a speech in a few minutes and you don't want to listen to me providing the same information twice over, so while we have a few moments to ourselves, tell me about yourself. I'm sure you get asked this all the time, but what is the granddaughter of a British earl doing living in New York?"

"Hanging out. Earning my keep." Melody let her eyes lock with his for just a moment too long, then hastily glanced away as if caught off guard by her attraction to him. "I work at the Van der Meer gallery as executive assistant to the owner, Jasper Fowles."

"And you would rather work in a New York gallery than one in London?"

"Actually, at one point I planned to open my own gallery

in London, but then my mother died and the financing fell through, and I found myself at loose ends. When Jasper offered me a job, I was delighted to take him up on his offer. Painting—art in general—has always been a love of mine, ever since I was a small child."

"I imagine you grew up surrounded by magnificent examples of great art."

"In my grandparents' home, you mean? Yes, they've inherited some fabulous paintings."

"The paintings and the family portraits in the great country mansions are wonderful, of course, but it was the antique furniture I fell in love with when I was over in England."

"Then you would love High Ridgefield." Melody's cheek muscles were beginning to ache from all the smiling. "My grandparents were fortunate enough to have an ancestor who gambled away the family fortune at the beginning of the nineteenth century—"

"Fortunate?" Zachary interjected. "Losing your family's inheritance was fortunate?"

"Well, yes, as it turned out. An economist friend of my grandparents worked out that our ancestor gambled away the equivalent in today's money of seven million pounds—"

"Good heavens!"

"Yes, my thought exactly. Anyway, my Victorian ancestors had barely a penny of ready cash to bless themselves with. There was no question of wasting money on redecorating, so they had to put up with all the old-fashioned eighteenth-century furniture they'd inherited. And by the time the family fortunes had recovered, the First World War had broken out. Which is how my grandfather came to inherit a selection of Chippendale, Hepplewhite and Sheraton pieces that are not only lovely, they're also extremely valuable. Our gambling ancestor turned out to have done us a huge favor."

"What a splendid story. I can't even imagine living with genuine eighteenth-century furniture scattered through my home. I'm definitely jealous." Zachary chuckled to show he was joking.

"Well, next time you plan a trip to England, let me know. I'll ask my grandmother to show you around High Ridgefield. She loves the place so much that she makes a fabulous tour guide."

"Oh, my goodness. That would be a rare treat." Zachary's gaze traveled to her mouth and then back up to her eyes. He was, Melody thought, intrigued by her, and she could detect a definite flash of sexual attraction each time their eyes met. Despite that, Unit One's order to seduce him struck her as potentially difficult to achieve in the short time frame available. Given the way women had been flirting with him tonight, it occurred to Melody that he would never be short of bedmates if he wanted them. He might find her significantly more desirable if she kept her clothes on and beguiled him with stories about England and her aristocratic forebears. Sleeping partners were a dime a dozen. The promise of inside access to an earl's country estate was harder to come by.

"What about you?" she asked. "Where is your family from originally, Zachary? Wharton is an English name…."

"My parents anglicized the original Arabic. They were immigrants from Damascus, in Syria," Zachary said. "And very poor immigrants, at that. They were so busy trying to clothe and feed the three of us kids that we had almost no exposure to any of the arts. Or any other leisure-time activities come to that. Plus the neighborhood in Detroit where we lived was devastated by urban blight, so I grew up assuming all cities are ugly and dirty and covered in foul graffiti. It wasn't until I went to Oxford as an exchange student that I realized just how beautiful a city could be."

"Oxford is beautiful," Melody agreed. Her briefing file had included warnings that Zachary was captivating in his role of poor-boy-made-good, but she was still impressed by how well he managed to sketch in the deprivations of his childhood without sounding sorry for himself.

"It was early April when I arrived in Oxford for the first time," Zachary said softly. "The grass was that amazing shade of green you can't find anywhere except in the British Isles, and the spring flowers were in full bloom. I'd never seen anything like the masses of daffodils and tulips that rioted in every garden. I walked around for at least a week, drunk on the colors."

"'Oh to be in England, now that April's there,'" Melody said, quoting Robert Browning. "Although I often wonder if English hedgerows and chaffinches seemed so appealing because Browning was toasting himself under the Italian sun at the time he wrote that poem. It's a lot easier to admire the green grass and the blooming flowers if you don't have to walk everywhere in a drizzle of rain."

Zachary laughed, then shook his head. "You're exaggerating. Sometimes the weather in April is glorious. Even in the rain, the countryside is magnificent. When I looked around Oxford on that first afternoon, I told myself that I'd just been given a glimpse of what heaven must look like."

For the first time, Melody would have sworn that Zachary was entirely sincere, and she was caught off guard by a flash of nostalgia for High Ridgefield and its beautiful gardens. The wave of yearning was all the more intense in contrast to her prevailing numbness, and the artificiality of most of her conversation with Zachary.

"What is it?" he asked, his voice low and yet subtly commanding. "Have I said something to offend you, Melody? You look—sad."

"Your description of Oxford made me homesick, that's all." He was tall enough that she had to tip her head back just a little to meet his gaze. "I enjoy living in the States so much, the sensation caught me by surprise."

Zachary's smile radiated warmth and he placed his hand reassuringly on her arm, the gesture comforting rather than sexual. "I love the States, too," he said. "I wouldn't want to live anywhere else permanently. But you'll understand better than most people why the nine months I spent at Oxford were a magical experience for me. A kid from the Detroit ghetto studying in buildings that have been around for more than a thousand years. What a trip!"

"In lots of different ways! Have you been back to England since you were there as a student, Zachary?"

"Only once, about five years ago—" He broke off as Amelia returned. He glanced at his watch, grimacing ruefully. "Good heavens, it's nine-fifteen! I hadn't realized Melody and I had talked for so long. You've probably come to tell me that I must stop monopolizing her."

"Not at all, but I have come to take you away, Zachary." Amelia gave them both a speculative glance. "Sorry to break up the tête-à-tête, my dears, but I think it's time to make your speech. We don't want to wait too long and find some guests have already left."

"Of course, I'll come right away. Business before pleasure." Zachary turned to Melody. "I hope we'll have the chance to talk again?"

"I'd like that…very much."

"Do you need to leave early tonight, or could you stay a little?"

"I'd love to stay," Melody murmured. "I'll look forward to hearing some more about your experiences at Oxford."

"Great. But I'm giving you fair warning. Once I start reminiscing about England, it's like a train with faulty brakes running down a mountain track. There's no stopping me without a derailment." With a final parting gesture, Zachary followed Amelia to the podium set up amidst a bank of potted ferns in the corner of her main reception room. His speech was short, eloquent and perfectly adapted to his audience. Outlining the unique features of his treatment program, he delivered a concise balance of grim statistics and hopeful human interest stories. Melody was sure he convinced ninety-one of the ninety-two people in his audience that their donations would effect real change in the lives of many disadvantaged teens. As the sole holdout, Melody made a mental note to check on the progress of Bob Spinard's investigation of Zachary's bank accounts.

Watching Zachary deliver his speech, she had to work hard to resist the contagious enthusiasm of the rest of his audience. She would probably have been as spellbound as everyone else if she hadn't already seen the videotape of his sermon in White Falls, Melody mused.

The contrast between the two speeches was significant. In the safe surroundings of his most devoted followers, Zachary had preached a sermon designed to inspire fear of Islam, and hatred for individual Muslims. Tonight he made no mention of the menace of Islam. In fact, he made no mention of anything remotely political or even overtly religious. Instead he stuck to his theme of young people finding renewed hope, and lives being saved through hard work, prayer and the generosity of tonight's donors.

Amelia's guests were more inhibited in their reaction to

his speech than the devil-stomping enthusiasts of the Soldiers of Jordan congregation. Nevertheless, Zachary managed to bring even this sophisticated audience to its feet as he invited them to share with him in the joy and glory of young lives pulled back from the very brink of destruction.

Zachary Wharton was a seriously slick operator, Melody decided, joining in the loud applause. Apart from Nikolai Anwar, she couldn't think of any other man she'd met with more impressive powers of crowd manipulation, not to mention one-on-one charm. She had no hesitation in designating Zachary as highly dangerous, given his dubious sincerity.

It was a pity that Unit One couldn't recruit Zachary, she thought bitterly. He'd fit right in with all the other liars and deceivers who called Unit One home.

Eight

Mac pulled open his office door and grunted by way of greeting when he saw Melody standing on the threshold. "Come in. Got your interim report. You've had seven meetings with Zachary Wharton already, and you plan to leave for White Falls tomorrow?"

"Yes, my flight's arranged."

"Bob was looking for you. He's got gadgets for you to take. Have you picked them up?"

Melody indicated her shoulder purse. "I have them here, including a cell phone that Bob guarantees will work throughout the country. He also replaced my tracking chip and gave me an update on his research into Zachary's various bank accounts. So far, Bob is in agreement with the FBI investigators. There's nothing in the money trail that raises major red flags where Zachary is concerned. The ninety thousand donation from Amelia's party, for example, has already shown up in the appropriate account."

Mac's mouth turned down. "Well, we've been warned that he's too smart to slip up on anything obvious." He closed the door behind her. "Want coffee? Help yourself." Since Nick was seated directly in front of the espresso machine and showed no sign of moving, Melody refused the offer of coffee and sat down in a chair as far away from Nick as possible. It was infuriatingly difficult to pretend the man didn't exist when she had to report directly to him, but she was doing her best to treat him as invisible, or at least unworthy of her notice. Neither pretense delivered as much satisfaction as she would have hoped. The truth was that whenever Melody allowed herself a moment of honesty, she recognized that she missed Nick like hell, and not just for the amazing sex.

Mac waved a piece of paper in front of her nose. "Your report states that Zachary Wharton has been working hard to recruit you," he said, peering at her over his reading glasses. "He's been eager to convince you that the Soldiers of Jordan are creating heaven or earth, right here in Idaho."

"We've been together every night for the past week," Melody agreed. "At his suggestion at least as much as mine."

Mac set down his glasses and tugged at his necktie, which was imprinted with a hologram of a hula dancer. "Does that mean you've already established a sexual relationship with Zachary Wharton?"

Given that Nick was listening, Melody was tempted to say yes, and that the sex had been awe-inspiring. So fabulous, in fact, that she couldn't wait for more.

"Zachary and I haven't had sex yet," she said, settling for the more mundane truth. "Right now, he's concentrating on healing my soul, which I've indicated to him is deeply wounded. So far, he seems a lot more interested in encouraging me to come to Idaho to join the Soldiers of Jordan than he is in taking me to bed."

Mac took hold of the end of his tie, squinting at the hula

dancer and then back at Melody as if comparing their attributes. "Any reason why you haven't pushed him toward a sexual relationship?"

"Yes, precisely because I don't want him to feel pushed.
Zachary is either sincerely religious, or he's damn good at
faking it. I've studied the FBI files, plus our own background
investigations, and I'm not at all sure that sex is the best way
to get to him. In all the information we've generated on him,
nobody has found any evidence of sexual affairs. He preaches
chastity outside marriage—"

"Both FBI agents reported that they didn't believe he was
celibate," Mac said.

"But they never found a woman who claimed to have had
sex with him, did they?"

"No," Mac conceded. "But the investigation was called off
before they really had a chance to look."

"Or maybe there isn't any such woman," Melody suggested. "Perhaps the FBI agents were reflecting their own dislike of celibacy rather than Zachary's. He's told me he
believes sex should only be part of a loving and committed
marriage. It's possible he means exactly what he says."

Mac pursed his lips. "Easy advice to give. Not so easy to
follow."

"But Zachary needs to follow it unless he wants to prove
himself a hypocrite," Melody said. "He made a big point that
Nick's affair with Jacyntha Ramon was inevitable given that
I had made the mistake of allowing Nick to—quote—slake
his lust without first making a loving and permanent commitment to me. How can Zachary initiate a casual sexual affair
after making a claim like that?"

Nick made a strangled sound and started to rise to his feet,
fists clenched. Intercepting a withering look from Mac, he

swung around and confronted the espresso machine instead. "I need some more coffee," he muttered.

Melody was obscurely pleased to have provoked Nick. She'd been pretty sure that the remark about slaking his lust would get to him, which was partly why she'd repeated it. She tried to decide which of Zachary's other comments about Nick were most likely to provoke a similar reaction.

She was still debating when Mac spoke again. "Okay, Melody, give us your best guess. If you pursue Zachary, is he likely to break his own stated rules and initiate a sexual relationship with you?"

"I'm not sure," Melody said. "I need to spend more time with him before I can decide. Right now, my best guess is that Zachary genuinely believes most of what he's preaching and that he's chosen to remain celibate in pursuit of some goal he considers more important than sexual gratification."

Nick let rip with some harsh-sounding Russian. Melody had no difficulty guessing that what he'd said could be translated as a cruder version of *bullshit*.

"Bottom line," Mac said. "From Unit One's perspective, is it worth your while going to White Falls?"

Melody shrugged. "We have nothing to lose, do we? Right now, I have the impression that Zachary is spending as much time with me as he can possibly squeeze away from his fund-raising schedule, which suggests he's interested in me at some level or other. But since he believes I'm both rich and potentially a huge donor if I can ever be persuaded to buy into the Soldiers of Jordan philosophy, I suspect he's more interested in my money than my sexual attributes."

"So if Zachary is never going to take the bait and initiate a sexual relationship with you, why do you recommend going to White Falls?" Nick demanded.

Melody swiveled in her chair, telling herself that she was over him—way over—and she couldn't possibly feel pain merely because their glances met. "I didn't realize that my mission for Unit One was to have sex with Zachary Wharton," she said with false sweetness. "I was under the impression that my mission was to infiltrate the Soldiers of Jordan campus—"

"Your mission is to discover what the Soldiers of Jordan are plotting, and to do that you need to be in Zachary's confidence," Mac said, ignoring both her sarcasm and Nick's thunderous scowl. "It's not enough for you just to be in White Falls. We don't have time for you to take months to infiltrate the inner sanctum—"

"I *have* Zachary's confidence," Melody said. "In my opinion, playing the role of pastor to my spiritual needs is a real power trip for him. As it happens, the publicity surrounding Nick's affair with Jacyntha Ramon has provided the perfect opening for me, although not in the way we first imagined. Instead of approaching Zachary as a single woman on the prowl, I've approached him as a lost soul searching for a mentor. That helplessness on my part really appeals to his ego. He admires me, envies me even, because I grew up in a house full of servants and have grandparents with a title and a big mansion in the country. It gratifies him to believe that I'm looking to *him* for spiritual guidance. I believe that positioning myself as a vulnerable woman, with a healthy trust fund and a yearning for spiritual enlightenment, will provide me with the best chance of infiltrating the inner workings of Zachary's organization. Once I'm in White Falls, there's no reason why I can't initiate a sexual relationship if Zachary appears receptive and if it seems appropriate."

"Once you're in White Falls, you're surrounded by approximately a hundred and eighty fanatical Soldiers of Jordan," Nick said. "At last count, one hundred and five of the Soldiers were men, all of them armed."

"And how does my having sex with Zachary, or not having sex, change those statistics?" Melody asked.

"If you'd slept with Zachary, you would have better protection from the other men on campus even if he becomes suspicious of your motives," Nick said.

"How?" Melody was genuinely puzzled. "Why in the world would you think that?"

"Men tend to be protective of their sexual partners," Nick said.

She laughed. "Yes, I've noticed that." She stood up, not bothering to make any further comment. She kept her gaze fixed on Mac. "If you have no other specific instructions, I'd like to get back to my apartment. I still need to pack, and my flight for Boise leaves early tomorrow morning."

"One more question." Mac studied her intently. "Are you sure your failure to initiate a sexual relationship with Zachary is based on your assessment of his character, and not on your own reluctance to have sex with a man you don't much like?"

The fact that Mac asked such a question meant that Nick had shared details of what she'd told him during their final night together. Melody tried not to feel sick to her stomach. She replied curtly, her gaze focused rigidly ahead, screening Nick out of even her peripheral vision. "Yes, I'm sure."

"Then I trust your judgment," Mac said. "Handle Zachary as you decide is best. Nick, do you have anything to add?"

"Not on that subject," Nick said brusquely. "We do have one fresh piece of intel. Senator Cranford's wife, Eleanor, visited her daughter last week. She stayed for three days in White Falls and then left—without Rachel."

Which could mean almost anything, Melody decided. Eleanor could be the senator's messenger, up to mischief. She could equally easily be a caring mother, worried about her barely adult daughter.

"Sam is working on a plan to plant a couple of bugs inside the senator's home, which may generate some useful information," Nick said. "Unfortunately Cranford's offices in the senate building are too well protected for us to gain access. Plus they're swept routinely every week, so the bug would only be operational for a maximum of six days. I'll keep you posted if we learn anything useful, of course."

"What about Eleanor Cranford?" Mac asked. "Any chance you could extract useful intel from her, Nick?"

"I'm working on it," Nick said shortly. "If I find anything out from the senator's wife, I'll make sure the information is passed to Melody immediately."

It was less than two weeks since Nick had last made love to her, Melody reflected wearily. A mere twelve days had passed since he'd been romping in the sack with Jacyntha and now Nick was clearly planning to seduce Eleanor Cranford. How could she ever have thought that their relationship meant something important to both of them when Nick seemed to regard sex as little more than a lever with which to pry out secrets from susceptible women? How could she have misread him so completely?

Realizing she was about to slide into a swamp of self-pity, Melody jumped back. It was time she stopped wondering why so many people in her life betrayed her and started to ask herself instead why she was such a rotten judge of character.

"I'll report in from White Falls within twelve hours of my arrival." Melody directed her comment to Nick, acknowledging him with the barest of nods as she moved toward the door.

"Which reminds me of one final point," Nick said, intercepting her. She stepped back a couple of paces, protecting herself from the force of his up-close presence.

Nick's gaze narrowed, and she read frustration in his eyes. His voice, however, remained professionally neutral. "Just so that you won't be caught off guard, your communications device links directly with my cell phone, and not with central command. When you call in on your cell phone, you'll be talking with me, not with anyone on Bob's staff."

Bob Spinard hadn't informed her of that, but since Nick was chief of operations, there were no legitimate grounds for Melody to object. Bob's entire department was inundated with work in the wake of Dave Ramsdell's escape, and reporting directly to Nick would ease some of the burden on Bob and his people. She glanced at Mac, who appeared totally absorbed in the wiggling motion of the hula dancer on his tie.

Melody sure as hell wasn't going to award Nick the importance of making a protest. How hard could it be to talk to him on the phone every twenty-four hours? "I understand," she said curtly. "Expect my first report before midnight tomorrow."

"I'll be waiting. Please bear in mind that there is no backup team anywhere close to you and it will take us several hours to assemble one and fly in. If things start to go bad, don't play the hero. Call us. Ask for help. And get the hell off campus. Those are orders."

"I understand."

"Good luck with your mission." Nick hesitated for a moment. "Stay alert, Melody. Don't be lulled by the peaceful scenery, or by Zachary's apparent sincerity. If Zachary's a fraud, he's dangerous. If he isn't a fraud, that's worse. There are few things in this world more dangerous than a religious fanatic with violent tendencies who truly believes what he's preaching."

"I haven't forgotten that Jodie Evanderhaus is dead," Melody said. "I plan to be very cautious."

"You can go, Nick. I know how busy you are." Mac finally stopped staring at his tie. "Melody, stay. I need to speak with you for a moment."

Melody was surprised by the request, but Nick had apparently been expecting it. He nodded briefly to Mac, then allowed his gaze to lock one final time with hers. For a moment he dropped the shield that normally guarded his expression and she could see the passion blazing. Melody's stomach clenched and her heart began to beat in double-time.

"Take care, Melody. Stay safe."

She nodded, which was all she could manage. Frowning, Mac watched Nick's retreat. He switched his attention back to Melody, still frowning, but he made no direct comment on the tension between the two of them, even though the room vibrated with its aftermath. With a final flick of his tie, he hopped up from his seat.

"This way," he said. "Hurry up. Time's a-wasting." He marched over to the cupboard in the corner of his office, a cupboard that contained stationery supplies, liberally interspersed with cans of his special-blend coffee, imported in bulk from Italy.

Melody took a couple of steps toward Mac and then stopped. Hurry up to do what? Were they about to brew coffee? Make copies of a document?

"Come on," he repeated, opening the cupboard door. He pushed a stack of pink memo paper to the left and pressed his thumb against the concealed touch-pad his action had just revealed. The entire wall of shelving swung inward, providing access to a large office, windowless as everywhere was at headquarters. The fake door was itself steel-reinforced, Melody saw, indicating this was an area designed to be extra safe, even within the already super-tight physical security of Unit One.

Melody had been in Mac's office upward of a hundred times, had even taken fresh coffee beans from the cupboard, and yet she'd never been aware that an inner office lay concealed behind the wall of shelving. She understood that the need-to-know principle was an effective security tool but, rational or not, she felt a flash of resentment at this reminder of how many Unit One secrets remained hidden from her, some of them relatively trivial like this one, and others huge, like the identity of her father.

Her rancor turned to outright dismay when she followed Mac into the hidden room and realized that the man seated behind the imposing desk was Jasper Fowles. She was still raw from her breakup with Nick and the last thing she needed right now was to be forced to cope with the father figure who had betrayed her.

"The commander wants to speak to you before you leave for Idaho," Mac said. He nodded toward Jasper and exited the room, closing the back panel of the cupboard behind him.

Jasper took off his reading glasses and looked at her without speaking. Melody had the disconcerting sensation of the world around her blurring, then subtly shifting focus. The change was caused by seeing Jasper in this new environment, she realized. It was six months since she'd learned that he was the commander of Unit One, but she'd never seen him at headquarters until now. Hadn't even thought about where he might have his office. Was that because she'd assumed he was merely a figurehead, and that he only dabbled in Unit One business?

Seated behind the document-littered desk, he didn't look like a figurehead. Nor did he look much like the easygoing man she had known for the best part of twenty years. A row of computer monitors were lined up on the credenza at right angles to his desk, all streaming different information. As she watched, he turned in response to a soft, repeated beep, keying in a command with quick, decisive strokes.

His appearance was significantly less effete, a lot more disciplined and—she was forced to admit—slightly intimidating. Melody couldn't imagine curling up on the sofa next to this man and teasing him about his tiny bald spot, or his love of coconut ice cream.

"I decided it was time for us to talk," Jasper said, and his voice sounded subtly more authoritative, stripped of the underlying affection that she had accepted as her due from him since childhood. Even over the past six months, when she had barely been willing to speak to him except on matters of gallery business, Jasper had maintained his previous affectionate, faintly indulgent, manner toward her.

"I thought you were in Europe, buying art for the gallery," she said.

"Yes, you were supposed to think that." Jasper leaned back in his chair, continuing to hold her gaze, his expression unreadable. "You've been avoiding me at the gallery. You've refused all my personal invitations to lunch or to my apartment, so I concluded that I was left with no choice other than to confront you here."

With a shock of rueful self-awareness, Melody recognized that she was hurt by the distance Jasper was placing between them. Apparently it was okay for her to offer him the cold shoulder, but Jasper wasn't allowed to return it.

As always when she was hurt or confused, she withdrew

into herself. "Why do you want to see me?" she asked, her voice even more distant than Jasper's. "Do you have instructions for me regarding the Soldiers of Jordan mission?"

"Indirectly." Jasper pointed to the chair on the opposite side of his desk. "Please sit, Melody. Our conversation may take a while."

It was an order, not a request. Clearly, Jasper was conducting this meeting as the commander of Unit One, not as her oldest and most important friend. Melody's sense of disorientation increased, but she sat down. When this new Jasper gave an order, it was hard to imagine disobeying.

Jasper leaned back in his chair, elegant hands resting lightly on the leather arms. "According to the reports I've received, as well as my own observations, you have integrated rapidly and effectively into Unit One operations. However, as a junior operative and a very new recruit, you haven't been kept informed of the full scope of our activities. Let me outline them for you. In the past three months, Unit One has investigated four cases of white-collar corporate fraud. We've also investigated two judges, the police chief of a major city, the head of a private security firm who also happened to be Chicago's biggest drug dealer, and a company that was importing illegal aliens to work as virtual slaves in its meatpacking plants. Regular law enforcement agencies had been unable to secure the evidence necessary for a conviction in any one of these cases. Unit One succeeded where everyone else failed. In the same three-month period, we didn't take on a single mission where we were unable to accomplish our objectives."

Melody's mouth was so dry, she had to swallow before she could speak. "It's an impressive record."

"Yes, it is. Unit One provides a vital service to our country." Jasper's manner warmed, just slightly. "You yourself played a role in two of these investigations. Your contributions were invaluable, and you know from firsthand experience that the positive outcomes could never have been achieved by normal law enforcement methods."

"I'm very well aware that Unit One is involved in important work," Melody said.

"Are you? It doesn't always seem that way to me. I sometimes have the impression that you consider the dedication of the people who work for Unit One to be…excessive."

"You're wrong. I admire the dedication I've witnessed here."

"But you don't share it."

Melody hesitated. "Not entirely."

"Why? You've seen the value of what we do and you're the sort of person who normally gives a hundred and ten percent when the goal is worthwhile."

She was happy to deliver a barb that was also the truth. "The way I was recruited left a nasty taste. It's hard to give a hundred and ten percent when you're being coerced."

Jasper leaned forward, hands clasped on top of one of the piles of documents. For the first time, Melody detected a hint of uncertainty in his manner and she wondered if perhaps he was not as confident as he appeared.

"You're angry with me because I didn't tell you I was the commander of Unit One," Jasper said finally. "You're furious with me because you believe I exploited our long-term friendship so that you could be manipulated into joining Nikolai's team as a field operative."

"Yes," she said. "You're right. I'm angry with you for precisely those reasons."

"Then you need to get over it," he said coolly.

She gave a mock salute, accompanied by a short, mirthless laugh. "Yes, sir. I'll change my feelings immediately."

Jasper frowned impatiently. "Can you dismount from your high horse long enough to notice that you're leading the damned animal straight into a swamp?"

"I'm sorry, I don't understand your metaphor. Sir."

"You're determined to blame me for your recruitment into Unit One and that's distorting your judgment and your understanding of your own motives. It's true that I believed—that I still believe—you have the basic attributes that make for an outstanding undercover operative."

"What attributes are those?" Melody asked, deliberately cynical. "A natural talent for lying? An inability to form normal relationships due to a childhood of extreme emotional deprivation?" As soon as she'd said that, she wished like hell that she hadn't.

She saw the flash of sympathy in Jasper's eyes and wasn't grateful for it. "I was thinking more along the lines of courage, integrity, intelligence and an outstanding ability to think fast on your feet," he said.

Melody wished she could believe him, but for the past two weeks she had been feeling about as courageous and intelligent as a stomach virus. She experienced a sudden fierce yearning for a return to the good old days, when Jasper had been nothing more than a wonderful companion, an indulgent adoptive uncle with a talent for making everyday life fun. Most of all, perhaps, she was angry with Jasper because he'd destroyed half a lifetime of cherished memories. The one rock in her erratic childhood turned out to have been resting on a turret of wet sand.

"I was blackmailed into joining Unit One," she said, not caring if she sounded immature as well as resentful. "If I'm so full of courage and integrity, why didn't you simply ask me if I wanted to join?"

"You're usually more honest with yourself," Jasper said softly. "You weren't blackmailed into joining Unit One, Melody."

"It sure felt like blackmail to me."

"Then let me refresh your memory. You were recruited when you stumbled over Lawrence Springer's body. You were illegally burglarizing Springer's house at the time. And although Nikolai at first attempted to blackmail you into joining our team, you called his bluff. In the end, you joined Unit One because you saw the organization as the quickest, easiest way to achieve what you wanted most in the world at that time: the downfall of Wallis Beecham. If we exploited you, you exploited the skills and resources of Unit One every bit as much."

"Maybe I did. But I seem to recall one of my nannies teaching me that two wrongs don't make a right. They just make two wrongs."

"Not always," Jasper said. "Sometimes a marriage of mutual convenience can turn out better than either party could possibly have hoped."

"You lied to me," Melody said, her voice harsh with hurt feelings. "I trusted you, Jasper, more than anybody else in the world, and you lied to me."

"You'll hear no apology from me. Lies are part of the price we pay for the existence of Unit One. The organization is only effective as long as it remains secret. Telling you the truth about my profession wasn't an option, but I never lied to you about anything else, Melody."

"How can you make such a farcical claim? Of course you lied to me!" She pushed back her chair and jumped up, so clumsy with exploding emotions that the chair clattered to the floor. She was too busy pacing to bother with picking it up.

"When I came back to your apartment—our apartment—after basic training, you didn't tell me you were the commander of Unit One and that you knew exactly, almost to the minute, what I'd been doing for the previous six weeks! You let me go through the absurd pretense that I'd been undergoing physical therapy after a car wreck—"

"Yes, I did." Jasper's determined calm merely set Melody to pacing faster, clenched fists at her side. "And in case you haven't noticed the giant flaw in your self-righteous anger, you were lying to me, too. Not that I'm blaming you, of course. You lied because you'd sworn an oath to Unit One, and you intended to keep that oath even if it meant deceiving me."

"But I was only lying because you hadn't told me the truth about your connection to Unit One! I didn't have a choice. You did!" Melody drew in a deep breath and then another. She had an appalling suspicion that at any moment she was going to start crying. Bawling, more like it. The ice that had encased her feelings for the past two weeks was cracking, and the tumult of suppressed hurt and rage was bubbling up with the force of a Yellowstone geyser. She had just enough self-possession to recognize that Jasper and Nick had become confused in her mind to the point where their respective sins had merged into one giant betrayal, with Unit One as both cause and symbol of their treachery.

Jasper folded the earpieces of his glasses. "The name of the Commander of Unit One is traditionally revealed to no more than four or five operatives, usually after several years of service—"

"Dave Ramsdell knew," Melody said. "That was a really

smart decision to let him in on the big secret. You'd have done better to trust me."

"I certainly would have. But my silence wasn't about lack of faith in you, Melody, and it certainly didn't mean that I don't care about you."

"No, I'm sure you loved me to pieces. Just not quite enough to tell me the truth!"

"Think back to your own experience after you were recruited," Jasper said tersely. "You went through the whole of basic training without dropping the smallest hint to me about what you were doing."

"That's because Unit One monitored all my conversations with you—"

"No." Jasper shook his head. "You lied to me about what you were doing because you separated what you owed me in terms of our friendship from what you owed to Unit One. Can't you accept that I did precisely the same thing? You were a new recruit. It was possible you wouldn't make it through training, or that you'd fail on your first mission and be dismissed. It would have been irresponsible of me—deadly irresponsible—to give you information that could harm the effectiveness of our organization."

Melody's hurt feelings churned inside her, a giant furball that she couldn't dislodge. She'd loved Jasper for twenty years and it was hard to cling to her anger when part of her wanted very much to let it go. Unfortunately his explanations didn't justify the biggest lie of all.

"You're conveniently forgetting something important," she said. "Maybe I overreacted to the fact that you never told me you're the commander of Unit One. Maybe it's time for me to move on and put that particular slice of the past behind us. But you also lied to me about something that's entirely personal. Something that you knew I cared about deeply—" She stopped because her voice had started to crack.

"You're talking about Nikolai's claim that I concealed the identity of your biological father," Jasper said quietly.

"Yes! You know how much I want to find out who he is, but you let me believe you had no information. No idea where I should start looking, even. Worse, you kept *me* in the dark, but you let Mac and Nick know that if they ever needed a stick to beat me back in line, then this was the perfect weapon for them to use."

"You're misinterpreting the facts."

"Am I? How?" Her voice broke on a sob, but she was past caring. "I don't believe I'll ever forgive you for hiding the truth about my father."

Jasper flung down the pen he'd been playing with. It was an old-fashioned fountain pen and a blob of ink splattered over the file in front of him. He ignored the blob, pushing to his feet and planting himself in front of Melody, blocking her demented pacing.

"Nikolai was completely out of line when he revealed the fact that I know who your father is," Jasper said curtly.

Melody's smile was bitter. "Out of line maybe, but that doesn't change the fact that he was truthful. You do know my father's identity, don't you, Jasper?"

He looked straight into her eyes, but it was a long time before he finally answered. "Yes, I know."

"And that's all you've got to say? Just yes, you know. No apologies? No slick excuses?"

"I can't apologize for carrying out your mother's wishes. And that's not a slick excuse, it's the simple truth. Your mother asked me not to reveal the name of your father until a certain set of conditions had been met." Jasper paused for a moment. "As of now, those conditions haven't been met."

"How very convenient for you to have such a cast-iron alibi for behaving badly." Melody gave a mocking smile. "How noble of you to carry out my mother's wishes so precisely. And what do you know? By coincidence, Roz is dead, so there's nobody to dispute you, is there?"

"I have a letter from your mother that I received only after she died. She made her wishes very clear—"

Melody's tangled emotions finally unknotted in a burst of liberating rage. "What about *my* wishes?" she demanded, fists balling in sheer frustration. "Don't I have the right to know the name of the man who is responsible for half of everything that I am?"

She felt scalding tears streak down her cheeks but for once she let them flow. "My mother lied to me my whole life about who my father is and then she chose the cruelest method possible to announce the truth. Even Wallis Beecham didn't deserve to be publicly humiliated like that. And now I'm supposed to excuse your lies over the past two years because my mother invited you to participate in one of her sick games and you agreed? Sorry, Jasper, but I'm all done with being a good girl and trying hard to understand everyone else's point of view. I'm mad as hell and I'm not willing to listen to excuses anymore."

She stopped, chiefly because between the tears and the self-pity she'd run out of breath.

"Here." Jasper handed her a wad of tissues and she scrubbed her cheeks, her emotions nowhere near as easy to tame as her tears. In the past, she'd always been able to read Jasper's expression without any trouble. Now, though, she had no idea what he was thinking.

He waited until she was more or less in control of herself before he spoke again. "Nikolai told you that he struck a bargain with you. If you agreed to infiltrate the Soldiers of Jordan on behalf of Unit One, then he would see to it that I shared with you everything I know about your father."

"That was what we agreed," Melody said. Her rush of anger drained away, leaving her exhausted. "Are you about to renege on the deal, Jasper?"

"In a way." Jasper paused for a moment. "Your father is Johnston Yates," he said.

Melody's knees wobbled. She leaned against the desk for support, knees literally shaking. "J-Johnston Yates is my father? *Johnston Yates*—the vice president?"

"The former vice president," Jasper agreed.

Melody was stupefied enough to state the obvious. "My mother must have had an affair with Johnston Yates while he was holding office."

Jasper nodded. "Yes. Yates was about eighteen months into his term when the affair started and Roz had been married to Wallis Beecham for barely a year. Yates was married, too, of course. As Roz explained it to me, she and Yates met at a White House reception for the British prime minister and were immediately attracted to each other. They started a secret affair that lasted more than six months."

"Six whole months! What a touching demonstration of devotion." Melody's irony didn't quite mask her pain. "Another couple of years, and they'd have outlasted fifty percent of celebrity marriages."

"They genuinely cared about each other," Jasper said, ignoring her sarcasm. "But there was nowhere for the relationship to go. Thirty years ago the family values lobby wasn't as powerful politically as it is now, but Johnston Yates was a leading voice in the movement, such as it was. Revealing that he'd impregnated another man's wife would have cost him the vice presidency. It would probably have cost his party the next election as well. So, despite a lot of misgivings on her part, your mother eventually agreed to say nothing, and to stay married to Wallis Beecham. The truth is, Johnston Yates didn't offer her any viable alternative."

The depressing thought occurred to Melody that she'd lost Wallis Beecham as a father and acquired another uncaring, fully-paid-up hypocrite in his place. It was a while before she could speak. "Does Yates know he's my…father?"

"Yes. Your mother told him as soon as she knew she was pregnant. She hoped it would persuade him to divorce Cynthia and marry her, but Yates refused even to consider the possibility." Jasper's voice softened. "It's no surprise if Roz's attitude toward men tended to be on the cynical side after her experiences with Yates."

"How in the world did Yates manage to keep their affair secret all these years?" Melody asked. "Why hasn't some Secret Service guy bought early retirement by selling a tell-all book?"

"I assume because nobody in the Secret Service knew what was going on. Yates and your mother avoided the mistake of confiding in anyone, and they weren't found out. Remember they both moved in the same social circles, so it wasn't difficult for them to arrange to be in the same place at the same time, presumably often with their respective spouses in tow, which would provide them with some cover. And Roz might have been young, but she was smart enough to realize Wallis would crush her if he ever found out the truth, so she had every reason to be discreet. Keeping an affair secret is a lot easier when both parties are completely motivated to hide the truth. Roz needed to hide the truth from Wallis and Yates needed to hide it from Cynthia. They were motivated by a mutual need for total secrecy. In those days, too, security around the vice president was a lot less intrusive than it is nowadays."

Melody listened to Jasper's explanation, thirsty for every scrap of information, although she had trouble taking it in. She tried to digest the fact that Johnston Yates knew she was his daughter, but had never made the slightest attempt to get in touch with her, or establish a connection, however tenuous. The brutal truth was that for more than thirty years he'd totally ignored her. He hadn't even watched her from afar, Melody reflected. When she'd approached him last November during the course of Unit One's investigation of the Bonita project, he hadn't recognized her until she identified herself by name. He had so little interest in his daughter that he didn't know what she looked like. She supposed he would excuse his silence on the grounds that he couldn't let his wife discover the truth, but Melody wasn't prepared to allow him that excuse.

She struggled to assess the ramifications of what she'd just heard, but the reality was too big and kept slipping out of her emotional grasp. Did she want to confront Yates and demand an explanation for his silence? For his neglect of her, even after Roz died? She wasn't sure. At some level of her subconscious, she'd assumed that learning the truth about her father would be miraculously liberating. Now she realized that possession of a name was light years away from possession of a father. Part of her wanted to run home and pore over every photo of Yates she could find, searching his features for evidence of their kinship. Another part of her wanted to find some harsh way to reject him. She wanted to throw his paternity in his face, and at the same time let him know that she regarded him with the same chill indifference he'd always demonstrated toward her.

Shock was making her feel cold. Melody hugged her arms around her waist. "Why did you tell me?" she asked Jasper. "You've kept their secret at least since my mother died and I suspect a lot longer. Why break your silence now?"

"Mostly because I realized I agree with you," Jasper said. "Your right to know the truth is greater than the right of your mother and Johnston Yates to keep their secret hidden."

"That's been true for the past thirty years. Call me cynical, but I'm guessing the reason you told me right now has more to do with Unit One than anything else. Nick put you on the spot and this was your way out of the mess."

"Nikolai has certainly demonstrated less than his usual excellent judgment where you're concerned," Jasper said mildly. "However, my decision to tell you the truth was motivated by concern for you, not for Unit One. You're about to undertake a dangerous mission. You need to have your head in the right place while you're in White Falls if you're going to operate safely and effectively. That means you need to take on the mission for the right reasons. A burning desire to find out the name of your biological father isn't the right reason, so I took it away."

"You're assuming I'm still going to undertake the mission. Now that you've revealed the name of my father, I have no reason to go to White Falls. I'm sure Nick has given you a blow-by-blow account of our last private conversation, so you know I had every intention of quitting Unit One as soon as I pried my father's name out of your vault of secrets."

"I'm aware of what you said to Nikolai. I'm a lot less convinced it's what you meant."

"Then believe it now. I quit."

"Do you? I've been honest with you, Melody. Now I need you to return some honesty to me. I'm fairly certain that you weren't planning to put your life on the line in White Falls because you wanted to squeeze the name of your biological father out of me."

"You're wrong. Dead wrong."

"Am I?" Jasper said quietly. "Here's what I think. I believe you recognized months ago that you belong in Unit One. Not because Nikolai found a bribe to entice your cooperation, but because you know you're an outstanding undercover agent. You agreed to go to White Falls because you feel an intense need to protect innocent people from becoming victims of Zachary Wharton's twisted world vision and you know that you're more likely to succeed in this mission than anyone else."

Melody wasn't about to admit that he was right. "You're overestimating my dedication to the cause, Jasper. In fact, it sounds to me as if you have me fatally confused with somebody who gives a damn."

"Flip phrases aren't going to hold me at bay, Melody. I've known you too well and too long to be put off by your protective shell, however hard and shiny you make it. Your problem is that you not only give a damn, but you also care way too much. But since I recognize that, wouldn't it be easier on both of us if you just dropped the pretense and acknowledged you have every intention of going to White Falls and finding out what Zachary and the Soldiers of Jordan are planning?"

"What will happen if I refuse to go to White Falls?" she asked.

Jasper shrugged. An elegant gesture that reminded her of the old Jasper, the debonair owner of the Van der Meer gallery, as opposed to the intimidating commander of Unit One.

"You'll be assigned to a desk job until you've fulfilled your contractual obligation to Unit One," he said.

Melody shook her head. "No, I didn't mean what will happen to me." Although Jasper's version of her punishment sounded significantly less draconian than the extraction, summary judgment and imprisonment that Nick had threatened. "I meant what will happen to Unit One's investigation of Zachary Wharton and the Soldiers of Jordan?"

"It will be delayed while we establish a different mission profile and arrange to infiltrate a different operative." Jasper paused. "We'll have to hope that the delay isn't disastrous in terms of whatever Zachary is planning. And, of course, that the operative we substitute will have as much success as you would have in penetrating the inner councils of the Soldiers of Jordan."

Melody's emotions might be in turmoil, but she could still recognize when she was being manipulated. "You think I'll go to White Falls anyway, despite the fact that I already know my father's name."

"Of course I do."

He'd never have told her otherwise. The insight didn't bother Melody as much as she would have expected. She held Jasper's gaze. Unfortunately he was correct in claiming that he knew her well. He'd gambled and—damn him—he'd won. "I'm still angry with you," she said. "Very angry."

She heard Jasper expel a short breath. "But you'll go to White Falls?"

"Yes," she said. "I'll go to White Falls."

Nine

When Melody and Zachary were finalizing arrangements for her stay in Idaho, Melody had suggested renting a car at the airport in Boise. Zachary rejected her idea with the deceptively low-key, rock-solid obstinacy that Melody had come to expect from him after only a week of acquaintance.

"There's no need to waste your money renting a car. I'll arrange for somebody to pick you up." Zachary had patted her hand, all smiles. His rejections, she'd noticed, were always sugarcoated to disguise the fact that they were nonnegotiable. "It wouldn't be hospitable to have you visit our community and not send anyone to welcome you."

Melody managed to return the smile, squelching her irritation. She hadn't recognized how much she relished the sharp parry and thrust of her dealings with Nick until she found herself smothering under Zachary's exaggerated courtesy. Disagreeing with him was like trying to punch a cloud. However hard you swung, you made no impact. After a while, you realized you were suffocating, not to mention exhausted from all the useless swinging.

Melody really wanted to have access to transportation, so she gave it another shot. "I appreciate the offer, Zachary, but I might need a car if there's an emergency—"

"We have vehicles and plenty of people to drive them if, God forbid, you run into any sort of a problem while you're our guest." Zachary squeezed her arm, the gesture paternal rather than sexual. The more time she spent in his company, the more convinced Melody became that attempting to seduce him was a lost cause. Some evangelists might get caught with their pants down, but Zachary wasn't about to fall into a sexual trap, however enticing she made the bait.

"You must learn to let friends help you out, Melody. Life isn't a journey you're required to make alone, you know."

"I'm beginning to understand that," she said, wondering just how far she could push the breathless admiration before Zachary would become suspicious. Based on his reactions so far, quite a long way. At Amelia's party, Zachary had struck her as not only smart, but also charismatic. She was finding him less impressive the more time she spent with him. Perhaps it was the tight-ass Brit in her, but she had a low tolerance for smarm, which seemed to be Zachary's defining characteristic—closely followed by smug.

Melody gave the car rental one last shot. "I was planning to explore some of the national parks while I'm in Idaho. I've been wound way too tight the past couple of years, and it would be great to drive around without any real schedule. Just relaxing and taking in the beauty of nature, you know?"

Zachary's gaze became gently reproachful. "Traveling wouldn't be a good idea," he said softly.

"Why not?" She sounded way more aggressive than she'd intended, but her frustration had heated to the boiling point.

"Exploring the national parks isn't why you're coming to

Idaho, is it, Melody? You're looking for a new direction for your life, and it's important to commit yourself fully to the retreat experience. You need to plan on spending at least a month right in our little town of White Falls. Focus is important, so you need to avoid outside intrusions."

All the better to brainwash you, my dear. Melody could practically see the wolf's ears poking through Zachary's cloak of fake charm. Much as she had disliked the prospect of being stuck on the Soldiers of Jordan campus with no access to a getaway vehicle, she realized that any more protests would damage the image she had projected of a woman, bruised by past relationships, who yearned for firm guidance, if not outright male domination. Zachary was determined to have her confined, and she had no choice but to suck it up.

"Oh, I *am* committed to finding new directions," she had said, reverting to her breathless and eager mode. "I have this really strong feeling that joining your community is going to mark a turning point in my life. I so much admire the work you're doing, Zachary."

"I'm glad, because if you feel that way, then your stay will almost certainly be significant for you and for our community. Don't think of what you're giving up, Melody. Remind yourself of all that can be gained. Remember, God never closes a window without opening a door for us to walk through."

Melody resisted the urge to tell him that she'd seen *The Sound of Music* and remembered the quote.

Zachary gazed deep into her eyes and she returned his gaze with an expression of mute adoration. "Our community is a healing place, Melody. You'll be amazed at how much spiritual growth you'll experience when you're surrounded by loving people, all committed to the same goals. The thing is, though, you need to close yourself to outside distractions so that the inner you can absorb the nourishment your soul craves. You can't be a tourist enjoying the Idaho scenery at the same time as you seek the sort of deep self-awareness that comes from closer, more intimate contact with God."

Melody had swallowed the urge to retort that her God would be a lot easier to find in the Idaho wilderness than hemmed in by fanatics on the Soldiers of Jordan campus. But in the interest of maintaining her role, she listened with feigned meekness while Zachary delivered one of his vaguely New Age lectures on the combined benefits of meditation and communal love. He made a great salesman, she mused. His spiel was always perfectly pitched to what he assumed was the personality and interests of his audience.

Eight days after her first meeting with Zachary at Amelia's party, she arrived in Boise. As promised, one of Zachary's senior lieutenants waited to pick her up at the airport. Jason Cushman was a burly man in his early fifties, the muscles of his huge forearms straining the seams of his flannel shirt, his creased and leathery face set into an expression of amiability. If there was one thing Melody prided herself on, it was her ability to persuade people to talk about themselves, but Jason was so friendly and outgoing that she barely needed to exercise her skills.

By the time they turned off the interstate and onto the narrow road that was sign-posted for White Falls, she knew that Jason had three grown daughters and two grandsons, that he'd been twice divorced, that his ex-wives had every right to be mad at him because he'd been a lousy husband, and that he was an alcoholic in his eighth year of recovery.

Eight years was also the length of time since he'd been baptized into the Soldiers of Jordan. He wasn't quite a founding member, but Reverend Zachary had only started to gather supporters about six months before Jason joined the flock. Right from his first meeting, at a church hall in a rundown Detroit neighborhood, Jason had been attracted to Zachary's goal of a self-sufficient community, built somewhere far removed from the stresses of urban life. Beaming, he assured Melody that he had never regretted his decision to join the Soldiers of Jordan.

"My kids all think I've gone nuts," he said cheerfully. "I tell them they shouldn't knock the simple life until they've lived it. Praise God, I finally got my head in the right place and I know what's important and what's not."

Jason struck Melody as a decent man, proud of his victory over alcohol, and deeply regretful of the fact that he'd spent most of his daughters' early years bombed out of his mind. Melody was as sure as she could be without getting inside his skin that Jason was sincere in his praise for Zachary and committed to living a godly life. It was impossible to visualize him sabotaging the mayor's farm machinery, much less conspiring to cover up Jodie's murder. Of course, Jason's sincerity didn't prove anything about Zachary. If Zachary was as smart as his past actions suggested, he would make sure he had plenty of genuine converts sprinkled around campus to provide cover for his more sinister plans.

"We're here," Jason said as he swiped a plastic keycard through an electronic reader set into the post of a chain-link fence. "This is White Falls." His voice thickened with pride. "Our town."

The bar that formed a security barrier across the narrow road swung slowly upward. Melody wondered if Jason or the other Soldiers ever questioned why they needed roadblocks for a supposedly peaceful community in the heart of rural Idaho.

She risked asking him about the perimeter fence and the electronic barrier. Jason wasn't offended by her question, but he clearly considered the answer self-evident. He simply shrugged and told her that even in rural areas, there was no telling when you might get intruders and Reverend Zachary had decided to build the perimeter fences last year. Jason was glad to have them. They made him feel extra safe, especially since they were wired and an alarm would sound if anyone unauthorized tried to enter.

Getting off campus was not going to be easy, Melody reflected, making a mental note of state-of-the-art surveillance cameras lining the access road.

The car rounded a bend, revealing a cluster of single story buildings set on the crest of a rise. "Nice place, huh?" Jason gave a satisfied sigh. "I can tell you, this sure ain't nothin' like the dump I lived in those last few years I was in Detroit."

"It's very attractive," Melody agreed. "It's…peaceful looking."

"Yep, that's just what our town is. Peaceful." He indicated the center building. "We call that big building Jordan House. You'd never know it was once a motel, would you?"

"No, you wouldn't," Melody said, genuinely admiring of the way the long, low building had been spruced up. Built of cinder blocks with a roof of asphalt shingles, it had been painted a delicate sage green, with the doors highlighted in a darker shade of the same color.

"We just finished repainting," Jason said. "Had to wait for the weather to warm up some. The colors are real nice, I think."

"They're great," Melody agreed. "The flowers are lovely, too." The concrete walkways surrounding the former motel were standard ugly, but flower beds stretching the length of the building were bright with tulips, clustered around leafy shrubs. As they drove closer, passing along the front of the motel, Melody saw that the doors to individual units weren't numbered. Instead hand-carved wooden plaques indicated the names of the occupants.

"Which unit is yours, Jason? I don't see your name."

"That's because it's not there. Right now, I'm living in Forest House with the other single men." Jason pointed to a distant building, much newer than the motel, with exterior walls faced to look as if they were made out of natural, unvarnished logs.

"We built Forest House ourselves, right from the foundations up," he said. "There's six rooms in that building, with space for six men in each dorm. And there's six bathrooms, too, one for each dorm. It's real nice. Everything designed for easy maintenance, and easy to keep clean, too. Plus we don't never need to paint the exterior because them logs are treated to last forever."

"Is it difficult to share sleeping quarters with so many other people? I think I'd miss my privacy." Melody didn't want to sound too gushing and enthusiastic about White Falls. Surely most recruits had doubts about communal living when they first arrived, even if they were already committed to the Soldiers of Jordan philosophy?

Jason shrugged. "You get used to sharing everything real fast. Fact is, a lot of the men here are like me. We've spent more nights than we want to remember sleeping rough, or in shelters. It's not much of a hardship to share a room with people who are clean, and who don't have no interest in robbin' your stuff."

"Do the single women live in a dorm situation, too?"

"Yeah, they live on the opposite side of town in River

House. It's the exact same plan as the men's dorm." Jason cleared his throat. "As a matter of fact, I'm gettin' married on Saturday, and then Sally and I will be movin' into one of the units in Jordan House. That's where the married folks live."

"Congratulations," Melody said. Given that Jason had two failed marriages behind him, he was apparently allowing hope to win out over experience. "You and Sally must be very excited."

"Thanks. We are, I guess. The Reverend says it's the right thing for us to do, so I'm sure it is."

Melody bit back a comment to the effect that Zachary wasn't the person getting married. "You have a lot of faith in the Reverend's judgment."

She would have to watch the irony that kept jumping into her voice, Melody warned herself. Fortunately Jason took her words at face value and agreed that he trusted the Reverend's judgment completely, since the Reverend was both wise and smart. "Educated, too," Jason added. "He's a lawyer, you know."

"Yes, I do know. His qualifications must be useful to the Soldiers."

"I guess so." Jason looked as if he'd never given Zachary's professional qualifications a thought. Parking the Dodge minivan in front of another log-faced building, he turned to her with a cheerful grin.

"This is our admin building," he said. "We call it the White House. That's kind of a joke because it's real small, as you can see. But it's where we have the offices and such like."

"It's the center of government for your community, just like the White House in Washington is the center of government for America," Melody said.

"Exactly." Jason seemed pleased that she understood the

joke. "Come on. I'll take you in and introduce you to Terri Bodowski. She's in charge of handicrafts, and she's the lady that's goin' look after you. She'll take you around until you get the hang of things. Help you find out where everything's located, and what your job is and so on."

"Great. Do you know what my job will be?"

"Nobody told me. That's for the Reverend to decide, anyway."

Zachary had already informed Melody that everyone on campus was required to work. Even guests were supposed to pitch in and help. With a smile to show he was joking, he'd reminded her that the devil makes work for idle hands, so one of the rules was that every Soldier had to work or study seven hours a day, six days a week. Melody had been pretty sure that when Zachary was in White Falls, he didn't bother to smile when he made remarks like that one.

Jason removed her suitcase from the van and carried it inside the already open door of the admin building. Melody slung her carry-on bag over her shoulder and followed him inside. The tiny lobby was pleasantly rustic, decorated like the reception area for a country inn, with three closed doors opening off the entrance area, presumably leading to more offices. This building would be a prime target for her to search once she could determine how to gain access without detection, Melody decided, but she could already see that avoiding detection was going to be difficult. A single quick glance was all it took to show her that there was plenty of sophisticated security in place.

"Hi, Jason. Back already? And you must be Melody Beecham. Welcome." A middle-aged woman sat behind the counter, crocheting an afghan in multiple shades of brown, from palest beige through to rich dark chocolate. Her fingers flew as she hooked the yarn.

"Your blanket is exquisite," Melody exclaimed. "And you're working so fast, too!"

The woman put down the afghan, and smiled with evident pleasure. "Well, I crochet seven hours a day, so I ought to be fast by now! I must have made a hundred in this pattern alone. But different colors, you know, so I never seem to get bored."

"Melody, this is Terri Bodowski. Like I mentioned, she's in charge of the women's handicrafts," Jason said. "We sell everything the women make over the Internet, and Terri's afghans are one of our most popular items. Terri, this here is Melody Beecham. I explained as how you'll be takin' her under your wing for a few days."

"That'll be my pleasure, God willing. I hope you had a good flight, Melody?"

"Well, as good as it gets these days. La Guardia airport is a nightmare with all the extra security. Would you believe my luggage was searched three times before they'd let me on the plane? Still, I suppose the government's just trying to keep us safe from terrorists." Melody paused for a second or two, wondering if Terri or Jason might make a comment, either about the government, or about terrorists, but neither of them said a word.

Melody continued smoothly, gliding over the slight pause. "At least the plane arrived in Boise on time so I didn't keep Jason waiting."

"Speakin' of keepin' people waitin', I promised Tom I'd help him with that set of shelves he's tryin' to get put together," Jason said. "Real nice to have met you, Melody. Bye, Terri. I'll see you both at dinner tonight. God bless."

"God bless," Terri said warmly. "See you soon, Jason."

Giving both women a smile and a quick wave, Jason returned to the van and drove off. It was no wonder that Agent

Harry Cooper had advised the FBI to shut down their investigation, Melody thought. This whole place was idyllic. Jason and Terri were so friendly they seemed like characters plucked from an old TV show. *Mayberry,* perhaps, or *Leave it to Beaver* brought up-to-date with vibrant color and additional outside shots.

The comparison had no sooner occurred to her than Melody realized Jason and Terri would fit even better onto the more sinister set of *The Truman Show.*

Terri spoke while Melody was still debating whether she'd landed in cozy Mayberry or frightening Truman territory. "Single women usually board in River House," Terri said. "That's the dorm at the east end of the campus, down by the Allagash River. But Reverend Zachary instructed that you were to stay in the guest room right in Jordan House, since you're just a visitor, not a true Soldier yet."

"I'd be happy to stay in the women's dorm if it's easier for everyone," Melody said.

"Oh, no. Reverend Zachary has assigned you to the guest room in Jordan House." As far as Terri was concerned, that clearly ended the discussion. "You can visit the women's dorm anytime you want, though. I'd be happy to show you around if you'd like to get an idea of where you would be living if you did decide to join our community. But Forest House—that's the men's dorm—is off-limits to women. And vice versa, of course."

More shades of the 1950s, but Terri's cheerful expression suggested that she felt no resentment at being barred from entering Forest House. She folded her afghan, and stuck the crochet needle into her ball of yarn.

"You must be anxious to get settled. I'll walk you to your room. It's not very far. Oh, drat!" Terri almost stumbled over

Melody's big suitcase as she emerged from behind the counter. "I should have asked Jason to drive this over to your room before he took off."

"No problem," Melody said. "It's on wheels. It shouldn't be too hard to pull."

"Oh, no, leave it here," Terri said quickly. "You don't want to drag that heavy load over all those rough concrete paths. You'll ruin the bottom of the case. Why don't we go on ahead and I'll call one of the men to deliver it to you later?"

Terri sounded just a fraction too insistent about leaving the case right where it was, Melody decided. She could only assume that Jason had deliberately "forgotten" to deliver it to her room so that the Soldiers could search it first.

"It's fine to leave your luggage here," Terri assured her. "That's one of the lovely things about our town. It's safe as can be to leave your belongings wherever it's most convenient."

"What a wonderful change from New York," Melody said, falling into step next to Terri. "Although it may take a bit of getting used to after years of living in Manhattan."

"You don't sound much like a New Yorker." Terri waved to a group of half a dozen boys, who all waved back, even the two oldest, who were in their midteens. The boys were tossing a soccer ball from one to another as they ran, apparently heading for a patch of level grass alongside the White House. They looked to be having a grand time, laughing and jostling as they made their way toward the makeshift soccer field. More escapees from the *Mayberry* soundstage, Melody reflected, unnerved by the sight of so much good humor.

"I was born in England," she said, responding to Terri's comment about her accent. "My mother was English and my father is American, and I spent time in both countries when

I was growing up. People tell me I have this strange middle-of-the-Atlantic Ocean accent that's neither one thing nor the other."

"You sound more like a Brit than a New Yorker, that's for sure!" Terri laughed. "I'm envious of all your traveling. I always wanted to go to Europe. Idaho is about as far as I've gotten, and you might say it's in the wrong direction, but I'm real glad I came here. There's something special about the West."

"Where are you from originally?" Melody asked.

"Michigan. I grew up in the suburbs near Detroit. The lake's lovely, but the weather's not so great and the schools in our district were flat-out terrible."

"Do you still have family in Detroit?"

"Oh, some. But my husband's here, and our son, and I wouldn't go back for anything. Our David is a changed boy now that he's being taught by teachers who care."

Anyone listening to Terri and Jason would have to conclude that Zachary and the Soldiers of Jordan were more about providing social services and family therapy than plotting to blow up the world, Melody thought wryly. She followed Terri through a breezeway and emerged onto what must once have been the motel parking lot. Only four vehicles were parked on the worn asphalt, but the lot was ringed by young conifers, and each corner was anchored by a giant tub of spring flowers. The Soldiers of Jordan really seemed committed to making their surroundings as attractive as possible.

"The flowers are Jillian's pride and joy," Terri said, indicating the tubs. "She's in charge of landscaping, and she works real hard to make the place look nice. She had the children planting bulbs last fall as an after-school project, and the tulips have come up just fine. Here we are." She turned toward the end unit. "This will be your home away from home, so I hope you like it."

The door Terri approached was decorated with a wooden plaque inscribed Welcome Guests. With a sinking sensation, Melody saw that Terri wasn't carrying a key. Sure enough, Terri simply turned the handle and the door swung inward. Guests might be welcome, but it seemed that they weren't accorded much privacy.

"My husband just repainted this room," Terri said, moving to stand in front of the window. "I chose the color scheme myself. It's fresh looking, don't you think?"

"I do. It's lovely." The walls were a cheery daffodil-yellow, and although the Formica-topped furniture and dark brown tweed carpeting had clearly been inherited from motel days, the furniture surfaces gleamed with polish, and the smell of lemon cleansers lingered in the air. The yellow gingham bedspread appeared crisp and new, and the windows were covered by attractive white wooden shutters. There was a chest of drawers affixed to one wall, standard motel-style, but there was no TV perched on top. Instead a Bible and several slender paperbacks were stacked between a pair of gilded plaster bookends, painfully bad replicas of Raphael's famous cherubs.

"I know you'll be comfortable here, Melody." Terri gestured to the heating unit under the window. "That unit works just like you'd find in any motel, but I don't expect you'll need heat or AC at this time of year. The weather's been lovely this past couple of weeks."

"I'm sure everything will be terrific." Melody set her bag and purse on the table, wondering how far she could go before her enthusiasm began to sound as fake as it was. She pushed open the bathroom door, pretending to explore her quarters. Without drawing attention to her search, she tried to identify any fixtures that might conceal audio bugs and/or cameras. Zachary's unmasking of two experienced undercover agents—almost as soon as they set foot in White Falls—had happened too fast. It was possible, of course, that Zachary was brilliant at assessing the sincerity, or lack thereof, of potential converts. Melody would have found that theory easier to believe if Zachary had shown any sign of doubting *her* sincerity. In fact, though, he seemed to have accepted everything she said at face value. All things considered, it seemed more likely to her that Zachary had a source inside the Bureau, or else that he spied on every newcomer to the campus. If he was spying on new converts, Melody was determined not to be caught out.

"The bathroom's got brand-new fixtures," Terri said, hovering. "I know this isn't a five-star room, or anything close, but it's clean and everything works. That's what's important, isn't it?"

"It's just lovely. I'm sure I'll be very happy here." Melody smiled, and then exclaimed, as if the thought had just occurred to her. "Oh, by the way, do you have the room key, Terri?"

Terri's smile became just a little strained. "We don't use keys here, Melody. I thought you understood that. You have absolutely nothing to worry about, though. I assure you, your belongings are as safe here in this open room as they would be under lock and key in any other town."

Melody decided that any newcomer might find that statement a bit hard to swallow. She risked a mild protest. "The idea of leaving my door unlocked makes me nervous."

"It took a bit of getting used to for all of us," Terri said. "Then after a while, you begin to wonder how you ever lived another way. Don't worry, Melody. You won't have any problems. Nobody in White Falls would dream of taking anything that belongs to you. It just won't happen."

Unless it was a cell phone or something else the Soldiers deemed dangerous to her moral health, Melody reflected cynically. She supposed Terri justified the search of newcomers' belongings on the grounds that it was better to remove sources of temptation before they could cause a problem.

Terri gestured to the phone. "Maybe it'll make you feel safer to know there's always someone on guard duty and you can reach them at any hour of the day or night. Just call 911, like you would in any other city. The only difference is, help here arrives in less than two minutes, instead of half an hour, or whenever the dispatcher gets around to it. Plus you know the person who arrives on your doorstep."

"Well, it's certainly reassuring to hear that."

"Isn't it?" Terri smiled. "You can reach everyone in White Falls with that phone. There's a list of contact numbers in the drawer right beside your bed."

"And how about long distance calls?" Melody asked, although she was pretty sure she could guess Terri's answer. "How do I get an outside line? I'll pay the charges, of course."

"We only have an internal phone system," Terri said, just as Melody had expected. "We don't make outside calls. There's no reason for us to call outside White Falls."

"Then how do you stay in touch with your family?"

"The Soldiers of Jordan are my family," Terri said simply. "Here we try to keep ourselves to ourselves as much as we possibly can. It's the best way to stay focused on what's really important. "

"I understand," Melody said, mentally blessing Bob Spinard. "But how am I going to let my friends know that I'm okay? They'll worry if they don't hear from me."

"You can write a letter," Terri said. "There's a basket where you can put mail at the end of the counter in the White House."

And bets were on that all the mail got scrutinized before it was sent out. "I can't remember the last time I wrote letters to a friend," Melody said. "Unless it was e-mail." She smiled to show she wasn't complaining.

"You'll soon get used to it, and it's real nice when they write back. Taking phone calls always seems like an interruption, but getting letters seems a treat." Terri's attitude was determinedly upbeat.

"If you don't need me for anything more, Melody, I'll be getting back to the office. I'll call Jason about your luggage, and I'll pass word to Reverend Zachary that you've arrived. He'll be real pleased to know you had a safe journey and that you're getting settled in."

"Great. Thanks for all your help." Melody glanced at her watch. "My goodness, it's five-fifteen already. That's seven-fifteen New York time. No wonder I'm feeling hungry! Could you explain to me what we do about dinner? Where exactly do I have to go?"

"I'll come and pick you up a few minutes before six. We all eat together in the dining room. Three meals a day, and afternoon snacks for the kiddies." Terri produced another of the warm, encouraging smiles that seemed to be a Soldiers of Jordan specialty. "We have some wonderful cooks and I know you're going to love our food."

"I'm looking forward to the meal, and to meeting everyone." Melody gave a nervous laugh. "It's a bit intimidating being the new kid on the block."

"You don't have to worry, not for a moment. Everyone will make you welcome and you'll soon feel as if you've lived here forever."

In fact, the whole damn place was just so sugar-sweet and friendly she was at risk of going into a diabetic coma. Melody dredged up one final smile. "Well, I'd better hurry if I'm going to get freshened up before dinner."

"I'll leave you to it," Terri said. "My extension number is 448. Just give me a holler if you need anything at all." She paused in the doorway to the small room. "Welcome to White Falls, Melody. I can already tell that it's going to be a true blessing to have you with us."

Ten

As soon as Terri left, Melody gave an exaggerated yawn, then folded the gingham coverlet, draping it over the back of the chair. She removed her shoes and lay down on the bed, resting her hands behind her neck. Trying to look like a woman unwinding the kinks after a long flight, she flexed her muscles and stretched her legs, squirming around the bed until she was in the position that gave her the best possible view of the ceiling fan.

After a few moments of staring, Melody was nearly sure the decorative whorls at the hub of the fan were designed to conceal the lens of a camera. Unfortunately she couldn't think of any way to confirm her suspicion. If there was a camera inside the fan, scooting down the bed and standing up to take a closer look would simply alert whoever was watching her to the fact that they'd been found out.

The idea that guests were routinely spied on gave the lie to the image of peaceful do-gooders that the Soldiers of Jordan tried to project. Still, provided she gave no clue she'd noticed the camera, the fact that she was being watched could be made to work to her advantage. She would make sure that the watchers saw nothing except an eager prospective recruit to the Soldiers of Jordan lifestyle, which might help them to lower their guards in her vicinity.

With another fake yawn and a final stretch, Melody got up from the bed and took her travel pouch of toilet articles into the bathroom. She set the contents out on the counter, then cleaned her teeth, washed her hands, combed her hair and dabbed powder on her nose. At least the fan-mounted camera couldn't penetrate in here once she closed the door, and as far as she could determine, there was no second camera anywhere inside the small bathroom. That final invasion of personal privacy was apparently too much, even for this spooky crew.

If she was right in her assumption that she was being watched, it was logical to conclude that she was also being listened to. Bob Spinard had provided her with an excellent bug detector. Unfortunately she couldn't utilize it because her actions would be recorded on camera. No genuine recruit was going to arrive on campus with sophisticated electronic monitoring equipment. However, she didn't really need to conduct a search to be confident the room was wired for sound. Given the presence of a camera, she had to assume that the bedroom and possibly the bathroom were loaded with bugs. Obviously she wasn't going to be checking in with Nick from inside her room unless she wanted everything she said to be overheard.

In fact, she might as well make use of the camera to convince the people watching her that she'd been successfully defanged. She would make a call using her cell phone. She was confident the Soldiers of Jordan would then send somebody to confiscate it. With any luck, they wouldn't consider the possibility that she'd come equipped with a second phone.

Melody pulled her phone from her purse and keyed in the speed dial code that connected with her assistant at the Van der Meer Gallery. Since it was heading toward eight o'clock on the East Coast, there was no chance she'd find Ellen still at work. The point of the exercise, though, wasn't to talk to Ellen. The point was to show Zachary and his followers that she had a cell phone.

Ellen's voice-mail box invited her to leave a message. "Hi, Ellen, it's Melody. Everything was so rushed yesterday, I forgot to tell you that the Simona gallery is complaining that we haven't paid their invoice from January. It was for the nineteenth-century portrait of Dante Alighieri that we sold to the First Commercial Bank in Greenwich. Could you follow up, please? Thanks. Oh, and tell Jasper that I've arrived safely in White Falls, would you? The people here are all very friendly, and the town is much prettier than I expected. I think this is going to be just the break I needed."

Melody had barely returned the phone to her purse when she was interrupted by a knock on her door. It was a relief to discover that the Soldiers did at least knock before barging in. Unannounced visitors, however smiling and friendly, would have been pushing the limit of what she could stomach.

The boy on her doorstep was one of the teens she'd seen going off to play soccer, and he'd come to deliver her suitcase. He was as abnormally cheerful as Terri and Jason, but Melody didn't get the impression that the good cheer was a cover for darker emotions. He politely informed her that his name was Tyler Wildhelm, and that he looked forward to introducing her to his parents and sister. He lifted the suitcase off the dolly, but placed it barely inside her doorstep, presumably because carrying it any farther into her room would have been a breach of the rules about separation of the sexes.

There were still fifteen minutes or so left before Terri would be arriving to escort her to dinner. Melody opened her suitcase and carefully checked the contents, but there was no way to ascertain if it had been searched by the Soldiers. Her clothes weren't folded quite as she'd left them, but that could have been caused by security workers at the airport, or even by the baggage handlers tossing the case onto a conveyor belt.

Proof or not, she was confident the case had been searched. If she'd been a dog, the hair on her spine would by now be standing up in an angry, bristling line. Her instincts had been shouting warnings ever since she arrived in White Falls, and she had considerable faith in her instincts. Paranoia was definitely called for, Melody decided. Suspect everyone and trust nobody. It was a great maxim to live by, even if it had been suggested to her by Nick.

She had to assume her room would be searched while she was at dinner, which was worrisome. Her suitcase had contained nothing that would identify her as anything other than what she claimed to be, but her room was another matter. Discovery of any one of Bob Spinard's gadgets would guarantee that she get tossed off campus immediately. Should she try to hide Bob's gadgets? Unfortunately, with the likelihood that there was a camera scrutinizing her every move, hiding the gadgets would do nothing except draw attention to them. Bottom line, she would just have to rely on Bob's camouflage to be effective.

Melody started hanging up clothes in the tiny closet and stashing underwear in the drawers, which had all been lined with fresh, rose-scented paper. At ten minutes to six, there was another knock on her door.

"I'm almost ready, Terri," she called out. "Be right with you. I'm just putting on my shoes."

"It's not Terri. It's me." Zachary pushed open her door a crack, but didn't peek in. "May I come in?"

Melody opened the door, doing her best to look thrilled. "Zachary! I'm so happy to see you. Come in!"

Apparently Zachary was exempt from the rule of no single men and women alone in the same room, although she noticed that he did leave the door wide-open when he stepped inside. He shook her hand, smiling broadly. "Well, it's terrific to see you, my dear, even though we only said goodbye three days ago. Welcome to White Falls, Melody. It's great to have you here."

"It's great to be here. You didn't tell me how beautiful White Falls is."

"It is lovely, isn't it? I'm glad you like it. Our little town is still a work in progress, but we're very proud of all that we've achieved in the past three years. I should show you some pictures of how run-down the place was when we first arrived. As Winston Churchill once said, there's a lot of blood, sweat and tears gone into building our community."

Churchill had been talking about a nation at war. Melody wondered how literally she should take Zachary's reference to the blood and the tears. "You all have every right to be proud," she said. "It's amazing what you've accomplished in such a short period of time."

"With God, all things are possible."

Zachary invariably got a pompous look when he mentioned God. Which, Melody realized, was part of the reason she doubted his sincerity. She always felt as if he were quoting, never as if he were speaking from the heart. Something stirred at the edges of her consciousness, an incongruity connected to the video filmed by Jodie Evanderhaus, but the thought wouldn't quite take shape and there was no time to pursue it with Zachary watching her.

"I'm looking forward to meeting everyone," she said, wondering if her conversation sounded as stilted to Zachary as it did to her. "Jason and Terri were both so kind. They seemed truly anxious to make me feel welcome." Usually she was quite good at role-playing, but there was something about the aura of this place that froze her facial muscles into an expression that felt more like a grimace than a smile.

The Stepford Wives, she thought suddenly. She wasn't walking through the set for *Mayberry* or even *The Truman Show.* She was right in the middle of the town of Stepford, with its dark secrets waiting to be uncovered.

"People here are happy. It's easy to be kind when you're feeling content with the way your life is working out." Zachary's words formed a bizarre contrast to the sinister nature of what she was thinking. He sat down in one of the room's two chairs, without waiting to be asked. Obviously he'd forgotten that he was nominally a guest in her room, Melody thought.

"Sit for a moment, would you?" he asked, gesturing to the chair opposite him. "I need to bring you up to speed on a couple of our community rules before we go into dinner."

"Of course." Melody sat opposite him and he leaned across the table, his manner both confiding and earnest.

"In order for our community here to remain strong, we have guidelines about the way our members are expected to behave. You and I have already talked about the fact that the Soldiers of Jordan don't approve of sex between men and women who aren't married to each other."

He paused and she gave him the reply he wanted. "I wouldn't dream of starting a sexual relationship with anyone here, Zachary. That part of my life is behind me."

"Maybe. But you're a very beautiful woman, Melody, and

there are a lot of single men living here. We don't want any mishaps, and I've learned that it's best for everyone if we have clear rules, so that we make it as easy as possible for members of our community to live up to our high principles."

"Yes, I understand. What are the rules?"

"Single men and women should avoid being alone together as much as possible. I know Terri has already told you that we prefer men and women not to enter each other's dorms. You probably think that's old-fashioned of us, but we've found that it's much easier to control a situation before it gets started, rather than when it's already halfway to conflagration."

"Terri explained about avoiding the men's dorm, and it seems a simple rule to follow." Melody gave him a wide-eyed gaze, wondering why it was that fringe religions and hang-ups about sex so often seemed to go together. She matched her solemn expression to his. "After my recent experiences with Nikolai Anwar, I can promise I'm not in the mood to start a casual sexual relationship ever again. I've learned my lesson."

"You've been hurt," Zachary murmured. "Nikolai took advantage of you and you ended up humiliated in a very public way. However, I've seen a lot of women put promiscuous lifestyles behind them, and I promise that if you dedicate yourself to our program, you'll find your wounds are not only healed, but that they have left no scars."

The pompous baboon was accusing her of having a led a promiscuous life? Melody clasped her hands beneath her chin and gazed at Zachary submissively while she fantasized about delivering a swift, Unit One-style kick to his balls. "It would be so wonderful to be free of emotional pain," she murmured.

She was afraid she'd overdone the gushing, not to mention

the wistfulness, but once again Zachary seemed to sense nothing amiss. He gave her one of the quirky smiles that always
preceded his attempts at humor. "And that brings me to my
next rule, which is one most of our guests find a lot harder to
follow than giving up casual sex!"

"Are you about to warn me that I have to live on bread and
water?" Melody asked.

He laughed. "No, nothing quite that grim! Good, healthy
food is surely one of God's greatest gifts to us, and we try to
make each meal into a small celebration."

"Well, thank goodness." She returned his smile. "So what's
this strict rule that nobody likes? If I'm allowed to munch on
the occasional cookie, then nothing else seems too unbear-
able."

Zachary became solemn again. "While you're here, it's really important for you to focus your energy and your attention on our program," he said. "That means no phone calls to
your family and friends—"

"Terri's already explained that the phones will only reach
numbers within White Falls," Melody said. "It'll be hard, but
I suppose I can learn to live with that."

"I wasn't talking about our internal phone system," Zachary said. "I was talking about your cell phone. I'm sure you
must have one? Everyone does these days."

Zachary tried to make his question sound routine, but Melody's hackles bristled into full alert. *He knew she had a cell
phone because he'd watched her make the call to Ellen on his
damned hidden camera.* Melody was a hundred percent sure
of her conclusion, but she debated how to respond. Since
most people nowadays felt naked without their cell phones,
she decided it would be more credible if she didn't hand hers
over too easily.

"I have a cell phone," she admitted. "I won't use it except in an emergency, but I can't give it up, Zachary. What if Jasper Fowles needs to reach me? There could be a crisis at the gallery—"

"Then somebody else must handle it," Zachary said gently. "Now is the time for you to take care of yourself, Melody. Haven't you earned the right to at least a couple of weeks entirely to yourself?"

"Well, yes, I suppose so. But what if my grandparents need to talk to me?"

"They'll reach the central switchboard and I'll personally reassure them that you're well and happy but not available to take their call." Zachary held out his hand. "This is important, Melody. You need to get rid of your phone. Handing it over to me is a sign that you're willing to commit seriously to our program."

She didn't stir. "I feel so isolated without it…."

"I know." His voice throbbed with compassion. "I understand exactly how you feel, but you need to give our program a chance to work its miracles. Give yourself the gift of freedom from the tethers of your past." Zachary's eyes locked with hers. "Give me your phone, Melody. I'll keep it in my office, and whenever you're ready to leave White Falls, it will be waiting for you."

She let doubt suffuse her voice. She shifted uneasily on her chair. "Well, if you really think it's essential…"

"I do. Absolutely."

She'd just bet he did. Indoctrination would be a hell of a lot more difficult if she kept in contact with her friends. Melody took the cell phone out of her purse and stared at it for a moment. Then, hesitantly, she handed it to Zachary. As he took it, she gave a tiny sigh, as if she were wishing she could snatch it back at the last moment.

Zachary's fingers closed tightly over the phone. He smiled at her as he slipped it into his jacket pocket. "See, I warned you that giving up your phone would be harder than giving up sex."

He clearly expected her to laugh, so she obliged with a small chuckle. "That's better," he said approvingly, as he rose to his feet. "That's the sunny-natured Melody I came to admire so much during my stay in New York. Trust me on this, my dear. You'll soon wonder why you ever thought that darn cell phone was so important."

"Yes, Zachary. I'm sure you're right."

"Oh, and another thing, my dear. Now that you're here in White Falls, it's probably not a good idea for you to call me Zachary. Most people here call me the Reverend."

"Then that's what I'll call you, too." She flashed a smile. "Reverend."

She could feel the smug satisfaction oozing out of him. He nodded at her, the high priest acknowledging his acolyte. "Good girl. Now, let's go to dinner. Everyone will be waiting for us."

Eleven

The dining room, originally the motel restaurant, had a full commercial kitchen, Zachary informed Melody as they strolled through the lengthening evening shadows toward the end of the building, with its serene view toward the river. Twelve women worked two separate shifts preparing meals for the entire congregation. He pointed out the vegetable gardens, which were freshly tilled but mostly bare. The Soldiers grew as much of their own produce as possible, although the growing season had only just begun and they were using canned provisions at the moment.

It was only a minute or two after six when Melody and Zachary arrived at the entrance to the dining room, but there were no more than half a dozen empty spaces left in a room that held twenty-two tables, each set for ten. Agents Bostwick and Cooper had reported that the Soldiers of Jordan numbered less than a hundred and fifty, including children. The group had increased its numbers since the FBI investigation, Melody reflected.

She and Zachary were apparently the last to arrive for the

evening meal and the Soldiers assembled in the dining room stood up as Zachary came through the double doors. Smiling, Zachary made motions with his hands urging everyone to sit. He moved through the room like the famous conductor of a symphony orchestra receiving accolades from the admiring audience before he'd even begun to play.

Exchanging greetings with a few favored adults, and tousling the hair of every child he passed, Zachary led Melody to a table where Terri Bodowski and Jason Cushman were already seated. An awestruck hush fell behind them as they walked past and Melody could feel Zachary drawing power and energy from the waves of admiration flowing toward him. He held Melody's chair, waiting for her to be seated, and then picked up the mike that lay on the table, ready for him to use.

"I apologize for keeping you waiting for your dinner," he said. "As you can see, we're fortunate enough to have a guest with us tonight. I know you'll welcome her into our community and find a place for her in your prayers." He lifted his outstretched hands, palms facing upward, and the entire roomful of people instantly lowered their heads.

"Let us thank God for directing Melody Beecham's footsteps to our congregation. We pray that she will find new meaning for her life while she is with us. And let us also offer thanks for the food we're about to eat and for the cooks who have labored to make it delicious as well as nourishing. We thank God for the day now drawing to a close, and ask for His blessing on the night that approaches. If we have offended any of our brothers and sisters, we ask for their forgiveness and ask God for his help in being kinder and more considerate of others tomorrow. Amen."

The moment everyone had repeated Amen, a dozen women

stood up and disappeared through a set of double doors that presumably led to the kitchens. They returned with serving trays loaded with bowls of steaming food and quickly distributed the bowls to each table. Meanwhile, a cluster of little girls, none older than twelve and all dressed in ankle-length ruffled aprons, carried out baskets of hot bread that filled the room with the appetizing smell of fresh baking. It was startling how many subtle pressures Melody had already observed that pushed the men and boys toward pursuits that emphasized strength and the outdoors, while the girls were confined inside, pursuing domestic chores. As it happened, these girls all looked as if they were having a fine time, but heaven help the girl who fancied the idea of becoming a carpenter, or a boy who would like to become a chef.

The meal was a simple chicken and vegetable casserole, but Melody was impressed by how well cooked it was, given the number of people needing to be served. Dessert was apple pie, bursting with fruit and with a crust tender enough to win an award at the county fair. There was even drinkable coffee to end the meal. In comparison to the sort of food she'd been served at boarding school, Melody considered that this meal registered somewhere between ambrosial and heavenly.

Unfortunately the conversation was a lot less inspiring than the food. Terri introduced her husband and son, who were men of few words, contriving to pass the entire meal without saying more than a few sentences. Jason introduced Sally, his bride-to-be. Sally was a thin, homely woman of about forty, with work-worn hands and a subdued manner. For a woman who was about to marry Jason, Sally spent an awful lot of time staring at Zachary. And, if Melody was any judge, Sally's rapt stares were spliced with a healthy dose of sexual desire for her spiritual mentor.

Perhaps Zachary got off on the adoration of his groupies and didn't need actual intercourse to feel sexually satisfied, Melody speculated. If he fed on silent adoration and the suppressed sexual longings of his female followers, it would be easier for him not only to preach celibacy outside of marriage, but also to live by his own rules.

The older couple seated across the table from Melody introduced themselves as Dr. Harvey Leonard and his wife, Betty, who had been her husband's nurse until they both retired ten years ago. They were in charge of basic health care for the Soldiers of Jordan, and they'd trained a cadre of twenty volunteers in rudimentary first aid. Unfortunately Harvey was deaf, and Betty had taken on the task of acting as his hearing aid. Every remark addressed to Harvey, or likely to be of interest to Harvey, was repeated at double volume by Betty. Which, Melody thought wryly, might be part of the reason that her dinner companions were smart enough not to say much.

The tenth and final person seated at the table was Rachel Cranford. Rachel mumbled a greeting, but she made no reference to the fact that she and Melody had met two years earlier in England, at the memorial service for Lady Roz. Melody wondered if Rachel felt awkward about broaching the topic of Roz's death, especially since she'd been aboard Johnston Yates's yacht when Roz died. Still, given that Zachary had most likely hand-picked the people seated at his table, it was clear that she needed to identify Rachel up-front as somebody she was acquainted with. She simply couldn't afford to be found out keeping secrets.

"Rachel Cranford?" she queried. "Oh, my goodness, I do believe we've met before. What a small world this is! Aren't you Senator Lewis Cranford's daughter?"

"Melody says Rachel is Senator Lewis Cranford's daughter," Betty bellowed for her husband's benefit.

"I didn't know that," Harvey said. "Is that true, young lady? Is your father a United States senator?"

Rachel flushed bright scarlet and looked as if she wished she could disappear under the table. "Er…yes," she said. "I'm the senator's oldest daughter."

"Which state does he represent?" Betty forgot she wasn't talking to Harvey and yelled the question. "I recollect seeing him on the TV, but I don't recall where he's from."

"He represents Kentucky," Rachel said. She yelled, too, then flushed when she realized how loudly she'd spoken. She lowered her voice. "My parents were both born and raised in Lexington but they spend most of their time in Washington nowadays."

Her voice was neutral to the point of flatness, but Melody got a sudden sense that being forced to spend so much time in Washington might be an issue for Rachel. Teenagers tended to have strange decision-making processes, but running to rural Idaho and joining a cult struck Melody as overkill for solving the problem of not liking the D.C. lifestyle.

"You were at my mother's memorial service two years ago," she said, wanting to demonstrate for Zachary how slender her past connection to Rachel had been. "The service was held in Malmesbury Abbey, in England. Do you remember?"

"Oh, yes, I remember. There were gazillions of pictures of you in the paper afterward." Rachel stared at her glass of water, refusing to meet Melody's eyes.

And that was another odd thing for Rachel to mention. Why would she even have noticed the tabloid coverage?

Melody disguised her interest behind another overbright

smile. "What an amazing coincidence to find you here!" When this assignment was over, she thought she might never smile again. "How long have you been a member of the Soldiers of Jordan, Rachel?"

"Five months. I arrived in White Falls three months ago." Rachel finally lifted her head high enough to meet Melody's eyes. "Did my father send you to bring me home?"

"Senator Cranford has sent Melody to bring Rachel home," Betty bellowed for Harvey's benefit.

Hell and damnation, Melody thought, wishing Rachel hadn't asked that particular question, and especially wishing that Betty hadn't roared out a repeat. She didn't want to put ideas into Zachary's head about her motives for coming to White Falls, especially one that cut just a bit too close to the bone. Still, it would have been even more undesirable to hide the fact that she and Rachel had acquaintances in common and had met previously, albeit briefly. She couldn't afford to arouse Zachary's suspicions by concealing anything that he might already know.

"Why would you think that your father sent me?" she asked Rachel, her brow wrinkling in fake puzzlement. "The senator and I haven't spoken for months." She gave an embarrassed laugh. "To be honest, your father is a bit annoyed with me. My stepfather, Wallis Beecham, seems to have encouraged him to make some dubious financial investments, and I had the impression last time we spoke that your father blames me by association. It's unfortunate, because the senator used to be a good customer of the art gallery where I work."

"Oh." Rachel looked back down at the table, but Melody sensed a faint lessening in the hostility beaming from her direction.

Zachary took control of the conversation at that point, and kept control of it for the rest of the meal, strengthening Melody's suspicion that he'd deliberately sat back and waited to see how she would react to Rachel's presence. She was more than happy to let Zachary sermonize while she drank a second cup of coffee and watched the interactions of the other people at the table.

Sally wasn't the only woman at the table mesmerized by Zachary, Melody concluded. Poor Rachel wasn't good at disguising her feelings for him and it was clear that she was in the throes of a major crush. It was equally clear that Zachary was aware of her crush and did nothing to dampen it. On the other hand, Melody was forced to admit he did nothing to encourage it, either. He could scarcely be blamed for the fact that Rachel blushed every time he so much as glanced toward her, and that the poor kid melted into a hormonal puddle on the rare occasions he smiled directly at her.

It was a good job she wasn't hanging too many hopes on Mac's plan to seduce Zachary, Melody reflected wryly. She'd have been fighting her way through a phalanx of rivals to get to him. With so much repressed sexual passion already on offer, she would probably need to strip naked in his bedroom in order to catch even a flicker of his attention, and then he'd most likely tell her to get dressed and remember the community rules.

Despite Mac's and Nick's view that sex was the ultimate tool for promoting intimacy, she was becoming more convinced by the moment that there were more effective ways to gain Zachary's attention. At the first possible opportunity, she'd start dropping gentle reminders that she had something unique to offer him: namely, her family's money and aristocratic connections, a combination that still packed prestige and power in England. In her judgment, Zachary would opt for money and power in preference to sex any day.

Zachary was the first person to leave the dining room, having told Melody that she should report to the White House at eight next morning, following early morning prayers and the communal breakfast. Her job assignment would be in the office, working on the Internet mail order business that provided an important part of the income earned by the Soldiers of Jordan. She lowered her gaze modestly, hoping she concealed a flash of delight that he was assigning her to precisely the location she most wanted to investigate.

Zachary was followed from the dining room by five men, all white, all early middle-aged. Betty helpfully identified the men as the governing council for the Soldiers of Jordan. Harvey pointed out—as if Melody hadn't already noticed—that there were no women on the council. "In White Falls, women know their place," he said, in the loud voice of the hard-of-hearing.

"And what is their place according to you?" Melody was stung into asking. After less than four hours on campus she was already suffering from a severe overdose of enforced meekness.

"Women are partners with men," Harvey responded promptly. He shot an unexpectedly shrewd glance in her direction. "Partners, young lady, not inferiors, but not rivals, either."

"I agree. But I'm not sure we would agree on what it means to be partners."

"Partnership means that women should do what they do best and leave men to do what they do best." Harvey's patronizing attitude suggested that he was explaining the obvious. "Men enjoy fighting their way through the corporate jungle, or climbing the ladder in a profession, because it's their nature to be competitive. Men have competed to be top dog ever since cavemen went out to slay the woolly mammoth and bring home meat for their families. Women, on the other hand, are designed to be mothers and homemakers. The hand that rocks the cradle rules the world, and that's not just old-fashioned wishful thinking, it's the truth. Women have the most important job in the world and they neglect it at their peril. Our society has literally been going to the devil ever since women chose to step outside the role that God and nature designed them for. Women have no place in public life. They belong inside the home."

Melody clamped her teeth together. Rappelling down the sides of buildings was beginning to seem like one of the easier tasks Unit One would ask her to undertake. With superhuman restraint, she refrained from telling Harvey what she thought of his opinions. She sipped the dregs of her coffee until she was sure she could open her mouth without asking how women who didn't want to be wives and mothers fitted into his world view, not to mention men who would have preferred an alternative to hacking a path through the corporate jungle.

"I've always wanted to have children," she said, setting her cup back in its saucer. "I'm sure motherhood is a great joy for many women." It was one of the few truthful but conciliatory remarks she could come up with and Harvey told her approvingly that she had her values in the right place.

Afraid of blowing the moment of harmony, Melody rose to her feet. "Will you all excuse me, please? I still have a lot of unpacking to do." She smiled. "I'll see you tomorrow morning, at prayer service. I'm looking forward to it."

"Rachel, why don't you walk Melody back to her room?"

Terri's voice rose in a question, but Melody had the distinct impression this was more of an order than a suggestion.

Apparently three months with the Soldiers hadn't been long enough for Rachel to vanquish her natural teenage surliness. She greeted the order with a definite scowl. However, she didn't consider refusing to do Terri's bidding. She accompanied Melody outside, still looking sulky, their departure followed by repeated cries of goodnight and God bless from the Soldiers remaining in the dining room.

"Why have you really come here?" Rachel asked as soon as they were outside and out of earshot. "My father sent you, didn't he?"

"No, he didn't," Melody said. "I told you, I'm one of the last people your father would ever approach with a request for a favor. I'm here because my life needs a new direction and I was impressed by Reverend Zachary's message of spiritual renewal."

"Why would your life need a new direction? You're beautiful. You're famous. You're rich. You have a great job—"

"Trust me, fame isn't all it's cracked up to be." About to explain that she was anything but rich, Melody stopped herself just in time. She wanted Zachary and the Soldiers to believe she had inherited lots of money so that she would be an especially desirable recruit.

"There have been plenty of not-so-great things in my life recently. My mother died in a horrible accident. I learned that Wallis Beecham isn't my father, and then had to cope with the fact that he tried to kidnap me, and now he's been indicted for conspiracy to commit murder. On top of that, my former boyfriend just ditched me in about the most public and humiliating way you could imagine. Why is it hard to believe that I need some time to regroup and maybe discover a new way to look at my life?"

"I'm sorry about your mother," Rachel said, not meeting Melody's eyes. "She was really nice to me on that horrible trip my father made us take on the Yates's yacht. When I admired the gold bracelet she was wearing, she gave it to me. And then, on her birthday, when the wind started to kick up and I began to feel sick, she gave me some of her travel-sickness pills."

Lady Roz, for all her sins, had been capable of unexpected moments of generosity, especially to young women who were plain, or socially ill-at-ease. A stab of grief for her mother's loss came out of nowhere, catching Melody so much off guard that she spoke without censoring herself. "Did my mother enjoy her birthday, do you think? It bothers me that we hadn't seen each other for more than two months when she died. I would like to think that her last day on earth was happy."

The question was not only unplanned, it came from the heart. But as soon as she asked it, Melody realized she'd just broached an excellent topic for lessening Rachel's hostility. Rachel knew the details of Roz's final hours on earth and Melody didn't. That made for a subtle reversal of power in their relationship. A reversal that might encourage Rachel to be more open, and eventually to confide something about the reasons that had brought her to White Falls.

"Lady Roz seemed really happy when we were at lunch," Rachel said. "She laughed a lot and told a bunch of funny stories. I remember she talked about how one day when she was still in her teens she had tea in the garden at Balmoral Castle with Queen Elizabeth. One of the queen's corgis ate all the cucumber sandwiches and then puked them up over the footman's shoes. But Lady Roz said the queen wasn't upset one bit. She just got up and walked to another table, under a different tree, and sent a footman off to get more cucumber sandwiches. Lady Rosalind said she felt as if she'd walked into the Mad Hatter's tea party when they all got up and changed tables. She had this way of telling stories, you know? It made the dog puking sound funny instead of gross."

It was bittersweet to hear an anecdote from the final few hours of Roz's life. "My mother had a real talent for making people laugh," Melody said. "Sometimes, though, she was at her most amusing when inside she was feeling quite sad."

"I guess laughing is better than crying, right?" Rachel appeared relieved when she saw that they'd arrived at Melody's room, although her hostility had lessened as soon as she began to talk about Roz. "Oh, look, we're here already. Good night, Melody. See you tomorrow at morning prayers."

"Why don't you come in for a minute?" Melody's invitation was motivated as much by her personal needs as by the needs of Unit One's mission. "It's such a long time since I talked to anyone about my mother. You'd be doing me a huge favor if you'd tell me some more about what happened in those final few hours of her life. The reports from the police in Mexico were not only bare bones dry, they raised more questions than they answered."

Rachel hesitated. She glanced at her watch, the only jewelry she wore with her white blouse and plain blue skirt. "I can't stay long. I have to be back in River House by nine."

"That gives you at least forty-five minutes." The note of pleading in Melody's voice wasn't faked. For the first eighteen months after her mother died, she hadn't questioned the ruling by the Mexican authorities that Lady Roz's death had been accidental. But six months ago she'd realized during a conversation with Johnston Yates that she didn't believe the ruling was correct, and that Roz was one of the last women in the world who would choose to commit suicide. Which had left Melody confronting the possibility that her mother had been murdered.

Lady Roz was an all-too-likely target for murder. She had been blackmailing Wallis Beecham over the Bonita partnership, seducing her own stepson along the way. Most of the guests on board Johnston's yacht had been members of the Bonita partnership, and all of them were in the public eye, with lots of prestige and money at stake if the project went awry. If Roz had blown the whistle, almost every guest on board the yacht would have had something to lose.

Until very recently, Melody had suspected that her mother's death was ordered by Wallis Beecham for reasons connected to the Bonita project. The fact that Wallis had explicitly denied being involved meant little, given that he lied as easily as he drew breath. With Wallis Beecham behind bars, she had considered her mother's murder avenged.

Jasper Fowles's recent revelations had blown away her comforting certainty that Wallis was to blame. Now that she knew Johnston Yates was her father, the fact that Lady Roz's death occurred on his yacht raised chilling alternatives to Wallis Beecham's guilt. It was possible that her mother had been blackmailing Yates for reasons that had everything to do with their long-ago affair and nothing at all to do with the Bonita partnership. She couldn't ignore the possibility that Lady Roz had been invited to join the cruise specifically so that Johnston Yates could murder her, thus burying the secret of his connection to Melody deep in the ocean. How ironic it would be if she had finally learned the identity of her biological father from Jasper Fowles, only to discover a few days later that he was also the man who'd killed her mother.

Rachel's voice brought Melody back to the present. "I

don't know if your mother was unhappy," she said, still hovering at the entrance to Melody's room. "But I do know everyone on board wasn't as friendly as they tried to pretend."

That had to be something of an understatement, Melody reflected wryly. Her guess was that the blades of some pretty vicious knives had barely been concealed beneath all the sunscreen and polite chatter. "I'm sure you're right, Rachel, but did something specific happen to make you think that some of the guests were unhappy or mad at each other?"

"Mostly it was little stuff. I know my mother really disliked Lawrence Springer, although I'm not sure exactly why. And then I overheard Mrs. Yates and Lady Roz arguing the afternoon before Lady Roz died—"

"My mother was arguing with Mrs. Yates?" The question sounded sharper and more aggressive than Melody had intended.

Rachel looked as if she wished she hadn't started this conversation. "I've never talked to anyone except my father about what I heard," she said. "After your mother died, I told him what had happened, and he said I shouldn't mention the argument to the police because it wasn't relevant. I thought my dad was mostly covering his own butt, like he usually is, but in those days I always did what he told me."

It didn't require special training as an investigator to deduce that Rachel's opinion of her father was less th— owing. It was also apparent that her conversion to — d proper ways of the Soldiers of Jordan didn't — ing the senator for past failures. Her bo— every time she mentioned him.

Rachel lifted her head, me— time that night. "If I tel— make you sad. Som—

about our parents." For a moment, she sounded unexpectedly mature.

Melody certainly hadn't anticipated coming to White Falls and finding herself in a situation where she could glean fresh information about the last hours of Lady Roz's life. Did she really want to open old wounds and hear details about her mother's final hours that might lead nowhere except to more grief?

"Whatever you have to tell me, I want to hear it," she said, making the choice. She hadn't forgotten that her room was bugged, but she could see no harm in allowing the Soldiers of Jordan to eavesdrop on her conversation with Rachel. The fact that Lady Roz had died on board Johnston Yates's yacht had been reported in almost every media outlet on two sides of the Atlantic, so it wasn't as if she was blowing a dark secret.

"My sister and I were sharing the cabin next door to Lady Roz's," Rachel said. From the promptness with which she spoke, Melody concluded that at some level she had been wanting to share what she knew for some time. "Most of the guests were up on deck playing quoits. It was hot and sunny, the calm before the storm, I guess, but I didn't feel like playing a stupid game, so I went downstairs to our cabin. I started to read a book, but that got to be way boring, so I decided to go back up on deck and talk to one of the crew. At least they were fun to hang out with."

Rachel was transforming into a regular teenager in front of Melody's eyes. Her body language changed from meek submission to aggressive slouch, and her hands kept sliding down her thighs, as if she were trying to shove her hands into the pockets of jeans that she was no longer permitted to wear.

just as I started to leave the cabin to go on deck arguing with Lady Roz," she said.

Melody was surprised that Roz had risked a dispute with Cynthia Yates. Roz had little time for women, but she usually took care not to offend wives who had the power to issue pleasurable invitations. Melody would have expected her mother to be especially careful around Cynthia given the secret Roz and Johnston Yates had been hiding from her and the rest of the world for almost three decades.

"Were the two of them angry enough that they were shouting?" she asked Rachel.

Rachel shook her head. "Actually, Lady Roz didn't sound angry at all. She sounded as if she was laughing. Mrs. Yates wasn't shouting, either, but I could tell she was mad. Mrs. Yates said that Lady Roz hadn't been invited to join the cruise in order to seduce Lewis Cranford, and that Roz was to leave the senator alone. *For God's sake, isn't there any man who's safe around you?* I remember Mrs. Yates saying that."

So Senator Cranford could be added to the list of men her mother had been sleeping with in the days and weeks before her death. Melody was surprised that Rachel didn't seem more angry with Lady Roz. The gift of a gold bracelet didn't seem much compensation for the fact that Roz had seduced the senator.

"How did my mother respond to Mrs. Yates's accusations?" Melody asked.

"She just laughed again. She said my father—" Rachel broke off, her cheeks flushing bright red. "She said th[...] [L]ewis was such a bore in bed that she was sure Elea[nor would] [b]e grateful to have his attention diverted els[ewhere for a few] nights."

Melody could visualize the sce[ne] [...] with unwelcome clarity. She'd [...] teen that her mother cons[...]

conquests as proof that she remained desirable. Still, it was always painful when the details of a specific affair got filled in, and it must have been even worse for Rachel, who could only have been fifteen or so at the time. If Rachel had trained herself to view her parents' marriage through rose-tinted lenses, those lenses would have been abruptly shattered.

"I'm sorry you had to overhear such an unpleasant discussion," she said. "Mrs. Yates might have been mistaken, you know. My mother flirted with every man who crossed her path, but it doesn't follow that she tried to seduce your father, much less that she succeeded. Just because Roz claimed your father was…unexciting…in bed, it doesn't mean she really knew, or that your father had been unfaithful. My mother sometimes said things just for the sake of being outrageous."

Rachel shot her a look of cynicism that was startling in contrast to her earlier sullen timidity. "Of course Lady Roz succeeded. It was obvious if you looked at the two of them together. Not that she would have to work very hard to get my dad in bed. Hint that sex might be available, and he's unzipping his fly."

Melody winced at the pain behind Rachel's crudeness. "I'm really sorry. Roz could be thoughtless and she must have hurt you."

Rachel shrugged. "I'm not mad at her. I'm mad at my father. He's been cheating on my mom for years—"

"You can't be sure of that…"

"Yes, I can." Rachel's conviction was absolute. "Mom doesn't even try to hide the truth anymore. Not from me, anyway. His junior legislative aides are chosen on a rotating basis from Stanford, Harvard and Princeton. They're always ___ and their most important qualification is that my fa___ they look. He rotates hair colors, you know, right along with the different schools. At the moment he has a blonde from Princeton. The next one will be a brunette from Stanford, and the one after that will have a Harvard degree and raven-black hair. For some reason he skips redheads and Yale. Go figure."

Melody didn't mistake Rachel's flippancy for indifference. The poor kid was hurting badly. "It's difficult to find out that our parents aren't quite the great people we wanted them to be." God knew, she could testify to that.

Rachel gave another shrug. "I just wish Mom would divorce him, that's all. He's a pig. I don't care that your mother seduced him. I wish she'd lived long enough to convince him to leave my mother. He'll never do that unless some really clever woman tricks him into it. Mom is too valuable with the voters back home, and my father would never get rid of a vote-getting advantage."

At the cost of finding out more than she wanted to know about her mother's sexual activities during the final days of her life, Melody realized that she'd just been provided with valuable insight into what Rachel was doing in White Falls. The Cranfords's marriage sounded disastrous enough that it wasn't surprising Rachel had run away from it. Melody wasn't yet ready to trust Rachel, but she certainly felt a great deal more sympathy toward her. Sometimes teenagers had every right to be sullen and hard to get along with, she reflected.

"I've met your mother on a couple of occasions and she's a smart woman," Melody said. "If she's chosen to stay with your father, I'm sure she has good reasons."

"Sure she does. She thinks she's doing me and my sister a favor. I wish she'd wise up to the truth." Rachel bit her lip, perhaps regretting having said as much. "Well, anyway, those are my problems, not yours. You can see Lady Roz was having a pretty good time right before she died. I read that lots of people thought she might have committed suicide, but I'm sure she didn't. She wasn't unhappy at all."

"It's good to hear that. Thanks for talking to me, Rachel. It can't have been easy to share those details about your dad and I appreciate it."

"You're welcome." Rachel stared at her for a long, silent moment. "I thought you must be having an affair with my dad, but you're not, are you? You didn't care one bit when I told you about his aides and how he seduces them all."

"No, I'm not having an affair with your father."

"But you still might be working for him. He's brilliant at calling in favors and you could easily owe him something." Her mouth turned down in a bitter smile. "Sometimes I think everyone in the world owes my father something."

"Well, I don't. I told you the absolute truth when I said your father has been angry with me for months."

Rachel's smile faded. "My father is more than capable of using somebody whether he likes them or not. So if you're working for him, you can give him a message from me. Tell him that I'll leave White Falls the day he gets rid of his mistresses." She laughed. "Which means that I'll be here until the guy croaks."

"I'll try this one more time. I'm not working for your father, Rachel."

"It doesn't matter if you are. I'm an adult. He can't order me to do anything. It's a great feeling." Rachel flicked her braid over her shoulder. "See you tomorrow at breakfast." She left the room without waiting for Melody to say good-night.

Twelve

There was no time to ponder what Rachel had just told her. She needed to call Nick within the next hour or he would activate the signal to send in a rescue squad, and finding a safe place to call from wasn't going to be easy. She couldn't risk making the call from her room, given that it was almost certainly under audio and visual surveillance. She was almost sure the bathroom had no camera, but almost wasn't good enough for an activity that could blow the entire mission. That left no choice but to call from outside, far enough away from all the buildings to be out of range of the security lights and cameras.

Melody laced on running shoes, changed into shorts, and threw a zippered cotton jacket over her T-shirt without attempting to hide from the camera. Then she went into the bathroom. On the remote chance that there was a camera she hadn't detected, she made a show of rummaging around in her bag of toilet articles until she found a Scrunci, which she used to tie her hair back in a ponytail. Keeping her left hand over the top of the bag, she used her right hand to palm a compact of pressed powder. She slipped the compact into the pocket of her jacket, her action shielded by the bathroom counter on one side and her body on the other. With the compact safely transferred, Melody permitted herself a small sigh of relief. Based on the Bureau reports, she and Nick had anticipated surveillance when establishing the mission profile, but they'd underestimated both its scope and its sophistication.

Dusk had given way to full dark outside, but her options for finding a place to call Nick weren't much improved over the daylight hours, since the entire campus was so brightly lit. Going for a run was the best excuse for leaving her room that she'd been able to come up with, although it was only marginally credible that she would choose to jog at this hour of night, especially in a direction that led away from the lighted paths surrounding the campus buildings. But since there were no better options, she'd have to go with marginally credible.

Melody left her room at a fast jog, circling the almost empty parking lot until she reached a narrow footpath that she'd noted when Terri first escorted her to her room. The path led toward the woods that marked the southern boundary of the campus at the rear of the motel. Luckily, there was a full moon, so the path wasn't entirely in darkness, but if she'd genuinely been intent on exercising, this was one of the last directions she, or anyone else with half a brain, would have chosen.

Melody ran as fast as she dared down the shadowy path, which had been rough-graded and graveled, making for an especially slick running surface. The physical action helped to ease her tension, but she was acutely aware that her window of opportunity, already narrow, was closing fast. Whoever was monitoring the surveillance camera in her room would soon realize that she wasn't in her bed, at which point Melody was sure somebody would be sent to track her down. The camera concealed high in the branches of the spruce in the corner of the parking lot would reveal the direction she'd taken, but she planned to strike off the path as soon as she rounded the first bend, where a convenient stand of trees would conceal her movements. She could only hope that the sheer size of the undeveloped acres in that part of the campus would then help her to avoid detection until her call was finished.

She rounded the bend in the path and saw at once that her plan wasn't going to work. The trees that had appeared to offer such a useful screen for her activities also concealed a sturdy shed built at the edge of the path and backing up to a grassy field. The field was fenced with barbed wire and a row of sinister figures loomed on the far side of the field.

Melody dropped to the ground. Jesus, they'd already sent an entire posse to search for her! She rolled sideways and looked back at her potential attackers, adrenaline sending a flush of heat over her skin despite the damp ground beneath her. Was it better to try to hide, or to brazen it out?

Then the moon came out from behind a cloud and she saw that the menacing figures were nothing more than two-dimensional cutouts. Feeling sheepish, she got to her feet and resumed her run. She must have been more on edge than she'd realized to have been intimidated by a set of plastic cutouts. The life-sized targets were suspended from a line that worked on a pulley system so that they would move, although the threatening action that had sent her rushing for cover had simply been caused by the night breeze. The realistic targets reminded her that the Soldiers of Jordan took the first part of their name seriously: they were being trained as an army, and taught to fire at images of people. How in the world had

Zachary managed to convince seemingly decent men like Jason and Harvey that they faced a threat so dangerous that they needed to learn how to shoot down human targets?

A second stand of trees loomed on her right, fifty yards before the edge of the forest proper. It was just the cover she needed. Melody ran off the path half a mile farther from campus than she'd anticipated, lying down in the rough grass at the edge of the copse. She hoped her footfalls had been loud enough to scare away the snakes, spiders and assorted rodents who might otherwise have chosen to frolic in this particular patch of territory.

She rolled onto her stomach, turning toward the campus buildings and scanning the horizon for any sign of movement. Her view was partially obscured by the trees surrounding the shooting range, but she could see sections of the two dorms and, as she watched, the lights inside both buildings went out. A couple of seconds later, the flicker of pallid yellow in a few of the windows suggested that a night-lighting system had switched on. Almost simultaneously, the lights inside the former motel turned out one after another, although the exterior lights remained on. Within a minute every window on campus was dark, except for those inside the White House.

Melody was torn between amusement and disbelief. It seemed the Soldiers were not only required to be back in their dorms by nine, but they had to be lying down to sleep by nine-fifteen. No wonder Rachel had been so anxious about returning to River House promptly. She would barely have had fifteen minutes to get ready for bed. Melody wondered what the punishment was for Soldiers who weren't tucked in at the designated hour. Extra chores? Humiliating public rebukes in front of the rest of the community? Both FBI agents had insisted there was no evidence of corporal punishment being administered to anyone, so Zachary must have discovered some other means of enforcing his rules.

Only the White House remained brightly lit. No doubt Reverend Zachary stayed up late, laboring on behalf of his flock. Alternatively, of course, he might be sipping a good brandy while reading *Playboy* magazine. Melody, accustomed to summing up people rather fast, discovered that in Zachary's case she couldn't decide which of those two scenarios struck her as more likely.

She scrutinized the exterior of the White House as well as she could, given the distance separating her from the admin building. She detected a trace of movement that might be the guards the FBI agents had reported as being posted each night, but she saw no sign of the sort of activity that would suggest they were forming a search party. If the Soldiers' watchdogs weren't already searching for her, she probably had at least fifteen minutes in which to make her call to Nick.

Satisfied that she was alone and unobserved, Melody pulled out her compact. She flicked open the gold-colored case and shook out the disc of pressed powder, revealing a smooth metal touch pad. A touch to the corner of the mirror released a tiny spring and the mirror popped out to expose the audio receiver. Bob Spinard's communication device had no dial pad or keyboard, but she only needed to be able to dial one number. She pressed the lone button in the center of the compact base, and waited through a single ring before she heard Nick's voice.

"Yes. Go ahead."

"I'm on site."

"Great. Any problems to report?"

"Nothing major. My cell phone has been confiscated,

which we anticipated, and my luggage has been searched, but otherwise everyone has been very friendly."

"Any special reason why your luggage was searched?"

"No. I'm pretty sure it's standard procedure, which suggests something about the general level of paranoia here. I believe there's also a surveillance camera in my room, but I can't confirm without arousing suspicions. I'm assuming my room is wired for sound. Again, I can't confirm without giving myself away. The security here is skintight."

Nick didn't waste time asking where she was calling from, and if she was sure it was a safe location. After six months of working together, he trusted her to have taken care of finding somewhere protected from surveillance before calling him. "What's your preliminary assessment of the situation?" he asked. "Are the Soldiers just a weird but harmless religious community or something more menacing?"

"Too early to say for sure, although the security seems excessive for a group of religious believers with no goal other than to live worthy, God-fearing lives."

"Except that paranoia and fanatic religious belief often go together," Nick said. "When you believe you're in direct communication with the Almighty, you also tend to believe you're a prime target for attacks by the devil. You have to be vigilant or Satan will send in his assault troops to bring you down."

"If Satan pays a visit to White Falls, he can count on being filmed when he arrives," Melody said dryly.

"Just make sure the Soldiers don't decide you're working on the side of the devil."

"As long as Zachary accepts me, the rest of the Soldiers will, too. From what I've seen, he exerts complete control over every aspect of community life. My strictly personal reaction—not my official report—is that this whole damn place is somewhere between creepy and downright scary."

"And your official report is….?"

"As I said, it's too early to tell. But I believe I'll be in agreement with Agent Bostwick. I think there's something more dangerous going on here than Zachary Wharton and his followers trying to march back into the lifestyle of the pilgrim fathers."

"Has there been any attrition in the numbers since the last Bureau report?" Nick asked.

"The opposite. There were two hundred and twenty people at dinner tonight, so the community is growing."

"What's the ratio of men to women and children?"

"There's still an excess of men, but they're mostly middle-aged and Zachary seems to be working hard to get all the single men married off. That strikes me as counterintuitive if he wants to build them into an effective army. Wouldn't they be easier to train if they didn't have the distraction of wives and families?"

"Possibly not. Don't count on your definition of logical behavior holding true for Zachary and his followers. You're surrounded by two hundred and twenty people who were fanatical enough to give up their previous lives and move halfway across the country to pursue a religious belief. There's no way to assess how much further their fanaticism can be increased if Zachary knows how to push the correct triggers."

"Don't worry, there's no chance I'll underestimate the potential dangers of this place." Melody spoke with heartfelt sincerity. "I keep feeling as if I've walked onto the set of a horror movie. The surroundings look inviting, but that's just to lull me and the rest of the audience into relaxing. I'm expecting the bogeyman to jump out of his coffin at any minute."

"I have it on excellent authority that the bogeyman lives in a cave." Nick's voice softened with an almost imperceptible hint of laughter.

Melody smiled into the darkness, her first genuine smile in days. "I think you should double-check the source of that intel."

"I will. In the meantime, you could compromise," Nick suggested. "Keep a sharp lookout for coffins, caves and all other potential hideouts for bogeymen."

Melody knew Nick well enough to understand the real message behind his banter. He was concerned for her safety. "I'm working on the assumption that most of the Soldiers are sincere, trying to build new lives with no clue that anything is going on here other than the development of a Christian community with old-fashioned values and strict rules about behavior. That doesn't mean I've let down my guard. I assume it's only a small inner circle that's using the place as a cover for something more sinister, but everything I've seen suggests that the inner circle is willing to be ruthless in carrying out its goal."

"I agree with both points," Nick said. "It's unlikely that all the Soldiers would be in on the secret plan, if there is one. How would Zachary manage to keep a secret that's shared by more than two hundred people? Look at how hard we have to work to keep information confidential within Unit One, and we're trained professionals, with elaborate security protocols in place."

"And what about people who leave White Falls?" Melody said. "If every initiate gets let in on the secret plan, then Zachary would have to kill everyone who dropped out of his program." She stopped in midbreath, caught by the implications of her own comment. "Good grief, we'd better check into that.

Did anyone at the Bureau think to investigate if ex-Soldiers are being killed off?"

"The Bureau didn't," Nick said. "But this morning I assigned two Unit One agents to tracking down ex-Soldiers and interviewing them as soon as they're found. So far, my people are having a hell of a time even collating a list of ex-Soldiers. Zachary reports membership totals and donations for tax purposes, but there's no requirement for him to turn in the names of individual members of his church, so there's no easy way to track when somebody leaves the community."

"Especially if they just disappear," Melody said grimly.

"True, but my guess is that ex-Soldiers aren't being eliminated, or there would have been rumblings from family members by now. The mayor of the township and the local sheriff's office are already suspicious of the Soldiers and they'd jump at any complaints that gave them an excuse to investigate. Still, if you could manage to acquire a complete listing of the names and original home addresses of all the Soldiers, my two agents could start running some really interesting crosschecks."

"I'll do my best," Melody said. "Although finding the list might be easier than transmitting it to you. Regular mail is monitored. I assume e-mails are, too. That means I could only transmit the list to you by going off campus. I don't know how I'd do that without making a huge song and dance."

"Don't worry about transmission methods right now. If you access the list, I'll find a way to get it from you."

"I've been assigned to work in the main office, which is an unexpected bonus. I'm sure I'll be watched, but in a couple of days I may be able to find a way to work around their security systems."

"That's excellent," Nick said. "What about Rachel Cranford? Have you seen her already? Spoken to her?"

"Yes to both. She was seated at my table for dinner tonight. She jumped to the conclusion that I'd been sent here by her father and she wasn't pleased about it. Apart from that, she seems well and is definitely here by her own choice."

"You denied any connection to the senator, of course."

"Of course." Melody asked her next question with careful neutrality. "What about your part of the mission? Have you made contact with the senator's wife?"

"I'm in Washington right now. I met with Eleanor today and we're getting together again tomorrow."

Melody's stomach lurched slightly at the news, even though she'd been expecting it and should have been prepared. "Did you get any info from her?"

"Only that the Cranford marriage is as messed up as you would expect, given the senator's personality. I'm hoping for some more useful insights tomorrow."

Knowing Nick's skill at seduction, he no doubt anticipated having Eleanor Cranford in his bed by tomorrow afternoon. In the languid aftermath of sexual satiation, Eleanor would be beguiled into revealing secrets she barely knew she possessed. Melody stared up at the star-splattered sky, wishing she didn't have such a vivid imagination. Not to mention enough practical experience of Nick's lovemaking to fill in any blanks.

"Do you have any intel from Bob Spinard to pass on to me?" she inquired with what she considered admirable cool, all things considered.

"Nothing new in the past twelve hours on the Soldiers of Jordan. On another front, though, there's a possibility that Dave Ramsdell chartered a plane and flew to Mexico. Monterey, to be precise. We're actively following the lead."

"If you picked up his trail this fast, then I'd bet it's a hundred percent certain that wherever Dave is headed, it isn't to Mexico, and especially not to Monterey."

"That's what I concluded. Still, we have to follow the lead."

"Meanwhile, Dave is enjoying watching us waste our resources."

"Yes, I'm sure he is." There was a tiny pause before Nick spoke again. "I miss you, Melody."

His voice had about as much expression as a computer announcing the arrival of an airport tram, but the admission brought a lump to Melody's throat. She knew how much it must have cost him to break protocol and introduce a personal comment into their conversation. Her fingers tightened around the cell phone as she strained to resist the urge to respond that she missed him, too. Quite desperately, in fact. Unfortunately, much as a part of her longed to patch their affair together again, she was fairly sure that she and Nick would be doing each other a huge favor if they allowed their relationship to die before it caused them more pain than it already had. With the advantage of hindsight, it was hard to believe that she'd ever been delusional enough to convince herself that their complex characters could be made to mesh into a smooth, perfect whole. Despite the wildly passionate and wonderful sex they'd shared, and the magic moments of sweet laughter, the bitter truth was that she and Nick weren't well suited to each other. They both needed generous, uncomplicated partners with no sharp edges to rip at each other's emotional wounds. Once you got past their physical compatibility, she didn't fit the description of the woman likely to make Nick happy any better than Nick met her pressing need for security, reliability and total faithfulness.

Melody waited until she was sure her voice would be steady before she spoke. "Good night, Nick," she said softly. "I ought to get back to my room. I'm breaking curfew as it is. I'll call you tomorrow, probably a little earlier than tonight." She snapped the lid of her compact shut, breaking the connection before she could weaken.

The night wrapped around her, cool and lonely. Why was making the right decision always so damned hard? It felt way too quiet without the sound of Nick's voice. The urge to press the button that would recall him was almost overwhelming.

She got to her feet, shoving the communicator into her jacket pocket. She ran blindly toward the path, heart beating stupidly fast, and almost stumbled over a root before she snapped back into focus. Dammit to hell! Did it really take no more than a few tender words from Nick to destroy her concentration? Seconds later she heard the sound of voices coming from the shooting range and realized how lucky she'd been to trip. This was a dangerous moment to have let her emotions take over from her professional expertise.

There was nowhere to hide, so if the voices meant that she'd been tracked down by security guards, she would have to lie her way out of trouble. She slowed her pace from a sprint to a slow jog. No point in providing the watchers with a free demonstration of how fast she could run.

"Melody!" Zachary's voice summoned her from the field to her right. "What in the world are you doing out at this hour of the night?"

He and another man were standing in the field next to the shed, but there was no way to tell if they were on their way in or out of the small building. Zachary sounded surprised as much as angry, Melody decided, which suggested he might not have come searching for her because he had known she was missing from her room. Perhaps this encounter was accidental.

Belatedly Zachary seemed to recollect that she wasn't yet a committed member of his flock, and he visibly reined in his urge to scold. He covered his surge of temper with one of his most winning smiles. "My dear, it's not wise to wander so close to the woods at this late hour of the night."

Because the big, bad wolf would eat her? Melody unclenched her jaw—since she arrived on campus, Zachary's presence seemed to set her teeth permanently on edge—and greeted him with feigned surprise, her hand fluttering to her throat. "Goodness, Zachary…I mean Reverend. You startled me."

The man standing beside Zachary still hadn't gone into the shed, or even moved away, but he didn't speak to her and Zachary didn't make any introductions. Melody wondered if this silent man was one of the five members of the governing council. She had managed no more than a glimpse of the governors as they exited the dining hall after dinner, but she didn't think this was one of the five, although she couldn't be entirely sure. The man was above average height, of medium build, with short brown hair that was streaked with gray. In this poor light, she couldn't determine the color of his eyes. He stood quietly, his gaze downcast, looking as humble in Zachary's presence as Terri and Sally and every other Soldier Melody had met. She was beginning to find the universal subservience to Zachary seriously annoying. Was she really the only person on campus who felt a frequent urge to deliver a swift kick in the region of Zachary's pompous butt?

Zachary allowed his smile to fade, gazing at her more in sorrow than in anger. "We try to keep White Falls as secure as possible, but this isn't a safe area for you to be wandering alone, Melody. There have been reports of mountain lions in the vicinity and a mountain lion is not an animal you'd want to meet alone at night. Remember those cyclists in California who got killed a few months ago when they were attacked by a mountain lion?"

"Yes, I remember. Gosh, I had no idea there were such dangerous predators in this area." She gave a nervous laugh. "I was just out for a jog."

"For a *jog?* In the dark? At this time of night?" Zachary sounded justifiably astonished.

"Well, I'm not used to keeping such early hours and it was the first chance I had to get out. I jog every day." She gave another embarrassed laugh, as if confiding a deep personal secret. "It's the only way I can keep my weight under control. I'm sorry if I alarmed you. I never gave a thought to wild animals."

"You'll have to find time to exercise during the daylight hours," Zachary said shortly.

"Yes, of course. I can see that would fit much better into the program."

Zachary appeared mollified by her instant agreement. "We can certainly go over your schedule to make sure we leave you some time for physical fitness. Keeping ourselves strong and healthy is a primary goal for the members of our community."

Melody noticed that he never referred to his followers as Soldiers when he was talking to her. Perhaps he didn't want to scare her off with hints of their militaristic underpinnings. "Physical fitness is important to me," she murmured. "I'm glad it's important to you, too."

"I think we're going to discover that we share many of the same goals," Zachary said. "Now, my dear, I have an extra flashlight, so I'll escort you back to your room. You need a light. This path isn't designed for running, especially at night."

"I already discovered that. I tripped a couple of times." She brushed grass from her shorts to emphasize how she'd fallen and saw his gaze follow the movement of her hands. For the first time, she sensed a wave of sexual desire coming from Zachary. Not sure whether she wanted to encourage his interest, she turned to the man still standing silently behind him and held out her hand.

"Hi, I'm Melody Beecham. I don't believe we were introduced at dinner tonight? You probably already know that I'm new here. Fresh off the plane from New York City and obviously not too well-informed about Idaho wildlife."

"I'm Ed Harris," he said in a voice gruff enough that it sounded almost as if his vocal chords might be damaged. "I'm from New Jersey, and glad to be out of there. Idaho's a beautiful state." He seemed friendly enough, but he didn't shake her hand, and she wondered if the Soldiers of Jordan disapproved of unmarried men and women sharing even that brief physical contact.

"It's nice to meet you, Ed." She let her hand drop to her side.

"Likewise. But the Reverend's right about not running in the dark, Melody. You and the other ladies need to watch out for predators at night."

Melody bit back a distinctly unladylike response. "I will, Ed. Thanks for the warning. Trust me, I haven't the slightest desire to find out if mountain lions are as fierce as their reputation."

"There's bears, too," Ed said, with a definite hint of relish.

"Don't terrify her." Zachary laughed. "She's learned her lesson, haven't you, Melody?"

"Oh, absolutely." The last time somebody had asked her if she'd learned her lesson she'd been about seven. She'd lied then, too.

Zachary turned to speak to Ed. "Melody and I had better be getting back. You and I can continue our discussion tomorrow morning after prayer service."

"Yes, Reverend." Ed Harris bobbed his head in acknowledgment, a gesture that was as obsequious as the rest of his body language. He turned back toward the shed as Zachary indicated that Melody should precede him back up the path toward the campus buildings. Did Ed sleep in the shed? she wondered. And would that be a reward or a penance for some previous transgression? Personally she would consider the privacy compensation for a lot of physical discomfort.

She jogged at a moderate pace back to the parking lot. Unfortunately Zachary was quite fit and he had no trouble keeping up. He even had plenty of breath left to deliver one of his lectures about the need to conform to community rules. Strictly for her own sake, of course. He threw in a couple of jokes to take the edge off his rebukes, but Melody was left in no doubt that if she wanted to remain in White Falls she was going to have to obey the rules to the letter. She let Zachary's comments flow over her while she worried about how the hell she was going to find somewhere safe to call Nick tomorrow night.

Zachary didn't come into her room, which gave her cause to be grateful for the strict rules, and the fact that Zachary was willing to obey them. He stopped outside her door, taking her hands and staring deep into her eyes. Apparently he had no clue that she'd found his latest lecture anything other than inspirational. It puzzled her that a man smart enough to mes-

merize two hundred and twenty followers was so blithely unaware of her own insincerity. Was she really that brilliant an
actor in comparison to two experienced FBI agents? It seemed
unlikely, and she tucked the worry away to be mulled over
later.

Zachary held her gaze. "Good night, Melody, my dear.
We're so happy to have you here in White Falls."

"I'm glad to be here," she said. "It's been a wonderful
day."

"That's what I like to hear." He carried her hand to his lips,
pressing a kiss against her knuckles. "I believe God has
brought you here for a very special purpose, Melody."

"You think?"

"I do indeed. Sleep well, my dear. We'll talk more tomorrow."

She slipped her hand behind her back, wiping it surrepti-
tiously on her shorts. She stared up at him with limpid adoration, wondering if she had been mistaken about his
dedication to the ideal of celibacy for unmarried adults. She'd
felt a definite and faintly disgusting hint of damp tongue sliding over her knuckles when he kissed her hand.

"Good night, Reverend. Thank you again for making me
so welcome."

"It's been my pleasure. I know you're going to grow to love
our community." With a final patronizing smile, he strode off
toward the glowing lights of the White House, humming underneath his breath.

Remembering the surveillance cameras, Melody resisted
the urge to pull a face and waggle her ears at his retreating
back.

Thirteen

The charmingly decorated Virginia Beach condo was right on the waterfront, close enough to the ocean that the sound of waves breaking on shore could be heard through the doors that led from the living room to the balcony. The sun slanted through wooden blinds discreetly adjusted to insure privacy while letting in breathtaking glimpses of sky and water. It was the perfect setting for an after-lunch seduction in late spring, which was precisely why Nick had chosen it. Among other benefits, he and Eleanor Cranford could enjoy a leisurely breakfast tomorrow morning and still be back in D.C. by noon, six hours before her husband and his chief legislative aide would be returning from their "business" trip to Lexington.

Nick carried a glass of white wine over to the sofa where Eleanor Cranford was sitting, her tightly crossed legs and ramrod straight back shouting a message of tension mingled with guilty excitement.

"This is a pinot grigio from the Alto Adige region of Italy," he said, handing her the glass. He avoided doing anything obvious like letting their fingers touch. Eleanor wasn't an experienced adulterer, and he suspected her sexual tension would vanish if there was any suggestion that he was performing by rote and not by desire. "It is a light wine, but there is a pleasant subnote of fruit. I think you will like it."

As always when he was about to undertake a seduction on behalf of Unit One, his Russian accent had thickened, although without any conscious intent on his part. He was self-aware enough to realize that adopting the persona of Nikolai Anwar, exotic Russian entrepreneur, helped to distance his emotions from the physical actions his body was engaging in. He didn't choose to probe that awareness, however. Especially not today, when he was already expending far too much energy to suppress the knowledge that—despite what might have seemed to be the case with Jacyntha Ramon—he hadn't had sex with any woman other than Melody in six long months. Since the first night he'd taken Melody into his bed, in fact.

This seduction of Eleanor Cranford was work, he reminded himself brusquely. There was nothing in what would happen here today that could be considered a betrayal of his relationship with Melody. Besides, Melody had made it crystal clear that their personal relationship was over. Which, surely to God, was what he wanted, or at least recognized was best for both of them. Neither his profession nor his past made him a candidate for promises of commitment and eternal devotion.

"I enjoy Italian wines," Eleanor said. She took the wine from him and sipped nervously. "Most of the Russians I've met never drink anything but vodka."

Nick smiled easily. "I am only half Russian, remember. But I drink vodka, too. When the moment is right, it is an excellent drink." He managed to make the remark sound

Jasmine Cresswell

faintly sexual. He sat down next to her and raised his wine glass, holding her gaze. "Here's to a long and pleasant afternoon," he said softly. "With plenty of time for vodka—later."

"Oh. Yes." Eleanor blushed and buried her nose in her glass.

Nick waited until she'd gulped down most of the wine. Then he leaned across and took the glass from her hand, setting it on the coffee table. He despised seductions that depended on alcohol to wash away inhibitions, and they'd already consumed a bottle of wine during lunch. Eleanor hovered right on the cusp of tipsy, ready to topple over into drunk quite soon. Drunken decisions only led to regrets and recriminations later, and Nick prided himself on sexual affairs that never led to recriminations, and especially not to regrets.

Except with Melody, where he ached with regret for all that they no longer shared, the little intimacies as much as the grand passion.

He slammed a mental door against that intrusive thought and laid his hand across the back of Eleanor's neck, massaging in a slow, erotic rhythm. Eleanor gave a deep sigh and dipped her head forward, eyes closing.

"That feels good," she said, her voice low.

"For me, too," Nick said. "Your skin is so silky."

She turned toward him and slipped her hand inside the buttons of his shirt, the tips of her fingers circling hesitantly against his skin. Then she blushed again, the color a delicate pink along her cheekbones, before she nestled her face against his chest, hiding from his gaze.

His compliment hadn't been a lie. Eleanor had unexpectedly lovely skin for a woman of forty-four, and her thick hair gleamed in the sunlight filtering through the blinds. He had a suspicion that her body would turn out to be a great deal sexier than the conservative clothes covering her. Even so, looking down at her, Nick experienced an emotion that felt closer to abstract appreciation than sexual desire. Shaking off an unexpected reluctance to take advantage of Eleanor's vulnerability—hell, Unit One had targeted her *because* she was so obviously vulnerable—he reached toward her, pulling the pins from her hair. She opened her eyes, murmuring a halfhearted protest, but he silenced her by leaning across and kissing her with calculated expertise.

Eleanor resisted for a moment, but her resistance was easy to overcome with a few light touches and whispered words of admiration and desire. Nick had researched her background intensively and the brutal truth was that he had a damned good idea of exactly what he needed to do and say to maximize her pleasure and minimize her guilt at starting an illicit affair.

He knew that she was the first member of her rural Kentucky family ever to graduate from college, and that she'd been both class valedictorian and head cheerleader at her small-town high school. Eleanor's marriage to Lewis Cranford, an ambitious young lawyer at one of the largest and most prestigious law firms in Lexington, had been the ultimate jewel in her crown of overachievement.

From everything Nick had been able to discover, the marriage had been a love match on both sides. Certainly, from Lewis Cranford's point of view, there couldn't have been much motive other than love to marry somebody as devoid of money and connections as Eleanor. Nick found it depressing that in the space of a mere twenty years the Cranford marriage had descended from love, through indifference, into double adultery and stolen afternoons of illicit sex.

He knew from his research that Eleanor wasn't simply a

bored Washington wife, in the habit of looking for sex to enliven an empty hour between shopping and cocktails. She was a woman of intelligence and warmth, whose pride had been beaten down, and whose love had been spurned by her husband. At some point during the complicated process by which Lewis Cranford completed his metamorphosis from eager young congressman to corrupt and ruthless player in the game of national power politics, his love for his wife had vanished. He hadn't looked at his wife—really looked at her—in a decade, except to make sure that she was still the sort of friendly, nonthreatening spouse likely to win approval with the voters back home in Kentucky.

Nick was fairly sure Eleanor hid a well of anger a mile deep behind her submissive facade. The trick for him was to tap into that anger without allowing it to become displaced from Lewis and directed toward Nick.

Softened by his compliments and mild foreplay, Eleanor had already slipped off her shoes and unfastened the buttons on her Armani silk jacket. She let him slip the jacket from her shoulders with no more than a token murmur of protest. Nick was a little surprised to discover she wore nothing beneath the jacket, not even a camisole. Eleanor gave off vibes that suggested a woman whose body would be protected by layers of sensible underwear.

He kissed her for a while, making sure that she was as compliant as the lack of underclothing suggested before he went to work unfastening her bra—a one-handed skill he'd mastered several years earlier so that his other hand could be employed more excitingly. The hook on the front of her bra separated, freeing her breasts. Nick slipped the straps from her shoulders, kissing as he went, and immediately felt the increasing heat and urgency of Eleanor's response.

"You're as skillful a lover as your reputation suggested," she murmured, reaching for the buckle of his belt.

"No," he said with calculated arrogance, trying not to think too hard about the implications of what she'd just said. "I'm much better."

"I never guessed committing adultery would be this easy." She gave a small, tight laugh. "Doing something so wrong ought to be more difficult, don't you think?"

"It is very American to believe that all pleasures must be guilty. Fortunately, in such matters, I am entirely Russian." He smiled teasingly, then kissed her throat, where a pulse beat very fast, working on smothering her doubts with desire. "Is it wrong to find delight that is denied to you by your husband?"

"Yes," she said, but she didn't move her hand away from his crotch, and she shuddered with anticipation when he kissed her breasts. "It's wrong because I made a promise to be faithful to Lewis for the rest of my life, and I'm breaking my own promise."

"It is common knowledge that your husband broke those same promises to you many years ago."

She shrugged in silent acknowledgment. "Lewis has been unfaithful so many times, I don't even bother to count anymore."

"Then there is no reason for you to feel guilty." He took her hand and kissed the tip of each of her fingers, investing his words with total confidence.

Eleanor turned away, but not before he saw the brightness of unshed tears in her eyes. "I don't feel guilty about betraying Lewis. I feel guilty about betraying my own standards of what's right."

Nick wasn't accustomed to seducing women who succumbed to moral qualms during the process of shedding their clothes. Most of his sexual partners had been so busy ripping off his pants that they wouldn't have recognized a moral scruple if it had jumped up and bitten them on their shapely butts.

He pushed aside his qualms and returned to kissing her. Her passion reignited but Nick's stomach was churning and there was a hard lump in his gut that was growing more constricting by the moment. He sensed an element of desperation in Eleanor's actions that was becoming more and more difficult to ignore. He slowly straightened, his hands covering hers, holding them against his chest to prevent her unzipping his fly.

In the past, he'd always made it a point to concentrate strictly on the physical gratification of his partners because he'd found that was a great way to avoid emotional and ethical complications. He chatted during sex, because most women seemed uneasy with silence, but he limited his remarks to flattering comments about the physical attributes of his partner. With a sinking feeling, Nick realized that his six months as Melody's lover had weakened the wall he'd previously been able to maintain between sexual activity and his feelings toward women he seduced on behalf of Unit One. Now Eleanor's remarks had punched a giant hole through the already tottering structure that kept the segments of his life separate.

He looked at the woman lying half beneath him and no longer saw a target in possession of useful information. Instead he saw a woman poised so close to the edge of emotional destruction that, once he allowed himself to think about it, he could see she was holding herself together by sheer force of will.

He reached out, catching her chin and gently turning her head around to face him. He brushed his thumbs over her eyes, wiping away the barely formed tears. The gesture was practiced, but for the first time since they entered the condo, Nick's emotions were honestly engaged. "If you're so unhappy with Lewis, why do you not divorce him?"

"I could tell you that I stay with him for the sake of my daughters."

"Would that be true?"

She sighed. "No. It was once, but not anymore."

"Then what?"

Eleanor smiled without mirth. "I stay with him because I was dirt poor and now I'm filthy rich. And, trust me on this, rich is a whole hell of a lot better."

"At least you are honest."

"Not until recently." She pulled away from him, picking up her bra and jacket and holding them as a shield in front of her breasts. "I'm sorry. This isn't going to work, is it? I was using you to solve my problems, and now I've discovered that I can't even use people without making a fool of myself."

Nick knew that if he'd carried out his seduction of Eleanor Cranford with his usual single-minded expertise, she would at this moment be writhing beneath him, doubts and questions at least temporarily forgotten. With a flash of sardonic humor, he realized he was feeling guilty because he *hadn't* had sex with a married woman.

"Why don't I pour us another glass of wine while you get dressed?" he suggested, getting up from the sofa.

She grimaced. "I think I've had more than enough wine. Ice water might taste better right now."

"Then we will have ice water."

"Are you sure you don't want to go back to Washington?" Eleanor looked at him uncertainly. "I'm not going to change my mind, you know."

"About the sex?" Nick shrugged. "That is not so important to either of us, I believe. And why would I wish to be trapped inside the Beltway on such a fine spring day? The view of the ocean from the balcony is beautiful. The sun is warm and you are a lovely woman. What better way to spend the next hour or two than sipping a cool drink and talking about whatever subject we decide is interesting to us?"

He walked away from her before she could reply, going to the bar that divided the kitchen from the living area. After a moment of silence, he heard Eleanor walk into the bedroom. He ought to have been assessing how best to redeem the situation and elicit the information Unit One needed. Instead he found himself thinking longingly of Melody and how much he wished she could have been the woman about to join him on the balcony.

When he realized what he was doing, he swore viciously and carried a bottle of sparkling water outside, along with ice, slices of fresh lime, and two glasses. He adjusted the awning to cut out the full glare of the afternoon sun as he swiftly ran alternate save-his-sorry-ass scenarios through his mind. Without sex as a warm-up, he would have to work a hell of a lot harder to induce Eleanor to confide in him.

She joined him on the deck ten minutes later, her hair once again coiled neatly at the nape of her neck and her silk jacket rebuttoned. She took the water he offered and drank thirstily before setting the glass down on the wrought-iron table. Instead of looking at him, she kept her gaze fixed on a motor launch speeding across the horizon, the roar of its engine drowning out the lap of the waves and the caw of seagulls circling overhead. When the boat had passed, she finally turned to look at him, her expression hard to read.

"You didn't seduce me," she said.

He inclined his head, his regret not entirely feigned. "I am not sure why I was foolish enough to allow my more virtuous instincts to deprive me of what I am sure would have been a delightful experience. I hope for both of us."

"No, that's not what I meant." Eleanor poured herself more water, but she kept her gaze fixed on Nick. "You imagined *you* were picking *me* up at the Russian ambassador's reception last weekend. You weren't. At least not after the first couple of minutes."

"I'm sorry. I do not understand." Nick was, for once, being totally honest.

"You thought you were the instigator in our assignation. You weren't. You imagine that since I'm not especially sexy or desirable, men never make passes at me. You're wrong. There are always men on the Washington party circuit who find it amusing to have affairs with the wife of a powerful senator, even when the wife is past forty and looks more like a soccer mom than a movie star. I've had enough experience rejecting advances that I'm really quite good at giving men the brush-off. If I want to, that is."

"I see. But for some reason you decided not to reject me."

"That's right." She turned her gaze back out to sea. "I planned to have sex with you almost from the first moment I realized it was a possibility. I'd already decided to go ahead with whatever proposition you came up with, even before we had lunch yesterday."

Nick swirled his glass, watching the sunlight refract from the rim. "I will take a wild guess and suggest that your favorable response to my invitation to spend the night here in Virginia Beach had nothing to do with my dazzling charms?"

"You're right. Although, as it happens, I do find you attractive." She gave a wry smile. "A million years ago, I had a healthy sex drive, and you're one of the most attractive male packages to have crossed my path in the past twenty years. But if you hadn't asked me to have lunch with you yesterday, I'd probably have invited you. It just made it easier that you're so astonishingly good at playing the game."

Nick made some rapid adjustments to his mental image of Eleanor Cranford. The fact that she'd stood submissively by her husband's side for the past twenty years might mean that she was a doormat, but she sure as hell wasn't unaware of the choices she'd made. She was a well-informed doormat, in other words, and her observations were shrewd enough to be unsettling. "What game is that?" he asked.

"The game of making women feel desirable. Convincing them they're beautiful and sexy even when they're no more than mildly attractive. Like me."

"You are much more than mildly attractive, Eleanor."

She smiled sadly. "You see? You play the game even when the prize has been declared off-limits. But I'd much prefer that you didn't patronize me, Nikolai. I have no illusions about how I look. I have medium brown hair. I'm average height—"

"You have a beautiful body—"

She shook her head. "I'm slim, and my breasts don't need implants, but my legs are too short and you have enough experience to be able to guess that my abdomen is covered in stretch marks from two pregnancies. Better than average for my age, maybe, but there's nothing in the package to entice a man whose last two lovers were women as spectacular as Melody Beecham and Jacyntha Ramon."

Nick leaned back in his chair, more than a little alarmed. He'd analyzed Eleanor Cranford to his complete satisfaction five days ago, before he ever approached her at the ambassador's reception. It was disconcerting to discover that she wasn't fitting into his preselected pigeonhole. In fact, she wasn't coming anywhere close.

"You underestimate your attractions," he said, his Russian accent strong. "But let us agree that we are here because you chose to spend time with me and not because I persuaded you against your better judgment. Naturally, I am flattered that you wished to spend time with me." He sent her a glance that was openly assessing. "Or perhaps I should not be? Why do I have the feeling that you are about to tell me something that will slice my masculine ego into very small shreds?"

"Your ego is in no danger from me." She shrugged. "You can have almost any woman you choose as your lover. Why would you care two shakes of a pig's tail whether or not you add me to your list of conquests? I'm sure I attracted your attention for precisely the same reason that I decided to start an affair with you. I'm Senator Lewis Cranford's wife."

Nick's first reaction was to smile charmingly and pretend not to understand. A moment's reflection warned him this would be an irreparable mistake. For whatever reason, Eleanor Cranford had apparently moved to a point in her life where social lies, and courteous facades had ceased to be important to her. If he persisted in playing dumb, she'd give up on him and leave. The only way to salvage anything from the wreckage of the afternoon might be to return her honesty with a dose of his own.

"You will have to forgive me if I seem slow on the uptake, Eleanor. Leaving aside my motives in asking you to spend the day with me, why would the fact that you are Senator Cranford's wife inspire *you* with a sudden desire to accept my invitation and take me to your bed?"

"Because my husband hates you," she said simply.

"There's almost nothing I could do that would infuriate him more than to take you as my lover. And recently, I've discovered within myself an intense longing to infuriate my husband."

Holy shit! He hoped like hell she wasn't planning to tell the senator about their assignation. "Revenge can be a dangerous indulgence," he said with a pretense of calm. "The senator would not react kindly to hearing that the two of us had become lovers."

"Oh, don't worry. I never planned to tell him what we'd done. The satisfaction would have been all the more intense because I'd be deceiving him." She gave a mocking smile. "That would make a change in my relationship with Lewis, wouldn't it? For me to be the one doing the deceiving?"

Score one for Eleanor Cranford, Nick reflected wryly. Not only had she devised an effective way to get revenge on the senator without compromising her lavish lifestyle, but he'd be well and truly put in his place in the process. Eleanor wasn't really attracted to Nick, except in the most superficial sort of way. He was simply an object with which to punish her husband. Which, of course, was exactly how he'd been intending to use her. Nick took a long swallow of ice water, adjusting to his new status. It was a good thing Eleanor had rejected his suggestion of more wine; he definitely needed to keep his wits about him.

"Why does your husband hate me so much?" he asked, tacitly acknowledging the accuracy of her comment. He knew perfectly well why Lewis Cranford disliked him, but he wondered if Eleanor had any inkling as to the real truth of the matter.

"There are several reasons," she said. "I expect you can guess them all."

"Humor me. Give me your version of the list."

"It all started three years ago, when that Russian oil deal went so disastrously wrong. Everyone knew the president was looking for a new running mate for his second term. Lewis was number one on the list of possible candidates. He had Johnston Yates's backing, which is crucial for anyone hoping to get the inside track to higher office. But once the scandal broke, he could barely get an invitation to a White House fund-raiser, much less to one of the intimate private dinners he craved. His chances for the vice presidency vanished in a deluge of Russian oil. Johnston Yates stopped taking his phone calls. He even lost his chance for chairing any high profile Senate committees. To this day, Lewis is still trying to recover from the debacle and claw his way back onto the lower rungs of real power. His hatred for you has built from there. And I guess Yates isn't exactly one of his favorite people, either."

"Ah," Nick said softly. "I understand that the senator is an ambitious man who probably regrets having succumbed to the lure of easy profits. But on the other hand, you have to consider that those profits were real, and the senator retained all the financial benefits of his dealings with me. Thanks to my expert advice, he was able to keep all of his gains from our oil deals out of the American banking system. There are people who would say that the size of the senator's offshore bank account is a fine consolation prize for the loss of the vice presidency."

"Lewis yearns for power even more than he wants money. Besides, you know he didn't keep the money. You went on and took most of his illegal profits away from him, too. So for him, his dealings with you were lose-lose. Not many people tangle with Lewis and leave him a two-time loser."

She was absolutely right on both counts. Lewis Cranford played to win, and obstacles in his path—human or inanimate—tended to end up destroyed. Removing Cranford from the list of candidates for vice president had been a highly successful Unit One operation, and Nick prided himself that America was a better place without the senator one heartbeat away from the Oval Office. Nevertheless, Nick feigned surprise at Eleanor's remarks.

He raised an inquiring eyebrow. "What makes you believe that I was involved in the senator's recent financial losses? How could I possibly have had access to his offshore accounts?"

"I've asked you not to patronize me, Nikolai. I know you were involved in bringing down the Bonita partnership. Lewis lost a great deal of money when Wallis Beecham was jailed and the partnership dismantled. A very great deal of money."

"My heart bleeds for his loss." The sarcasm was inappropriate, but Nick couldn't resist. "By my calculations, the senator must be down to his last five or six million."

Eleanor gave a thin smile. "That's enough for a comfortable retirement. It's not enough to buy his way back into power. As far as Lewis is concerned, five million dollars is chump change."

It had been an afternoon of surprises, but the discovery that Eleanor Cranford was aware he had played a part in the destruction of the Bonita partnership was perhaps the biggest surprise of all. There was only one way she could have found out about Nick's involvement, and that was from the senator himself. And that was more than odd, since Unit One had very reliable intel to the effect that the senator confided nothing at all about his business dealings to his wife.

"Has the senator discussed the Bonita project with you?" Nick asked.

"No." Her expression was bitter. "Lewis never discusses anything with me."

Which was precisely what the intel suggested. "Forgive me, but if that is so, what makes you think that I had anything to do with the failure of the Bonita partnership and the resulting bad publicity for your husband? My financial interests are limited to Russia and its oil industry—more than enough for one man to cope with, believe me, especially since the Russian government is now involved in a running battle with the major oil cartels. I had no investment in the Bonita partnership, none. You have my word on that."

She didn't answer him for a full minute, but Nick was smart enough to wait her out, and not to prompt her. "I never believed you were an investor in the Bonita partnership," she said finally. "I simply believe you were active in destroying it."

"Why would you believe anything so improbable?"

"It's not improbable. On the contrary. Wallis Beecham is Melody Beecham's stepfather. You are…were…Melody Beecham's lover. Wallis would never have attempted to kidnap Melody if she hadn't been causing him trouble. Until prison humbled him a little, he had too much of a god-complex to bother himself about anyone who wasn't actively interfering with his plans. And if Melody was actively causing trouble for Wallis Beecham, it's not much of a leap to suppose that you were helping her defend herself."

"You are building a fragile cobweb of connections out of very shaky facts."

Eleanor smiled tiredly. "Cobwebs aren't fragile, Nikolai. Ever try to brush one off your skin? They cling tenaciously. Besides, Lewis has accused you of direct involvement in the destruction of the Bonita partnership, and that's enough for me. On this sort of thing, my husband's suspicions are always correct."

As explanations went, it was perfectly reasonable. However, in an afternoon filled with surprises, Nick added one more. Eleanor Cranford was telling him a half truth in order to conceal something more important. It was a technique that required some skill and he wondered where she'd learned it. From dealing with her irascible husband, perhaps?

"Forgive me, but I am puzzled. In one breath you inform me that the senator never discusses business matters with you. In the next breath you state that your husband has accused me of direct involvement in the destruction of the Bonita partnership. Those two statements cannot both be true. Which one is the lie?"

Eleanor considered his question. "Neither," she said, but added no further explanation. "You still haven't told me, you know, why it was that you so completely screwed Lewis over on those Russian oil deals. You not only left him twisting in the wind, but you cranked up the wind machine and made sure as many people as possible were there to see him twisting. Why? I would have expected you to be eager for Lewis to win the vice presidency. That way, you would have had a connection to a man almost at the summit of world power. Instead you very nearly got him dismissed from public office. If his opponent in Kentucky hadn't been so inept, he'd never have won reelection to the Senate. I want to know why you worked so hard to bring him down."

"Because the senator is corrupt to his core." Nick couldn't identify the precise moment he decided to stop beating around the bush and admit the truth. But this afternoon, his instincts kept prodding him in the direction of honesty, even if only limited honesty.

"I worked to bring the senator down *because* he was number one in line for the vice presidency, and because I nourish this naive, idealistic hope that the person elected as vice president of the United States will be honorable. I knew enough about your husband's activities over the past decade to be quite sure that he is not even a pale imitation of an honest man. If you want to know the truth, I'm astonished that the voters of Kentucky didn't toss him out of the Senate at the last election. I expected that they would, despite the lousy campaign waged by his opponent."

Eleanor abruptly pushed back her chair and walked to the railing of the deck. Nick followed her, not breaking the silence, following her gaze as she watched a somewhat amateur crew attempt to tack a sailboat against the wind. Finally she swung around and looked straight at him. In a flash of sensory awareness, he felt the late afternoon sun burning against his back and heard the sound of children laughing somewhere far along the beach. Above all, he was aware of the fact that Eleanor was watching him with an intensity that bordered on the ferocious.

"Three months ago my eldest daughter left home, dropped out of college and went to join a religious cult in White Falls, Idaho," she said. "I need your help to bring her back."

In his most optimistic fantasies Nick had never expected to be handed such a powerful entrée into the subject he wanted to discuss. Eleanor's request wasn't a spur of the moment thing, he decided, and definitely not the consequence of too much wine, or a sexual assignation gone awry. Even more than the need to have sex with her husband's enemy, he would lay odds that this request concerning Rachel was the major reason Eleanor had accepted his invitation in the first place.

Nick framed his reply with extreme care, trying to extract maximum information without tipping his hand. "I am flattered that you would ask for my assistance, and in such a personal matter. But again, I am curious as to why you believe I am qualified to help you."

Eleanor leaned back against the balcony railing. "If you could scam my husband out of the vice presidency of the United States, I'm pretty sure you could find a way to rescue my daughter from a bunch of religious kooks waiting for the Second Coming in a motel in Idaho."

Nick laughed. "When you express it just so, I believe you are right. The task does not seem difficult. A few phone calls from your husband and surely your daughter will be on the next flight home."

She frowned. "It's a lot more difficult than you might expect. Lewis has made several calls. There was even an attempt by the FBI to investigate the group, but they uncovered no evidence of wrongdoing, and Rachel simply refuses to come home."

"Is it wise to pressure her, then? If she was in college, I am guessing she is already eighteen? Perhaps it would be best simply to ignore her?"

"We can't risk that. It's dangerous. I truly believe her life could be at risk."

Nick schooled his features into an expression of courteous disbelief and Eleanor rushed on, cutting off his protest that she was surely exaggerating. "You must be asking yourself why on earth I'm expecting you to waste valuable time and energy helping me. Well, I have something to offer that would make your efforts worthwhile."

Nick allowed the silence to stretch out, and Eleanor suddenly looked flustered again. "I didn't mean sex," she said.

"I have something to offer that I believe you really want. Valuable information about my husband."

He sure as hell hoped Eleanor was right. "If I am going to offer my help, you must tell me more." Nick managed to sound a tiny bit bored. "Why is your daughter in…White Falls, did you say? Let's start there."

"She's escaping from the pressure of being Rachel Cranford, or trying to."

"Is that such a difficult role?"

"Yes, it is."

"Why is that? Because she has specific problems, or simply because she is the daughter of a senator who has received a lot of media attention?"

Eleanor's voice was harsh with self-reproach. "I wish I could blame Rachel's unhappiness entirely on Lewis, but I can't. Not anymore. When she ran away, I woke up from my dream world. Until then, I'd been kidding myself that I stayed with Lewis for the sake of our daughters. Rachel and Megan are both bright, wonderful young women and although Lewis doesn't spend much time with them, he's always paid for the best schools and seemed proud of their achievements. Last year, for example, when Rachel applied for admission to Princeton, he called in a couple of favors and insured that she made the cut." She shrugged, explaining her actions perhaps to herself as much as to him. "I guess I'm not above taking advantage of my husband's ability to pull strings when it's for something I want. And I desperately wanted Rachel and Megan to have all the chances that I didn't have as a young woman."

"That is not a reason to blame yourself," Nick said softly. "You were just being a good mother."

"Was I? In retrospect, I realize that Princeton was where

I had always dreamed of attending college, not where Rachel wanted to go."

"You were offering her the chance of a wonderful education. Do not make it sound as if you condemned her to a life of stuffing the meat into hot dog casings."

Eleanor didn't smile. Instead she made a curt brushing motion with her hand. Nick wasn't sure if she was dismissing his comment, or trying to get rid of an unpleasant memory. "Rachel worked as an intern in her father's office over the Christmas break. I suppose she saw him in a different light once she was working for him. She started paying closer attention to how he brokered his political deals, and she became very angry with him. With me, too."

"Why was she angry with you?"

"For having no backbone," Eleanor said tightly. "For never standing up to Lewis when he was in the wrong. Rachel's known about her father's extramarital affairs for a while and she didn't make any secret of the fact that she was disgusted with me for staying with him. For tolerating being constantly humiliated, as she put it. Then she uncovered the details of a specific deal Lewis was working on. He'd traded off his vote on an environmental issue in exchange for federal dollars for a highway project in Kentucky—something that meant big bucks for one of his business cronies back in Lexington. Undoubtedly there was some sort of kickback involved from the Lexington business crony. On the surface, there was nothing illegal about what he did…."

There never was, Nick thought bitterly. Senator Lewis Cranford was a master of the sleazy deal that pushed right up against the boundaries of what was legal—and never crossed over far enough to risk indictment. You could bet your ass that the kickback would be disguised as "consulting fees" or some such impossible-to-dispute payoff.

"But Rachel tried to stop him making the deal anyway?" Nick guessed.

Eleanor nodded. "Environmental issues are important to her. She prepared a fact sheet, demonstrating why her father needed to vote against the proposed relaxation in pollution standards. Lewis basically laughed in her face, then gave her a lecture on political realities. He was actually proud of the way he was bringing federal tax dollars home to Kentucky. Rachel assumed I must know about the deal her father had made, and about the kickbacks, just as I knew about his sexual affairs—"

"Did you know about the deal?" Nick asked.

"No, but only because I always took care never to inform myself about my husband's business activities. Anyway, as far as Rachel was concerned, my failure to take her side on the environmental legislation was the final straw." Eleanor gave an unsteady smile. "She has all the sharp-edged black and white clarity of a very young woman and she accused me of aiding and abetting her father's corruption."

"I remain surprised that her disappointment over a single vote was enough to send her running off to a religious commune in Idaho."

"She didn't leave at once." Eleanor's voice became weary. "After Lewis cast his vote, she tried to interest a journalist in writing an exposé of the corruption that's involved in so many Washington insider deals, using her father's recent bargaining as an example of how the needs of the larger community constantly get traded off to the commercial benefit of the few. Unfortunately she was naive enough to take her information to a journalist she'd met at one of her father's parties.

Not surprisingly the journalist turned out to be in her father's pocket. He strung her along until he found out exactly how much damaging information she had, then he went to Lewis and told him everything."

"I assume Rachel was extremely disillusioned by the journalist's actions. And very angry."

"You're right about the first part. She was extremely disillusioned. Frankly, though, I wish she'd been more angry. There are plenty of journalists out there who would have grabbed her information and been thrilled to run with it. Rachel wasn't interested in trying to find one of them. Instead she seemed to give up. She'd already told me how impressed she was by this preacher, Zachary Wharton. After the incident with the journalists, she fell totally under Zachary's spell."

"I've never heard of this…Zachary Wharton. Is he a TV evangelist?"

"No, I don't think Zachary approves of television. Much too corrupt and modern for his taste. He's a devastatingly handsome charlatan who's swept my daughter off to his creepy commune in the wilds of Idaho." Eleanor's voice shook with suppressed anger. "My smart, lovely daughter is wearing clothes taken straight out of an illustration for *Little House on the Prairie*. She's hemmed in by so many rules and regulations, she just about needs to ask permission if she wants to sneeze. She seems to have decided that since she can't change her father's way of doing business, she's going to opt out of participating in the world of the twenty-first century."

"I am sorry," Nick said. "Most sorry. I can barely guess how frustrating it is when teenagers behave…well, like teenagers. But you should not take this experiment of your daughter's too much to heart, Eleanor. I have heard from friends who have children that wonderful things happen when a young man or woman turns twenty and their hormones finally stop controlling them. Your daughter is still young. There is time for her to learn that there are better ways to stand up to the senator than running away."

"I realize all too well that she'll be a different person in five years from now. The problem is, Rachel doesn't realize it." Eleanor sounded almost despairing. "And in the meantime, Zachary is going to marry her off to one of his cult members, and she'll be pregnant before her next birthday."

"Your husband cannot possibly want that for his daughter any more than you do," Nick said. "What is he doing to get Rachel out of the clutches of this preacher?"

"Nothing. Absolutely nothing." Eleanor's anger was quieter now, but no less intense. "Oh, he went through the motions, just to appease me. But for some reason, Lewis doesn't want Rachel to leave White Falls—"

Why not? Because the bastard needed to have a convincing reason for calling in Unit One? "Unfortunately, Rachel is an adult, in law if not in experience," Nick said. "Legally you and the senator are on shaky ground in demanding her return. But the senator may be going through back channels of some sort that he does not feel comfortable revealing to you."

Eleanor glanced back out to sea, obviously debating what she should say next. "I know that Lewis has approached a covert organization called Unit One, supposedly to ask for their help in shutting down Zachary Wharton. What this organization doesn't know is that they're being set up. Lewis needs Rachel in White Falls to explain his sudden interest in what's going on there. But Rachel isn't what he really cares about. He has something else entirely planned, and Unit One is going to find itself in the middle of a major disaster. Somehow, Johnston Yates is involved, too."

The fact that Eleanor knew of the existence of Unit One stood all of Nick's hackles on end. For the first time, he wondered if Eleanor might be something quite other than an unhappy wife. What if she was Senator Cranford's ally? He didn't believe he'd misread her that completely, but it was a possibility he needed to consider.

"Why are you telling me this?" he asked quietly, playing for time.

"Because I'm pretty sure you work for Unit One." She turned slowly to face him. "It might save a lot of time for both of us if I tell you that I've been bugging my husband's home office ever since the week after Rachel left for White Falls. He sends in sweepers to check for bugs, of course, but I'm the person who lets them into the office, and so I can always remove the device before they come and plant it again when they leave. Lewis should have realized that if you're planning criminal activity, it's a really bad idea to ignore your wife." Her smile was bitter. "Anyway, I heard your name mentioned in connection with Unit One, which is obviously some sort of covert government agency. I decided it was time for me to talk to you. So here we are."

After fifteen years with Unit One, Nick would have sworn that it was impossible to shock him into incoherence. Eleanor Cranford had just proved him wrong. He gazed at her for at least a minute before he found his voice. "Start at the beginning of what you learned from the tapes," he said grimly. "And go from there."

Fourteen

Melody hummed to herself as she jogged down the road heading toward the main gate. At this hour of the evening the chiggers were out in force, but she swatted them away and ran on, her mood too upbeat to be spoiled by a few bugs. She'd had a really successful day and was looking forward to calling Nick and letting him know how much useful intel she'd gleaned in less than twenty-four hours. She relished the prospect of rubbing his arrogant nose in the fact that she hadn't needed to have sex with anyone in order to acquire her information. All she'd had to do was act a little dumb.

When she arrived at the White House after breakfast, the first task she'd been assigned was to print out shipping labels for the mail orders that would be sent out that afternoon. The computer program correlated the address labels to the correct order form, and automatically produced a packing slip. Judging by the number of address labels she'd printed, the Soldiers of Jordan were selling their handmade quilts, afghans and baby blankets at a spanking pace. The wooden curio cabinets made by the men in a workshop next to their dorm were equally hot-selling items. Even Zachary's book, *Raising Spiritually Healthy Children,* had shipped a half dozen copies—and that was in a single day. At twelve bucks a pop, she calculated that he'd probably netted close to fifty dollars to be tossed into the communal kitty.

The Soldiers charged premium prices for their products, but the handiwork Melody had seen was exquisite and worth the cost. The profits from the mail-order business must be considerable, but she'd done some quick sums and concluded that even though the Soldiers were providing their talents and labor for free, the cost of housing, feeding and providing health care for the community probably amounted to a sum at least as large as their business was generating. Zachary wasn't raking in profits at the expense of slave labor by his recruits. The Soldiers of Jordan was a self-sustaining community, but not a huge profit center.

Throughout the morning, Melody had worked enthusiastically at her assigned tasks, taking care not to finish anything too fast. She also asked plenty of not-too-smart questions about the computer program she was using. She wanted to create the impression that she knew the basics of how to find her way around a word processor, but not much more. She guessed the Soldiers would keep financial and personal records on the office computer system, but anything confidential would be protected by security protocols. If she was ever going to be left unsupervised long enough to have a chance at hacking into the good stuff, then she needed to convince everyone that she not only lacked any motive to access their private records, but also lacked the expertise to break through even the simplest of security protections.

Jennifer and Lisa, the two other women working in the office, paid her little attention after the first hour except to offer the occasional friendly word of advice in response to one of her questions, or to toss out a comment on the lovely spring weather, or the excitement of waiting for the birth of Jennifer's first baby, which was due in another month. Jennifer's job was to deal with all the phone calls relating to the mail-order business, known as White Falls Handicrafts, and Lisa rather proudly identified herself as Zachary's administrative assistant and the community's bookkeeper.

Terri once again sat behind the counter in the reception area, dealing with the mail and fielding any phone calls that weren't related to the mail-order business, including requests from the main gate for entry. She also had a row of monitors set on a low shelf behind her desk that displayed the information gleaned from the various surveillance cameras mounted along the road and outside the two dorms. But there was no feed from the camera hidden within the ceiling fan in her room, Melody noted. That monitoring screen was apparently located elsewhere, presumably along with the display screens for any other surveillance equipment the governing council preferred not to make known to run-of-the-mill members of the community.

Gossip Central would have been a perfect job title for Terri, Melody concluded by midmorning. Still, for all that she clearly enjoyed chatting, Terri's fingers were in constant motion. The afghan she'd been working on the previous day was finished before eleven, and she immediately started another one, this time in shades of yellow.

"I like to challenge myself with different patterns, too," she said to Melody, whose workstation was directly opposite the reception area, making her the recipient of many of Terri's conversational gambits. "Next week I'm going to start on a set of baby blankets. I always enjoy that. We're running low on blue." She chuckled. "Must have been a sudden burst of boy babies arriving in the world."

Zachary poked his head out of his corner office. "Melody, could you come and give me your advice for a moment, please? We have a new brochure advertising our handicrafts that we're going to send out to some specialty stores, and I'd like your opinion. You must have considerable expertise with sales brochures, having worked for the Van der Meer Gallery."

"I'd be happy to help," Melody said, getting to her feet. She had no trouble sounding eager to oblige, since she was delighted to get the chance to check out Zachary's inner sanctum. She wondered if the monitoring equipment for the security camera in her room was housed in Zachary's office, then dismissed the idea. He would never have invited her into his office if the monitoring station was there.

Zachary had been working all morning behind closed doors, but once she entered the office, he left the door open so that Terri, Lisa and Jennifer could all see what was going on. He had the brochure samples laid out on his credenza. Walking around the desk to stand next to him, Melody's stomach gave a little jump when she saw that he'd left his computer on. For about twenty seconds before the monitor switched to a scrolling screen saver, she saw that he'd been studying a blueprint, and that the header at the top of the screen displayed an address in Dearborn, Michigan. She managed to catch the name of the street, Oak Avenue, but not the number.

Since Zachary came from the Detroit area, the blueprint might be nothing more significant than the plans for his old house. Or for some drug-rehab project he was planning to underwrite with profits from his fund-raising efforts. Still, Melody decided it was definitely worth passing the news to Nick that Zachary had been studying the blueprints of a building on Oak Avenue in Dearborn.

She quickly turned her attention to the brochures. Zachary's comments made it plain that he himself had designed them, and she was careful at first to temper her critique with plenty of praise. She soon realized that Zachary's ego was strong enough to withstand criticism and that he was genuinely anxious for her input. She sighed in silent frustration. Just when she felt she had his character pegged, he behaved in a way that surprised her. She began to give him serious suggestions for improvements until they were interrupted by the same recording of ringing church bells that had woken her at six that morning.

"Lunchtime!" Terri chirped from the outer office. "My, hasn't the morning flown?"

Melody rose to her feet, responding to the summons, but Zachary gestured for her to sit down again. He stepped out into the main office. "Terri, this brochure has to be at the printer's by three this afternoon. Melody and I need to wrap up the final corrections right away. Could you ask the ladies in the kitchen to send us up a couple of sandwiches? And perhaps you'd ask Elderman William to offer the prayer before the meal?"

"Yes, Reverend. Of course." Terri replied swiftly enough, but the look she directed toward Melody was slightly flustered, as if Zachary skipping a meal when he was on campus was unprecedented.

"Enjoy your lunch, ladies." Zachary smiled at the trio of women as they trooped out, then came back and continued working on the details of the brochure as if it were the most natural thing in the world to have ordered the two of them sandwiches at his desk. Which it would have been in almost any other office, of course, but Melody got the feeling it was unprecedented for the Soldiers of Jordan.

One of the young serving girls arrived fifteen minutes later, carrying a basket covered with a white cloth napkin. She was about eleven or twelve, Melody guessed, and she smiled at Zachary with a mixture of respect and friendship. "Here's your lunch, Reverend. Cook put in two apples, in case you and Miss Melody wanted something for dessert."

"Thank you, Courtney. And thank cook for the apples, will you? That was thoughtful of her." Zachary returned Courtney's smile. "We appreciate your help very much."

"Thank you, Courtney," Melody added.

"You're welcome. Enjoy your lunch." She ran off, the long ribbons of her apron flying behind her. You had to give it to the Soldiers, Melody reflected wryly. Zachary's program might be repressive and sexist, but at least half the parents of teenagers in America would probably be willing to sign on if they knew how content, not to mention well-mannered, all the kids in White Falls seemed to be.

"It's such a lovely day," Zachary said. "Shall we eat outside?" His question was rhetorical because he was already carrying the basket outside as he spoke. His office had a rear door that opened onto a small private patio, screened by a wooden fence and decorated with planters filled with pansies just beginning to bloom. Melody cast a surreptitious glance around for surveillance cameras and wasn't able to see any. Did that mean Zachary didn't want his privacy monitored? If so, she might eventually be able to access his office via the patio. Or did it mean that he liked his security to be well hidden, and if she climbed over the fence, she'd be instantly busted? Like everything else about the Soldiers, the answer wasn't at all obvious.

Melody sat in the full glare of the sun, so that she would have an excuse later to switch positions and scan the patio from a different angle. As unobtrusively as possible, she continued to search for surveillance equipment as Zachary talked.

"You've probably realized that I used the brochures as an excuse for us to have lunch together," he said, spreading the napkin over an iron mesh table top, and removing paper plates and wrapped sandwiches from the basket.

Actually, she hadn't realized any such thing, but Melody wasn't sure if she should express her astonishment, so she played safe and smiled, which was fast becoming her all-purpose response in White Falls. Just call me Little Mary Sunshine, she thought ruefully.

Zachary took her hands across the table, and bowed his head to say a short grace. Then he handed her one of the sandwiches and started to unwrap the other one for himself. Melody had eaten pancakes for breakfast and would have sworn she wouldn't be hungry again before dinner, but the smell of home-baked whole-wheat bread wrapped around slices of roasted turkey breast and fresh alfalfa sprouts was so delicious that her mouth began to water. Her lie of last night was coming home to roost with a vengeance, she thought in amusement. She'd soon have to start jogging for miles a day or she'd be twenty pounds heavier by the time this assignment was over.

Zachary took a sip of water and a small bite of sandwich. "I'm anxious to hear how you feel about our community now that you've had almost twenty-four hours to get to know us. I hope your impressions are favorable?"

"It's been an amazing experience," Melody said with perfect truth. "I never expected the countryside to be so beautiful. On top of that, everyone has been so friendly. I can feel my priorities readjusting. It's almost a physical sensation. A lot of things that seemed important when I was in New York just don't seem to matter much now I'm here."

Zachary nodded, obviously pleased with her answer. "People ask why God never works miracles anymore. They seem to forget that a spring day as beautiful as this is a miracle all of its own if we would only take the time to enjoy it."

"Just having the time to appreciate the weather is definitely a miracle as far as I'm concerned," Melody said, and smiled—again.

Zachary set down his sandwich and reached across the table, resting his hand over hers. "You could be such an asset to our community. Do you think you'll be making the decision to stay with us permanently, my dear?"

She looked down at his hand and, with a deliberation equal to his, covered it with her other hand. When she looked up to meet his eyes, she detected a definite gleam of sexual awareness in his eyes. "I need a little more time, Zachary." She purposely left off his requested title of reverend. Dammit, the guy was coming on to her, albeit mildly, and she wasn't going to pretend she hadn't noticed. "I'm really loving it here, but staying would mean changing my whole life, and all my plans. It's a huge decision."

"Perhaps bigger than you know," he said.

And what the hell did that mean? Melody wondered. "I don't understand," she murmured. "How can the decision be bigger than I know?"

"Now isn't the right moment for me to explain. We'll talk again tomorrow." Zachary flashed her a smile that earned him a full nine out of ten on the patronization scale.

"I'm not sure I can wait until tomorrow." She was back to being breathless and eager. Being with Zachary had the effect of reducing her responses to an emotional range of faked shy admiration through faked not-so-shy admiration. Melody thought with unexpected longing of the ease and naturalness of her defunct relationship with Nick and was flooded by a rush of desire intense enough to cut off her breath.

"Patience is a virtue," Zachary said, patting her hand. He delivered the cliché without any trace of irony in his voice.

"I know." Melody couldn't think of anything more productive to say. She found Zachary's inconsistencies bewildering enough that they deadened her capacity to improvise. Half an hour earlier he'd discussed sales brochures with the incisiveness of a trained marketing executive. Now he was chiding her with the paternalism of a Victorian schoolteacher. It was like dealing with a person suffering from multiple personality disorder, and she was never quite sure which Zachary she was talking to.

"The sun's shining right in my eyes," she said, standing up and rubbing her eyes as she walked into a patch of shade near one of the planters. She admired the flowers, then walked casually to the opposite corner. There were no cameras hidden among either tub of pansies, not unless they were buried deep in the soil.

She came back to the table, adjusting the position of her chair, ostensibly to get away from the sun, and let her gaze roam over the patio from this new angle. Once again, there was no obvious sign of surveillance equipment. The patio was looking better and better as an access point for searching his office.

"The sun is unusually bright today," Zachary agreed. "There isn't a cloud in the sky."

"Does it get very hot here in summer?" She liked the subtle implication that she was planning to be in White Falls during the summer.

"It depends what you're comparing it to. In comparison to England, we roast. In comparison to New Orleans, we're cool and dry."

"Mmm. That sounds like a perfect compromise!"

"Yes, most people who make the decision to remain in White Falls enjoy the climate." He leaned across the table, pushing the picnic basket to one side. "I want to know more about you, Melody. Talk to me about yourself. Tell me about your studies at the University of Florence. Do you speak Italian?"

She talked about her courses in art history, but took care not to let the conversation get too technical, and left the impression that she'd been taking an easy course for foreigners with too much time and money, rather than a demanding graduate degree for people planning a career with a major museum or art gallery. Some gut instinct that she would have been hard put to justify analytically inspired her to sprinkle her conversation with references to every Italian countess, prince and wealthy landowner she'd ever met during her frequent stays in Italy.

Zachary's expression remained no more than polite and friendly, but she had the distinct impression that he was avidly sucking up every reference to the countess of this and the count of that.

"Of course, in Italy it sometimes seems as if everyone who doesn't descend from sturdy peasant stock claims to be a prince or princess." Melody laughed as she tossed out the comment, but she watched Zachary closely.

"Is that so?" he asked smoothly, giving away nothing. "I've never had the pleasure of visiting Italy, but I'm sure it must be a fascinating place. Anyway, thank you so much for sharing your experiences with me, Melody."

"You're welcome. I hope I didn't bore you with all that chatter about the Italian Renaissance."

"You could never bore me," he said. "You're a fascinating woman." He let his gaze linger on her mouth for a moment before he rose to his feet. "Let's save Courtney a trip and take the picnic basket back to the kitchen," he said.

Melody repacked the basket and slipped it over her arm. By the puritanical standards of the Soldiers of Jordan, Zachary was coming on to her. Why? He would wreck his reputation with his followers if he started an affair with her. So what was the point of singling her out for special attention?

No answer came to mind, so she added one more item to the list of character inconsistencies she needed to puzzle over later. As they walked back through his office, Zachary glanced over at his computer, then bent down to give a couple of quick mouse clicks to close out the program he'd had running. She stood right behind him and was rewarded when the file containing the blueprint flashed momentarily onto the screen before shutting down. She looked instantly to the corner of the blueprint that contained the street address, and managed to register the number before the file vanished: 345 Oak Avenue. At least it was a starting point for Bob Spinard if Oak Avenue turned out to be ten miles long.

She didn't want to be caught staring at the computer screen. A second before Zachary finished closing down the program, she twisted around and stared at the first thing to catch her eye—a framed sepia photo, identified as Souk el Hadimayeh, Damascus, 1926.

"Did your family bring this with them when they immigrated to the States?" she asked, pointing toward the picture. "The composition is perfect, with the foreground in shadow and the sun striking the street deep in the background."

"Yes, my parents brought that with them. I'm glad you like it. It's always been one of my favorites. My grandfather took the picture himself. He had a store in that particular Souk."

"He was obviously a skillful photographer with real artistic talent."

"He was a silversmith by trade, so I guess he had a few artistic genes sprinkled into the mix."

"Was your father a silversmith, too?"

Zachary shook his head. "The family store was burned down in the early thirties and everything was destroyed, right down to the last piece of silver. My grandfather was devastated and seemed to lose interest in passing on his skills to my father. He even stopped creating new pieces of his own. We have no examples of his work, which was rumored to be magnificent."

"That's a terrible shame." Melody's sympathy was sincere. "Was the fire one of the things that prompted your family to immigrate to the States?"

"Yes. My family's wealth was wiped out and they had to start over from scratch. My grandfather never really recovered from the trauma, though, and he died when my dad was still in his teens."

"I'm sorry. I guess you can't have known your grandfather?"

"Only from family stories. I don't remember my grandmother, either. She died when I was a baby, reportedly from a broken heart."

"The fire in Damascus seems to have had a devastating effect."

"It did. And the worst part is that it was deliberately set, but the arsonists were never brought to justice, even though everyone knew who they were. My family was Christian, you see, and even back in the late twenties and early thirties there were fanatic Muslim nationalists who believed that Syrians shouldn't be allowed to belong to other religions. Islamic terrorism isn't new. The only difference is that these days, America happens to be the target so our government has started to pay attention."

It was the closest he'd come to making a political statement since she'd met him. Seeming to regret having spoken with too much vehemence, he turned abruptly. "Anyway, enough of this sad subject. The lunch break's almost over. Let's get this lunch basket back to the kitchen, shall we?"

His grandparents' story certainly suggested a possible root cause for Zachary's dislike of Islam, and the virulent anti-Muslim rhetoric of his sermon that Jodie Evanderhaus had managed to capture on film. Zachary claimed that the identity of the arsonists who had destroyed his grandfather's business was well-known. If the descendants of those arsonists were now in the States, might he be planning vengeance against them? It was an intriguing idea, but it would be impossible to follow up. Digging into the details of an unsolved crime that had taken place in Damascus seventy-five years ago was beyond the skills of even Bob Spinard's team of research geniuses.

Zachary went straight from the dining room to attend a meeting of the governing council. Melody returned to the White House and tackled a stream of boring clerical chores assigned to her by Jennifer and Lisa. Lisa received a letter that obviously upset her when she came back from lunch and became increasingly grumpy as the afternoon wore on. She finally snapped out a comment to the effect that they'd all work a lot faster if Melody didn't ask so many idiotic questions.

Melody apologized humbly, swallowing a laugh, in complete agreement with Lisa's assessment. Jennifer and Terri rushed to assure her that she was doing very well for her first day on the job and they appreciated her efforts. Melody wished she could tell them that Lisa's mild flash of temper seemed about the most normal behavior she'd encountered since arriving in White Falls.

When Melody got up to go to the rest room, Terri followed her. Thrilled to pass on juicy gossip to a fresh pair of ears, she confided that Lisa's husband, Phil, had left White Falls eight months ago, and that Lisa was mired in the morass of a messy divorce. The papers Lisa had received in today's mail were yet another stalling tactic on the part of Phil's obnoxious lawyer.

The Soldiers proclaimed that marriage was for life and beyond, an unbreakable sacrament that lasted into eternity. However, they also asserted that marriage was only valid in the eyes of God if it had been celebrated in the presence of at least one of the twelve elders of their church. The fact that this meant fewer than seventy couples in the whole world were legitimately married while the remaining billion or so were living in sin didn't appear to strike Terri as at all odd.

In terms of Soldiers of Jordan theology, Lisa's marriage to Phil didn't exist and she had been engaged to a fellow Soldier for more than six months. George, her fiancé, was a former teacher, currently in charge of the half dozen students of high school age resident in White Falls. George was a lovely man, according to Terri, who would make a wonderful husband. The only fly in the ointment was the fact that the State of Arizona held stubbornly to the view that Lisa remained legally tied to Phil, and her "true" marriage to George couldn't take place until her divorce was finalized. Her voice lowered to a whisper, Terri confided that George and Lisa were both getting a tad frustrated waiting for the intimacies of married life.

Hearing Lisa's story, Melody felt a sneaking admiration for the way Zachary made damn sure he covered any and all bases that might provide the slightest grounds for criminal prosecution of the Soldiers of Jordan. Apparently he had no intention of getting into trouble with law enforcement because of bigamous marriages taking place under his ministry. She felt a burst of sympathy for Lisa, trying hard to be a good Soldier and demonstrate sweet charity toward her neighbors. No wonder the poor woman's frustration at the delay in her wedding poked through the facade of good cheer every now and again.

Later in the afternoon, Lisa delivered a pinched-lipped apology, then asked for Melody's help in checking the dozens of new addresses she had added into the master list of donors in the wake of Zachary's trip to New York. For once Melody had no need to pretend to work slowly. It required painstaking attention to compare the original list with the amended printout, and by the time Melody had finished, finding four mistakes in the process, Lisa had moved on to another task.

Lisa sighed when Melody pointed out the mistakes. Then she remembered Soldiers weren't supposed to be grouchy and forced a smile. She closed the file she was working on and gave the command to switch back to the file containing the list of donors. A message box popped up on the screen, asking for Lisa's password.

Melody had been on the way back to her workstation. But seeing the message box, she halted in her tracks so abruptly that she felt like Road Runner, sliding on heels and tail feathers as she screeched to a halt. She strolled casually back toward Lisa and picked up the printout of addresses she'd just put down. Then she justified her return by standing behind Lisa's chair as if waiting to read off the corrections.

Melody held her breath, expecting to be sent away at any minute, but Lisa typed in her password without seeming to give a thought to Melody's presence. Against all the laws of good security practices, Lisa had chosen her fiancé's name as her password—easy to remember, but easy to guess, too. As soon as the password was entered, an entire directory of confidential personnel files appeared on the screen. Lisa scrolled her cursor down the list until she found a file that was headed Drug Rehab/Donors.

Melody expelled the breath she'd been holding, scarcely able to believe the ease with which she'd been handed the key to accessing the Soldiers' records. For all their intermittent paranoia, not to mention their shooting range for military training and their high-tech surveillance cameras, she was reaching the conclusion that the Soldiers were incredibly naive about some aspects of security. Or perhaps Lisa assumed that since Zachary had assigned Melody to work in the office, she must be trustworthy?

"Okay, here we are," Lisa said, clicking open the file of donor addresses. "What were the corrections again?"

Melody read them off, then returned to her workstation, careful to keep her jubilation under tight control. All she needed was a few minutes of privacy at her computer and she'd be able to search for the address list Nick had requested last night. Unfortunately, privacy was a rare and precious commodity in White Falls, and evading observation by Zachary and all three of her fellow office workers was going to require luck as well as planning.

Zachary returned from his council meeting just long

enough to inform Lisa and Terri that he would be driving into the local town to hand the revised brochure into the printer.

One down, three to go, Melody thought. Fifteen minutes after Zachary's departure, the UPS man arrived at the entrance gate and was admitted by Terri to pick up the day's quota of mail order packages.

The UPS man was exactly the sort of diversion Melody had been waiting for. The driver's trips back and forth to his van created a constant flurry of activity. Jennifer was occupied signing the shipping authorization and checking packages off against her master list. Lisa was filing in the back office. Unfortunately that left Terri. Nosy, gossipy Terri whose seat was directly opposite Melody's desk.

Melody was frantically racking her brains to think of some way to distract Terri's attention when the phone rang. Terri responded. It was somebody asking for Zachary and apparently leaving a complicated message. For the first time during the entire day, nobody was paying a lick of attention to Melody.

Melody's fingers had keyed in the name *George* before she'd consciously decided to grab the chance. In less than ten seconds a directory of confidential files appeared on the screen. She scrolled her cursor down the list of headers, searching for something that might indicate it contained a membership list. She found a file labeled Social Security Numbers and clicked on it, hoping for the best. She was stunned when she found herself staring at columns containing the Social Security number of every Soldier who had ever been baptized into full membership in the community, along with the date of their baptism and the amount of money they had donated to the Soldiers as their "baptismal gift."

Melody turned a triumphant gasp into a smothered cough.

This was even better than finding an address list. With Social Security numbers as a starting point, Bob Spinard's team would be able to generate basic financial and personal information on most of these people within a couple of hours.

Terri hung up the phone, but was still preoccupied as she wrote out a note, presumably recording the details of the call. Melody could hear Lisa opening and shutting metal drawers as she continued to put papers into the filing cabinets and Jennifer had actually gone outside to take the driver a package that had been left behind.

Making a copy of the Social Security file was going to be a high risk project whenever she did it, but Melody concluded that she couldn't hope for a better opportunity than this. She slipped a CD-ROM into the drive, then hesitated, seized by last-minute doubts. Could it really be this easy? Maybe she was being set up. Lisa's password seemed trivial protection for such important records. Did the Soldiers really have nothing more effective in place?

Or maybe the laxness of the office security was something of an illusion. If she hadn't been assigned by Zachary to work inside the admin building, she wouldn't have been able to access the computers, much less download confidential information. The FBI agents, for example, had never been able to penetrate the admin building, which was partly why their information about the financial underpinnings of the group was so limited.

Bottom line: the only way she was going to discover if the files were booby-trapped was by giving the command to copy them. *Stop debating and download the damn file.*

Stomach churning and palms sweating, Melody clicked the mouse and gave the command to copy the data. Her heartbeat sounded deafeningly loud in her ears as the computer whirred into action, but no alarm bells rang, and nobody jumped up to demand an explanation of what she was doing. The familiar adrenaline rush that always accompanied a risky stage in a mission heightened Melody's senses, making her acutely aware of the rustle of Terri's yarn—which meant she'd started crocheting again—and the sounds of Jennifer's footfalls dashing in the direction of the rest room.

It took two nerve-racking minutes before the CD-ROM drive opened with a *ping,* indicating that the copying was complete. The *ping* sounded like an explosion, but Melody forced herself not to look up in guilty expectation of her illicit activities having been discovered.

Before she even took the newly minted disk out of the drive, she initiated the series of commands that Bob Spinard had taught her to obliterate all trace of her clandestine activity. This was the most time-consuming part of the copying process, and she could feel the pressure build, her fingers clumsy with tension as she went through the complex procedure of accessing the basic code of the hard drive.

It was finally done and her screen reverted to a display of innocuous inventory forms. Melody leaned back in her chair, slipping the disk into the side pocket of her flared skirt. At least that was one reward for deferring to the hokey dress code of the community and wearing a long full skirt, she thought, giddy with relief. The outline of the disc would have been easy to spot if she'd worn her usual hip-hugging short skirts, or tailored slacks.

After the drama of copying the disk, the rest of the afternoon was uneventful. As they closed up for the day, Melody had made sure to drop a casual comment to the effect that she planned to jog to the gate between the end of work and the start of dinner. Jennifer, massaging her pregnant belly, expressed envy of anyone able to run, and the other two women both swore they were going to start a serious exercise program some time soon. Fortunately, neither of them volunteered to start tonight and join Melody in her run.

Jogging toward the main gate, Melody mentally reviewed the day's events. On the surface, everything she'd experienced suggested that the Soldiers of Jordan were exactly what they claimed to be: a group of fervent religious believers, striving to lead lives dedicated to God. So why, when she finished copying the Social Security file onto a disk, had she experienced such overwhelming relief at evading detection? It wasn't as if she was a stranger to high-risk activities. Ever since her mother died and she had begun her investigation into Wallis Beecham's business affairs, her life had been filled not just with stress, but with moments of real danger. Since starting to work for Unit One six months ago, risk-taking had become the norm. And yet, this afternoon, inside a pleasant office in rural Idaho, surrounded by three friendly women, she had felt a fear that was as intense as any she had ever experienced.

Her problem was that she didn't trust people who were too cheerful, Melody decided ruefully. Which probably said more about the people she usually hung out with than it did about the real dangers of White Falls. After all, other than the death of the reporter and the sabotaged farm equipment, there wasn't any suspicion of violence in connection with the Soldiers. On the contrary, both FBI agents had been unmasked as spies, and their only punishment had been a courteous request to leave White Falls. Nobody had even been rude to them, much less subjected them to physical abuse.

But the feeling of imminent danger persisted. Thank God for Bob Spinard's communications device and the fact that she could call Nick each day. The prospect of reporting to him had kept her grounded when she'd felt in danger of flying apart. Despite her rage—her hurt?—at his concealing the fact that Unit One knew the identity of her biological father, she trusted him completely in terms of their professional relationship.

She still had to tackle the problem of finding somewhere safe to call him from, but Melody was optimistic she had that problem licked. After watching the desultory fashion in which Terri monitored the security cameras along the road leading from the highway to the former motel, she no longer viewed them as quite such a serious threat. Besides, they were designed to monitor cars, rather than pedestrians, and they were mounted in a staggered fashion along the road, each one at least a quarter of a mile from its counterpart on the opposite side of the road. When she drove in yesterday with Jason, she'd counted at least eight cameras looming overhead. That count might be accurate, but for anyone on foot, there were plenty of gaps in the coverage. Since the perimeter of the campus was protected by an electric fence, the Soldiers apparently didn't feel any need for closer monitoring of the road. All she had to do was find a convenient clump of bushes at the midpoint between two sets of cameras and she would be out of sight and hearing for placing her call to Nick.

The route down to the main entrance was lined with trees, mostly conifers, and the undergrowth hadn't been cleared, which provided her with adequate cover. Of course, the undergrowth provided convenient hiding places not only for her but also for snakes, rats, mice, chipmunks and all manner of other beasties, Melody reflected gloomily. How many types of poisonous snake were there in Idaho anyway? Maybe she could demand a new clause in her contract with Unit

One: no sex on the job, no climbing down the sides of high buildings and definitely no sharing of ground space with poisonous reptiles.

She'd been running for ten minutes, but she'd traveled less than a mile, since she didn't want the cameras to record how fast she could move when she really pushed herself. She estimated she was halfway to the gate, which would be a good place to stop.

Safely out of camera range, she found a suitably wooded spot and ducked into it, kneeling behind a juniper bush. The ground was covered with dead pine needles and felt rough against her legs, but she didn't move until she was sure she was alone. She heard the chatter of a distant squirrel and smelled the aromatic bark of a few nearby ponderosas. After another minute of waiting and listening, she decided that she was temporarily safe from predators, both human and animal. She risked sitting down, tucking her legs close to her body, so that she was obscured by the juniper bush.

Aware that she was looking forward to hearing the sound of Nick's voice a great deal more than was good for her, she drew her communicator out of her shorts pocket. She hoped that Nick wouldn't be in bed with Eleanor Cranford when she called. If he was with Eleanor, he'd still take the call, but he'd ask her to wait a moment. Then he'd make an excuse to go into the bathroom, or some other spot where Eleanor wouldn't follow him. She *really* hoped he wouldn't ask her to wait.

Melody pressed the button that would connect her to Nick's cell phone.

Fifteen

Nick's phone, the one that linked him directly to Melody, lay on the desk in his hotel room, within easy reach of his hand. He grabbed it on the first ring. "Yes."

"I have to be at dinner in less than an hour." Melody's voice was soft, but vibrant with energy. "I have a lot to tell you."

Are you safe? Do you miss me as much as I miss you? How in hell did our relationship manage to get so totally fucked up?

Nick drew in a sharp breath. Jesus Christ, he needed to get a grip. "Wait a moment, please," he said.

He stood up, put down the phone, and walked over to the window, staring out at the view of Washington in the rain. After a few seconds, he picked up the phone again. "Yes, I'm ready now."

When she spoke this time, it seemed to him that Melody's voice had become distinctly cooler. Focus on the goddamn report, he ordered himself. Stop microanalyzing every nuance of her speech pattern.

He listened, impressed by the clarity of Melody's explanation, as she told him about the blueprint she'd seen on Zachary's computer, and gave him the address.

"Great work," he said. "Bob Spinard should be able to identify the building with no difficulty. Once we know what it is—a house, a store, an office building—we might be able to guess why Zachary was studying it."

"Do you think it could be a mosque? I know there are several quite large ones in Dearborn."

"If it's a mosque, then you've just provided us all with something very interesting to talk about in terms of possible targets. I'll let you know tomorrow what Bob Spinard finds out. Anything else?"

"Yes. I also have a CD-ROM that I made this afternoon. It contains the Social Security numbers for every baptized member of the Soldiers of Jordan, past and present."

Melody sounded almost offhand, but Nick could picture her clearly and knew there would be a gleam of satisfaction in her eyes that belied the casualness of her voice. She had every right to be pleased with herself. In less than twenty-four hours, she'd collected more useful information than the two FBI agents had generated in their combined stay of three weeks.

"Well done, kid," Nick said softly.

"Thanks. Now we get to the next problem. How am I going to transmit the disk to you?"

"I'll collect it tomorrow, in person," he said. Nick had never been more delighted to have an excuse to visit an operative on the job.

"I don't know, Nick. How will we make contact? The perimeter of the property is guarded by an electric fence. The campus buildings are all monitored by surveillance cameras—"

"We can't meet secretly. Way too much risk of blowing your cover."

"Then what are we going to do? I'm fresh out of clever ideas about where we might meet. I'd suggest off campus, but there's no way for me to get off the grounds without telling everyone where I'm going. I'm not entirely sure Zachary would let me leave and then come back. He'd certainly insist on sending an escort."

"We won't try for subtle or secret. I'll simply drive through the gates and demand to talk to you. Pretend to be annoyed that I've come. You can tell me to get lost and refuse to speak to me. I'll eventually overcome your objections—"

"That figures," she said dryly. "How very true to real life."

If he'd been hoping for her to sound excited at the prospect of seeing him, he was disappointed. "Expect me late in the afternoon, and meanwhile work on finding somewhere out of surveillance range where you can hand over the disk to me."

"That's going to take some planning." She waited a beat. "Did your meeting with Eleanor Cranford produce any useful intel?"

"More than any of us expected. First, Eleanor made comments that convince me Senator Cranford invited Unit One's help with the deliberate intention of setting us up. The senator's planning for our investigation to go down in flames."

"How? How in hell could he achieve that?"

"Wish I knew. But there's one marginally bright spot. I don't believe Rachel is part of the senator's plans, which should make things a bit easier for you. Eleanor made it clear that her daughter has serious issues with her father and joined the Soldiers of Jordan at least in part to annoy him."

"Rachel may have issues with her father, but the major reason she joined the Soldiers of Jordan is that she's infatuated with Zachary Wharton," Melody said.

"Interesting. But if she's looking for a father figure with plenty of moral absolutes, Zachary's just about perfect, isn't he? Anyway, the important thing from your perspective is that if Rachel volunteers any information, or offers any suggestions, you can probably take the offer at face value. It isn't likely to be part of a Senator Cranford-inspired setup."

"That's useful to know," Melody said. "Although it's frustrating that we still don't have the least idea how he's planning to set up Unit One. Didn't Eleanor provide *any* insights into what he might be up to?"

"No. However, she did provide some information that confirms our basic supposition that Zachary is unaware of the senator's plans—whatever they are."

"I certainly haven't detected any signs that Zachary's suspicious of my motives, although that doesn't make me as comfortable as it should. Maybe I just can't read him."

"That's unlikely. You're especially good at assessing people's motives. As you just did with Rachel Cranford."

"Not with Zachary, though. Even the fact that he's put me to work in the central office is a two-edged sword. It could mean he has no clue I'm working against him. Or it could mean that he suspects I'm an undercover operative and wants to keep me up close and personal while he feeds me a bunch of misinformation. In which case the blueprint may have been left on his computer monitor because he wanted me to see it, and the Social Security numbers may be fakes."

"Bob Spinard will know if the Social Security numbers are fakes within a few moments of running them," Nick pointed out. "And if they're genuine, it confirms that Zachary trusts you enough to bring you right into the heart of central office operations."

"Yes, the Social Security numbers are a good test," Melody agreed. "I'll look forward to hearing what Bob turns up."

"Is Zachary really capable of bluffing you so completely?" Nick asked. "I'm surprised you would even consider the possibility."

"He's absolutely capable of deceiving me." Melody's response was swift and firm. "I can't get a handle on what makes the guy tick. I still don't even know if he sincerely believes all of the stuff he's preaching here, or only most of it. Or whether he's simply running some huge scam."

That was a pretty basic question to remain unanswered, Nick reflected. Melody was probably the best field operative Unit One was currently running in terms of ferreting out what made people tick. If she couldn't assess Zachary's sincerity, then his acting ability was either enormous, or his character was exceptionally complex.

"What about the paramilitary activities for the male recruits?" he asked. "You haven't mentioned that. Did you have a chance to observe their training this morning?"

"No. Women aren't encouraged to venture near the men's training area, and I want to avoid as much as possible doing anything that makes me stand out from the obedient crowd. However, it seems all the men between the ages of eighteen and fifty spend the first two hours after breakfast doing jumping jacks, crawling around in the bushes and learning to shoot straight."

"How does Zachary integrate military training into his spiel about a community dedicated to living together in love and harmony?"

"The Soldiers view the world outside White Falls as a threatening place, but the military training is the most surprising aspect of the whole community for me. I can't reconcile the happiness of the kids, and the homebody friendliness of most of the women, with the fact that their men go out in the fields each morning and fire bullets at cutouts of human beings. Zachary's sermon this morning was about the need to treat each day as a special gift from God. It was a great sermon and we all chanted an enthusiastic amen. Then we sang a happy hymn and the men raced out to go and practice shooting up fake people. It's much more than creepy—it's flat out weird."

"People's beliefs don't always fit neatly together," Nick said. "The Soldiers aren't alone in that. Remember Data, the android in *Star Trek?* The whole premise of his character was that he had to learn to be illogical if he wanted to become more human."

Finally—finally!—Melody's voice warmed with laughter. "You score half a point for that one, Nikolai. Data's lack of logic only seemed to apply in episodes where he was trying to understand the concept of how human beings fall in love." She stopped abruptly and the moment of warmth and laughter vanished beneath a layer of instant ice. "Getting back to the point, did you learn anything else relevant during the course of seducing Mrs. Cranford?"

Her sudden change of mood actually lifted Nick's spirits somewhat. From the juxtaposition of Melody's remarks, he realized she was thoroughly pissed off about his supposed affair with Eleanor Cranford, which had to be good news for him. Presumably, if her feelings for him were irretrievably dead and buried, she wouldn't care. That thought cheered him considerably.

"I learned a great deal from her, as I told you, but it's not directly relevant to your situation right now. She gave us one major lead, but the details are complicated. I'll fill you in tomorrow."

"I'm glad she provided you with enough information to make the time you spent seducing her worthwhile." Melody's voice was fake-sugar sweet.

He'd been burned yesterday when he injected a personal note into their conversation and she flatly rejected the opening. But he couldn't resist giving it one more try. "Melody—I didn't have sex with Eleanor Cranford."

She was silent for a very long time. Eventually she asked, "Why not?"

"It seemed unfair to everyone to have sex with Eleanor when I was trying to pretend she was you."

Once again, she took a while to answer and when she finally spoke, her response was oblique. "Sex was never the problem in our relationship, Nick. It was everything else that we couldn't handle."

"Not everything else." He forced himself to acknowledge the truth. "The main problem was my refusal to acknowledge how important you are to me." He swallowed hard. "I love you, Melody, and that scares the hell out of me."

He waited through an excruciating few seconds, but Melody didn't say anything. The silence stretched out, dragging his nerves with it.

"Jesus, Melody, I just admitted that I love you. Could you find *something* to say at least?"

There was still no reply. Nick stared at his cell phone in frustration, then realized he was talking to dead air. Melody had disconnected their link.

Sixteen

The thud of several pairs of feet pounding on pavement came from the direction of the road, no more than thirty yards from her hiding place. More than two runners were approaching, Melody guessed, but less than eight. Whoever it was had come way too close for comfort before she heard them, filtered out of her awareness because she was mooning over the husky timbre of Nick's voice when he denied sleeping with Eleanor Cranford.

Melody hurriedly closed her communicator, shoving it into the pocket of her shorts, regretfully cutting off whatever Nick was saying in midsentence. If she could hear people running, then they could just as easily hear her speaking. She couldn't even risk saying goodbye.

Taking care not to make any sound, she squeezed back behind the juniper bush, seeking to narrow her profile relative to the road. The scraggy branches suddenly seemed to provide very inadequate protection. If the runners looked in this direction, she would be seen.

The loudness of the footfalls peaked, then started to fade,

indicating the runners had passed her hiding spot without stopping. Expelling a shaky breath, Melody risked peering around the bush, keeping her face low to the ground. She saw the rear view of four men running hard in the direction of the main gate. They wore shorts and mesh shirts, and the sort of two-hundred-dollar performance shoes preferred by Unit One operatives for intensive training. These men were clearly serious about their physical fitness. Even from her incomplete view, Melody could see they were pushing themselves to the limit. Their shirts weren't just sweat-streaked, they were totally soaked, and the air seemed to vibrate with the fierceness of their concentration. Lucky for her that they were so focused or they would surely have noticed her.

She couldn't identify any of the men, although she thought one of them might have been Ed Harris, looking a great deal younger and fitter than she would have imagined after their brief encounter last night. More like a man in his thirties than one approaching fifty, as she'd assumed.

She waited until the four runners were out of sight—thank God for the multiple bends in the road—and then quietly eased her way out of the brush and back onto the road. If the men were heading toward the main gate, which seemed logical, she could maintain her former moderate pace and still have time to get back to her room before they turned around for the return leg and spotted her running in front of them. She didn't want to raise questions in their minds as to why they hadn't passed her somewhere along the road when they were outward bound. As it was, she already might have some explaining to do if anyone ever reviewed the surveillance tapes. The cameras were going to pick up on the fact that she'd disappeared from view for several minutes. She'd have to invent a debilitating leg cramp if anyone questioned her about what she'd been doing during that missing stretch of time.

She showered and changed and made it to dinner with seven minutes to spare. Tonight Zachary was greeting the Soldiers outside the dining hall as she arrived. He greeted her with the same smile and murmured welcome that he gave to all the Soldiers, but when she started to go inside, he put out his hand, touching her lightly on the arm to indicate she should wait.

"It's a lovely evening. Stay outside with me until I go in." He smiled to show it was a request, not an order.

"Of course." Melody stood beside him, listening as Zachary greeted the last few arrivals. One of the final people to put in an appearance was Ed Harris, looking freshly showered and with his short hair still wet, which confirmed her suspicion that he might have been one of the four men subjecting themselves to the grueling training run she'd observed half an hour earlier.

"Ed, could you join me in my office after dinner?" Zachary asked. "I'm sorry to ask you to work at night, but I have some papers we need to go over together."

"No problem. See you then, Reverend." Ed seemed to be a man of few words. He nodded toward Melody and strode into the dining hall without saying anything more.

At Zachary's request, Melody once again sat next to him, but their other table mates had all changed from the previous night. She saw Rachel at the next table over, but Terri and her family were seated clear across the room, as were the doctor and his wife. Rachel seemed to have reverted to her former mood of total animosity. She ignored Melody's smile and sent a furious scowl winging toward a woman she clearly considered as her rival for Zachary's affections. If only the poor kid knew how little cause she had to be jealous, Melody thought wryly.

Melody's companions tonight included Lisa and her fiancé, George, who seemed nice enough until the conversation chanced to settle on the events of 9/11. Poor George had apparently lost a firefighter brother in the aftermath of the attack, and he was filled with rage at the plight of his widowed sister-in-law and two orphaned nephews. He spewed venom at the terrorists who'd killed his brother, and at the religion that made them believe that killing innocent, peaceful people was acceptable.

Melody expressed deep sympathy for George's loss and glossed over his rants about the dangers of Islam. She noticed that Zachary was watching her reaction with covert intensity, and when George finally paused for breath, she forced herself to inject a comment to the effect that Islam had become a dangerous religion, and that it was time for Americans to stand up and defend traditional Western values or drown in a wave of terrorist attacks. She managed not to let her mouth curl in distaste as she spoke, which was a significant triumph of training over instinct.

Zachary nodded approvingly at her remark. "We Christians are going to have to find new ways to defend ourselves against fanatical followers of false beliefs," he said, without a trace of irony. Apparently he had no clue that the Soldiers of Jordan might be considered a little on the fanatic side. "This country is under siege and we need to take steps to protect our way of life."

There were murmurs of consent from everyone around the table. Either Zachary was tapping into a preexisting well of racial and religious bigotry in his recruits, Melody mused, or he'd indoctrinated his followers to the point that they believed their freedoms and way of life were at profound risk not just from terrorists, but from hordes of ordinary, peaceful Muslims.

The conversation at their table glided smoothly from anti-Muslim rhetoric to racist comments about the number of black Americans who'd chosen to convert to Islam, and then on to all the tired clichés about crime, the breakdown of the family and the way African Americans were "taking over" wholesome mainstream media with profane rap music and degenerate displays of lewdness that were misnamed dancing.

Melody smiled and nodded and felt sick enough to lose her appetite, despite the luscious homemade ice cream that was being served for dessert. Only a little over twenty-four hours and she was apparently enough of an insider to be allowed a glimpse of the hate-filled underbelly of the Soldiers of Jordan. She found the sight loathsome.

To distract her attention, and prevent herself saying something that might well be dangerous in this group of bigots, she occupied herself by looking around the room and trying to identify the other three men who'd been running with Ed Harris. She could discount two-thirds of the men on the basis of age and body built, but she needed to see the remaining two dozen or so stripped if she was to have a hope of picking the runners out from the crowd. And in this community, her chances of seeing any of the men stripped weren't very promising.

Melody felt a surge of impatience at her passivity. In an undercover op, it was often best to sit back and let events unfold according to their natural pattern, but she couldn't shake the feeling that the Soldiers were moving from a generalized state of paranoid defensiveness into a more active state of fighting back against the forces that they saw as oppressing them. Ed Harris was going to be meeting with Zachary immediately after dinner, and he was in charge of military training. Any late night business sessions with Zachary struck Melody as cause for alarm.

She needed to take advantage of the fact that both Zachary and Ed were going to be occupied elsewhere. What better chance could she hope for to sneak a look at the inside of the shed she'd discovered last night? She'd slipped a small flashlight into her pocket before leaving her room, hoping she might find a chance to go exploring. Well, here was her chance. She was just going to go for it, she decided.

The fact that she had a plan helped to keep her smiling and friendly for the rest of the meal. Just before they broke up for the night, Zachary leaned down and whispered to her, ignoring the fascinated glances of their table companions.

"I've so much enjoyed our conversation tonight. I thought the first time we met that you were going to be something very special in my life, Melody. Now I'm sure of it."

"I felt it, too," she said softly. She *really* hoped the bozo wasn't rethinking his attitude toward extramarital sex. For all her brave disclaimers to Nick, she wasn't sure just how easy it would be to fend Zachary off if he ever decided he was going to have sex with her.

She stared into his dark eyes, and realized anew how charismatically handsome he was. "From the time we met at Amelia's fund-raising event, I've felt a real spiritual connection between the two of us." She emphasized *spiritual* and hoped he would get the message.

"I wish we could spend some time together this evening, just the two of us." Zachary gave a sigh. "Sadly, duty calls."

Thank you, Jesus. "We have tomorrow," Melody said. She barely concealed her relief when Zachary nodded in agreement and got up to leave without saying anything more directly to her. He strode through the dining hall, smiling, nodding and waving to his fans. Once again, he was followed from the room by the five-member governing council—of which Ed Harris was not a member, Melody noticed.

She made her way out of the dining hall, taking care to speak to everyone she knew, and managing to convey the impression to each group of Soldiers that she was planning to spend the ninety-minutes before lights out with somebody else. The Soldiers didn't believe in solitude, and anybody standing alone was instantly invited to join some activity or another.

The sun was setting as she walked outside, tingeing the sky in a glorious rainbow of vermilion, purple and pink. She would have preferred to wait for darkness to explore the shed, but she didn't have that luxury. Yesterday she could plead ignorance as an excuse for wandering around the campus in the dark. Today she had no such excuse. She had to be back in her room before lights out or risk raising serious suspicions about her motives.

When she had been standing next to Zachary greeting the last stragglers arriving for dinner she'd noticed an overgrown footpath, probably dating from the time when the dining hall had been part of the motel. The section of the footpath that she had seen led in the direction of the target practice field and the storage shed she wanted to investigate, and there didn't seem to be any surveillance equipment anywhere along the route. Melody still worried about the pervasive cameras. Although Terri's daytime monitoring of the security system seemed somewhat haphazard, she knew that at night a guard was posted inside the White House. He would have nothing much to do except watch the monitors, and she wanted to avoid showing up on any of his screens.

Her best defense was to appear entirely open and above-board, Melody decided. She strolled around to the side of the building and was just about to step onto the path when she noticed Rachel Cranford lurking at the corner of the dining hall, clearly watching to see where Melody planned to go.

The poor kid probably thinks I've got an assignation with good ole Reverend Zach, Melody thought wryly. How in hell was she going to shake Rachel from her tail? She almost laughed out loud as she got the answer—a very simple one.

"Hi, Rachel!" she called, waving vigorously. "Want to join me in a little stroll? Do come!"

Rachel, with predictable teenage rudeness, instantly disappeared, making a feeble pretense that she hadn't seen or heard Melody. Melody grinned. Then, amusement fading to concentration, she set off down the path, keeping a close watch for anyone who might be following her.

Nobody seemed to be paying her any attention. She'd guessed correctly and the path ended up at the target field, at a point about fifty feet from the path she'd taken yesterday. She strolled along the perimeter fence until she reached the storage shed where she'd encountered Zachary and Ed Harris last night.

The storage shed measured roughly twelve feet by twelve, and although it appeared neglected, closer inspection revealed that the scuffs and dents were all superficial. Structurally the shed was more than sound, Melody concluded. There was also a stack of chopped firewood to one side, not exactly concealing a near-new heating and cooling unit, but certainly making it less visible at first glance. There were no windows, but the fancy air-conditioning unit suggested the interior of the shed would be climate-controlled.

A night breeze rattled the life-sized targets on the other

side of the field, attracting her attention. Melody stared at them, her brow furrowing in thought. Until now, she could claim that she'd simply been taking a stroll and admiring the countryside before bedtime. The moment she attempted to enter the shed, her excuses would vanish. Was it worth compromising her acceptance by the Soldiers, which so far seemed pretty complete, for the sake of peeking inside the shed and possibly finding nothing more than a collection of canned goods, or sleeping quarters for Ed Harris?

She took one last, careful look around the exterior of the shed. She couldn't see any surveillance equipment, but that might simply mean that it was well hidden.

All the better to trap you with, my dear.

She needed to stop scaring herself half to death. Melody drew in a deep breath, tucked her skirt up, and climbed over the gate. Clinging to the pretense, however fragile, that she was simply an innocent visitor, she knocked on the shed door, her hand curling around the small flashlight that was going to provide her excuse. She planned to tell Ed Harris, should he by chance be there instead of with Zachary, that she believed she'd seen him drop it at dinner tonight.

There was no answer to her knocks. She listened, straining to pick up the slightest electronic whir that would suggest surveillance equipment, or some other electronic booby trap, springing into action, but she heard nothing. She turned the handle and the shed door swung inward with no resistance. Anywhere else, that would have suggested the shed contained nothing incriminating. In White Falls, absence of locks didn't necessarily indicate absence of secrets.

Melody's heart pounded. She was dry-mouthed with fear, she realized, swallowing to moisten her throat. It took a real effort of will to step over the threshold into the nearly pitch-black space beyond.

She switched on the flashlight, half expecting to find herself confronting an armed guard. Instead her suspicion that she might find nothing but canned goods turned out to be close to the mark. The flashlight beam revealed racks of paint cans, rollers, brushes and drop cloths, along with a few heavy-duty industrial cleaning fluids. So much for her hope of finding stacks of illegal weapons, or something that might provide a clue as to whether the Soldiers' military training was merely neurotic self-defense or something more threatening.

Melody switched off the flashlight and turned to leave, her heartbeat still not quite slowed to normal. Something about this harmless scene didn't reassure her as much as it should. What was setting off her internal alarms?

She had one foot out the door before the answer came to her: the interior of the shed was too small for the exterior, and the shape was different, too. With proper lighting, she'd have noticed the discrepancy sooner. The exterior was a square, approximately twelve by twelve. This internal storage room was a rectangle. She guesstimated its dimensions as twelve by nine. What had happened to the missing three feet?

Obviously there was a fake wall concealing a long, narrow closet. Which set of shelving was most likely to cover the entrance? The one stacked with drop cloths and cleaning rags, she decided. If they fell as the hidden door swung out, or in, or whatever, they would cause least commotion.

Melody dragged a can of paint across to those shelves and stood on it, so that she could reach the point where the wall and ceiling met. She rapped on the wall, which sounded faintly hollow—just enough to encourage the idea that she might find a closet hidden behind the shelves.

The laminate that supported the shelves was designed to look like wood paneling. Not an extraordinary choice for a storage room, but now that she was actively looking for a concealed doorway, it occurred to Melody that the vertical grooves in the panels made for a convenient way to conceal the seam of an opening. The paneling was covered with nicks, scratches and blotches of greasy dirt—a great way to disguise the fingerprints that would come from frequent pressing in the same spot to activate a spring lock.

Melody ran her flashlight over the wall, starting at the top and searching inch by inch for the smudge marks most likely to mark the presence of a concealed lock. She had reached the third shelf from the top when she saw a smear that looked to her as if it could have been caused by multiple fingers applying pressure at that precise spot. She pressed a few times in that general area, hopes high, but nothing happened. Muttering curses under her breath, she carried on searching and pressing.

The knowledge that Ed Harris might return at any moment added spice to her simmering state of fear. While the FBI agents had been able to leave the campus unharmed, she guessed they owed their easy escape to the fact that they hadn't discovered anything incriminating. By contrast, Jodie Evanderhaus had taped a film of an inflammatory sermon of Zachary's and a week later she had been dead. Too much information about the inner workings of the Soldiers of Jordan seemed to prove fatal to a person's health.

Melody's first exercise for Unit One, even before she knew she was being recruited by the organization, had been to escape from a featureless, enclosed space with no visible doors or windows. At the time of the exercise, she had no way of knowing that she hadn't fallen into the hands of thieves and murderers. Despite that, she had been almost more angry than scared as she attempted to figure a way out of that room. Because she'd known at some gut level that Nick wasn't going to harm her? How odd if that was the case. When she first met Nick, there had been a dead body on the floor at his feet, and he was both armed and masked, which surely provided reasons enough for her to be terrified. Zachary, by contrast, had never done anything more threatening than smile too much, and yet she kept waiting for something truly dreadful to happen, and by his direct orders, too.

Melody was more than halfway down the wall when she found another promising smudge pattern that suggested multiple fingerprints. She pressed in the precise center of the splodge and felt the click of a spring lock releasing beneath her fingers. The wall cracked open along a groove in the paneling. Expelling her breath in a triumphant hiss, she moved the can of paint so that it propped open the door. She didn't want to go into the secret room and discover that it was booby-trapped to close behind her.

She stepped over the paint can and squeezed into the long, narrow room. The pale beam of her flashlight illuminated the back of a metal chair, and a shelf that served both as a desk and as the support for a computer, along with a maze of heavy-duty electronic wiring. She had found the monitoring station for the secret surveillance equipment, Melody realized, moving her flashlight in a small arc. A corner shelf held a tape deck that presumably recorded whatever came from the voice-activated bugs scattered in various strategic locations around campus. A printed list indicated the locations of all the bugs, with numbers assigned to each station. In addition, there were five monitors stacked on a shelf at what would be eye-level for an operative seated at the computer desk. One monitor showed Zachary's office. A second showed the darkened patio where she and Zachary had eaten their picnic lunch. From the angle of the patio that was visible, she assumed the camera was mounted under the eaves of the roof, behind and above where she'd been seated. Thank goodness she hadn't decided to climb over the patio fence and break into his office tonight or she'd already be toast.

A third screen displayed the empty guest room that had been assigned as her room, and the fourth screen showed her bathroom. She stared at that screen in silent fury. The slimey bastards had even invaded that last normal refuge of privacy. If she'd called Nick from the bathroom last night, her cover would have been blown within a couple of hours of arriving in White Falls. No wonder both the FBI agents had been unmasked so easily.

From the section of bathtub displayed on the screen, Melody concluded that the surveillance equipment must be hidden inside the fluorescent fixture above the mirror. She mentally reviewed her actions when she'd slipped Bob Spinard's communication device into her pocket both yesterday and today. She'd been careful, but since she hadn't known the location of the camera, she hadn't known exactly what to hide. She couldn't decide whether her movements would have gone unobserved, or whether whoever reviewed the tapes had seen her slip her compact into her pocket and had simply assumed she was a woman who chose never to leave her room without makeup. Either way, judging from Zachary's attitude, it seemed that her motives in coming to White Falls weren't being questioned, at least for the moment.

The idea of Zachary or Ed Harris watching her in the bathroom left Melody shaking with anger. Now that she knew she was being observed, she was tempted to dance naked in the shower, or fake a self-induced orgasm just to give them something shocking to drool over.

The final monitor displayed a room stockpiled with enough arms and munitions to outfit a company shipping out for combat duties in Iraq. There were M9s, the standard sidearm of the US military; a selection of Glocks, a few M16s and an entire rack of AK-47s along with sufficient ammunition to sustain at least a mini war. In addition, there were four top-of-the-line Dragunov sniper rifles, outfitted with PSO-1 scopes and infrared technology that enabled the shooter to "see" the outline of the target in darkness. The carton of ammo alongside the Dragunovs suggested that the Soldiers of Jordan planned to use incendiary, armor-piercing bullets on some unlucky target.

The fact that there were four sniper rifles and that she had seen four Soldiers pounding through a training run earlier this afternoon struck Melody as an ominous coincidence, or more likely no coincidence at all. It wasn't much of a leap to conclude that four of the most physically able Soldiers were training for an assassination attempt. Perhaps the Soldiers were preparing to invade a mosque, shoot up the congregation, and then send in their elite team to take aim at some important Islamic leader?

The major flaw in that scenario seemed to be that the Soldiers would inevitably be identified as the culprits, and nothing Melody had observed since she arrived in White Falls suggested that the Soldiers were expecting to spend the rest of their lives in a federal prison. Everyone was working hard to build a viable commercial enterprise with their handicrafts, and poor Lisa couldn't even marry her George because Zachary was so intent on not breaking any laws. Most of the people she'd met in White Falls struck Melody as dedicated to the ideal of creating a viable community right here on earth, unlike other cults, where the leader prepared his congregation to die in a blaze of bullet-driven glory. However, the stockpile of weapons and the paramilitary training for the men suggested that—at a minimum—the Soldiers had a paranoid fear of being attacked and were willing to defend themselves with force if they felt threatened. Violence stewed and bubbled beneath the peaceful surface of White Falls.

She was going back and forth without ending up anywhere useful, Melody decided. Time to return her attention to the strictly practical. She searched the images on the computer screen to see if she could spot any clue as to where the cache of weapons might be hidden. Unfortunately the room was devoid of any identifying features. Based on the evidence of this shed, a good guess might be that there was some room-within-a-room in another storage shed, or even somewhere as trafficked as the men's dorm. The possibilities were regrettably endless and she couldn't afford to hang around any longer. Zachary had implied that the business he and Ed needed to deal with wouldn't take too long, and either one of them could return here at any moment.

With a final glance to register as many details of the weapons stockpile as she could, Melody eased out of the closet. She closed the section of wall behind her and carefully removed all trace of her incriminating presence in the shed. She made it back to her room without seeing anyone, and undressed for bed, fighting the urge to stick out her tongue at the hidden cameras. Bastards.

Nick would be here tomorrow. Melody realized she was smiling. She wouldn't have believed two weeks ago that she could be looking forward to his arrival with such heart-thumping eagerness.

Seventeen

Nick drew his rented Toyota Camry to a halt outside the electronic gate that barred the entrance to the Soldiers of Jordan campus. He was planning to play the role of Nikolai Anwar, temperamental Russian Mafioso, to the hilt, and the car didn't exactly fit Nikolai's dashing image. It was, however, as close as the rental companies at Boise Airport could come to his request for a Jaguar XKR or a Mercedes sports coupe.

A woman's voice spoke over the intercom. "This is Terri. Can I help you?"

"I wish to come in. Please open the gate."

"May I ask your business, sir?"

"I require to speak with Melody Beecham."

"Oh. Er...what's your name, please?"

"Nikolai Anwar."

"Er...one moment."

At least two minutes passed before the voice returned to the intercom. "Melody says that she has nothing to say to you Mr....um...Anwar."

"Open the gate," he said. "Or I will drive through it.

Whether Melody realizes it or not, she has a great deal to say to me. I will wait one minute for you to deliver my message to Melody, and then I am driving in. If the barrier is open, it will be more convenient for all of us. But if it remains shut, believe me, it will not keep me out."

There were risks to taking such an aggressive approach, but Nick had discussed various possible scenarios with Mac and they'd concluded that outrageous behavior on his part posed the least threat to Melody's continued acceptance by the Soldiers.

Nick waited while fifty-two seconds ticked away before the barrier swung open. Relieved that he'd avoided a confrontation before he even got onto the campus, he drove fast up the driveway, coming to a deliberately screeching halt outside the White House.

Zachary Wharton stood on the threshold of the admin building, his expression forbidding. Two large men flanked him on either side, reminding him vaguely of grizzly bears protecting their den. The men probably weren't carrying, Nick decided after a rapid assessment. There were no signs of a bulge on their upper torsos, and neither man looked agile enough to whip a revolver out of a leg holster. Still, they were undoubtedly capable of punching most unwanted visitors into unconsciousness with their bare hands. They might not be super fit, but they sure as hell were brawny.

Battle lines were being drawn early, Nick thought. Good. He got out of the car, aviator sunglasses dangling from his fingers. Feigning total indifference to the presence of Zachary and the accompanying guards, he gave the trio a brief, all-encompassing nod and strode past them.

As he expected, he was immediately seized by the two grizzlies, who held him in a straightforward but effective arm-lock. He allowed himself to be taken without a struggle, although he'd seen their move coming and could have evaded it without much difficulty. They turned him around, taking care not to loosen their hold, so that he was facing Zachary Wharton again.

Zachary's expression was smug, and his voice was suavely polite. "I am the Reverend Zachary Wharton, leader of the Soldiers of Jordan, and you are trespassing on private property, Mr. Anwar."

"Ask me if I give a damn. I wish to speak to my fiancée."

"Your fiancée? Melody Beecham is your fiancée?" Zachary's voice lost some of its cool and his expression switched from smug to astonished.

"You look surprised, Reverend. Could it be that Melody forgot to mention the small fact that she and I are engaged to be married?"

You had to give the guy points for swift recovery. Zachary's voice was polished to gleaming smoothness when he spoke again. "Whatever commitments Melody might have made to you in the past, obviously she now considers them at an end. No doubt the fact that she discovered you slaking your lust with Jacyntha Ramon caused her decision."

Slaking his lust? Oh, boy. Nick had heard the sound of soft footsteps and knew Melody was standing behind him, listening to everything that was being said. He was surprised at how badly he wanted to deny that he and Jacyntha had ever had sex together. But it would harm Melody's position to imply that their split had been caused by a misunderstanding, rather than by his bad behavior, so he merely gave an impatient shake of his head.

"Jacyntha Ramon is irrelevant," he said. "I wish to speak privately with Melody, and—trust me on this—I do not plan to leave White Falls until I have done so."

Melody must have decided the confrontation had gone on long enough to make the point that she was an unwilling collaborator. She spoke from behind his back. "Thank you, Reverend Zachary, for trying to save me unpleasantness, but perhaps I'd better speak to Nikolai and get it over with."

Nick twisted around to look at her. Melody stood in the entrance to the White House, three women lurking self-consciously behind her. Presumably this was Terri, Lisa and the pregnant Jennifer. With total lack of success, all three women tried to pretend they weren't avidly drinking in every last detail of what was going on.

Melody looked even more magnificent than usual. The afternoon sun caught the gold in her hair, turning it to white flame. It was a mere five days since Nick had last seen her, but as always after a separation, however brief, the sheer beauty of her face and the perfection of her body ripped the breath out of his lungs. Two days ago he'd told her that he missed her and she had changed the subject. Yesterday he'd told her that he loved her and she had hung up on him. A knot of panic twisted his gut as he again considered the terrible possibility that he might have screwed up their relationship to the point that it was irredeemable.

No trace of welcome warmed Melody's voice when she spoke to him. He reminded himself that she was acting. He hoped like hell she was acting. "Why have you come here, Nikolai?"

He gave the best imitation of a debonair shrug that he could manage with the two grizzly bears still clutching his arms. "I have come to speak with you. With my fiancée, in case you have forgotten what we are to each other. The question, surely, is what are you doing here, in this place where I am not even welcome?"

Melody looked at him with a mixture of scorn and pity. Nick wished he could be sure the emotions she was portraying with such skill weren't simply reflections of what she was truly feeling.

"You couldn't even be faithful to me before we were married, Nikolai, and yet you're still trying to claim we're engaged? I want a husband who'll be a trustworthy friend and a loving father to our children. It hurt when I found you with Jacyntha Ramon, but I've realized over the past few days that your insulting behavior was a blessing in disguise. It meant that I found out before it was too late that you aren't the man to fulfill either of those roles."

Since the day he saw his parents and sister blown up in front of his eyes, Nick had never been able to tolerate the idea of becoming a father. Until now, his opinion had always been that Fate was at best capricious and at worst downright cruel. Better never to have children, he had always thought, than to risk having them snatched from you in some wanton act of violence. The middle of a high stakes mission was an inconvenient time to discover that he quite badly wanted to become the father of any children Melody might choose to have.

"Nevertheless, I need to speak with you," he said, with all of Nikolai's arrogance, and none of Nick's doubts. "There are matters we must discuss. Financial matters, if nothing else. You owe me a large sum of money."

Melody looked past him, as if seeking counsel from Zachary. "Reverend Zachary, it's true. I do owe Nikolai some money. Perhaps if I could talk to him for a few minutes in private, it would be the quickest way for the two of us to resolve things? I'm really sorry that we've already disrupted everyone's work this afternoon with this unpleasant confrontation."

"My dear, it would be best not to speak with this man. Turn the matter over to your lawyer—"

"Like hell," Nick said. "Melody, one way or another, you're going to have to deal with me on this. Do you really want to call in lawyers, make depositions, waste days of our time? Wouldn't it be easier just to talk to me, for Christ's sake?"

Zachary looked pained at the blasphemy, but continued to address his remarks only to Melody. "If you feel you must speak with Mr. Anwar, I'd be happy to act as mediator. You could have your discussion in my office, where I would be available to offer you guidance whenever you might need it. Remember, I'm a lawyer myself and would know how to protect your interests."

"I do not care if you are a justice of the United States Supreme Court," Nick said quickly. "Melody, tell this man that we will not discuss our private financial concerns with him in the same room." He made a rapid mental review of his options if Zachary refused to allow them to speak alone. Could he kidnap Melody from right under the noses of the grizzly bears? Toss her into his car and just drive off? Yes, he could. The question was whether Melody would then be allowed back on campus.

As Zachary had done, Melody ignored him. "Thank you, Reverend, for making such a generous offer. But after only a few days here, I know how valuable every moment of your time is. Perhaps Nikolai and I could sit on the bench outside the dining hall while we make arrangements for me to repay the money I owe him? Once that debt's paid, our relationship would be over in every possible way."

Nick held his breath while Zachary considered Melody's suggestion. After a nerve-racking few seconds, Zachary nodded. "That seems a satisfactory compromise—"

"Then would you instruct your goons to let go of my arms?" Nikolai demanded, anxious not to give Zachary time to talk himself out of his permission.

A flicker of irritation crossed Zachary's handsome features. "The gentleman restraining you aren't goons, Mr. Anwar. They're simply two hardworking members of our community, dedicated to preserving its peaceful security from invasion by outsiders who don't share our values."

"How you view their job description depends on whether or not it is your arms they are holding in a deadlock," Nick said. "From where I stand, they are goons."

"You can let him go," Zachary said, sounding wearily patient with Nick's rudeness.

The men released him at once and Nick rubbed his arms, helping his circulation return to peak efficiency so that if he needed to act fast and with precision he could.

"The dining hall is over there," Melody said, pointing to a building about fifty yards away from the White House. She started to walk toward it, and he followed, not risking touching her in case it provoked second thoughts from Zachary or the grizzlies. He didn't look back, but he could feel six pairs of eyes fixed on him, and he was sure all six observers were simply waiting for an excuse to toss him off campus.

They made it to the dining hall without being stopped. Melody sat down on the bench, spreading out the folds of her full skirt. She very discreetly angled her index finger to point toward a pocket in the left side-seam of her skirt. Nick sat down on that side. Zachary and the women went back inside the White House, but the two guards remained posted at the door, making no bones about the fact that they were keeping Melody and Nick under close observation.

"Have you gone crazy?" Nick demanded, keeping to his

role until he was sure they weren't being overheard. "What are you doing living in this totally weird place, Melody?"

"These people are becoming my friends. They believe in honesty and integrity and leading a simple life," she said, twisting slightly away from him. To the observers, it would seem that she was giving him the cold shoulder. In reality, she was making it easier for him to slip his hand into the pocket and extract the disk. "Naturally, you would describe that as weird."

"Tell me you are joking, Melody. Why do you believe that you wish to live a simple life? There is nothing about you that is simple. You are one of the most complex women I have ever met." He reached beneath the folds of her skirt and extracted the disk, slipping it swiftly into the pocket of the fashionably loose-fitting slacks that he had worn expressly to make the transfer of the disk easier.

"Nikolai, could we please limit this discussion to the issue of the money I owe you? I assume you're talking about the stock you gave me in your company as an engagement present."

Nick glared in the direction of the two guards. "This is crazy. I resent the fact that I cannot be alone and private with you. Why are we talking with those two men staring at us? For all I know, they're listening to every word we say…"

Melody gave the slightest inclination of her head to indicate that he was quite right and there was a chance their conversation was being recorded, bugged, or otherwise eavesdropped on.

"Don't be silly, Nikolai," she said, jumping to her feet as if talking to him made her too aggravated to sit still. "Why would Jason and Tom care about what you're saying to me?"

"I do not know. You tell me. And while you are explaining, enlighten me as to why it is not possible to place a phone call to you, or send an e-mail. What is this place, anyway? A prison?"

She swung away, convincingly infuriated. "For heaven's sake, Nikolai, you're impossible. Of course it's not a prison! I *choose* to be here. Why won't you understand? I'm changing my life for the better, giving it the sort of purpose I never had before." She stormed away from him, aiming for a stretch of lawn where, Nick assumed, she believed they could talk without risk of being overheard. He allowed her to get all the way to the center of the grassy area—insuring maximum privacy—before he caught up with her and grabbed her arm, swinging her around.

He raised an inquiring eyebrow and she tugged at his restraining hand, freeing herself with an angry shake for the benefit of the two watchers. "It's as safe as we can be," she murmured, keeping the back of her head toward the grizzlies. "I'm almost a hundred percent sure there's no surveillance here other than Jason and Tom."

He took her word for it, and cut to the chase. "Bob Spinard confirms the address on the blueprint Zachary was studying yesterday is for a mosque in Dearborn," he said. "In fact, it's the site of one of the largest mosques in the country, and has a reputation for being fairly liberal. The FBI considers it low-risk for infiltration by fundamentalists. However, a new young imam, Sheik Mahmoud al-Ghrassi, has recently arrived from Damascus and he's from a radical family with long associations to activist, anti-Western forms of Islam."

"Any chance that the sheik could be from the family that burned down Zachary's family business?" Melody asked.

"A good chance. The sheik's paternal grandfather was in the right place at the right time. There's absolutely no proof that the sheik's family was responsible, of course, but it gives us a working hypothesis as to Zachary's possible target, as well as a possible motive for selecting that target, which is more than we had to go on a couple of days ago. Bob Spinard is working up a full report on the mosque, including all special religious holidays that are upcoming. If the Soldiers are planning an attack, they might want to hit the mosque when there are more people than usual on the premises. As soon as Bob's report is ready, we'll notify the FBI and request action. In the meantime, we'll keep you informed about any even marginally relevant intel that Bob generates."

Melody nodded. "Good. Here's my news. I found the monitoring station for the secret surveillance equipment last night," she said. "This place is more wired than Langley. They even have a camera inside the showerhead in my bathroom."

Nick let loose a string of Russian, and Melody eyes lit up with laughter. "Yes, I agree. In fact, whatever you just said probably doesn't get close to my low opinion of the slime buckets."

He gazed into her eyes, missing her at that moment with an intensity piercing enough to rip through years of training. He just barely resisted the temptation to pull her into his arms and kiss her with all the pent-up regret and passion of the past lonely weeks. How in *hell* had he been crazy enough to think that Unit One was more important than his relationship with Melody?

She looked away for a moment and he knew she'd seen his desire. Unlike the Soldiers, she was incredibly perceptive, and attempting to disguise his feelings from her was almost impossible. She didn't comment, of course, just waited for a couple of seconds, then turned to face him again, carrying on their conversation as if the shared flash of sexual awareness had never happened.

"Judging by the surveillance equipment I found, the monitoring activities are split about fifty-fifty between defending key places against intruders and overseeing the activities of the Soldiers themselves. Obviously the folks in charge are especially suspicious of new recruits. With cause, from their point of view, given that they know the FBI has already tried to infiltrate at least two undercover agents. I'm assuming they installed the cameras in the guest room after Jodie Evanderhaus managed to deceive them."

"Makes sense," Nick agreed. "Jodie's reporting exposed their vulnerabilities to outside interference and they probably decided they weren't going to run the risk of penetration ever again. Where is the monitoring station located, by the way? We'll add that to the campus map that we're constructing."

"It's hidden in a storage shed near the edge of the target practice area. The shed seems to be filled with paint supplies, drop cloths, that sort of thing. I was about to leave when I realized the interior was a rectangle and the exterior was a square. Which immediately made me think there was most likely a fake wall hiding something more interesting than paint cans."

Melody made it all sound easy, but the sheriff's department had searched the entire campus and found nothing, just as the two FBI agents hadn't spotted the surveillance equipment in their room. The risks Melody was running sounded greater the more he heard. With difficulty, Nick refrained from pleading with her not to go out tonight, looking for more secrets. No point in wasting his breath.

"How many Soldiers do you think are aware of the existence of the secret monitoring equipment?" he asked.

She shook her head. "Wish I knew. Not all of them, I'm

fairly sure. Perhaps none of the women, since they're ex-cluded from the official decision-making process. There's a governing council of five men. Those five, and seven more, make up the twelve elders of the church."

"Do the elders really make the decisions, do you think? Or are they Zachary's stooges?"

"I've no idea how much Zachary really shares with the eld-ers, either in terms of information or power. My guess is not much, but that's based on no evidence except my gut in-stincts. There's a man here called Ed Harris, who isn't even one of the elders, let alone a member of the governing coun-cil. He's in charge of military training, in his forties, doesn't speak much, but my impression is that Ed spends more time with Zachary than anyone else."

"I'll transmit the Social Security numbers to Bob Spinard as soon as I'm in the car and I'll ask him to run a check on Ed Harris first thing. If you call me tonight, I'll let you know what Bob digs up on his first run-through of the numbers. On Ed and anyone else."

"Great. Because Ed Harris and three other men that I haven't identified as yet are intensively training for some-thing. Remember how I hung up on you yesterday?"

Did he remember? Was she joking? Nick cleared his throat. "Yes."

"I had to cut the connection because I heard people run-ning on the road near where I was hiding. Four men. All su-perbly fit, and all training really hard."

Melody had hung up yesterday because she'd been in dan-ger of discovery! She hadn't hung up because he told her he loved her. She probably hadn't even been on the phone when he made his earth-shattering confession. Nick's spirits took a giant leap up the ladder of happiness.

"You can't even guess who the other three men might be?" He managed to prevent his voice squeaking with relief. "Just their level of fitness ought to make them stand out from the crowd."

"Not in this community. Remember, every Soldier under fifty has paramilitary training for a couple of hours after breakfast, so they're all at a certain minimum level of fitness. Enough that I can't look across the room and pick out the three who are in really topnotch shape. Long-sleeved shirts and long pants conceal a lot, and I'm never going to see a man who isn't fully clothed. That makes it impossible to judge their true level of muscle development. I only recognized Ed Harris because I'd encountered him the previous night and studied his body build fairly closely."

"That's frustrating."

"Yes, especially since the final discovery I made at the monitoring station is that the Soldiers have a room stockpiled with arms and munitions, including four top-of-the-line Dragunovs, complete with scopes and infrared sighting equipment. Those four men aren't training in a vacuum, Nick. They have a specific goal."

Dragunovs were sniper rifles. The bastards must be planning to assassinate somebody, Nick thought grimly. That tied in with what they'd heard on the tapes Eleanor had given him. The big question was who they intended to kill. The new imam at the mosque on Oak Avenue? It seemed a distinct possibility, and certainly worth issuing a warning to the imam that he should beef up his personal security.

The FBI had assumed that if the Soldiers caused trouble, it would be along the lines of Waco. The Soldiers would barricade themselves on campus and fight back if any law enforcement officials attempted to penetrate their territory. That idea had presumably gained currency because of the emphasis placed by the Soldiers on paramilitary training for all the men. Based on the film of Zachary's sermon, with its violent anti-Muslim rhetoric, Unit One had extended that risk to include the likelihood that the Soldiers were training not just to defend, but also to launch a mass attack. But if Melody was right, and the Soldiers weren't a suicidal group, their hate might be more finely channeled. Perhaps their plan was to assassinate Imam al-Ghrassi and then find some way to blame another group, Nick speculated. God knew, relations between the various religious communities were tense enough that the assassination of the imam could let loose a flood of violence. And these days, violence against Muslims in the States could all too easily be the precursor of an attack from abroad by enraged Muslim fundamentalists. If Zachary had delusions of setting off Armageddon, the assassination of Imam al-Ghrassi might be the match he had chosen to ignite the flame.

"I'm going to stay in Boise for the next few days at least," Nick said, the closest he could come to begging Melody to limit the risks she was taking. "I'd stay closer to campus, but I'm afraid that if I stopped in any of the small towns near White Falls, word of a stranger in the area might filter back to Zachary. If you need me, I can be here in an hour."

"Undoubtedly trailing a useful police escort at those speeds," Melody said, laughing.

Nick could resist her—well, he could sort of resist her— when she was serious. When she laughed, it was beyond his level of endurance not to respond. "You can slap me when I'm done," he said, wrapping his arms around her and pulling her close against his chest. He kissed her long, and slow and hard, as if he had been damn near dying for the taste and feel of her. Which, of course, was pretty much the case.

Her mouth was warm and soft beneath his, and her body melded to him with the ease of familiarity, spiced by a tantalizing hint of the forbidden. Her lips parted, accepting his kiss, and then returning it. For a blissful few seconds, he turned off all his mental guards and allowed his senses to fill with awareness of everything that was Melody. But after a minute of sheer heaven, the realization of the danger he was precipitating forced his senses back on to alert. As soon as he tuned back into their surroundings, he realized heavy footsteps were pounding in their direction. Damn. No doubt the grizzlies were flying to Melody's rescue.

Regretfully, he released her. She looked satisfying dazed and more than a little aroused but, well-trained Unit One operative that she was, she remembered her role and swung her arm, aiming a slap at his face.

He caught her hand at the last minute and whirled her around, giving them a final few seconds of precious privacy. "I love you," he said.

Her eyes widened with shock, but she recovered quickly and turned around just in time to greet the grizzlies. "Thanks for coming to my rescue," she said to them, ignoring Nick. "I'm going back to work now. If Mr. Anwar comes to the campus again, will you be sure to let everyone know that I have no intention of seeing or speaking to him?"

"We'll do that for sure," one of the grizzlies said. "You can count on us, Melody."

"Thanks, Jason. I knew I could." Melody walked away without giving Nick another glance. He could almost see the scorn radiating from her in disapproving waves. But this time Nick didn't care, because he knew the scorn was simply part of an act. He'd felt how she reacted to his kiss, and the news was all good. Melody might have dismissed him from her life two weeks ago, but she sure as hell was missing him.

She was a stubborn woman, and might not want to admit the truth. But he was an even more stubborn man, and in love for the first time in his life. When this mission was over, Melody would discover that love plus stubborn made for a killer combination.

Eighteen

He was getting too old for this game, Mac reflected, chewing a handful of antacids as he waited for his espresso machine to deliver an oversized mug of coffee. The machine hissed to a halt and he sipped gloomily, reviewing the morning's list of worries.

So far nobody had sniffed the faintest whiff of David Ramsdell's trail. The lead that suggested Dave might have chartered a plane and headed south of the border had petered out early yesterday, with no way to conclude whether Dave was actually in Mexico, or hanging out up north and laughing his ass off at the incompetence of his former employers. That wasn't merely cause for alarm, it was cause for major frustration. Mac was going to see the treacherous bastard back behind bars if he had to stay on the job till he was a hundred.

Then there was Melody Beecham. She was at huge personal risk in Idaho and Jasper Fowles was breathing down his neck demanding reassurances about her safety that they both knew Mac couldn't deliver. Add to that the fact that Senator

Cranford called on a daily basis requesting progress reports, and you pretty much had a recipe guaranteed to make a fifty-nine-year-old man yearn for the boredom of retirement. Hell, there had even been moments over the past couple of weeks when he'd wondered if he might actually be able to work up some mild enthusiasm for the game of golf.

A quick knock at the closed door of his office was followed by the entry of Bob Spinard. Mac greeted the arrival of his Director of Intelligence with a sigh of relief. Bob never voluntarily tore himself away from his computer unless he had something substantial to report. Even better, insofar as Bob's droopy bloodhound features could ever be arranged to look excited, they looked that way now. Maybe some threads in the Soldiers of Jordan puzzle were finally beginning to unravel. Mac sure hoped so.

"Okay, so what's the latest?" he asked, making a ritual offer of coffee that Bob ritually refused.

"I've run the data on the Social Security numbers that Melody downloaded to disk and Nick transmitted to us yesterday evening. Except in one case, they're valid numbers."

Mac grunted his pleasure. "Means the Soldiers aren't deliberately setting Melody up. Her cover's still intact."

"Yep, it's good news. And using the Social Security numbers as a starting point, I've been able to generate biographical data for almost all the current membership. I've also identified addresses for half a dozen ex-members. Who all seem to be alive, by the way. I know Nick had raised a question as to whether the Soldiers might be killing off anyone who tried to quit the group." Bob extracted a sheet of paper from the file folder he was carrying. "Here are the addresses for the ex-members, if you want to send somebody to interview them. I guess it's worth seeing what extra info we can pick up from them."

"Mmm." Mac skimmed down the list. The ex-Soldiers, four men and two women, had relocated mainly to Michigan, not surprising since that was the state where Zachary had done most of his recruiting. Since all six appeared to be alive and going about their daily business, it suggested Zachary didn't care whom they talked to, which meant they most likely had nothing useful to tattle about. However, he needed to cover all the bases.

He dialed a number on his internal phone. "Tony," he said. "Report to my office in half an hour, please. You're about to take a trip to Michigan."

"What was the Social Security number that didn't check out?" Mac asked, putting down the phone and turning back to Bob.

"Interesting case," Bob said. From him that was the equivalent of somebody else dancing a jig of jubilation around the room. "The number passed through the screening just fine the first time around. It even passed through our second level of screening. Which means the number's good enough to fool the vast majority of people who'd ever run a check. And that's what I reported to Nick last night. However, on the third pass this morning, I found some incongruities. Followed them back, and bingo—I've hit pay dirt. The number was originally assigned to a kid called Edward Michael Harris, who was reported missing in 1973. Kid was never found, dead or alive, but there were dozens of sightings, none of which ever checked out, unfortunately for his family. Perhaps because people kept on reporting that they'd seen him, his parents refused to have him declared dead, so the number's still on the government books as an active account."

"Did you find any financial history associated with the number?" Mac asked.

Bob nodded. "Plenty. Apartment rentals, missed credit card payments, a car that was repossessed, the whole shebang. But the financial activity only started fifteen years ago and tapered right off about six months ago,"

"Suggesting what?"

"Suggesting somebody who needed a new identity fifteen years ago saw the potential in resuscitating Ed Harris," Bob said.

"And the absence of reports for the past six months?"

"Whoever was using the ID hasn't made any credit card purchases during that period, or rented an apartment, or maintained a bank account, or done anything else associated with daily living."

"Why not?" Mac demanded. "He'd been doing all those things for years. Why stop?"

Bob shrugged. "Well, nobody using Ed Harris's identification has died, or that would have been noted in the Social Security database and the account would have been closed. The most likely guess is that Ed's identity was being used by an illegal immigrant who left the country. He's not in jail, or I'd have found the record of his sentencing."

"So if Ed was originally brought back to life by an illegal immigrant who's now left the country, the Social Security number might have been up for sale again quite recently?"

"Yes. That's exactly how I figure it."

"Do any of the Eds have a driver's license?"

"Yep. Just one. Issued by New Jersey." Bob pulled a piece of paper out of the file he was carrying. "Here's a copy of the license photo, which was taken in 1995, and here's a computer-generated update as to how the guy in the photo might look now. Not all that much change. Ed was thirteen when he disappeared, so whoever was using the card had to be able to pass for thirty-five when the license was issued. And he'd be coming up on forty-five now. The descriptive details on the license aren't much help. Brown hair, brown eyes, five feet nine inches. That's exactly average height, so the guy wouldn't have stood out in a crowd. There's no screen on the communicator I made for Melody, so I guess there's no way to get a copy of the picture transmitted to her."

"Nick can describe the picture to her and see if it bears any similarity to the Ed Harris she knows," Mac suggested. "If the guy in White Falls is six feet, for example, we know he's not the man in the photo."

"I'm guessing the ID has changed hands more than once since 1996," Bob said. "No surprise if the Ed Harris in White Falls doesn't match the driver's license photo. He'll just turn out to be one in a long line of people taking advantage of the poor kid who disappeared."

"Bottom line," Mac clarified. "As of now, all we know for sure is that there's a man in White Falls who calls himself Ed Harris and he's either come back from the dead, or he isn't who he says he is."

"That's about it."

"Interesting stuff," Mac said. "Especially since Melody has reported that Zachary seems to spend more time alone with Ed Harris than with anyone else."

"Yeah. That's why I gave the number a third pass. Otherwise I might have been satisfied with two."

"Nah, not you." Mac swallowed the dregs of his coffee, ignoring the burning in his gut. "Good intel, Bob. You got any more hot stuff for me? You look like you're bustin' your buttons with whatever you're holdin' back."

"I don't know if it's hot stuff or a blind alley," Bob said. "But for sure it's a strange coincidence. Then again…"

It wasn't like Bob to beat around the bush. "Spit it out," Mac ordered.

"Okay, here it is. I automatically ran a check for military service records. It sometimes provides a useful extra perspective on a person's bio. Most of the Soldiers don't have military backgrounds, but five of them do. Dr. Harvey Leonard and his wife, Betty, both served in the navy. He was a doctor and she was a nurse and they got married while they were still in uniform. Thomas Clifford served in the air force right out of high school. He was assigned to McDill Air Force Base in Florida, working as a mechanic. No combat missions, but a decent record with an honorable discharge at the end. He's twenty-nine now, and has been with the Soldiers eighteen months. There's a similar record for William Kowalski—"

"Great. And the significance of this is…?"

"I've saved the best till last." Bob drew in a deep breath, his grooved cheeks flushing with suppressed excitement. "The best is a man called Richard Mitchell. He and Ed Harris—whoever Ed Harris really is—are the most recent recruits to the Soldiers of Jordan. Turns out they were baptized together, barely a week before Melody arrived on campus—"

"Surprising," Mac commented. "Given that Melody is reporting that Zachary and Ed Harris appear to work so closely together."

"Yep, it's very surprising. You'd have expected Ed to be an old-timer the way Melody described his position, but he's the opposite. Anyway, back to Richard Mitchell's military service. He's forty-two and he served for seven years with the army's special forces unit. The 75th Rangers, to be precise. He was awarded two purple hearts for battlefield wounds he sustained during covert combat ops conducted in partnership with CIA personnel. The ops were in Afghanistan, back in the eighties when the Soviets were trying to stop the Taliban taking over the government and we were secretly helping the Taliban to resist. Richard got a medical discharge in 1989, but that seems to have been a fudge. The records don't tell much, just a hint here and there, but it's pretty clear that the medical discharge was a payoff from the army brass for past bravery. The real reason for his dismissal was something quite different."

"Failure to follow orders?" Mac guessed. "That's the trouble with Special Forces. Recruits have to be self-starters, but they can't take themselves too far out on a limb."

"Yeah, that's what I get from reading between the lines. He attacked a village without authorization and killed a bunch of little kids instead of the Soviet troops he thought were hanging out there. But that's not the important point." Bob actually grinned, a huge, jowl-shaking grin. "Richard served with the 75th Army Rangers. Ask me which company he served in."

Mac suddenly understood. He went ice cold. "Which one?" He bit the words out through pinched lips.

"Richard Mitchell was in Delta Company." Bob's grin vanished, replaced by a ferocious scowl. "Now ask me the name of the lieutenant in charge of Richard's platoon."

"Who?"

"David Ramsdell, later promoted to captain of Delta Company." Bob sank back on the chair and let out his breath in a huge gushing sigh, his bombshell delivered.

The reverberations of what he'd just heard ripped through Mac with a force that drove out every other sensation. He didn't respond, but his thoughts raced into automatic overdrive. Dave Ramsdell had escaped from Leavenworth more than three weeks ago. Almost simultaneously, Senator Cranford requested assistance in uncovering a plot that he claimed was centered on the Soldiers of Jordan campus. Ten days ago, Ed Harris and Richard Mitchell arrived in White Falls and were immediately baptized. Richard Mitchell had served in the army's Ranger regiment with Dave Ramsdell.

Mac's mind went blank again, stopped by that final stunning fact. He really was getting too old for this, he thought wearily when his brain function kicked in again. "Coincidences happen all the time," he said.

"Yeah, they do."

Mac scratched his chest. His skin itched all over from tension. "Okay, which one of us is going to say it first?"

"I will," Bob said. "Ed Harris might be a cover name for Dave Ramsdell. I think Dave might be hanging out with the Soldiers of Jordan."

Mac swallowed over the huge lump that had lodged in his throat, making it difficult to breathe. "If Ed Harris and Dave Ramsdell are one and the same person, he knows exactly who Melody is and who she works for."

"Holy shit." Bob turned white. "Jesus, Mac, I hadn't thought of that. Where the hell did I park my brains?"

"You were blown away by the discovery that Mitchell had served with Dave Ramsdell. Not surprising that you got stuck at that point."

"Backtracking here." Bob frowned. "Maybe we've both built too much on the simple coincidence that Richard Mitchell served under Dave Ramsdell. After all, if Ed Harris is really Dave Ramsdell, why hasn't he outed Melody? Everyone agrees that Ed has Zachary's ear. So the moment Melody arrived on campus, why didn't he go to Zachary and warn him that she was a government agent?"

Mac shrugged. "That's easy. Because it didn't fit with his plans. Whatever they are."

"But think of the risk he's running! Melody might recognize him at any minute. He's never safe while she's around." Bob's comments tumbled over each other as he tried to clarify his thoughts. "Dave must have guessed that Melody is in White Falls on a mission for Unit One, and he has enough firsthand experience to know that she's competent and dedicated. In other words, she's guaranteed to cause him a lot of trouble. So why did he allow her to get a job at the heart of the Soldiers of Jordan operation? The admin building is the one place on campus where she can download information like the Social Security numbers of all the Soldiers. Information that's going to point us straight to Ed Harris's fake ID and Richard Mitchell's army service with Dave Ramsdell. In other words, sooner or later she's going to generate intel that leads straight back to Dave. Why didn't he out her before she could point the finger at him?"

Those were good questions. Mac disciplined himself to reason as Chief of Unit One, and not as the man who might have sent Melody Beecham into a situation of impossible danger. "Dave's a risk-taker," he said. "He gets off on taking chances. When he was a Unit One field operative, his mission profiles were brilliant, but they were always more dangerous than they needed to be."

Bob shook his head. "The fact that Melody hasn't been outed makes me believe that Ed Harris is somebody else altogether. Jeez, Mac, it can't be Dave. For one thing, Dave is familiar with the checking and screening systems I utilize here, and he'd never buy an ID that's relatively easy for me to identify as a fake. Dave can't possibly want us to know that he's sitting in the middle of the Soldiers of Jordan campus—"

Mac's stomach lurched with the sudden, sickening conviction that they'd finally hit on the truth of what Dave was planning. "Yes, he does. That's exactly what the son of a bitch wants. He wants us to know he's in White Falls."

"He just escaped from military prison. Now he wants us to recapture him?" Bob sounded justifiably confused.

"No, of course not, but he wants us to send the FBI into White Falls. Which will immediately trigger a full-scale explosion of the paranoia Zachary's been drumming into the Soldiers of Jordan for the past two years. Before you know it, there will be a confrontation going on between the Bureau and the Soldiers—a confrontation that will make Waco look like a picnic at the rec center."

"If for no other reason than that Dave will fan the flames," Bob muttered.

"You've got it. And Unit One will be right in the middle of it," Mac said grimly. "You can bet that Dave will make sure there are dead bodies, and when the Bureau needs a scapegoat, they'll blame us. They can't name us in public, of course, but inside the administration, Unit One will take the fall. If we're not shut down, they'll decimate our effectiveness by clearing out the leadership and cutting our budget back to bare bones. There are plenty of people in the government who think that the money given to us would be better spent on antiterrorism. Fighting corruption in high places cuts a bit too close to the bone for some of the people who have to vote for us."

"People like Senator Cranford." Bob patted his pocket protector, as if for comfort. "What's the senator's role in all this? Was he setting us up all along?"

"I don't know. I'm going to listen again to the tapes Eleanor Cranford gave to Nick. Maybe they'll shed some light now we're listening to them from a different perspective." Mac rubbed his brow and realized his hands were shaking. If he sent in troops to arrest Ed Harris, there would be a pitched battle. If he didn't send in troops, he was quite sure that Ed would find a way to provoke a confrontation—probably by killing Melody.

"Senator Cranford's daughter is in White Falls," Bob said. "Okay, the guy has all the moral purity of month-old garbage, but I can't believe he'd risk the life of his own daughter just to wreak vengeance on Unit One."

"Rachel may not be at risk," Mac said. "If Cranford is working in alliance with Dave Ramsdell, he's probably done a deal whereby Rachel gets taken off campus before the shooting starts."

Bob stared at his hands in melancholy silence and Mac turned away, needing to clear his head. Thank God Jasper was at headquarters today. He would talk to Jasper right away, Mac decided. The Director of Unit One usually left operational details entirely to Mac, but on the rare occasions when Mac was at his wit's end, Jasper's cool intelligence invariably helped to bring him back on track, or open a fresh perspective. He hoped to God this was another occasion when dialogue with Jasper would work its magic.

"Set up a meeting in the command center for thirty minutes from now," Mac said. "I want Tony, Sam and Alec to be there." He named the three most senior field operatives who reported to Nick. "You, too, of course, Bob. And arrange a satellite link so that Nick can take full part in the meeting. I don't know how much time we have before the final countdown to disaster, but I suspect not much. Let's haul some ass here."

Bob stood up, clearly relieved to have been assigned a specific task. "I'm on it, Mac. See you in thirty minutes."

Nineteen

At lunch time, Melody noticed that Rachel Cranford wasn't in the dining hall. "Is Rachel sick?" she asked Lisa. "I thought I saw the two of you at the same table this morning at breakfast."

Lisa glanced around the dining hall, clearly surprised when she couldn't spot Rachel. "She didn't say anything about not feeling well. Oh, my, I hope nothing's wrong. We should ask Suzanne Bluhm what's up. Rachel works with her in housekeeping."

Melody managed to catch up with Suzanne as the Soldiers streamed out of the dining hall, on their way back to their afternoon's chores. "Hi, Suzanne. I don't believe we've met. I'm Melody Beecham. Lisa told me that Rachel works with you. Do you know if she's feeling okay? I didn't see her at lunch today."

"Rachel's gone," Suzanne said shortly.

"Gone?" For a heart-stopping moment, Melody wondered if *gone* was a Soldier euphemism for *dead*.

"She went back to Washington," Suzanne clarified.

"But why? What happened? She was so happy here." For once Melody could allow her astonishment to show. Two nights ago, Rachel had sworn there was no way to persuade her to leave White Falls. What had caused her to change her mind?

"I don't know why she left," Suzanne snapped. "I just know she's gone, and I've got nobody to help me with the ironing. 'Scuse me, please. I've got a lot of wash to get through this afternoon." Recalling that Soldiers were supposed to be cheerful at all times, she produced a smile. "Enjoy the rest of your day."

Melody decided to risk asking Zachary for more information about Rachel's departure. She was no doubt breaking a dozen unwritten rules by approaching him, but she didn't care. She badly needed reassurance that Rachel was still alive.

"I just noticed Rachel Cranford wasn't at lunch," she said, catching up with Zachary when they were still a hundred yards or so from the entrance to the White House. "Suzanne Bluhm says she's left White Falls and gone back to Washington."

"Yes, that's quite true." Zachary gave a mournful smile. "Sadly, Rachel decided that she didn't have the strength of character to stay with us here in White Falls."

"But she seemed so devoted to the program. What made her change her mind?"

"I'm sure she did her best," Zachary replied smoothly. "But we've seen this sort of sad failure before. Young adults like Rachel have an especially difficult time submitting to a life where the emphasis is on discipline and service, not pleasure and self-gratification. Perhaps Rachel will experience a burst of spiritual growth and come back to us."

"I wish I could have seen her to say goodbye."

"In fact, Rachel said the same thing about you. However, we've found from experience that when somebody decides to leave White Falls, it's better not to permit any goodbyes, or to make any official announcements. It's too unsettling for the remaining members of our community."

In view of Rachel's previous hostility, it was odd that she'd wanted to say goodbye, Melody reflected, following Zachary into the White House. Or perhaps Zachary was simply putting words into her mouth in order to cut off any more inquiries. She was about to return to her workstation when Ed Harris entered the building.

"I need a word with you, Reverend."

"Come into my office." Zachary held open the door and Ed walked past the four women without so much as a nod. Zachary closed the door.

"Ed isn't very friendly, is he?" Melody said.

"He'll warm up after a while," Terri replied, already at work on her baby blanket. "He's new here, you know. He and Rick Mitchell were baptized just a couple of weeks ago. Before that, they'd been working in the drug rehab center in Detroit."

Judging by the amount of time Ed and Zachary spent together, Melody would have expected to hear that Ed was one of the oldest members of the Soldiers of Jordan. "Ed and Reverend Zachary seem close," she said.

"They're working really hard to expand the drug rehab programs we sponsor." Terri's fingers hooked at lightning speed. She seemed to feel no curiosity as to why a drug program in Detroit would require Ed—presumably no longer in charge of the program—to consult at such frequent intervals with Zachary. In fact, Melody reflected, if there was one characteristic all the Soldiers of Jordan had in common, it was their almost willful lack of curiosity about what they were told. In an uncertain world, they longed for certainty and moral absolutes, and Zachary provided the certainty they craved—provided they never allowed themselves to ask questions.

"We're all very proud of the work we Soldiers do to help kids with drug problems," Jennifer interjected, massaging the side of her belly.

"That's how I first met Reverend Zachary," Melody said. "I attended one of his fund-raisers for drug rehab programs in New York City."

Terri asked a question about the fund-raiser and Melody answered mechanically. It had just occurred to her that the tiny window in the restroom overlooked Zachary's private courtyard. If he and Ed had gone out onto the patio, she might be able to hear what they were saying. Anything at all that she could overhear would give her more idea what their relationship was than she had right now, and there was almost no risk attached to the attempt to eavesdrop.

"I'll be right back," she murmured to Terri and walked quickly into the rest room.

She climbed up onto the toilet and slid open the small window, offering a silent word of thanks to Jason and his maintenance crew, who did such a fabulous job of keeping hinges oiled and windows gliding smoothly. Immediately she heard the blurred murmur of voices.

She kept her head below the level of the window, afraid that the mere act of looking out might send subliminal vibes that attracted the attention of the speakers. Zachary must be seated at the wrought-iron table with his back directed toward her. She could recognize his voice, but he was talking softly and she couldn't quite distinguish his words. Ed was probably facing her, because she could hear his reply without too much difficulty.

"I've been in contact with Senator Cranford," Ed said. "Rachel is safely en route to D.C. She's expected to land around four this afternoon."

The murmur of Zachary's voice was frustratingly indistinct. Melody could pick out only random words. *The senator...angry...inquiries.*

"I gave the senator a false name, of course," Ed said, sounding impatient. "Cranford isn't going to cause any trouble, but if he does send in the authorities, you have two hundred witnesses ready to swear that Rachel's stay here was entirely voluntary."

Most of what Zachary said next was inaudible. Despite the intensity of her focus, Melody heard only random words. *Detroit.....timetable....investigation...suspicion.*

"Bashy Alassan will be arriving in Detroit tomorrow afternoon," Ed said. Melody wasn't sure she had heard the name correctly. "His first meeting with Johnston Yates is scheduled for Sunday morning at ten-thirty."

Johnston Yates. Melody had barely allowed herself to think about her biological father since arriving in White Falls and Ed's mention of his name shocked her so much that she completely missed whatever Zachary said next. The Soldiers of Jordan seemed unimaginably far removed from the concerns of the former vice president. But Johnston Yates had been a partner with Senator Cranford in the Bonita project. Were the two of them working together again on a plan to bring down Unit One? The possibility that her newly-identified biological father might be dabbling in yet another illegal project sickened her. She'd so hoped that Johnston's involvement with the Bonita project had been a consequence of bad judgment, not a symptom of criminal intent.

"Rick and I leave this evening," Ed said. Melody realized that while she'd been scrambling to assimilate the mention of her father's name, she had missed a chunk of Ed's reply. She forced her attention away from personal concerns, and back to the problem she was supposed to be solving.

She heard the sounds of chairs scraping, suggesting that the men were standing up. Zachary must have turned around slightly, because she finally heard a complete sentence from him.

"What about Peter and Dillon? You told me that their training had gone well."

"It did. The fact that I'm not taking them has got nothing to do with how competent they are. Point one, the fewer people who know the target and the timetable, the less chance of leaks. Point two, you need somebody to lead the military exercises each morning, and those two are the best you've got."

"I expected you to need dozens of Soldiers to surround the mosque."

"I don't plan to surround the mosque. As I've mentioned already, increasing the size of the firing squad merely increases problems."

"You still haven't filled me in on the details of your plan. I need to know what's going to happen." Zachary sounded petulant, as well as worried.

"No, you don't," Ed said. "In fact, it's better for everyone if you don't know the details."

"I have a lot riding on this," Zachary said.

"Relax. Just remember that Rick is an okay marksman, but I'm the best there is. That's why you recruited me, remember?"

Rick is an okay marksman, but I'm the best there is.

An odd chill raced down Melody's spine, but she didn't

have time to analyze precisely why Ed's remark bothered her so much before Zachary spoke again.

"This is all happening too fast. It was supposed to be another week at least before Bashir Alassan arrived in Detroit."

Bashir not Bashy.

"Schedules change all the time. I'm on top of it." Ed changed the subject, clearly dismissive of Zachary's concerns. "I'll speak to you from Michigan, and keep you appraised of the situation."

"Are you flying? I don't even know how you're traveling to Detroit." The voices became muffled as the two men walked back into Zachary's office. Melody hastily slid the restroom window shut, climbed down from the toilet, and hurried back to her workstation. Her heart pounded hard and fast, but she managed to keep her breathing slow and even, and thankfully nobody paid her any special attention.

She had just sat down at her desk when Ed Harris came out of Zachary's office. He strode out of the admin building, giving Terri and Melody his usual cursory nod but calling out none of the good wishes that were standard operating procedure for the Soldiers.

But then, Melody thought, smiles and cheery greetings weren't likely to be part of the stock in trade of a man who was almost certainly a professional assassin. She would really like to know how Zachary had found and recruited him.

There was absolutely no way for Melody to contact Nick until the workday was over. Pleading ill health would be useless because she couldn't place a call from her room, and couldn't leave her room if she was supposed to be feeling sick.

The afternoon crept by on leaden feet, each slow minute ratcheting Melody's tension another painful notch tighter.

When the recorded church bells rang out the end of the work-day, she barely managed to conceal her relief. She rushed back to her room and quickly changed into running gear. Taking her communicator from her cosmetic purse, she slid it dexterously into her shorts. Now that she knew where the bathroom camera was located, it was fairly easy for her to slip the compact into her pocket in a way that would pass unnoticed by Ed, or whoever was monitoring the surveillance equipment.

She jogged out onto the road, heading for the main gate. This was an hour when most Soldiers were in their rooms, and she didn't encounter anyone. She was so anxious to talk with Nick that her pace kept picking up until she was running flat out, covering the mile to her hiding spot in less than seven minutes. It had occurred to her during the long heavy hours of the afternoon that she might have misheard the last name of the man Ed and Zachary had discussed. Bashir was a popular name for Syrian men, so perhaps the last name of the man Ed Harris had mentioned was al-Hassan, rather than Alassan. Hopefully, even with a degree of uncertainty, Unit One should be able to track down visitors from Syria who had recently flown into the States.

Melody turned off the road and hid behind the same juniper bush that had provided concealment two evenings ago. For a moment as she scrunched down behind the foliage she thought she heard a faint rustle of movement, almost like human footsteps. Instantly, she went still, her senses on high alert, but she heard nothing beyond the normal sounds of squirrels and chipmunks, and the high sweet note of a pipit calling to its mate. She waited for a full minute, just to be sure she wasn't missing anything, then flipped open her communicator, pressing the button that would link her to Nick. The weight that had pressed down on her chest all afternoon began to lift at the prospect of being mere seconds away from talking to him.

Except that the connection didn't happen. Melody pressed the button again but still no comforting buzz of electronic wizardry signaled a link to Nick's cell phone. She fought back panic, not on her own behalf, but because she had vital information and, without a functioning communicator, there was no way to pass it on. The frustration of being in possession of names and a possible target and having no way to inform Unit One was almost worse than having nothing to report.

She pried off the thin metal disk that formed the fake base of Bob Spinard's handmade device, exposing the tiny electronic chip that was the vital core of her communicator. She hoped against hope that she might be able to see an obviously loose connection, but all she saw was a microchip and some wires, not much thicker than pieces of thread. To her layman's eyes, everything seemed arranged as it should be. She hadn't really expected a quick and easy fix, but it was still disappointing to have her pessimism confirmed.

She left the communicator in her lap, pressing the connect button every so often as she mentally ran through her list of options. If she did nothing, by twelve midnight Unit One would consider her to be at risk and send in a rescue team. Nick had said an extraction team was on standby, so she could expect the team to arrive early tomorrow morning. But it seemed to her that time was of the essence. Ed Harris and his sidekick were leaving for Detroit tonight. Their plans— to assassinate Bashir al-Hassan?—could possibly have been put into operation before the rescue squad even arrived, much less before she could brief them and they could devise effective countermeasures.

Okay, so she needed to be in touch with Nick as soon as possible. Could she steal back her regular cell phone—the one that Zachary had confiscated on her arrival? No, she decided, that was a hopeless project. She had no clue where it had been stashed and couldn't search for it without showing up on half a dozen different surveillance cameras. Bottom line, she had to go off campus and find a phone. Fortunately, the town of Bridgerton was only five miles away. When Jason had driven her from Boise airport, she'd made mental note of a small grocery store in Bridgerton, as well as a gas station. Either or both must have public phones. It wasn't cold or raining, so she could make the five-mile trek into town in relative comfort and in less than an hour.

The only remaining question was whether she should make the break from campus right now, or return to her room and grab a purse so that she had money, credit cards and a driver's license. The lack of money was a relatively minor problem, she concluded, much less of a problem than the ticking clock. She could always call collect, and the urgent need to let Nick and Unit One know what she'd heard Ed and Zachary discussing outweighed any other considerations. Local law enforcement wasn't sympathetic to the Soldiers of Jordan, so if she could find a cop, she'd tell him she was running away from White Falls and he'd probably let her hang out at the police station until Nick could send help.

Her decision made, Melody pushed her useless communicator into her pocket and coiled into a crouching position as she listened to make sure that Ed and his trio of supporters weren't out on a final training run. Once again, she heard only the expected snuffles and chirps of a wooded stretch of countryside.

She made her way back to the road and started running,

resisting the urge to sprint since she had five miles to cover
and didn't want to end up with a leg cramp. She soon realized that she could hear people running behind her. Damn!
Ed Harris must have taken his trainees on a final run after all.
The way her evening was shaping up, she should almost have
expected the encounter. She slowed down, encouraging the
men to pass her. If she jogged slowly enough, by the time she
reached the gate, the four of them would be well on their way
back to the village.

Two of the runners passed her, moving directly in front of
her, and slowing down so abruptly that she either had to over-
take them or come to a halt. She could hear more runners behind her, presumably Ed Harris and his sidekick. Her stomach
gave a sickening lurch as she realized that the blockage of her
path was no accident: the four men intended to pin her between them. This wasn't simply an unlucky coincidence:
these men were coming after her. Why? What had caused Ed
Harris to target her?

Melody calculated the odds of being able to sprint fast
enough to outrun the men. The odds weren't good, she acknowledged. She'd watched their training run yesterday and
knew these four were the only people on campus as fit as she
was. And since she wasn't Lucy Liu, and this wasn't a movie,
she couldn't outfight four strong men simultaneously, even
though her unarmed combat skills were fairly impressive.
That left her with no choice but to change her plans and hope
she could bluff her way out of the confrontation.

She stopped running and stepped off the road, onto the
verge. She wasn't encouraged when all four men stopped, too.
They stood in a semicircle in front of her, menacing in their
silence.

She pretended to be unaware of their threatening body

language. "I guess I've given myself a stitch," she panted, doubling over as if exhausted. "Thanks for stopping, but I'll be okay. I'll go back to my room. Enjoy your run."

"Not so fast." Ed Harris shot out his arm, grabbing her as she started to jog back toward the village. His grip was bruisingly strong, but Melody made no attempt to shake it off. Her only defense—not a very effective one, she thought bleakly—lay in trying to convince these four men that she was harmless.

"Having trouble phoning your pals?" Ed inquired.

He'd been watching her? Was it some sound he'd made that she had heard when she first settled into her hiding place? Melody directed a puzzled look toward him, hiding her true thoughts. "You know Reverend Zachary has confiscated my cell phone. Soldiers aren't allowed to make unsupervised phone calls."

"Yeah, I know the rules. So why were you breaking them?"

"I wasn't—"

"You usually lie with more flair, Melody. But I'm in a hurry, so I can't waste any more time admiring your acting ability." Ed snapped the fingers of his free hand and the two men standing to his right immediately imprisoned her in an effective body lock.

"What are you doing? Let go of me! You're hurting!" She had to keep up the pretense of outraged innocence, but Ed was genuinely scaring her. His attitude hovered somewhere between vicious and gloating. Why? As far as he knew, she was simply a new recruit to the Soldiers of Jordan who had tried to make an illicit phone call. Why had he organized this elaborate posse, instead of simply notifying Zachary?

Ed removed a syringe from the nylon belt pouch at his waist. Using his teeth, he tugged a blue plastic cover from the needle. She struggled against the men holding her, but it was more a token psychological resistance than a realistic hope of freeing herself. With casual expertise but no gentleness, Ed plunged the needle into the muscles of her upper arm.

"Nighty-night, Melody," he said. And laughed.

Her coordination started to go immediately. Her brain lasted a few seconds longer. For some reason, his laugh reminded her of what she'd heard him say this afternoon, on Zachary's patio.

Rick is an okay marksman, but I'm the best there is.

Ed's laugh. His claim to be a great marksman. Something really important was lurking just out of her grasp. Melody tried to chase the thought, but it dissolved into fragments, her focus scattering. The ground rose up to meet her. She resisted falling, but she felt her knees buckle, and her head lolled weakly on her chest. She collapsed into the waiting darkness.

Twenty

"Here's my summary of where we're at," Mac said to the task force assembled in his office. "We have evidence—not conclusive by any means—that Dave Ramsdell is currently in White Falls, using the name of Ed Harris. Dave may have anticipated we would unmask him, or he may have hoped to go undetected. Either way, we can be sure he considered the possibility that we would track him down, and he's planned accordingly."

"If Dave is in White Falls, then he must have recognized Melody," Alec said.

"That's true. The fact that Zachary Wharton seems unaware of her identity as a Unit One operative confirms that Dave Ramsdell is pursuing his own agenda. The Soldiers of Jordan may believe he's working for them. In reality, we can be sure Dave is using them to achieve his own purpose."

"Now that we suspect Dave Ramsdell is in White Falls, why haven't we told Melody to leave?" Alec asked.

"We'll give her the order to leave as soon as we hear from her. Right now, we have no way to contact her without alerting Dave to the fact that he's been identified."

"We need to send in an extraction team," Sam said. "Go in through the woods and pull her out before anyone knows we're on site."

Mac grimaced. "Wish it was that easy. If we send in a team to extract Melody, Dave will be gone quicker than you can say tip-off. On the other hand, if we try to capture Dave without extracting Melody first, there's an excellent chance that she'll end up as a hostage. You suggested that the team should go in through the woods, Sam. Bob pointed out to us during his presentation that the electric fencing stops at the edge of the woods, so on the surface your suggestion seems reasonable. Trouble is, once the extraction team is on site, there's no way for them to get past the cameras without being seen. The Soldiers monitor their surveillance equipment 24/7, so they'll know we're coming long before we've found Dave. As of now, we don't even know where he sleeps, much less where he might be at any given moment during daylight hours."

"Can't we cut electrical power to the campus so that the Soldiers don't have access to their surveillance equipment?" Sam suggested. "How difficult can it be to find out where they're connected to the power grid and pull the switch? Bob could have the necessary info in five minutes."

"They have a generator on site," Mac said. "Remember, this is a cult with survivalist tendencies. They're off the grid as far as public utilities are concerned, except for their phone system. So it's a vicious cycle. We can't get to the generator to cut off power to the surveillance equipment without alerting them via the same equipment that we're on site."

Bob Spinard made a rare operational suggestion. "How about saying to hell with warning them? Who cares if they know we're coming? Let's just go in with overwhelming force. We could bring the FBI with us for backup."

Mac shook his head. "Won't work, Bob. First, Dave will have an escape route planned. He'll run at the first hint we're coming after him. So we'll storm up to the front door, and our target will run out the back. Metaphorically speaking."

"Besides, there's no way the Bureau is going to help us launch a full throttle attack," Sam said gloomily.

"Why not?" Bob asked.

"Waco and Ruby Ridge gave them enough bad publicity for the next decade or so," Mac said. "They aren't going to risk a head-on collision with a bunch of religious loony tunes based on the fact that Richard Mitchell served with David Ramsdell in the 75th Ranger division. That doesn't strike the director as overwhelming evidence that Ed Harris and Dave Ramsdell are one and the same person. He told me we're obsessed with Dave, seeing him under every pile of garbage. Those weren't his precise words, but it's the no-frills translation of what he meant. At best the Bureau might loan us a couple of agents."

"And they'd be more trouble than they're worth," Alec commented. "They'd be quoting law and damn Bureau rule books at us every step of the way."

"Despite their name, the Soldiers of Jordan are civilians," Sam said. "Why are we so scared to take them on? Why do we need the Bureau? We ought to be able to subdue them with a ten-man team. Hell, five of us should be enough."

"The Soldiers aren't civilians," Bob contradicted. "They're not even military. They're something much worse. They're fanatics, armed to the teeth, psychologically twisted, and badly trained. The moment they panic—which will be pretty much the moment they see our team moving in—they'll start shooting."

"And we'd be going in with our hands tied," Mac pointed

out. "So far, we have no proof the Soldiers have committed a crime. We can't go in with guns blazing, and that's what we would need if we're going to overpower two hundred people with a ten-person team."

"Maybe we need to wait for more convincing evidence that Ed Harris is really Dave Ramsdell," Alec said. "We get the Bureau on our side and go in with overwhelming force. With enough people, we can cut off Dave's escape routes—"

"Let me remind you all that the intel Melody has already generated suggests Dave and Zachary may be launching an attack against one of the largest mosques in the country," Mac said. "Melody believes the attack is going to happen soon. I don't know that we have time to sit around, scratching our balls, and hoping some time soon we can get the Bureau to see things our way.

Sam broke a brief silence. "All things considered, I'd say we're in deep shit."

"Anyone care to add to Sam's insightful analysis?" Mac asked. "Nick, you're being unusually quiet up there in Boise. Have you heard from Melody yet today?"

No, he hadn't, and he was trying not to obsess about that fact. Nick stood up and faced the videocam. "Negative," he said. "I'm expecting her call any minute. For the last two days, Melody has called me around five-thirty, after she finishes work for the day, so she's already twenty minutes late."

"Cause for alarm?" Mac snapped.

"Not necessarily. Melody has to find a location that isn't under surveillance before she can place the call. Could be she's having trouble with that for some reason." He didn't mention what everyone could figure out for themselves: that there were also a hundred or so less benign explanations for her silence.

One of his cell phones rang just as he finished speaking. "Is that incoming from Melody?" Mac queried.

"It's not Melody," Nick said. "Senator Cranford's wife is on the line. I need to take her call. I'll get back to you."

He scooped up the phone that was reserved for Melody's phone calls and put it into his pocket. He needed to be able to grab it the moment it rang. Then he flipped open his regular phone and said hello, moving out of range of the video uplink so that his conversation with Eleanor Cranford wouldn't disturb Mac's meeting.

"Rachel's home," Eleanor said, her voice lilting with relief and happiness. "Lewis arranged for a private plane to pick her up in Boise this morning. She left Idaho around ten and arrived in D.C. a couple of hours ago. It was a jet prop, not a regular jet, so it took longer than a regular commercial flight."

"Hey, that's great news," Nick said. "I'm glad for both of you." He forced himself not to leap ahead and make alarming inferences about Rachel's unexpected departure from White Falls. "Has Rachel explained why she decided to leave the Soldiers of Jordan?"

"She didn't decide to leave," Eleanor said. "As far as I can gather, she was forced out of White Falls. For once Lewis seems to have done the right thing. He called me this morning from his office in the Senate building and said he'd heard from his contact inside the Soldiers of Jordan—"

"Did the senator finally tell you the name of his mysterious contact?" Nick asked.

"No, of course not. Lewis would never reveal that sort of information to me. But you believe his contact is Steve Johnson, right? The man who came to see my husband two weeks ago?"

"Yes, that's our working theory," Nick said. "The snippets

of conversation your bug recorded before Steve Johnson jammed the signal suggest he's very familiar with Unit One, and that he was about to enter into some sort of partnership with your husband as a payback for past favors received from the senator."

That frustratingly truncated recording had also suggested that Steve Johnson and Dave Ramsdell were one and the same person and that Senator Cranford had been instrumental in aiding and abetting Dave's escape from Leavenworth. The membership list for the Soldiers of Jordan that Melody had stolen made no mention of anyone called Steve Johnson in White Falls, but that was no surprise. Dave knew enough to cover his ass from more than one direction. If Senator Cranford was acquainted with him as Dave Ramsdell and Steve Johnson, you could pretty much bank on the fact that the Soldiers of Jordan would be acquainted with him by some other name.

Nick considered it a huge bonus that Melody's theft of the membership list had enabled Bob Spinard's team to swiftly point the finger of suspicion at Ed Harris as a pseudonym for Dave Ramsdell. Mac's theory was that Dave Ramsdell didn't care if Unit One discovered he had infiltrated the Soldiers of Jordan community. Nick wasn't so sure. Zachary had granted Melody unexpected access to the admin offices, and she'd exploited the advantage that access gave her. In Nick's opinion, Dave hadn't anticipated Melody delving into the Soldiers of Jordan's confidential personnel records, at least not so quickly. In downloading the list of Social Security numbers, Melody had unearthed information Dave had planned to keep secret for a lot longer.

"So if Rachel didn't come home voluntarily, why did she leave White Falls at this particular moment?" Nick asked Eleanor. "Was she expelled for breaking one of the Soldiers' rules?"

"She's not talking too much," Eleanor admitted, some of the happiness leaking out of her voice. "But I'm not sure her leaving had anything to do with the Soldiers or even that dreadful Zachary Wharton. Lewis never gives me more than the minimum information, but reading between the lines of what he said, and the little bit that Rachel has confided, it seems Lewis was told to have a private plane waiting at Boise airport by nine-thirty this morning. His contact guaranteed that if Lewis came up with the plane, our daughter would be on it."

"Who drove Rachel to the airport? Have you asked her that?" Dave/Ed/Steve would presumably be smart enough, however, not to do the driving himself, otherwise the senator would be able to put two and two together and come up with the pseudonym Dave was using in White Falls.

"I did ask. She said that a man named Jason Cushman drove her into Boise. She seems very angry with him. She complained that he refused to talk to her or listen to any of her pleas. Zachary had ordered him to drive her to the airport, and Jason wasn't interested in hearing any reasons why she ought to be allowed to stay."

Everything he heard confirmed that Rachel had been removed from White Falls against her will. Nick considered the news ominous. Why would Dave/Ed/Steve go to all the trouble of getting Rachel out of White Falls unless he anticipated violence that would threaten her safety? If Dave had done a deal with Senator Cranford, it only made sense that part of the deal would include removing Rachel from the site of any potential danger. Unit One should consider Rachel's return to D.C. as a signal that major trouble was brewing in White Falls, Nick reflected grimly.

"Make sure your daughter doesn't catch the next flight back to Boise," he said. "This might be a dangerous time for her to return to White Falls."

"I'll do whatever it takes to keep her here," Eleanor said. "Rachel's absolutely furious with us for bringing her home, but her sister's here, and the two of them have always been close. Megan is pleading with her not to leave, and Rachel seems to be listening. I'm optimistic Rachel will soon realize there are better ways to express disapproval of her parents' lifestyle than retreating to the back of beyond and pretending she doesn't have a mind of her own."

"Thanks for letting me know that Rachel has left White Falls," he said. "Good luck with winning over your daughter, Eleanor. I'll be in touch."

He cut the connection and stared at the phone that would link him to Melody, willing her to call him. The phone remained stubbornly silent and delivering a string of Russian curses did nothing to make it ring. Scowling, Nick moved back to the other side of his hotel room and rejoined the video conference.

"Hope your conversation was more useful than ours," Mac said. "We've been dancing in circles here, doing nothing much except treading on each other's toes."

"My news isn't good," Nick said. "Eleanor Cranford called to let me know that her daughter is back home in Washington. Rachel didn't leave White Falls voluntarily. The senator was alerted by an informant within the Soldiers of Jordan organization and arranged passage on a private plane for her this morning. She was still committed to the community and wouldn't have agreed to board a commercial flight, but somebody was obviously determined to get her out of White Falls."

Nobody needed to ask why the news wasn't good. "Who

made the call to Lewis Cranford?" Mac asked. "Do we know?"

"Seems likely that it was Steve Johnson, otherwise known as Ed Harris," Nick said. "However, we have zero proof that Ed Harris and Steve Johnson are the same person. Which goes double for our suspicion that both of them are really Dave Ramsdell."

"Any suggestions as to how we might confirm our suspicions?"

Nick shrugged. "We should call Senator Cranford, tell him that we know Rachel is back in Washington D.C., and ask him how that happened."

"I'll make the call," Mac said, sounding weary. "The senator will tell me, of course, that the message he received was anonymous."

Sam pounded his fist into his palm in an outburst of frustration. "Dammit, I want to go to White Falls and haul Dave Ramsdell out by his treacherous ass. The bastard's playing us."

"You'll get no argument from me on that one," Mac said, staring into his coffee cup as if he'd forgotten what was in it.

Nick spoke directly into the videocam. "I'm still disagreeing with you on this, Mac. I'm not sure Dave is playing us, at least not to the extent you and Sam are suggesting. I tend to believe that we're not only smart, we've also gotten lucky. There's no way Dave could have anticipated that Eleanor Cranford would have bugged her husband's office, or that she'd confide in us, delivering hours of tapes implicating her husband in Dave's escape from Leavenworth. Dave knew from his dealings with the senator that we'd infiltrate an operative into White Falls, but he couldn't know that the operative we'd choose was Melody, and that Zachary would fall for her sufficiently hard to make him careless. He certainly couldn't anticipate that within four days of Melody being on campus, we would have identified Ed Harris's Social Security number as invalid. And despite his familiarity with our systems, he couldn't have anticipated Bob's brilliant move in linking Richard Mitchell to Dave Ramsdell and the 75th Army Rangers—"

"Your last three points are debatable," Mac said. "I agree about Eleanor. That's a bonus for our team. But Dave knows just how good Bob is. Dammit, he worked with Bob for years. And he knows Zachary's profile as well as we do. Why wouldn't we send in Melody? Dave can see she's the perfect trap for Zachary, same as we can. Maybe we've gotten lucky, but we can't count on it. Bottom line, any plans we make, we need to assume Dave knows we're coming. That he's woven our arrival into whatever scenario he has unfolding here."

"Which we still don't have a clue about," Bob said, reverting to gloom. "Melody saw an architectural drawing of a mosque in Dearborn. Does that mean the mosque is their target? Or does it just mean that Zachary is planning to rent their community room for a drug rehab project?"

"Melody ought to have more intel for us by now," Nick said. "Community rules require all Soldiers to be back in their rooms by nine, and lights out by nine-thirty, so she's not likely to be calling us after nine o'clock."

"If she doesn't call, are we going in?" Sam asked.

Mac didn't respond. Nick understood his boss's dilemma. If Dave Ramsdell knew he'd been identified, the very best way to guarantee the arrival of a Unit One team was to hold Melody hostage. But if Dave anticipated the team's arrival, then anyone Mac sent in was most likely going to be greeted by a hundred fanatical Soldiers, all lined up ready to play a live ammo version of the War of Armageddon.

"I'd like permission to pay a visit to the campus if Melody hasn't called me by nine-thirty," Nick said.

"No," Mac said at once. "Who do you think you are, the Invisible Man? Everything we've discussed about the problems of sending in an extraction team applies to you, too."

"Not in the same way," Nick said. "I'm one person. I've visited the campus before, so I have some idea what I'm getting into. I can go in on foot through the woods and keep out of sight of the surveillance equipment. Even if Dave has set the Soldiers up to expect a fight, I can get in under their alarm threshold."

Mac grunted, but didn't flat out refuse permission. *Perhaps because he knows I'd go in anyway,* Nick thought wryly.

Taking advantage of his boss's silence, Nick spoke quickly. "Bob, I'll need you to transmit the ground plan for the campus, with all the intel you have regarding location of security devices. Did we get any satellite time? Do we have sky photos of the campus?"

"We have pictures," Bob said. "And I've gotten a pretty good idea of the overall security system. The Soldiers have spent a lot of money, and their barricades are effective because they have somebody monitoring the security cameras at all times, but their perimeter defenses aren't designed to keep out a pro—"

"Wait a minute," Mac said. "You're getting ahead of yourselves. As of now, I haven't authorized anyone, pro or otherwise, to attempt an entry."

"It's almost six-fifteen and Melody hasn't called," Nick said. "If she reaches me at any point in the next three hours, I'll let you know, Mac. But I'm not waiting for the midnight deadline. If nine-thirty arrives and she still hasn't called, I'm going in."

Twenty-One

Melody woke up with a headache that threatened to blow off the top of her head, and her stomach roiling with nausea. Physically, the nausea bothered her, but mentally she felt peaceful and relaxed, floating somewhere that left her only loosely connected to her body and its ills. In the distance she could hear somebody singing, and the tune reverberated inside her head, the individual notes dissolving into a liquid stream of fantastic colors. The colors were entrancing, so she listened to them for a while, until the music stopped. She'd never known that singing looked so pretty.

She was lying in bed, wearing shorts and a T-shirt. She frowned. Something wasn't quite right about the bed. Or maybe it was her clothes that were wrong. She stared down at her legs, squinting to see her feet. The effort of focusing set her stomach churning almost to the point of vomiting, and then she couldn't remember why she wanted to see her feet anyway. She stopped moving, wishing the music would start again.

She had no idea where she was, or how she'd gotten there.

The room she was in didn't seem familiar. Melody felt a vague flicker of alarm. Should she be worried by the fact that she couldn't recognize her surroundings?

A man came and stood next to her. She recognized him, but couldn't remember his name. She wasn't entirely pleased to see him, but it was too much effort to tell him to go away so she closed her eyes and hoped he would disappear. Poof! She smiled. Yes, let him go poof. She *really* wanted him to disappear.

"I know you're awake," he said.

"Wan' sleep." Her contentment vanished at the sound of his voice, but the drowsiness lingered.

"You betrayed me," he said. "I trusted you. I was even ready to offer you marriage. You could have become Mrs. Zachary Wharton and gone on to glory at my side, but all the time you were working against me. For that you must be punished."

Whatever. Melody yawned and turned her head away. The man was a prick, even if she couldn't remember his name. She stared in fascination at the red light dancing on the bedside table. What a perfect shade of scarlet! *Flick,* and the configuration of the light changed again. How amazing. She was looking at a clock, she realized. Who knew that clocks were so fascinating? *Flick. Flick. Flick.* Counting off the seconds. A tiny knot of anxiety formed in the pit of her stomach. *Flick. Flick. Flick.* Time was passing and for some reason that wasn't good. She stopped watching the clock but the anxiety wouldn't go away.

"I thought you were a pure vessel," the voice droned on. "Now I see that you're just another whore without hope of redemption. Ed showed me your communicator and it's obviously a sophisticated piece of equipment. Who have you been calling, Melody?"

The man standing in front of her was taking off his clothes as he talked. Melody watched languidly. Definitely a prick, she decided. A prick with a small prick. She smiled at her own joke.

The man shed the last of his clothes and climbed onto the bed beside her.

She could have been Mrs. Zachary Wharton and lived with Small Prick Man for ever. She giggled. Yeah, that was just the future she wanted. Not. Mrs. Zachary Wharton. No thank you, sir.

A tiny sliver of coherence emerged from the kaleidoscope of her confusion. Zachary. *Zachary Wharton!* The Soldiers of Jordan.

Her head pounded worse than ever, but a flash of memory came to her. She'd been running, and Ed had caught up with her.

Ed. Injection. She'd been drugged.

Zachary was mauling her breasts. He was climbing on top of her. Oh, God! He was going to rape her.

Her whole body became drenched in sweat from the effort of making herself resist. Melody pushed weakly at Zachary's midriff, trying to beat him off. Her pummels had the force of a mouse, desperately flicking its tail to ward off a lion.

"You are from Satan, and must be punished. Punishing a whore is the Lord's work."

The Lord's work? Oh, please. Zachary wanted sex. And his desire had absolutely nothing to do with the Lord. Melody tried once again to beat him back, but her hands lacked both strength and coordination. He simply ignored her flailing and tugged at her T-shirt, pulling it up and making a frustrated sound when he saw that she was wearing a bra that closed in the back.

"Leave me 'lone," Melody mumbled. Her thoughts were becoming clearer, but making her mouth shape coherent words and sentences was still almost impossible.

"I can't leave you. It's my duty to conquer your evil body. This is how I punished Jodie Evanderhaus. She was sent by Satan, too, and it was my duty to remove her from the world. And you must join her. Another whore, sent to boil in the tar pits of hell."

Jodie Evanderhaus. The name was vaguely familiar, but Melody couldn't place it. Zachary was trying to turn her onto her side so that he could unfasten her bra, but she resisted with whatever puny strength she could muster. Her reluctance to move wasn't caused only by revulsion at the prospect of lying naked beneath Zachary's thrusting body. Her limbs felt so heavy that movement was excruciatingly difficult and her nausea was so intense that if she turned her head even a tiny bit she was sure she would vomit.

In a saving flash of clarity, Melody realized that the nausea might be her best hope of escape. Instead of struggling to conquer the drug-induced sickness, she let it grow. She waited until Zachary was collapsed across her body, one hand shoving at her shorts, the other reaching for the hook of her bra. Overcoming years of social indoctrination, she abandoned her inhibitions and allowed herself to vomit all over his neck and shoulder.

"What the hell!" Zachary rolled away from her and jumped off the bed, screaming curses that would have shocked his followers to the core if they could have heard. He rushed to the bathroom. Melody heard the shower turn on and grinned. Hey, she felt better already.

The drug pulled her back toward drowsiness now that Zachary was no longer an immediate threat. With an effort that was a triumph of will and training over body chemistry, she forced herself to sit up, wiping herself clean with the corner of the sheet. She dragged herself out of bed, but her legs buckled and she fell onto the carpet.

Teeth gritted, Melody used the mattress to haul herself to her feet, then lurched from piece of furniture to piece of furniture until she reach the door. Her sense of self-preservation was finally more powerful than the languor induced by the drug. It had just dawned on her that the only way Zachary could send her to frolic with Jodie in the tar pits of hell was by killing her, and she had no more intention of becoming his victim than she did of becoming his wife.

She turned the door handle with hands that trembled not only from weakness, but also from newfound urgency. The door refused to open. In White Falls, she'd finally discovered a locked door. Melody fought back a scream, her self-control weakened by the drugs in her system.

Calm down. Think instead of panicking. You're in a converted motel room, and this is a typical motel door. All you need to do is twist the latch counterclockwise and the door will open.

The shower water was still running. Good. She hoped Zachary would spend a long time scrubbing himself clean. It was difficult to force her fingers and thumbs to work in unison, but the threat of Zachary's return was enough to align her brain cells one step further along the path to coherence. In the end, she had to use both hands to get the door unlatched, one hand covering the other in order to steady it. She was dimly aware that it had taken way too long to accomplish something as simple as unlatching a lock, but she finally stepped outside, closing the door behind her. She wasn't sure, but she thought the shower water stopped running just as she closed the door.

The fresh air felt glorious and the fact that she'd thrown up seemed to reduce the level of her nausea, although her headache was still of pounding, epic proportions.

She started to run even before she knew precisely where she was. Except that she couldn't run. Her muscles remained partially paralyzed by the drug and she stumbled along, her pace little more than a drunken hobble. She oriented herself as she lurched from fence to wall to lamppost, searching for somewhere—anywhere—that she could hide.

She was close to the dining room, she saw. It was dark, except for the night security lighting system, and nobody seemed to be around. The Soldiers must all be tucked in bed for the night. She couldn't hear any sounds of Zachary following her. Was he calling the security guards to raise the alarm? Where were the guards that were posted each night, anyway? She knew at least one man was stationed inside the White House and that his job was to keep a close eye on the security monitors. If she showed up on his screen, would that be good or bad? Were Zachary's followers loyal enough to turn a blind eye to the fact that she had been drugged and that their leader had tried to rape her? Probably. If Zachary told them she was a spy, sent by the government to destroy their community, she would most likely find no refuge, so screaming for help didn't seem a safe option.

Melody staggered to the back of the dining hall. The overgrown path that led to the target practice field meandered off to her left. Power was returning to her body as she moved around, and her mind felt less fuzzy around the edges, but she still found it hard to keep her train of thought sequential. Where was Ed? Had he left the campus? Somehow, she was more afraid of Ed than she was of Zachary, even though the prospect of being raped by Zachary almost had her vomiting again. If only she could remember those final few moments before they shot her full of drugs. Something important about Ed had leaped into her mind, but now the information had vanished, leaving behind only a wisp of uneasiness. They'd probably used PCP on her and, unfortunately, PCP caused memory loss and hallucinations as well as overwhelming nausea.

With an effort as intense as pushing a boulder up a steep hill, Melody forced her attention back to the subject of her escape. Zachary would have to put on clothes before he chased after her, which was most likely why he hadn't already caught up with her. At last she'd found a reason to be grateful for the prudish dress code of the Soldiers of Jordan! Was there any chance that she could make it to the wooded area at the edge of the campus before he found her? Once there, she could go to ground and recoup her physical strength before tackling the problem of how she was going to cover the five miles to Bridgerton and phone in a report to Nick when her legs had all the stamina of overboiled noodles. If it was PCP that they'd used on her, the aftereffects could linger for hours, and some memories would be permanently wiped clean. All things considered, she could count herself lucky that her reaction was mild, relatively speaking. At least she remembered who she was and why she was in White Falls.

She tripped over a rock, and sprawled flat, so uncoordinated that she lay staring at the ground for a full minute before she could get her act together and stand up again. As she pushed her body through the laborious process of preparing to stand up, she heard the sound of footsteps pounding behind her. Damn! What to do? Where to hide?

Melody rolled to the side of the path and saw Zachary chasing toward her. She knew she didn't yet have the muscle strength or the coordination to outrun him, although in normal circumstances she could have outstripped him without any problem.

She didn't waste time or energy on an escape attempt she knew would be futile. Instead, utilizing every last gram of her strength, she levered up the loose rock she'd just tripped on, and hid it behind her back as she hauled herself to her feet. Since she couldn't hide, she'd have to attack.

Zachary reached her side, panting. Melody didn't wait for him to deliver another lecture about how she was a vessel of Satan, or whatever justification he planned to use this time around. She swung her arms out from behind her back and brought the rock up to thwack Zachary beneath his chin.

She was so weak that although she cut him, her punch didn't pack sufficient oomph to knock him out. Zachary gave an enraged bellow, blood spurting from the gash she'd inflicted. He lunged for her throat and Melody swung the rock again. This time, she managed to inflict a heavy enough blow that Zachary was knocked out. He fell at her feet with a satisfying thunk.

Hah! I am woman, hear me roar.

Melody dusted off her hands and resumed her dogged scramble toward the woods. The act of running shook off more of the lethargy that afflicted her, but her knees still buckled from time to time, and every so often she could feel her mind spinning off into a drug-fueled fantasy where the bushes reached out with clawed fingers to grab her.

The dividing line between fantasy and reality was sufficiently blurred that when she saw two men running across the target practice field, she wasn't sure whether the men were real or she was hallucinating. Was she giving life to the plastic targets?

Unfortunately it was soon clear that the men were real, that they were chasing her, and that they could run a lot faster than she could. She wished she hadn't been so quick to discard the rock she'd used to knock out Zachary, although even with the rock she had no realistic hope of escaping from two opponents in her current state. The skills in unarmed combat that Sam had spent dozens of hours drilling into her required both strength and agility, neither of which she possessed right now.

She refused to give up, even if her escape attempt was doomed. She ran stubbornly toward the woods at the boundary of the campus and managed to get three-quarters of the way there before her pursuers caught up with her. She recognized them as two of the men she'd seen running with Ed. The good news was that her brain was functioning well enough to assign identities to men she'd encountered only twice before. The bad news was that she didn't think that two men allied with Ed Harris were going to be sympathetic to her plea for sanctuary.

"Hold her," one of the men ordered the other.

The second man complied, ignoring her attempts to escape which, in truth, were feeble enough to be easy to ignore. The first man reached into his pocket and pulled out a syringe.

"No, don't!" Melody protested, her voice hoarse but her words no longer slurred. Determination to avoid being drugged a second time—with permanent memory loss as a possible result—provided her with a strength and cunning she hadn't realized she'd regained. Instead of continuing her struggles to escape, she suddenly went limp. For a split second the man holding her didn't react and she was able to free her arm. She swung her fist up, knocking the syringe out of her captor's hands just as he was about to plunge the needle into her arm. Her swing was wild, but she got lucky, and the syringe flew in a high arc, landing several feet away.

"Hold the whore of Babylon still!" the man commanded, kneeling down to hunt through the long grass for the syringe, which Melody sincerely hoped was broken. The fact that he'd referred to her as the whore of Babylon—why was that worse than a whore of anywhere else, Melody wondered—suggested that these men were motivated by the same peculiar brand of religious fervor as impelled Zachary. Her thought processes were still too hazy to decide whether that was good or bad.

She didn't struggle to escape, in part because her captor was holding her tight, and in part because there was nowhere for her to run. Better that she should concentrate all her attention on making sure that she didn't get drugged again. Obviously the two of them didn't have another supply of PCP with them, or the Soldier who'd accused her of being a whore wouldn't be scouring the ground for the missing syringe.

A black shadow slid through the grass, silent and swift, like a giant snake from a child's nightmare. Melody blinked, but the vision didn't go away. She watched as the shadow reared up, suddenly transformed from hallucination into the solid figure of a man wearing the night-ops combat uniform of a Unit One field agent.

Nick was here. He was *here*. Melody gave a smile of radiant happiness.

"Watch out!" The man who was holding her called out a warning to his partner, but he was too late. Almost too fast for her to catch the motion, despite the fact that she was watching intently, Nick swung out with his right leg, landing a blow on the head of the man still crouched in the grass. The man staggered to his feet and Nick gave a quick upward thrust, his joined and clenched hands landing beneath the man's chin. The Soldier crumpled, then fell to the ground and rolled onto his back, arms splayed.

Melody was afraid to help in case her lack of coordination screwed things up for Nick. Fortunately, the man holding her seemed paralyzed, either by shock, or by the need to prevent her running away. She finally felt him make a move to pull a weapon from the holster at his waist.

He was too slow and a second too late. Nick swung around and brought his fist down in a swift, chopping motion. Melody heard the crunch of wrist bone, followed by a howl of pain. Her captor dropped to his knees, his gun tumbling into the grass, but Nick wasn't taking any chances. He delivered a swift kick to the man's jaw and watched, ready to deliver another blow if need be, as the man keeled over, landing with his head resting neatly at his partner's feet.

"Fancy meeting you here," Nick said, stepping over the inert bodies and taking Melody's hands. He was barely breathing hard, she noticed. "Do you come here often?"

"Not if I can avoid it. The locals are seriously unfriendly."

"Then let's tie 'em up." Nick removed the Soldiers' weapons, shoving them into his belt, then unwound a length of cord from around his waist, cutting it in two with a knife he pulled from his ankle sheath. He handed her one of the pieces. "Here, you take the bozo on my left."

The remnants of the drug combined with relief at seeing Nick, and she felt tears prick at the corners of her eyes. "I'm not sure if I can tie strong enough knots. Ed Harris injected me with something—PCP or Rohypnol maybe—and I still don't have much coordination."

Nick realized she was on the verge of tears, of course. No way to hide her emotions from him when she was in this sort of a dippy state. He didn't comment on the tears however, but pulled her into his arms, resting her head against his chest. "Don't worry. I'll take care of the bozos."

His chest felt strong and warm beneath her cheek and Melody gave a tiny sigh of contentment. Later, she'd worry about her emotional dependence on a man she'd decided couldn't be trusted. For right now, she simply wanted to enjoy the closeness, the sensation of being reunited with a friend.

"If they gave you PCP you must be feeling sick as a dog," Nick said, handing her his flask of water and going to work on tying up one of the Soldiers. "Do you want something to drink?"

"I'm not sure. I'm still a bit queasy." She sipped the water with caution, but it eased the soreness of her throat and freshened her mouth. She handed back the flask. "Thanks, that seems to be staying down. The sickness hasn't been so bad since I puked all over Zachary. That was satisfying enough to make me feel quite a lot better."

"What had Zachary done to offend you? Other than be a hypocritical pain in the ass, of course."

"He tried to rape me."

"Then vomiting over him hardly seems sufficient punishment."

She smiled, knowing that he understood a lot that she hadn't put into words. "Don't worry, there's more. He's lying about half a mile back up the path, bleeding from the gash in his chin. At least I hope he's still lying there. I used a rock to knock him out, since I wasn't enthusiastic about becoming his latest express delivery to the tar pits of hell."

"That's my girl," Nick said softly.

She couldn't let that pass, even if she had missed him almost beyond endurance. "I'm not your girl."

"Aren't you?"

"Absolutely not."

"We'll fight about it later. Right now, we don't have time

to do the subject justice." He rubbed his hand up and down her back, and Melody realized that she was so cold her teeth were chattering. Warmth began to seep back into her, transferred from Nick's body.

"We need to get out of here before any more Soldiers come running out to defend their territory," he said, ruffling her hair. "Can you make it to the woods, do you think?"

"Yes, as long as I don't have to run fast, I'm good to go."

Nick soon had the second Soldier trussed and immobilized and they set off for the woods. Their trek was easier than Melody had expected. There were no footpaths, and Nick found their way out using a compass and the occasional tree that he'd notched on the way in, which meant that running was impossible. She simply followed his lead, leaning on him whenever her body shook from a muscle spasm. Apparently their disposal of the two Soldiers hadn't shown up on any security monitors because nobody gave chase.

The wood was half a mile deep—far bigger and denser than she'd realized—and backed up to a dirt road. Nick had parked his car behind a bedraggled hedge that looked as if it might once have marked the boundary of someone's property.

"This was a successful potato farm up until a couple of years ago," Nick pointed to the expanse of weed-infested fields as they got into the car. "Then the farmer's machinery was sabotaged, he believes by the Soldiers of Jordan. The machinery wasn't insured, and he went belly-up financially. Zachary just bought the whole property for a hundred thousand dollars. It's a steal, but according to Bob's research, none of the locals wanted to buy anything that close to White Falls and the Soldiers."

"I'd love to know where Zachary gets his money," Melody said, sliding gratefully into the front passenger seat.

"So would we all. Bob is double-checking the finances of the drug rehab programs Zachary runs. He's convinced those high-powered fund-raisers put a lot more money into Zachary's personal bank accounts than they do into programs for inner-city teens. Now he just has to track the mechanism that's being used to siphon off cash."

"I'm with Bob. It's how Zachary's doing it, not if." Melody tried to latch her seat belt, but her fingertips were still numb and Nick leaned across to fasten it for her. "Thank you," she said.

"You're welcome." He touched his hand to her cheek in a brief, gentle caress. "Still feeling sick?"

"Just a little."

"We have five miles of bumpy road ahead of us. Think you'll make it?"

She smiled wryly. "I'll keep the window open, just in case. What time is it, by the way?"

"Twenty-three ten." Nick handed her a phone. "Take your mind off your digestive system. Call Mac and tell him we're heading back to the motel in Boise. You can fill him in on what happened to you over the past twenty-four hours. I'll listen, and that will save you telling everything twice."

Melody took the phone and stared at it for a few seconds, relieved when she finally remembered Mac's number.

Mac picked up on the first ring, barking out his name.

"It's Melody. I'm with Nick."

"Humph." Mac's snuffle expressed satisfaction. "Are you both off campus?"

"Yes. Nick arrived just in time to rescue me from two Soldiers who were trying to inject me—again—with something nasty. Probably PCP."

"Humph. Why were you targeted? You were supposed to be acting the part of a sweet, submissive born-again virgin."

"Obviously I didn't quite nail the role," Melody said dryly. "Ed Harris somehow identified me as an undercover agent working for the government. I think he sabotaged my communicator, and when I tried to leave White Falls to find a public phone, he was lying in wait for me. I don't remember the precise details of what happened next, but he must have shot me full of a drug. Judging by my symptoms, I'm guessing it was PCP—"

"You sound fine now. Any significant memory loss? Vomiting? Headache?"

"All of the above when I first came around. But the blanks in my memory are pretty much filled in. The only thing I don't remember now is the last couple of minutes before I passed out."

"Any intel you need to pass on to us?"

"Yes. Something important. I eavesdropped on a conversation between Zachary and Ed Harris yesterday afternoon. Ed announced he was leaving for Michigan.... Actually, he's almost certainly left already."

"What's he going to Michigan for?"

"He told Zachary that a man called Bashir al-Hassan—I'm fairly sure that's the name—was scheduled to arrive in Dearborn late this afternoon. Ed also mentioned that Bashir al-Hassan was scheduled to meet at ten-thirty tomorrow morning with Johnston Yates. I'm not sure if the meeting is significant, or if Ed was just passing on information. Unfortunately I wasn't in a position to hear everything the two of them said, but I got the distinct impression that if Zachary has some grand plan to cause trouble in the Muslim world, then al-Hassan is probably the trigger, and Ed Harris is the man who's going to pull the trigger. It's less than twelve hours until the meeting tomorrow between Yates and al-Hassan. Obviously we need to find out everything we can about al-Hassan as quickly as possible. And we need to warn somebody in Detroit that he's the likely target of an assassination attempt."

"I'll take care of it. I'll check into al-Hassan's bio and get back to you. In the meantime, ask Nick to tell you what Bob discovered about Ed Harris." Mac, never prone to wasting time on social courtesies, cut the connection without saying goodbye.

Melody turned to Nick, handing him back the phone. "Did you hear Mac's last comment? He says you have some information to pass on about Ed Harris."

"Yeah." Nick paused for a moment. "Here's the short version. We have reason to believe Ed Harris may be a pseudonym for Dave Ramsdell."

Memory exploded, producing an almost visible flash of light inside Melody's head. In her mind's eye, she watched Ed running down the road toward the main entrance to White Falls. She could even feel the uneasy sensation she'd experienced: the sensation that she was watching something familiar. Of course, she had been. Dave could disguise his face and his voice. He could slump his shoulders and make his walk shambling. But when he was on a training run, operating under conditions that tested his physical skills to their limits, he could no more disguise his running style than he could change his height.

"That's the second time he's fooled me," Melody said, her voice thin with anger. "Shame on me. I should have recognized him. *I should have.*"

"Don't blame yourself. You were thrown headlong into a strange environment, with no reason in the world to expect Dave would be here. Also, remember that this is a man who was considered Unit One's master of disguise. He spent the last five years before he betrayed us perfecting his skills at impersonation—changing his voice, his walk, his gestures. He was simply the best at changing everything that helps us to recognize somebody over and beyond the way they look. And finally, we're not yet a hundred percent sure that Ed Harris is really Dave."

"It's Dave," Melody said flatly. "I heard him boast to Zachary that he was the best marksman in the country. His exact words were *Rick is an okay marksman, but I'm the best there is.* It sent a chill down my spine, although I didn't know why. Now I do. Dave said the same thing to me once, during my training period for Unit One. He told me I was an okay marksman, but he was the best there is. And he didn't laugh when he said it."

"No, he wouldn't. He took his marksmanship skills seriously, since he claimed they'd saved his life at least a half dozen times."

"But what is Dave doing here in White Falls?" Melody asked, still trying to get some logical backup for her instinctive certainty that Ed and Dave were one and the same. "Why on earth would Dave have decided to infiltrate the Soldiers of Jordan?"

"The only logical answer is that Dave must be working with Senator Cranford."

Melody's breath expelled in a sharp hiss. "Do you have any evidence of that?"

"Indirect. Not a damn thing that would convince the FBI to act, much less hold up in a court of law. We heard from Eleanor Cranford that Rachel is back in D.C., and her husband admitted that he'd been called by somebody in White Falls, who told him to send a plane and they'd guarantee that Rachel was on it."

Melody was very relieved to hear that Rachel was home safely. "That's more than indirect evidence, isn't it? Hasn't the senator compromised himself by admitting that he has a contact inside the Soldiers of Jordan organization?"

"Unfortunately not," Nick said. "Cranford's too astute to get caught out that easily. Mac contacted him and asked how and why Rachel had come home. He told Mac that the call he received was anonymous, but he figured the caller was probably a Unit One agent working undercover—"

"Of course! Dammit, the perfect excuse."

Nick nodded. "Yeah, as usual, the senator has his ass safely covered. The senator's story is that he had nothing to lose except a couple of thousand bucks for the plane, so he made the arrangements as instructed. He claims to be astonished and delighted that he got lucky and his daughter is home. Our take on the situation is that Dave Ramsdell got Rachel out of White Falls before the shit hits the fan."

"I want to nail Cranford almost as badly as I want to see Dave Ramsdell back behind bars," Melody said. "If the two of them are working together, you know they're planning to set up Unit One. Obviously the whole idea of sending in an undercover operative to investigate the Soldiers of Jordan was simply part of the senator's scheme to implicate us in whatever disaster is going to unfold."

"I agree," Nick said. "But we have to figure out exactly how they're planning to set us up or we can't avoid the trap. Based on what you've seen over the past few days, give me some scenarios for how they might expect to get us in trouble. If Ed Harris is Dave Ramsdell, and he's collaborating with Senator Cranford, what are the two of them planning?"

"I'd say it's almost a given that they intend to assassinate Bashir al-Hassan—"

"Why?" Nick asked. "Why would Lewis Cranford and Dave Ramsdell do that?"

Melody shook her head, and immediately regretted the action when her stomach churned in protest. "I can't answer that until we know something about Bashir's background...."

"Let's suppose he's a Muslim cleric," Nick said. "Let's go one step further and say he's somehow connected to the tragic destruction of Zachary Wharton's family business in Damascus seventy years ago. Okay, in Zachary's warped mind that may be justification for wanting al-Hassan dead, especially since he would like nothing better than to set off sectarian religious violence in this country. But why is any of that a reason for Dave Ramsdell to agree to carry out the deed?"

"Because assassinating al-Bashir was the price Dave had to pay in order to convince Senator Cranford to spring him from Leavenworth?" Melody suggested.

"Could be. Makes sense. But now go back a step. Why was Cranford willing to go to so much trouble just so that Dave could assassinate Bashir al-Hassan?"

The answer came to Melody with sudden, shocking clarity. "Because Cranford's target isn't really Bashir al-Hassan," she said. "You're right that it's Zachary who wants al-Hassan dead, not the senator. Senator Cranford's target is Johnston Yates."

Twenty-Two

Nick was still absorbing the implications of Melody's suggestion when his phone buzzed. He flipped it open. "Yes, Mac."

"I've arranged with the FBI for one of their planes to pick up you and Melody at Boise airport. Two pilots, Jeff Adams and Pierce Tripp. They'll meet you at the private plane reception area. Give your names to the security screeners. They'll take fingerprints, because they've been warned Melody has no documentation." As usual Mac plunged ahead without preamble. "The plane's being sent out of Salt Lake City. Should be in Boise within the hour. How far are you from the airport?"

Nick looked at the highway signs. "We're coming up to Kuna Mora Road," he said. "The airport is less than twenty miles from here. At this time of night the roads are empty so we should be there in fifteen minutes."

"Okay, great. They'll be able to turn the plane around as soon as it lands. Now as far as Bashir al-Hassan is concerned—"

"Wait a minute! Back up a bit, Mac. You told us you're sending the plane. You didn't specify where we're going."

"To Michigan, of course. Figure you and Melody have a better chance of spotting Dave Ramsdell than anyone else. Bob will transmit the most recent photo we can come up with for Richard Mitchell to the plane, plus the schematics for the mosque and any information about al-Hassan as it becomes available. You need to check the mosque out before al-Hassan and Yates get there. We'll intensify security around them, of course, but Dave must have anticipated the possibility of that, given the importance of al-Hassan. Try to think as if you were Dave. How are you going to bypass heightened security? Once you've figured that out, make sure you stop him."

"Right," Nick said dryly. "We'll do that."

"Good. You'll be pleased to hear Melody hit the jackpot when she heard the name Bashir al-Hassan. He's on the CIA registry, and the Department of Defense, too. He's a widely respected Sunni cleric, very popular with the rank and file of the Syrian army, who's somehow managed to avoid being imprisoned by the Alawite minority that governs Syria. The CIA smuggled him out of Syria a month ago—"

"Why? Sunni clerics with popular followings are a dime a dozen."

"I'll get to that. Al-Hassan turned up in Cairo three days ago, took a flight to London, and today flew into Detroit, landing around six this evening. Right now, Bob can't come up with his precise location. Security's tight. Officially, al-Hassan is the guest of the chief imam at the mosque on Oak Avenue—"

"The one that Zachary Wharton was studying the plans for?" Nick asked.

"Yeah. Looks ominous, doesn't it? There's been no official announcement about al-Hassan's visit, and his presence here is known only to a few officials in the CIA, the Defense Department and the White House. And the Senate Intelligence Committee, of course. Of which Senator Cranford is a member."

"You still haven't answered my question," Nick said. "Why did the CIA bring him here? And since he's their import, why is he in Detroit, not in Langley?"

"Because he refused to go there. He's a prickly creature, a strong Arab nationalist. His goal is to bring about regime change in Syria—get rid of the Assad family—and he certainly doesn't want to be known among his followers as a collaborator with the United States. However, he's looking to work a deal with Washington. He claims to have information about what happened to some of Saddam Hussein's weapons of mass destruction—"

"Ten percent of adult Syrian males claim to have information about Saddam's WMD programs," Nick said.

Mac grunted an agreement. "The difference is, Langley and the White House believe this guy knows what the hell he's talking about."

"In that case, I'm surprised we don't have half the Defense Department lined up in Detroit waiting to talk to him," Nick said. "If al-Hassan has definitive information about any of Saddam's weapons programs, he potentially has the power to influence the fate of the entire Middle East."

Mac gave a short bark of laughter. "As I understand it, at least half the Defense Department *is* lined up trying to get interviews with the guy, with the Secretary at the front of the line. But al-Hassan is choosy about who he talks to, and he's made it plain he'll talk only to Johnston Yates."

"Why?" Nick asked. "That's an odd choice, isn't it? Yates has been out of the public political arena for decades."

"Yeah, but he's still one of the biggest movers and shakers in the entire Republican party, so the White House is willing to let him represent them if there's no alternative. Anyway, al-Hassan first met Yates years ago, back in the seventies, when Yates was vice president and al-Hassan was a young cleric. Al-Hassan organized a resistance movement, trying to topple the rule of the Assad family in Syria. Later, al-Hassan formed a tactical alliance with the fundamentalist Muslim Brotherhood and the partnership didn't turn out well for anyone. Rumor has it that at least a thousand of al-Hassan's supporters got wiped out by Assad's forces during a botched uprising in the town of Hama. That was back in the early eighties. Yates conducted some secret diplomacy in the aftermath of the uprising and managed to save the life of al-Hassan's brother and cousin. Since then, al-Hassan has maintained sporadic contact with Yates. Anyway, bottom line, he wouldn't agree to deliver his information to anyone else except Yates."

"Does anything in al-Hassan's bio suggest why Zachary Wharton might be so anxious to see him dead?" Nick asked.

"Aside from the fact that assassinating the guy would send shock waves of horror throughout the Arab world?" Mac said dryly.

"I wondered if Zachary might have a more personal motive," Nick said. "Did Bob manage to trace any links between al-Hassan and Zachary's grandfather?"

"You're talking about records dating back seventy years, but the answer seems to be yes, it's at least possible that there's a personal link. Bob says al-Hassan's father and Zachary Wharton's grandfather were approximately the same age, and they were both silversmiths who worked in Damascus in the late 1920s. Syria was occupied by the French throughout the twenties and thirties, right up until the fifties, in fact, and Al-Hassan's father was identified by the French colonial authorities as a radical Muslim with a special hatred for Arab Christians."

"In other words, he's Zachary's dream target for elimination."

"You've got it," Mac said. "Okay, I'm off. We're juggling a lot of balls here and that's what I have for you so far—"

"Don't hang up," Nick said quickly. "Melody just made a suggestion that needs to be followed up. We were speculating as to why Senator Cranford would want to help the Soldiers of Jordan assassinate al-Hassan—"

"That's easy. Cranford doesn't care who the Soldiers kill, so long as Unit One gets blamed for not stopping the assassination."

"You could be right on that. But Melody suggested that al-Hassan might not be the senator's main target. Perhaps his real target is Johnston Yates."

"Humph." This time Mac's all-purpose snort seemed to indicate skepticism. "Why would Cranford want to get rid of Yates any more than he wants to get rid of al-Hassan? Cranford's intention is to make trouble for Unit One. Period."

"But what if he can make trouble for Unit One and pay off old scores at the same time? We know that Cranford was in line for the vice presidency until Yates campaigned against him. That's enough right there to piss Cranford off—"

"Enough to piss him off," Mac agreed. "But not enough to inspire murderous designs on Yates. That seems to be pushing it."

"Revenge is a powerful motivator."

"For some people," Mac said. "Zachary is the sort of person to kill for revenge, but is Cranford? I'd expect the senator to kill when he feels threatened, not because Yates screwed him over two years ago."

"Then we need to find out if Yates has the power to inflict fresh harm on Cranford," Nick said. "I'm betting he does."

"Humph. If there's any substance to Melody's theory, Jasper Fowles might be able to tell us where to look for dirt," Mac said. "He and Johnston Yates go way back. I'll contact Jasper and see what I can uncover. In the meantime, I'll make sure that Yates is notified that he and al-Hassan are both possible targets for assassination. Local law enforcement agencies in Dearborn have already been warned to anticipate problems, although they didn't seem to take the warning too seriously. Because of the number of Muslims in the Detroit area, law enforcement receives terrorist threats and antiterrorist warnings on a daily basis. That's another reason you and Melody need to go to Dearborn. Light a fire under the cops' tails and get 'em to haul ass."

"Sure, we'll do that. Right between saving al-Hassan and Johnston Yates from being murdered and negotiating world peace."

"Don't waste your time on world peace," Mac said. "You need to keep focused on what's important."

Nick decided his boss wasn't joking. One of the reasons Mac made such an excellent chief for Unit One was his relentless fixation on the goals of the organization. "I'm going to call Eleanor Cranford," Nick said. "She might be able to provide some clues about Cranford's plans. She already told me that her husband dislikes Yates. Perhaps the senator's dislike of him is stronger and more current than any of us assumed."

"It's nearly midnight," Mac warned. "If Eleanor's in bed, even if you call on her cell phone, the senator will hear you."

"She and the senator sleep in separate bedrooms. But I'll exercise caution. I'll hang up if she indicates Cranford is anywhere within listening range."

"Let me know what you find out," Mac said. "I'll be in touch again as soon as I've spoken with Jasper. The meeting tomorrow between Yates and al-Hassan is expected to begin at ten-thirty. I don't need to remind you we're working on a tight schedule here. Don't crash on the way to the airport." He cut the connection.

Melody buckled herself into one of the four window seats in the front section of the plane and gratefully accepted the co-pilot's offer of a diet soda. She was feeling almost human again. Her stomach had stopped imitating an out-of-control butter churn, and her headache had reduced itself to a level that was merely pounding as opposed to monumental. Better still, she was clean and warm. She'd used the airport rest room—deserted at this hour—to wash all over in scalding hot water and put on a fresh sweatshirt. Nick had stopped at a twenty-four-hour convenience store en route to the airport so that he could buy her a change of clothing. They hadn't been able to find a replacement for her running shorts, but instead of her thin, sleeveless athletic shirt, she now wore a sweatshirt emblazoned with the colorful logo for the Great Salmon Valley Balloon Festival.

Jeff, the co-pilot, handed her a ginger ale and indicated the fridge where she could find more. He returned to the cockpit, trading places with Nick, who had been conferring with the captain and picking up the transmissions from Mac.

"The captain is projecting a flight time of four hours five

minutes," he said, slipping into the seat next to Melody. "That means we should be landing in Detroit around five a.m." He clipped a sheaf of papers to the worktable that separated their seats from two others facing them, then pointed his thumb toward the rear of the plane.

"There are bunk beds back there behind the curtain. Once we're airborne, you might want to catch a couple of hours sleep."

"I'm too wound up to sleep," Melody said. "I've been fighting the PCP so hard, I think my system is flooded with adrenaline. I'm revved."

The captain's voice over the intercom told them that the plane had been cleared for takeoff and that they were to fasten their seat belts. She watched the tarmac speeding past them in a blur of landing lights, worrying about what lay ahead, afraid that Dave Ramsdell might once again escape and wondering if Johnston Yates...if her father...was going to be killed before she ever got the chance to demand an explanation as to why he'd spent the past thirty years ignoring her existence.

"These are the latest messages from Mac," Nick said, shuffling through the sheaf of papers he'd placed on the table. "The imam at the Oak Avenue mosque has been contacted and warned that there is an imminent threat to the safety of Bashir al-Hassan. The meeting between Yates and al-Hassan was scheduled to take place in the imam's own office, which has windows on two sides." Nick pointed to the printout of the architectural plans for the mosque, indicating a corner room. "He eventually agreed to move the meeting to a room without windows, closer to the center of the building." Nick pointed again, this time to a room sixteen feet by twenty, that had no doors or windows leading to the outside.

"We don't expect Dave to go inside the mosque, do we?"

Melody asked. "Dave prides himself on his marksmanship. Surely he plans to take them out as they arrive?"

"We'll check out the surrounding rooftops as soon as we arrive," Nick agreed. "Bob sent us aerial survey photos of the street where the mosque is located, and Mac arranged for the Bureau to provide us with a Remington M24 sniper rifle. The captain has it locked up right now, but he'll hand it over to us when the plane's on the ground."

Melody pulled a face. "The Remington wouldn't be my first choice of weapon, but I guess they're the best around for out-of-the-box accuracy."

They viewed the photo Mac had sent of Richard Mitchell, which Bob had reproduced from Mitchell's driver's license. The picture was typically unflattering, but accurate enough to be useful. She and Nick studied the plan of the mosque until they could draw it from memory, and discussed alternate scenarios that Dave might be planning until they were hoarse and exhausted.

"Okay," Nick said, going to the fridge and coming back with fresh sodas and a package of pretzels, "we're starting to say the same things three and four times over."

"I know." Melody linked her hands high over her head and stretched. "I'm just so afraid Dave is going to get the better of us. I couldn't bear it if Johnston Yates got killed because I screwed up."

Nick looked at her closely. "You're fixated on Johnston Yates. Why?"

She hesitated, not sure if she was ready to tell him the truth. Aside from a few moments after Nick rescued her from the Soldiers of Jordan, they had kept their dealings with each other tonight strictly professional. They were under extreme pressure, people's lives were in their hands, and the fault lines in their relationship that had been exposed at the start of this assignment were wide and complex. On the other hand, the three weeks since her breakup with Nick had shown her pretty clearly that her feelings for him were deep, and that she didn't want their relationship to be over, despite her sense of betrayal. If they were going to find some way to put together the pieces of their shattered relationship, they would have to start by taking some emotional risks. And there was probably no better way to uncover the insecurities they both fought so hard to keep hidden than by talking about their parents.

"Do you know the truth about Johnston Yates and me?" she asked finally.

Nick stared at her, his expression so tightly controlled, she knew he'd misunderstood her question. She wasn't sure whether to be furious that the idiot would believe she was capable of having an affair with a man almost old enough to be her grandfather, or to feel happy that his reaction indicated a level of paranoid jealousy that suggested where she was concerned, his emotions were definitely in control of his reason.

He responded to her question with a total lack of emphasis, like a politician trying not to offend anyone on the subject of gay marriage. "I didn't realize there was any truth about you and Johnston Yates for me to know."

"He's my father, Nick."

Nick's expression collapsed into unguarded astonishment but not, Melody realized, about the fact that Yates was her father. "I always knew Jasper loved you," he said. "I never realized how much."

"Why do you say that?"

"I've watched Jasper operate for the past six years, ever since I learned he was Unit One's commander-in-chief. I've never known him to give up a secret, or a lever that might be useful one day in the future, because of personal feelings."

"He owed me the truth," Melody said, and she heard the harshness in her own voice.

"Yes, he did. But Jasper doesn't usually let personal debts weigh too heavily in his accounting scales."

"He's trained you well," Melody said. "Do you really want to grow up to be Jasper, Nick?"

The accusation fell into a silence that seemed to envelop the whole plane. Even the roar of the engines sounded muffled, mingling with the blood drumming inside her ears.

"I deserved that," Nick said quietly. "The truth is, I owe you an apology. I manipulated you into taking on an assignment you didn't want because I wasn't willing to admit that our relationship was more important to me than Unit One."

"Is our relationship important to you? I've never been sure."

"It's the most important thing in my life. I love you, Melody."

The shock of hearing Nick make such an admission deprived her of words. Then she smiled, feeling a rush of tenderness. "You need to practice saying that without sounding quite so astonished."

"I love you." He took her into his arms and kissed her long and hard. "I love you. I love you, Melody Beecham. There, how was that?"

"Improving." She laughed. "Another few dozen times, and you'll almost be able to keep the squeak of surprise out of your voice."

"Show me how," he said, his voice husky.

"I love you," she said. "I love you, Nikolai Anwar."

"I love you," he said, sounding like the voice box on Tickle

Me Elmo. He shook his head. "Jeez, it's really hard to get the intonation just right. You know, I think I'd do much better if only we were lying down." He leaned across and unlatched her seat belt. "It's another ninety minutes until we land in Detroit. No point in letting those perfectly good bunk beds go to waste."

Melody couldn't have agreed more.

Twenty-Three

The mosque was freshly painted, the gold ribs of its dome gleaming in the early morning light. Flanked by a shuttered Lebanese restaurant and a Middle Eastern grocery store, the trio of buildings stood out in a street otherwise filled with warehouses and grungy office buildings. Melody scanned the nearly deserted scene as the driver of their car, an FBI vehicle ordered up by Mac, drew to a halt alongside the front entrance of the mosque.

"Where do you want me to park the car?" The driver sounded grouchy. Other than informing them that his name was Darren Reilly, and this was supposed to be his day off, he had barely spoken.

"Park in front of the grocery store over there," Nick said. "It's Sunday, so presumably there won't be much traffic, at least until later on in the day."

"Not for the warehouses," Darren agreed. He jerked his finger toward the mosque, swiveling around in the driver's seat to look at them. "But don't they have services today?"

"The Muslim holy day is Friday, not Sunday," Melody said, getting out of the car.

Darren shrugged. "But the kids still come for religious classes today and some of the parents hang out. Or at least they do in most of the mosques around here."

Nick and Melody exchanged horrified glances. The last thing they needed right now was the possibility of children arriving at any minute. "What time does Sunday school start, do you know?" Melody asked.

Darren shook his head. "I live north of the city. Never been here before. The local cops might know." He smothered a yawn. "You want me to stay with the car, or come with you guys?" He couldn't have made it more plain that he resented the fact that he'd been told to take his instructions from Nick.

"Stay close to the car, but take the keys out of the ignition. We don't want anybody using it as a getaway vehicle." Ignoring Darren's rolled eyes, expressive of his disgust at being told something so obvious, Nick showed him the picture of Richard Mitchell that had been faxed to the plane. "We're looking for two men with murder on their minds, and this is one of them. We believe this man plans to assassinate one or more of the people attending a meeting here at the mosque this morning."

"I know. My boss told me." Darren looked bored. "You know how many warnings we get like this in a month? Try a dozen, and then keep on counting."

"Take this one seriously. If you see the suspect, don't try to apprehend him, and don't alert him in any way. Just let us know you've spotted him."

Darren studied the picture of Richard Mitchell, scratching his jaw. "He's armed?"

"Yes. And definitely dangerous. His partner, Dave Ramsdell, is even more lethal."

"You have a picture of Ramsdell?"

Nick nodded. "We have a copy of his mug shot from Leavenworth, for all the good it will do us. Dave Ramsdell changes his appearance the way you change your socks. He's an escaped felon. Five ten, medium build, visibly fit—"

"Unless he chooses to pad himself and look fat and out of shape," Melody interjected.

Nick grimaced in rueful acknowledgment. "At least he can't do much to change his height. But hair color, eye color, skin color—could be anything. Richard Mitchell is the same build as his partner and half an inch taller. As far as we know, no particular skill in disguising himself. Unfortunately that's the best I can give you. Don't fool around on this one, Darren, even if you're pissed that I'm in charge."

Darren finally seemed to be paying attention and Nick decided to quit while he was ahead. Darren looked to be pushing fifty. The fact that he'd pulled the job of driving to the airport on pickup duty suggested that this wasn't an FBI field agent marked for future greatness. The best they could hope for was that his trained eye might spot any suspicious pedestrians.

Nick got out of the car, reaching back inside to hand Melody the dense nylon mesh case that held her borrowed Remington. Then he hoisted his own sniper rifle over his shoulder. He and Melody both scanned the nearly deserted expanse of Oak Avenue with dismay.

"I can see that local law enforcement is taking our warnings of imminent disaster to heart," Melody said with heavy sarcasm.

"Hey, they've sent one whole entire cop," Nick said wryly, using his rifle to point to a uniformed police officer standing at the gated entrance to the mosque. "If Darren's attitude is typical of local attitudes, they probably consider that overkill. No wonder we couldn't get the location of the meeting moved somewhere easier to protect. Nobody is taking the threat seriously."

Melody hoped to God that they wouldn't be bagging the bodies of Yates and al-Hassan before the locals wised up.

Nick approached the cop and showed him a badge that identified him as Nicholas Derwent, a Secret Service officer. Melody flashed a similar bade, identifying her as Melody Brodowski. The cop looked dubious and Melody could almost sympathize. Nick had washed the camouflage paint off his face and shed his flak jacket, but otherwise he was still wearing Unit One's night ops outfit, while she was still sporting her balloon festival sweatshirt and running shorts. Not exactly the clothes you'd expect to find on officers from a notoriously conservative government agency. However, if the cop was actually suspicious enough to call the Secret Service headquarters and ask for confirmation of their status, he would be assured that the badges were valid.

The cop decided to take their ID at face value. "I'm Tom Takane," he said. He sounded gloomy enough that Darren appeared almost cheerful by comparison.

"My partner and I need to conduct a safety check on the mosque and the adjoining community center," Nick told him. "We can leave the mosque itself until one of the clerics is here to escort us. That way we can avoid ruffling any sensitive religious feathers. In the meantime, we're under a lot of time pressure, and I'd like to get started on checking out the community center. Is the gate behind you locked?"

Takane eased his weight from one foot to the other, gloom shifting to worry. "The gates are padlocked. You can't even get as far as the courtyard until one of the clerics arrives. They should be here by nine, nine-thirty. Leastways, that's what I was told."

Nick inspected the heavy-duty padlock and thick, no-nonsense chain. Takane was correct. Short of an acetylene blow torch, the only way to open the gates was to know the combination of the lock. "Can you radio in to the station and arrange for one of the clerics to get here as quickly as possible to open the gate?" he asked.

The cop's expression became stubborn. "My instructions are to keep everyone outside the perimeter of the mosque until I hear from my sergeant. He didn't say nothing about the Secret Service, or any other feds turning up and wanting to get in here. Just that I wasn't on no account to let anyone into the building. Except the Muslims, of course."

Since Takane didn't have keys and Nick didn't have a blow torch, there was no point in insisting. He and Melody could always climb over the wall, but that wouldn't get them inside the mosque, and Nick had enough experience dealing with local law enforcement to recognize that he would ultimately get a lot more help if he didn't ride roughshod over Tom's sensibilities.

"I'll get my boss to call your boss," Nick said. "What's your sergeant's name? And his phone number?"

The cop provided the information, relieved not to be pressured to take immediate action. Nick called Mac, moving out of earshot casually enough that Tom didn't take offense at being excluded from the conversation.

"Hey, Mac, Melody and I are at the Oak Avenue mosque. The cop on site has been instructed to keep everyone outside the entrance gate, so we need authorization from his sergeant before we can gain access to the community center. Here's the contact number for the local police precinct, and the name of the officer you need to speak with." He gave the sergeant's name and repeated the phone number he'd been given. "We also need to get a cleric on site right away. The entrance gate is padlocked, so there's no way right now for us to get inside the mosque or the community center short of climbing over the wall." Nick paused for a moment. "You know, it would be a lot simpler all around if this meeting just got moved to the hotel where Yates is staying."

"The folks at Langley tried one more time to persuade everyone to move the meeting to the hotel," Mac said. "No dice. Yates is willing, but al-Hassan is paranoid about security—"

"He's paranoid about *security* but he refuses to move somewhere safer?"

"Yeah, he trusts the imam of the Oak Avenue mosque but he doesn't trust us to protect him, or even to be giving him the straight skinny. In fact, he's afraid we want him to move the meeting to the hotel because the CIA plans to take him into custody."

"So he's going to risk death because he's afraid of being arrested," Nick said. "Now that makes sense. For God's sake, can't anybody convince al-Hassan that the government has no plans to arrest him?"

"Apparently not. Yates has already tried. Al-Hassan's supporters will, nevertheless, blame the U.S. loud and long if anything happens to him, at which point everyone in Washington will be looking for scapegoats. And guess what, folks? That'll be us. Which means that it's essential for you and Melody to secure the site and keep the man alive. How many law enforcement personnel do you currently have available to help you?"

"One cop, from the local precinct."

"Holy shit, that's all?" Mac sounded suitably horrified. "Dearborn police have a sixteen-man SWAT team they can call on. Where the hell are they?"

"Not here," Nick said.

"And where the hell are the guys from the Bureau?" Mac demanded.

"Good question. Apart from the driver who brought us from the airport, we haven't sighted anyone from the Bureau. I guess I don't need to remind you that Melody and I lost two hours crossing time zones coming from Idaho so it's already eight forty-five local time. That means we have significantly less than two hours to get this place secured before Yates and al-Hassan arrive. We need extra bodies, Mac, and we need them fast. I don't care how much ass-kissing you have to do, or who you have to threaten, but get us some competent people here. Preferably a SWAT team. And make sure somebody brings a thermal infrared unit when they come. There's no time to search every nook and cranny of the community center to make sure that Dave and Richard aren't holed up inside. We need something that's going to penetrate walls and detect body heat, so that we can pinpoint where they are."

Melody left Nick to drum up personnel and equipment while she walked the perimeter of the mosque. She was familiar with the building footprint from having studied the architectural drawings intensively during the flight. As always, though, visiting the site in person created a subtle alteration in her perceptions. Had Dave already scoped out the mosque? He must have, she decided. No way he could plan an operation of this magnitude without walking the site, so he must be aware that the entire complex of buildings was surrounded by a wall, with a single gate serving as the only entrance from the street. The layout made sense from the point of view of the Muslim community: they wanted to have a walled court-yard surrounding their mosque, both for protection and for beautification. Unfortunately the walled design could have been custom-designed for an assassin, since the lone entrance meant that there was no way for visitors to enter the mosque except through the wrought-iron main gates. Yates and al-Hassan were going to be sitting ducks when their limos pulled up at the curb.

Melody tried to think like Dave. If she were planning to assassinate two important men, scheduled to arrive almost simultaneously at this mosque, where would she select her setup point? She wouldn't opt to go inside the mosque or its peripheral buildings, Melody decided, even though gaining access would be easy enough. On the plane she and Nick had noted that the air-conditioning ducts were more than large enough to crawl through. The ducts were also vented straight to the roof, providing easy entry. Dave could have arrived here while it was still dark, rappelled up the side of the mosque, landed on the roof, and then taken his time unscrewing the metal grille that covered the vent. It would probably take him less than ten minutes to get into the duct system unless the screws were severely corroded, and no more than another ten minutes to find a suitable point inside the deserted community center to drop down into a room.

However, taking up a position inside the buildings would mean that he was contemplating a suicide mission. Neither Dave nor his partner would have any realistic chance of escaping from inside the community center after killing al-Hassan, even though there would be rampant confusion in the wake of the shooting. The idea of going out in a blaze of glory might appeal to Dave, and maybe Richard, too, except that nothing about Dave's recent behavior struck Melody as being suicidal. Dave wanted freedom, and he wanted revenge on Unit One. He needed to be alive to savor both of those things.

Melody returned to her opinion that Dave was most likely to take his shot as Yates and al-Hassan arrived at the entrance to the mosque. Which meant that his most logical setup point would be in one of the buildings on the other side of Oak Avenue. Melody's stomach clenched as she calculated just how many windows overlooked the entrance and how easy it would be for Dave to hide in one of the warehouses waiting for the perfect moment. In the building located directly opposite the mosque gate the ground floor was windowless, with offices on the second floor, about twenty feet above street level. A perfect height for getting a target in your sights and keeping him there, Melody thought grimly.

"You look depressed," Nick said, rounding the corner and joining her in the parking lot. "Cheer up. I have good news. Our police force just doubled in size."

"The locals sent another cop?"

"Yeah. The age of miracles is not yet over. The sergeant has drummed up another warm body for us, although the kid is barely twenty and still in the stage where he knows it all. Which wouldn't be so bad if what he knows wasn't entirely things he's read in the training manual. Still, he promises me a cleric is on the way with a key to get us into the mosque, and Mac assures me the FBI has authorized three more agents from their field office. They're already on their way, too."

"We need to search the warehouse as well as the mosque," Melody said, her voice husky with tension.

"We will—"

"I just have this sickening gut feeling that Dave's already here, watching us. Nick, all he had to do was arrive a couple of hours before us and he's home free. He's probably set up inside that warehouse opposite the gate, ready to take aim at al-Hassan. And Yates."

Nick directed a look at her that suggested he knew perfectly well why she chose to refer to her father by his last name. Melody wondered if she should tell him that as a device for keeping her feelings toward the target strictly professional, it wasn't working worth a damn.

Apparently she didn't need to tell him. Nick touched her lightly on the arm, then took her hand. "Dave isn't going to succeed in killing your father, Melody."

She drew in a sharp breath, wanting to believe him. When she first learned that Johnston Yates was her father, she had felt so hurt by his lifelong neglect that she had wanted nothing to do with him. But now she knew she needed an explanation for his years of silence. It was painful to consider that Dave Ramsdell had the power to deny her even that much sense of closure to the mess that was her family background.

She let her hand remain in Nick's clasp, but she didn't respond directly to his comment. "I can't shake the sensation that we're missing something obvious. That Dave has been one step ahead of us the whole way, and that he's going to stay just enough in front that we won't be able to save al-Hassan. Or…my father."

"Good news," Darren said, jogging up to them in a surprising display of energy. "Your boss must know some really important people, Nick. Three more agents from our Detroit field office just arrived, and they've brought the infrared heat-seeking equipment you requested. Also a half dozen guys in abayas have just offloaded from their minivan, complete with an entire briefcase full of keys to get you into the mosque and the community center. Not to mention two guys from the Michigan State Police, who rolled up in their squad car a couple of minutes ago. Although God knows what they're planning to do. Hand out traffic tickets?"

"They could set up a check point at the north end of the street, and the two Dearborn cops could do the same at the south end," Melody suggested. "At least that way we would have control over the flow of civilians, especially Sunday school kids, and it would slow everyone down enough that there's a better chance of spotting Mitchell and Ramsdell."

"Not a bad idea," Darren said. "I'll take care of it." He jogged off at a spanking pace, energized by the arrival of his colleagues and the fact that Nick and Melody's unnamed boss was clearly a man with clout.

"I'll deal with the clerics," Nick said. "They'll work better with a man. There's going to be some resistance to the fact that I plan to go into the mosque with my rifle cocked and ready to fire."

"You can hardly blame them," Melody said.

"No, it's a violation, but I don't see any way around it. If Dave is in there, I need firepower. Anyway, there's no point in offending the clerics even more by having the weapon carried by a woman. So will you take care of bringing the Bureau guys up to speed?"

"I'll try," she said. "Assuming those three guys in suits and ties are the FBI agents, we'd better hope they have bright ideas about how to access a shuttered and locked warehouse other than climbing the exterior walls. Because they definitely aren't dressed for climbing."

The Muslim clerics were clustered outside the gates to the mosque, where they were engaged in agitated conversation with the local cops. The FBI agents stood off to the side, working on some equipment, and the two state troopers stolidly went about the business of setting up roadblocks.

Nick took Melody's hands and swung her around to face him, shielding her from the view of the clerics. "You're probably right that Ramsdell and Mitchell are inside the warehouse over there," he said, glancing across the street. "Take care, Melody."

"I will. I have no intention of allowing Dave to kill anyone this morning."

Nick raised her hand to his lips, turning it over and pressing a kiss into her palm. "I love you. Now go kick some butt."

"I love you, too. Now go pay your respects to the clergy."

The FBI agents greeted Melody with an icy courtesy that was indistinguishable from rudeness. Clearly they were no happier than Darren that they were being forced to take part in an operation where they weren't in charge. When she pointed out that the warehouse opposite the gate was the most likely place for would-be assassins to set up shop, the senior agent told her patronizingly that he'd been taking care of situations like this since she was in grade school, and he was capable of figuring out where the shooters were likely to be hiding.

Despite their condescending attitudes, the FBI agents were competent and worked fast. By ten o'clock, their infrared equipment had produced the unappetizing information that the warehouse opposite the mosque was riddled with rodents, but that there were no living human beings concealed anywhere within its walls. Melody greeted the news with relief, quickly followed by a fresh wave of fear. If Dave wasn't in the warehouse, then he had to be either in the mosque or the community center, and that wasn't good news. If he was treating this as a suicide mission, he might well be planning to end his life in a blaze of bullet-ridden glory, with dozens of dead bodies to mark his end as opposed to merely taking out Yates and al-Hassan.

The Muslim clerics, far from sharing Melody's sense of impending doom, considered the empty warehouse as proof of the fact that al-Hassan was protected by Allah, and that their imam had been absolutely correct to refuse to move the meeting out of the mosque and into Johnston Yates's hotel. With a grim-faced Nick accompanying them, the FBI agents moved on to check out the community center and the mosque itself with their specialized equipment.

The belated arrival of a two-man SWAT team from the Dearborn police struck Melody as anti-climactic. They looked impressive in their combat gear, with assault weapons at the ready, but there was nothing much for them to do. Mac's message about the need for infrared equipment had been passed on to them, and they'd brought a unit similar to the one in use by the FBI. The SWAT team might have been useful if Dave and Richard had been discovered and needed to be disarmed. As it was, there wasn't much for them to do. More to give them a sense of usefulness than anything else, Melody suggested they should start scanning the buildings on either side of the central warehouse. Perhaps Dave and Richard Mitchell had been willing to trade a straight shot at their targets in exchange for a better chance of avoiding discovery. The two SWAT team members, more friendly than the FBI agents, obligingly set to work scanning the buildings Melody had identified.

Melody tried to avoid hanging over the shoulders of the FBI agents and the SWAT team, begging for every scrap of information as it developed. Realistically she knew that if they found evidence of hidden assassins, they would immediately broadcast their discovery. Nick was still inside the community center, coordinating security and maintaining contact with the cops and Secret Service officers assigned to escort Imam al-Hassan and Johnston Yates to the mosque.

Melody occupied herself pacing up and down Oak Avenue, familiarizing herself with the heft and feel of her Remington, and wondering if she'd totally screwed up in White Falls. In only a few minutes, Yates and al-Hassan would be arriving for their meeting and so far there wasn't a trace of evidence that Dave or anyone else planned to assassinate them.

She was still convinced that Dave and Ed were one and the same person, and that Dave had been working with Senator Cranford to humiliate Unit One. But maybe this wasn't the time and place that Dave intended to use to make his point. A wave of panic swept over Melody as she contemplated the possibility that this was all a massive diversion, and that the real action was taking place elsewhere. Maybe the architectural plan on Zachary's computer had been a deliberate plant. If Dave wanted to embroil Unit One in a disaster, he couldn't do much better than to have Mac call in favors, drag local and federal law enforcement officers to the Oak Avenue mosque, while Dave staged a flamboyant murder in Milwaukee, or Los Angeles. Melody broke out in a cold sweat at the mere thought.

One of the Dearborn SWAT team members—he'd introduced himself earlier as Alan—came up to her. "We found a lot of rats, a few mice and a possum, but no humans hiding in either building, ma'am. I'd recommend against storing anything edible in them, but otherwise the buildings don't seem to represent any danger. If you like, Brad and I can wait in the van and keep the entrance to the mosque covered. Just in case there's a last-minute attempt to take out the targets with a drive-by shooting."

A drive-by shooting. My God! Could Dave have decided to fool them all and carry out the assassinations by the simplest method of all? A car roaring by at speed, spraying bullets into anyone clustered on the sidewalk? It could work, Melody thought, sucking in a gulp of air in a vain attempt to lower her stress. Zachary was obsessed with the idea of killing al-Hassan in revenge for the fire that destroyed his grandfather's business, but Dave didn't give a damn who died. He simply wanted to create mayhem. Even if Dave was collaborating with Senator Cranford, a pile of dead bodies on the sidewalk outside the mosque would work just fine. Instead of two carefully-aimed bullets, one for al-Hassan and one for Johnston Yates, Dave and Richard would spray the cluster of people at the gate with machine-gunfire. If a few cops and Muslim clerics died along with Yates and al-Hassan, it just meant a more newsworthy body count. Presumably Zachary would be pleased, too, given how much he hated Muslims.

"Ma'am? Is that what you'd like me and my partner to do?"

The two SWAT team members were still waiting for instructions. "Yes, it's a good idea to have the arrival of al-Hassan and Mr. Yates covered," she said. "In fact, you may be on to something, Alan. Since Ramsdell doesn't appear to be in the warehouse or the mosque, I guess he must be planning something along the lines of a drive-by attack."

"Glad to have been of help." Alan tipped his hand in a mock salute. "Okay, then. My partner and I will get set up inside the van. Don't worry, ma'am. Nobody is going to get past the two of us."

Melody sure hoped he was right. She watched his departure without really registering it. Nick came out of the mosque, trailing a trio of clerics. His face was completely without expression, which meant that he was as worried as she was. Melody quickly outlined Alan's theory about a drive-by attack.

"Makes a lot of sense," Nick said grimly. "Okay, let's run with it. We'll make the barricade at the south end of the block as impenetrable as possible, and warn the state troopers at the north end to move their cars into full blockade position the moment the limos with Yates and al-Hassan have passed through. You take care of that, will you, Melody? Communications are a nightmare, because there are so many different agencies involved and nobody's system talks to anybody else's. But I just had a phone call letting me know that Yates and al-Hassan are already in their vehicles. They'll be arriving from the north, and they have a motorcycle escort, as well as two Secret Service agents in each limo."

"How are you communicating with the Secret Service guys in the limos?" Melody asked.

Nick pulled a face. "It's insane, but I have to run everything through Mac. He's got a link to their communications system. I'll pass on word that we think Ramsdell may be planning a hit-and-run attack, and that the officers on escort duty should be on high alert for any vehicle that looks as if it might be attempting to follow the limos and crash through the barricade onto Oak Avenue."

It was the best they could do. Melody passed on the order about strengthening the barricades to the cops and the two state troopers. Now that the moment for the arrival of al-Hassan and Johnston Yates had come, tension levels were rising and the twenty-year-old rookie who'd been so bursting with confidence ninety minutes earlier was now visibly sweating. Even the FBI agents had shed their skepticism and were casting uneasy glances toward the northern end of the avenue.

Nick took up a position by the barricade, ready to fire at any vehicle attempting to crash through. Melody walked back toward the center of the block, coming to a halt opposite the mosque gates, which put her about fifteen feet to the left of the SWAT van. She lifted her rifle and sighted the gate, which stood wide-open, two clerics waiting in the center to greet the arriving dignitaries. She brought one of the clerics into her cross-hairs, adjusting the focus until she had a bead on his heart. The angle was perfect for a shot. However, once the limos drew up, they would block her view. In fact, the SWAT van was parked in the spot that was likely to provide the best view of Yates and al-Hassan as they got out of their limos.

She hoped to God the SWAT-team guys were as highly trained in marksmanship as they were supposed to be. Melody lowered her rifle and looked toward the van, checking that the two men were taking their roles seriously and were ready to fire if need be.

One of the SWAT team members had already positioned himself at the side window behind the driver, his rifle balanced on a special ledge to insure his weapon didn't move when it was fired. The other officer—Alan—was in the driver's seat, his rifle resting more casually across his lap, his fingers stroking the reinforced fiberglass stock of his weapon in an absent-minded caress. For some reason, the gesture troubled her with an odd sensation of familiarity.

The engine of the van was running, Melody noticed. A sudden flush of heat rushed from her head to her toes, but instead of making her warm, the heat vanished as quickly as it had come, leaving her ice cold. Why was the engine running? What possible reason could there be for the SWAT team to have turned on the engine of their vehicle? Not a one that she could think of, unless they needed to make a quick getaway. She stared at Alan's hands—his familiar hands—stroking his sniper rifle.

The son of a bitch had done it to her again!

The flash of recognition was as powerful as it was certain. Six months ago Dave had kidnapped her by posing as a Unit One security guard, lulling her suspicions because she'd looked at the uniform instead of the man inside it. In the end, though, Nick had rescued her. She'd escaped and Dave had ended up in military prison. Now he'd pulled the same stunt again, hiding behind the concealing uniform of a member of the SWAT team, confident that nobody would bother to look closely at a fellow law enforcement officer. The bastard was planning to wreak his revenge by killing her father from the very spot where she had recommended he should park his van.

Like hell he was going to get away with it.

The limos with her father and al-Hassan approached the barricades. In twenty seconds, they would pass through. Another thirty seconds and they would be parked outside the mosque. Without a body-mike, it was impossible for her to warn the drivers to turn back, or to let Nick know that she'd identified the assassins.

Melody was running before she consciously registered what she planned to do. It would have been safer—much safer—to approach from the side and fire into the van from the rear. But certain as she was of her identification, Melody couldn't take the risk of shooting two genuine SWAT-team officers in the back. She ran directly in front of the van, weapon in firing position, interposing herself between the two men and the approaching limos.

"Dave Ramsdell!" She yelled his name, fury giving her voice power. "Drop your weapon, you son of a bitch!"

She didn't expect him to comply and she saw the twitch of his finger on the trigger. She pulled the trigger on her own weapon before he had time to aim his rifle at her, as opposed to al-Hassan and her father. She aimed for his hand, and heard the clatter of the gun banging against the side of the van even as she squeezed off three more quick shots, one directed at his shoulder, the other at his left hand, the final one at his left shoulder. Dave almost certainly had more than one weapon, and she was taking no chance of leaving him with the power to take aim.

She swung her weapon and fired at Richard Mitchell. He dropped his weapon, cursing as blood poured from his wounded shoulders and she heard the sound of running feet pounding behind her.

Nick arrived a couple of yards ahead of a gaggle of cops and FBI agents. "Jesus, Melody, are you okay? What in hell happened here?"

"I'm fine." Her voice wobbled audibly enough to prove she was lying. "He's Dave," she said, gesturing toward the van with her rifle. "And that's Richard Mitchell." Any more detailed explanation was beyond her. She sank onto the pavement, drawing in shuddering gulps of air. Practicing target shooting with her grandfather on the lawns of High Ridgefield might be great for honing the accuracy of her aim, but it bore little relationship to firing live ammo at two crack marksmen who would kill you if you missed.

She was only vaguely aware of the roar of voices and waves of movement all around her. She watched blankly as, across the street, Secret Service agents hustled al-Hassan and Johnston Yates inside the mosque, followed by a cluster of terrified clerics. She'd saved her father's life, Melody thought. Good. That meant some time soon—very soon—she would have the great pleasure of telling the asshole exactly what she thought of the way he'd treated her.

The FBI agents were taking Richard and Dave into custody. Both men were fading in and out of consciousness, but Dave managed to use one of his brief spells of coherence to hurl a string of obscene abuse toward Melody.

Nick silenced him by delivering a heavy-duty punch to Dave's jaw. "It's at moments like this that I'm really glad I don't work for a regular law enforcement agency," he said, dusting off his hands.

"I thought you two were with the Secret Service," one of the FBI agents said.

"Not exactly," Nick replied.

"Ah. You folks report to Langley?"

"No." Nick didn't expand his response. "My partner and I are more than happy to leave you guys to take all the glory of thwarting an assassination attempt. In fact, I'll have my boss call your director. Between them, they'll come up with instructions on how you can get the paperwork taken care of. In the meantime, my partner and I would like to get out of here and find a motel. It's more than twenty-four hours since she had any sleep."

He bent over, offering Melody his hand to pull her up. Melody clambered to her feet, still a bit unsteady. He put his arm around her waist and led her to a spot away from the bustle of people and the rookie cop, who was doing a fine job of administering first aid to Ramsdell and Mitchell.

"You saved your father's life," he said softly.

"Yeah, I guess I did." She realized she was smiling. Tomorrow she would be furious with Yates again. For today, she would savor the knowledge that he was alive because of what she'd done.

"I believe you may have saved mine, too." Nick looked down at her, his emotions closer to the surface than she had ever before seen them. "Before I met you I was moving so

fast I didn't have time to notice I wasn't actually going anywhere. Now I have a destination."

"Where do you want to go?" Melody asked.

"Somewhere with you." He kissed her, tenderly at first and
then with passion. "Anywhere with you."

Epilogue

The housekeeper ushered Melody into Johnston Yates's book-lined study. He stood up, waiting in silence as she crossed the ten feet of space between the door and his desk.

The housekeeper finally broke a silence that was becoming awkward. "Would you like me to bring some refreshments, Mr. Yates? Coffee? Tea? I have lemonade, too."

"No, thank you." As an afterthought, Yates turned toward Melody, but he avoided eye contact. "That is, unless you would like something?"

"No, thank you." She spoke as coolly as he had done, although she wondered why Yates had insisted on seeing her if he was merely going to present her with a view of his patrician profile staring into space.

The housekeeper walked out, closing the door behind her. Yates seemed preoccupied with the documents on his desk, obscured from Melody's view by a polished mahogany in-tray. She looked at the man whose sperm had given her life and was furious with herself for feeling pain at this new example of his rejection.

The emotional barricade Yates had thrown up against her was all the more apparent because now she knew the truth, she couldn't avoid noticing the physical similarities between the two of them. Her mother had been petite and delicately boned. Melody's height, her athletic body build, the shape of her mouth and nose all came to her directly from Johnston Yates. She wished that she wasn't so deeply beholden to him, given that he appeared to resent every chromosome he'd donated.

Johnston Yates finally spoke. "I owe you a debt of gratitude. You saved my life."

"It was my job." Melody made no attempt to sound polite. "You owe nothing."

"You underestimate what you did. I would like to express how much I appreciate your courage and dedication, not to mention your skill in deducing that Lewis Cranford was using Zachary Wharton and the Soldiers of Jordan as a place to hide Dave Ramsdell until they could arrange for the assassination of Bashir al-Hassan and me. Bashir al-Hassan was able to provide information that will prove invaluable in tracking the whereabouts of some of Saddam Hussein's most dangerous weapons. His death would have been a tragedy for us, and for the prospects of peace in the Middle East."

"You're welcome." She could take pride in having saved two lives, even if one of those lives currently struck her as pretty damn self-centered.

Yates picked up a glass paperweight, then put it down again almost at once. "I assume you've been informed why Cranford made me his target."

"I was told he believed you had the power to ruin his political career."

"Yes, that's true. Ever since the debacle of Wallis Beecham's arrest and the dissolution of the Bonita partnership, I've been aware that Lewis Cranford doesn't deserve the honor of serving in the United States Senate. I had made it clear to Cranford that he needed to resign his Senate seat or I would make public knowledge that I have concerning some of his shadier financial dealings. I had set a deadline of the beginning of next month for him to announce his resignation. It was naive of me, perhaps, but I never considered that in pressuring Cranford to leave the Senate, I was putting my life at risk."

"Not only your own life, but other people's, too." Melody felt anger spew upward with all the force of emotion too long suppressed. Yates still hadn't looked at her, and she was getting more than a little tired of pretending that she didn't care. "Who appointed you judge and jury of the moral standards for America's political life? If you knew Lewis Cranford had broken the law, it was your duty to report his crimes to law enforcement, not decide yourself how he should be punished."

"Yes, you're right. Keeping silent was a serious error of judgment on my part. One of several I've made recently." Johnston Yates turned his back on her and walked a couple of steps to the narrow window that overlooked the small rear courtyard and its splashing fountain.

Look at me, you son of a bitch. Look at me! I'm your daughter.

Melody bit back the words. There was no point in forcing a confrontation that would inevitably end up hurting her far more than it healed. "Goodbye, Mr. Yates."

She was halfway to the door when he spoke. "I loved your mother, Melody. It was only after we parted—bitterly I might add—that I realized I loved her more than I had ever imagined it was possible to love another person."

Melody laughed, and swung around, her eyes blinded by tears she refused to let fall. "Right, Mr. Yates. I'm sure she was the love of your life—"

"It would be disloyal to my wife of forty years if I answered that."

"And God forbid that you should be disloyal to Cynthia! I guess committing adultery with my mother was just another way of showing your wife how much you cared."

Johnston Yates visibly winced. "I've already acknowledged that I made some pretty bad mistakes. If Roz were here, I'm sure she would tell you that she made mistakes, too—"

"And here I am. The result of two people's bad mistakes."

"Yes, that's exactly what you are," Yates said. "However, if I were a religious man, I would say that you are living proof of the fact that God can transform people's worst mistakes into something good and beautiful."

Melody didn't dare to allow her emotions to be touched. She protected herself with anger. "Cue the violins, Mr. Yates—"

"For God's sake, at least call me Johnston. I suppose father is too much to expect."

"Father?" She laughed mockingly. "And now I suppose you're going to tell me that for the past thirty years, you've been watching me from afar, yearning to acknowledge me but somehow never able to find the right moment."

"I could tell you that—"

"I'd be more inclined to believe that particular fairy tale if I hadn't attended a party here in this house six months ago. When I came up and spoke to you, it was clear you didn't even recognize me."

"I recognized you," Yates insisted. "My defense mechanism is always to become more aloof, more withdrawn when

I'm struggling to control intense emotions." He gave a brief, wintry smile. "I've observed precisely the same characteristic in you."

Melody wasn't about to be placated. "What an unfortunate trait for me to have inherited."

"Possibly. But I've always been extraordinarily proud of your achievements even if I had no right to claim any responsibility for them. "

"I'm sure." Melody's voice was sharp enough to slice glass. Then she realized she was doing exactly what Yates had talked about: she was withdrawing into coldness as a defense mechanism against potential hurt. The insight brought a renewed flash of rage. "The evidence of your interest in me is overwhelming. Let's see. I'm heading toward my thirty-first birthday and before today we must have spoken …oh, at least three times. I feel almost smothered by your attention."

Without speaking, Johnston Yates pushed the mahogany in-tray to one side, revealing a thick, leather-bound album. He drew back the cover, revealing the first page, on which a magazine article about Melody's christening was mounted. Silently, he turned the pages, displaying densely packed clippings and photos culled from magazines and newspapers in many languages.

He finally looked up and met her eyes, tossing her own words back at her. "For the past thirty years, I've been watching you from afar, yearning to acknowledge you, but somehow never quite able to find the right moment." He hesitated for a moment, and a note of pleading entered into his voice. "I was married… I am married…to a good woman, Melody. Cynthia didn't deserve to be hurt and humiliated because I fell in love with another woman."

"You didn't have to abandon Cynthia," Melody said. "You

were the vice president of the United States, and I understand your political career would have been ruined if you had acknowledged our relationship when I was born. But after my mother died and informed the world that Wallis Beecham wasn't my father, surely you had an obligation to tell me the truth. I spent two years with absolutely no idea who my father might be."

"You're right again," he said quietly. He closed the leather album with a snap. "The truth is, Melody, that I'm an ambitious man, but not a courageous one. I've been doing quite a lot of reflecting over the past couple of weeks since the assassination attempt. Looking back on my life, I realize that my ambition has almost always been undercut by my lack of courage. Which is supremely ironic when you think about it. You are fortunate that you inherited your courage from your mother and not from me."

"Why did you ask to see me?" Melody asked abruptly. "Did Jasper insist on it?"

Johnston Yates grimaced. "Perhaps I deserved that," he said. "No, Melody, I didn't ask to see you because of Jasper. I asked to see you because I very much hope that it isn't too late for us to get to know each other. I'm not foolish enough to believe that there's any way I can make up to you for three decades of neglect, but I would like to think that we might be able to establish some sort of friendly relationship."

"Have you told Cynthia that you're my father?"

"Yes." He hesitated for a moment. "She's known the truth for many years, in fact." As if realizing this belied his earlier argument about fear of hurting his wife's feelings being the reason for his silence, he hurried on. "I wanted to tell you the truth when you turned eighteen. It was Roz who wouldn't permit me to speak with you. She said that I'd lost the right to play any role in your life when I refused to divorce Cynthia and marry her. She pointed out that Wallis Beecham believed he was your father, and I had no right to take the gift of fatherhood away from him." He spread his hands, the gesture somewhere between resignation and a plea. "I felt she had some justification for her point of view."

Melody realized she had reached a clear crossroad in her life. She could either wrap her justifiable anger around her like a cloak, keeping her hurt warm and simmering. Or she could accept that Johnston Yates—that her father—was a man who had made mistakes and was now trying to the best of his ability to make amends. She could pay Yates back for years of neglect, or she could forgive him his past failings and move on.

It was amazing how appealing the idea of payback was, Melody reflected wryly. A part of her—the child who'd never been given the love she craved—wanted to fling Johnston's offer of friendship in his face and walk out of the study without a backward glance. Another part of her, the part that had blossomed since she fell in love with Nick, realized that in relationships, being right was likely to prove cold comfort in the darkness of a long and lonely night.

She looked at her father with the veil of her own hurt feelings pushed aside and saw a man whose outward calm barely masked the intensity of his inner emotions. God knew, she could identify with that particular coping mechanism. The fact that he wasn't rushing to hug her didn't mean that he didn't care. It was far more likely to mean that he cared too much.

"Would you like to have dinner with me one night next week?" she asked, her voice losing its brittle edge for the first time since she came into the study.

"Just the two of us?" Johnston cleared his throat. "That would be wonderful."

She smiled, and this time there was no edge to it. "We have a lot of catching up to do. I'm looking forward to it."

"Thank you," he said quietly. "You're a lot more generous than I deserve."

"Not generous. I'm selfish. I want to know the father I never had."

He came out from behind his desk, his arms outstretched. "I'm so sorry, Melody," he said huskily, sweeping her into a stiff, angular hug. "My dear child, I've wanted to hold you like this more than you can imagine."

She resisted at first. Then, hesitantly, she allowed herself to relax in his arms, resting her head against the starched white front of his shirt. His hand not quite steady, he stroked her hair. She closed her eyes, fighting tears.

They stood together for a minute without speaking, then she stepped away from him, holding his gaze. "Just don't let me down again. I don't think I could bear that."

"I won't," he said fiercely. "You have my word on it. From now on, Melody, you can count on me."

Turn the page for an exciting preview
of
FINAL JUSTICE
by Jasmine Creswell

available in May 2005
From MIRA Books

One

The motel room smelled of cigarette smoke and old carpet, overlaid by a thin veneer of cheap cleaning products. The heating unit was churning full blast, intensifying the stuffiness with intermittent blasts of hot, dead air. The sagging curtains had been drawn shut, not to close out the dreary view of rain falling onto the icy parking lot, but to conceal the identity of the occupants from any passersby.

Melody Beecham sat at the rickety table, her laptop open, her Sig Pro within easy reach. Her blank expression concealed the intensity of her focus on her partner, Nikolai Anwar, and the other two men in the room. So far, her role in Unit One's latest operation had merely been to look decorative, but in a few moments she would have to fake the transfer of two million dollars into Bryce Martin's bank account in Western Samoa, a newly popular hot spot for illegal bank-

ing activities, and it was important for the transaction to pro-
ceed with apparent smoothness.

Bryce was a lab tech employed the Seneschal Corporation,
where he worked under the direction of the renowned scien-
tist Dr. Simon Feng. Dr. Feng was one of the world's leading
authorities on the application on nanotechnology to the problem of energy generation. In return for two million bucks,
Bryce had promised to provide Nick with a CD-ROM he had
stolen from his employers. The disk reportedly contained
complete details of Dr. Feng's groundbreaking research into
photovoltaic materials that could generate electricity directly
from sunlight. Nick had heard rumors that the disk was for
sale during the course of another Unit One operation, and had
approached Bryce with an offer to buy. After two weeks of
hard bargaining, this afternoon's meeting had been arranged.

Bryce Martin's appearance was as greasy and unappetizing as his ethics, but provided he didn't get spooked and start
shooting, he didn't pose much of a threat. Although only a
few pounds overweight, he was seriously out of shape, his
body flabby and shapeless beneath his too-tight pants and
sweater. Melody didn't anticipate any trouble when they arrested him, even though he was flashing a pearl-handled
Beretta that he seemed to have no clue how to use. Amateurs
and guns often made for a dangerous cocktail, but Bryce was
arrogant enough to present a soft target and she was confident she would be able to disarm him without much difficulty.

Bryce's hired bodyguard wouldn't be so easy to handle.
Jesse was at least six feet two, and his body was bulky with
steroid-grown muscle. Jesse was carrying a businesslike Glock
and, in contrast to his client, he gave every impression of
knowing how to use it. He wasn't easy to distract, either.
Melody's short leather skirt and long legs encased in tight zip-

pered boots had won nothing from him beyond a single, assessing glance. Any longing looks Jesse cast toward her corner of the room had been aimed at her SIG rather than her body.

Unit One was a covert organization, not officially acknowledged by the government and not bound by the strict rules of agencies such as the FBI, or the CIA. Because Unit One operations were always secret, aimed at targets within the United States, and usually kept confidential even after they were completed, Unit One agents handed off most arrests to local law enforcement or the FBI. But today Nick and Melody would be acting as the arresting officers, which meant they were required to offer Jesse and Bryce all the protections guaranteed by the constitution. However, since both men were armed and likely to shoot their way out of the motel room the moment they felt threatened, Nick and Melody could legitimately disarm them before announcing the arrest. But first, they had to have evidence against the pair that would hold up in court. That meant Bryce and Jesse had to accept the two-million-dollar payment.

Bryce handed the promised disk to Nick with an elaborate flourish. "Here you are. Everything you need to start a revolution in the world's energy markets."

"I look forward to doing just that," Nick said. He spoke with a slight Russian accent, since he had conducted his negotiations with Bryce in the role of Nikolai Anwar, a businessman with connections to the Russian oil cartels and their associated criminal underworld.

Bryce gave a nervous laugh. "Hell, when you get down to it, I'm a regular patriot. By selling you this research, I'm fucking over all those Arab dictators who want to hold America to ransom by charging a fortune for their oil."

"I am overwhelmed by the intensity of your desire to serve your country," Nick said.

"Yeah, well, we can't all be heroes." Bryce scratched at a pimple on his chin. "Anyway, I've given you the disk and now it's your turn. I want my money."

Nick tapped the slim plastic case containing the CD-ROM. "Before I hand over any money, I need to be sure that you are not selling me something worthless."

Bryce appeared insulted. "You have my word that the disk contains all of Feng's current research materials."

"Your word?" Nick allowed a moment of withering silence and then smiled coldly. "Thank you, but I prefer to review the disk for myself."

Bryce Martin flushed, stung by Nick's contempt, although he tried not to show it. He shrugged, almost visibly consoling himself with a reminder of how much sun and fun he would be able to buy with two million bucks.

"Be my guest," Bryce said. "Here, use my laptop." He sat on the edge of one of the beds and slipped the disk into his computer. He keyed in a command and the computer hummed quietly. After thirty seconds or so he swiveled the screen around so that it was facing Nick.

"There you go, hotshot. I've pulled up the table of contents. Take your pick of any file. They're all loaded with good stuff. Feng has no clue about how to keep his files secure. You know what his password is in the lab? His wife's name." He shook his head, genuinely appalled. "What a loser."

"In fact, he almost deserves to be robbed," Nick said. Melody admired the way he managed to keep all trace of irony out of his voice.

"You got that right," Bryce said. "Feng may be a genius at

physics, but he hasn't a grain of common sense. The guy needs a minder to help him tuck his dick inside his pants."

Nick sat down on the bed. He actually understood no more about nanotechnology than Melody, which meant he understood next to nothing. However, he'd been extensively briefed by Dr. Feng, and he knew which files contained the most confidential and innovative elements of Seneschal's research project. He swiveled Bryce's laptop around the bed, opened an appropriate file, and started reading, searching for the crucial equations that Feng had helped him memorize in order to identify the contents of the CD-ROM as stolen property.

In fact, Nick's insistence on examining the contents of the disk was mostly for appearances' sake, since Bryce Martin was toast once he took the two million bucks, even if the disk contained nothing but garbage. If he couldn't be arrested for the sale of stolen property, he could be arrested for extortion.

Melody watched Nick as he read, ruefully aware that she must have fallen dangerously deep into the minefields of love when even his frown of concentration struck her as sexy. Neither Bryce nor Jesse spoke, and the roar of the heating unit fan sounded loud in the stuffy room, the only other sound being the creak of Jesse's boots as he rocked backward and forward in monotonous rhythm.

After less than five minutes, Nick ejected the disk, slipped it into its case and tucked it into his shirt pocket. The fact that he put the disk into his pocket using his right hand was a prearranged signal to Melody indicating that, as far as he could tell, the disk contained exactly what Bryce had promised. Honor among thieves, if you could call it that, had apparently prevailed.

Nick pushed the laptop back across the bed to Bryce. "I'm satisfied you have delivered Dr. Feng's research materials."

"Impressive stuff, right?" Bryce sounded as proud as if the research were his own.

"Very impressive," Nick acknowledged. "Dr. Feng is clearly a genius."

"Yeah." Bryce grimaced. "Also a major pain in the ass." He glanced toward Melody. "Okay, enough with socializing. Let's move on to the good stuff. Where's my money?"

Melody looked at Nick. "Shall I start the transfer?"

He nodded. "Yes, that is acceptable to me. You can transfer the money now."

"The motel only has a dial-up connection," she said as she entered the codes that connected her laptop to the computer system at Unit One headquarters. She keyed in the numerical combination and password that indicated she was ready to begin the fake transfer of two million dollars. "It's going to take several minutes to complete the transaction."

"That's okay." Bryce smiled. "My plane doesn't leave for another four hours."

"Where are you going?" Nick asked.

Bryce laughed, increasingly excited now that the money was almost in his grasp. "That would be telling, wouldn't it? Somewhere warm, that's for sure. I'm sick to death of freezing my ass off through five months of goddamn winter. That bastard Feng insists on starting work at seven in the morning." He sounded genuinely outraged. "You know what it's like getting up before dawn at this time of year? Fucking miserable, in case you couldn't guess."

The link to Unit One was finally established. Thanks to the outstanding computer skills of Bob Spinard, the director of intelligence, Melody's laptop took only seconds to display what appeared to be a Nigerian bank account in the name of Nikolai Anwar. Bob had enjoyed himself, Melody saw, and given Nick a supposed balance of over seventeen million dollars.

Melody gestured to Bryce, indicating the screen and showing him that sufficient funds were available to make the transfer. "You notified us that you want your two million dollars transferred to the Presidential Bank of Western Samoa," she said. "I'm accessing the Web site of that bank now."

The monitor went blank for a full minute and then displayed a screen that welcomed her to the Presidential Bank. So far, so good. "For the next step I need to enter your account number, Mr. Martin." She moved her mouse to highlight the box asking for account details.

"I'll type in the account number myself," Bryce said hoarsely. Now that the two million dollars were only moments away from his possession, his excitement had escalated to the point that his breathing had become audibly quick and shallow. "I'm not stupid enough to give my passwords to you. You could take the two million back out of my account as soon as I leave here."

"We never expected you to give us your account passwords," Melody said, turning her laptop toward him. "Go ahead. Enter them yourself."

Bryce merely grunted. Hunching one arm over the keyboard so that nobody could see what he typed, he pecked out a series of numbers using only his left hand. The screen blinked and then returned with a request for him to enter his password. Bryce repeated his one-handed entry system, which effectively prevented anyone in the room from learning his password even if they had a clear view of the screen. Unfortunately for him, every stroke was being recorded back at Unit One headquarters, giving Bob Spinard immediate access to Bryce's account.

From Bryce's perspective, however, all was well and he

gave a satisfied grunt when a window popped up on the screen asking him what transaction he wanted to complete. He clicked the box for *Make a Deposit*.

"Okay, it's all ready for you to transfer the two million bucks into my account," he informed Melody, stepping aside so that she could access the keyboard. He moved behind her, hanging over her shoulder, and she pointedly asked him to move away while she typed in the codes that supposedly gave her access to the funds in Nick's Nigerian account.

"I'm transferring the money now," she said, entering the final command that created the illusion of two million dollars winging their way into Bryce's account in Western Samoa.

Bob Spinard was such a computer whiz that Melody had never anticipated any serious problems. Still, it was a relief that there hadn't been a glitch in this crucial part of the operation and she let out a breath she hadn't realized she'd been holding when a window finally appeared announcing that the transfer was complete.

Bryce used the sleeve of his sweater to wipe his forehead. "Show me my new balance," he demanded.

Melody switched the laptop in his direction. "You need to enter your password again for that screen to come up."

"Okay, I'll type it in." For a second time, Bryce hunched over the keyboard and pecked away. A few seconds later, a banner flashed onto the screen containing the information that his account now held two million, two thousand, three hundred and eleven dollars and sixty-three cents.

Thank you, Bob Spinard.

"Hey, how's that for a healthy bank balance?" Bryce's face broke into a beaming smile. "Two million and change!" He gulped in air and then laughed as he zipped his laptop into its carrying case. "Come on, Jesse, let's get out of here. We've got a plane to catch."

"Not so fast." Jesse spoke almost for the first time since the meeting began. He stepped in front of Bryce, extending his arm to stop his partner's rush toward the door. "You need to check that transfer of funds again. This time run the check on your own computer."

Bryce's gaze narrowed. He clearly wasn't a man who reacted well to having his decisions questioned. "Why?" He jerked his head toward Melody. "I watched what she did. I keyed in my account number myself. There's no way for her to have screwed us over."

"Humor me. Check the balance on your own computer and make sure she really put the funds into your bank and didn't just make pretty pictures on her computer."

Melody rose to her feet, tucking her SIG into her waistband, the movement fluid and deceptively casual. Bob Spinard had considered the possibility that Bryce would insist on checking the transfer of funds on his own computer and had promised to arrange a link to the Presidential Bank in Samoa so that anyone attempting to access Bryce's account for the next twenty-four hours would actually be diverted to Unit One. Instead of accessing Bryce's genuine account, they would access the fake account generated on the Unit One system. She hoped to God the link and the diversion were in place, and would function as advertised. It would be much easier to disarm Bryce and Jesse if they were relaxed and happy, not anticipating problems. She didn't want this afternoon's operation to end in a shootout, or serious injury to Bryce and Jesse, even if the two of them were slightly less appealing than pond scum.

"Check all you want," she said to Bryce. "The money's in your account, as you'll discover."

"It'd better be." Scowling, Bryce shoved his revolver into the holster hidden under his sweater. Then he slid his briefcase onto the table Melody had just vacated. He extracted his laptop, plugging in the modem, his fingers tapping impatiently as he waited to get online. Standing behind him, Melody hid a rush of relief when his Presidential account came up, once again displaying a supposed total in excess of two million dollars.

"Nasty suspicious minds you and your partner have," she said mildly.

"Better safe than sorry." Bryce produced the cliché with as much aplomb as if he'd just invented it.

Melody shrugged, using the gesture to conceal the fact that she was looking to Nick for instructions. This operation had gone on long enough. Bryce had incriminated himself a dozen times over, and Jesse was apparently never going to put away his gun, so they might as well get on with the business of arresting them.

Nick clearly shared her opinion that it was time to move. His hand hanging loosely at his side, he pointed his index finger almost imperceptibly toward Bryce, their agreed signal to indicate that she should disarm him while Nick, who was a master of unarmed combat, concentrated on taking down Jesse, the stronger and more dangerous target.

She gave Nick the briefest of nods, an acknowledgment that she would move in five seconds. Melody counted off the seconds as she positioned herself directly in front of Bryce, her attention focused on getting his gun away from him without injury to anyone. On the count of five, she threw a hard punch to the region of Bryce's solar plexus. Her hand sank into an inch of flabby flesh, which must have cushioned the blow, but Bryce reacted as if she'd sliced his liver with a stiletto. He shrieked and doubled over, probably as much from shock as from pain. Melody quickly moved in close, screening out the thuds and bumps of Nick's fight with Jesse so as not to become dangerously distracted.

She grabbed Bryce's right arm. Almost simultaneously, she brought her right leg forward and hooked it around Bryce's leg, forcing it toward her. He fell backward, crashing into the table. She pulled his fancy Beretta out of his holster as he careened off the table and collapsed onto the floor. He lay there moaning, although his total injuries didn't amount to much more than a few bruises and maybe a couple of pulled muscles.

"You're under arrest," she said, keeping the Beretta aimed squarely at his heart. "Don't move until I say you can. You have the right to remain silent. If you choose to speak—"

"You're a fucking *cop?*" Bryce spat the words out.

"Something like that," Melody said.

Behind her, she heard the crash of a chair tumbling to the floor and the thud of hard blows landing on flesh. Nick yelled out her name almost at the same moment as she heard the explosive sound of a gun firing.

A sudden searing heat knifed through her side. Pain blossomed, spreading out to envelop her body so completely that her mind couldn't think, only experience the pain. She tried to focus on keeping the Beretta aimed at Bryce, but it was impossible. Her eyes were open—weren't they?—but she couldn't see. The room had gone dark.

More noise. More shots. More crashes. More thuds. She was on the floor, Melody realized. Then Nick was suddenly close to her. She felt him take her hand.

"Stay with me, Melody!" he pleaded. "Melody, for God's sake, you can't die on me, dammit!"

I'll try not to. The thought popped out of the darkness.

"I'm calling the paramedics now. Just hang in there. Promise me you'll hang in there."

She would have answered him. Promised him that she would fight to stay alive, since he seemed so frantic, but the world went black. She slid into quietness, where there was no more pain.

MIRABooks.com

We've got the lowdown on your favorite author!

☆ Read an excerpt of your favorite author's newest book

☆ Check out her bio

☆ Talk to her in our Discussion Forums

☆ Read interviews, diaries, and more

☆ Find her current bestseller, and even her backlist titles

All this and more available at

www.MiraBooks.com

JASMINE CRESSWELL

32012	DECOY	___ $6.50 U.S.	___ $7.99 CAN.
66931	THE THIRD WIFE	___ $6.50 U.S.	___ $7.99 CAN.
66838	THE CONSPIRACY	___ $6.50 U.S.	___ $7.99 CAN.
66712	DEAD RINGER	___ $6.50 U.S.	___ $7.99 CAN.
66608	THE REFUGE	___ $6.50 U.S.	___ $7.99 CAN.

(limited quantities available)

TOTAL AMOUNT	$_____
POSTAGE & HANDLING	$_____
($1.00 for one book; 50¢ for each additional)	
APPLICABLE TAXES*	$_____
TOTAL PAYABLE	$_____

(check or money order—please do not send cash)

To order, complete this form and send it, along with a check
or money order for the total above, payable to MIRA Books,
to: **In the U.S.:** 3010 Walden Avenue, P.O. Box 9077, Buffalo,
NY 14269-9077; **In Canada:** P.O. Box 636, Fort Erie, Ontario,
L2A 5X3.

Name:_____
Address:_____ City:_____
State/Prov.:_____ Zip/Postal Code:_____
Account Number (if applicable):_____
075 CSAS

*New York residents remit applicable sales taxes.
  Canadian residents remit applicable GST and provincial taxes.

MIRA®

www.MIRABooks.com

MJC1104BL